Augustus Henry Beesly

Life of Danton

Second Edition

Augustus Henry Beesly

Life of Danton
Second Edition

ISBN/EAN: 9783337332747

Printed in Europe, USA, Canada, Australia, Japan

Cover: Foto ©Raphael Reischuk / pixelio.de

LIFE OF DANTON

'Few such remarkable men have been left so obscure to us as
this Titan of the Revolution.'—CARLYLE

> Who, doomed to go in company with Pain
> And Fear and Bloodshed, miserable train,
> Turns his necessity to glorious gain :
>
>   *   *   *   *   *
>
> He, who though thus endued as with a sense
> And faculty for storm and turbulence,
> Is yet a soul whose master-bias leans
> To home-felt pleasures and to gentle scenes.

WORDSWORTH

BY

A. H. BEESLY

AUTHOR OF 'THE GRACCHI MARIUS AND SULLA'
'LIFE OF SIR JOHN FRANKLIN' 'BALLADS AND OTHER VERSE'
'DANTON AND OTHER VERSE'

SECOND EDITION

PREFACE

TO

THE SECOND EDITION

In criticisms of the first edition it has been surprising to find Danton so often acquitted of organising the massacres. Some have gone so far as to style defence of him on that count mere slaying of the slain. This is sufficiently refuted by the fact that in other criticisms he is still, as of old, held to be guilty. And it would have been simply impossible in a life of him to pass over without thorough examination charges till quite recently, at all events, almost universally credited. No farther back than 1893 M. Aulard—in France too—wrote : '*Aujourd'hui c'est presque un lieu commun d'attribuer à Danton et à la Commune la préméditation et l'accomplissement de ces massacres.*' It is difficult to imagine that in England a favourable verdict, though notified by fair-minded historians, like Mr. Morse Stephens and Mrs. Gardiner, can have been more generally accepted than in France, the more so as it was not within the scope of either of those writers to go into the evidence in detail.

Other critics still insist that Danton might, had he chosen or had the courage to do so, have stopped the massacres. I would ask such writers to define precisely what they think that he should and could have done. The moment they try to do so they will find that generalities about his 'power' and his 'eloquence' are no answer. He was not a Member of the Assembly. He had no party there. He had only spoken there twice before the second of September. Vergniaud, whom no one assails, was its eloquent man. Danton, whom it suspected and dreaded, would have been the very last man to whom it would have entrusted force, could force have been procured by urgent decree, the very last man whom it would have followed if he had proposed to lead it into the streets to confront the mob, as its successor confronted the mob (how uselessly!) in 1793.

Nor would Palais Royal eloquence to the mob have been more efficacious. The mob, as Danton knew, was Marat's mob. Because he could persuade men to enlist against a hated enemy it is argued that he could dissuade men from murdering a hated enemy. It would be as reasonable to argue that Peter the Hermit's voice could have checked the excesses of the Crusaders because irresistible in preaching a crusade. Michelet, it is true, suggests that Danton should have gone into the streets with a flag, and a Gordon would very likely have sallied out with a walking-stick. But a commander is not usually expected to play the part of a private, still less that of a martyr. If he cannot do all that he will he must do what he can. Danton must, to be judged fairly, be judged as leader and as man. I firmly believe that as leader he did all he could, and more than the more responsible Roland or anyone else did, to prevent the massacres; that, failing in his attempt, he felt that there was one thing which he, and, in view of the flight proposed by the other ministers, only he, could succeed in doing, viz. save Paris from the Prussians, and that this feeling, and neither fear nor ferocity, actuated him in the awful crisis of September. He was neither saint nor martyr, but a sorely beset political leader unwilling to see even enemies lawlessly murdered, unwilling also that he and his friends should be murdered by Brunswick after murderous civil war in the streets. Walking on the razor-edge of two precipices he has been condemned as if his path was easy and his foothold sure.

As man he was no guiltier than anyone else in Paris. 'Why,' says Mr. Carlyle, 'was I not there with some sword Balmung or Thor's hammer in my hand?' But if he had had no sword Balmung, nor any sword at all—what would he have done? Moralised in his hotel, as that evidently kindly and courageous Englishman, Dr. Moore, did. Yet unless to confront death in order to prevent murder is merely a local obligation, and one not binding on a Parisian in London or a Londoner in Paris, Dr. Moore was as much bound to risk his life for the prisoners as Danton.

In this edition I have corrected errors (mostly clerical and often corrected by the context) which were due partly to my manuscript having been copied by another person for the press, partly to a pen ἐπιορκήσασαν ἰδίᾳ τῆς φρενός, when eyes and brain were overworked. With one immaterial exception they escaped the notice, or were left unnoticed by the charity, of reviewers.

At the end of Chapter VIII. I have dealt at length with M. Aulard's view of the affair of the Champ de Mars and of Danton's attitude then, which, ably though that lucid writer argues, appears to me in some respects erroneous.

At the end of Chapter XII. I have given further specimens of Taine's method of aspersing Danton which I commend to critics who continue to put faith in that historian, and have examined a positive allegation made by Von Sybel and not hitherto refuted; appending the results of an inquiry made for me in the archives of Angers by an expert, for whose services I am indebted to the courtesy of M. Charavay.

I have altered the English of a few sentences for greater

clearness &c.—in some cases to correct inaccuracies—and also the spelling of some French names.

The parallel chronological columns, and the year's date, from 1789, at the top of the pages will, it is hoped, be useful.

Numerous references are given ; contemporary journals and documents being as a rule cited only when such authorities as Aulard, Bougeart, and Robinet, who quote them in profusion, are cited also. Where identical information is to be found in a variety of books I have as a rule chosen the handiest, or the one which will help anyone, who wishes, to explore farther. If there are errors I hope the non-hypercritical reader will bear in mind the labour involved, for which there will be certainly no other return to me than his convenience and appreciation.

IN THE NOTES

Rév. Fr. . .	stands for	*La Révolution Française, Revue Historique, &c.,* edited by M. Aulard
M. . . .	,,	Moniteur
M.-T. . .	,,	Mortimer-Ternaux's *Histoire de la Terreur,* in 8 volumes
S. . . .	,,	Sorel's *L'Europe et la Révolution Française*
Michelet . .	,,	Michelet's *Histoire de la Révolution Française*
L. Blanc . .	,,	Louis Blanc's *Histoire de la Révolution Française*
Bougeart . .	,,	*Danton, Documents Authentiques, &c.,* by Bougeart
Procès. . .	,,	Robinet's *Le Procès des Dantonistes*
Vie Privée . .	,,	Robinet's *Danton, Mémoire sur sa Vie Privée,* edit. 1884 except in ch. i.
Homme d'État .	,,	Robinet's *Danton, Homme d État*
Bat. du 10 *Août* .	,,	Pollio et Marcel's *Le Bataillon du* 10 *Août*

In the case of Claretie's ' *Desmoulins* ' I have occasionally quoted from Mrs. Hoey's translation, but the references, unless specified, are to the original. So also I have used both the French and English versions of Mme. Roland's *Appel à l'Impartiale Postérité.*

August 5, 1899.

PREFACE

TO

THE FIRST EDITION

DANTON was long regarded as the Catiline of the French Revolution, with the same gift of speech—' satis eloquentiæ '—the same mental characteristics—' animus audax, impurus, dis hominibusque infestus ; alieni appetens, sui profusus ; ardens in cupiditatibus '—and the same physical—' magnâ vi corporis ; colos exsanguis ; fœdi oculi.'   And even the most mendacious of eighteenth-century memoirs hardly match the rancour with which writers like M. Taine have ransacked the rag-bags of history for materials to malign him.   In repelling such charges it is hardly possible not to write as an advocate or to avoid repetitions of the same kind of disproof.   For the accusations themselves have a certain horrid family likeness, and in dismembering an octopus there is little scope for variety of stroke. But such advocacy will neither be attributed to a childish itch for paradox nor be pooh-poohed as whitewashing by those who call to mind how long ago he was weighed in quite other scales than those of the Peltiers and Prudhommes and was not found wanting.   This is what the philosopher Condorcet [1] thought of him :—

I have been reproached for voting for Danton being Minister of Justice : Here are my reasons : A man was

[1] Who in 1791 had disowned all connexion with Danton.

necessary in the Ministry who possessed the confidence of the people which had just overturned the throne, and who could keep under control the extremely contemptible agents of a revolution in itself glorious, useful, and necessary. It was necessary, too, that this man should have eloquence, intelligence, and character which would not be unworthy of the members of the Assembly with whom he would come in contact. Danton was the only man possessing these qualifications. I chose him, and do not repent it. He may have deferred too much theoretically to the opinions of the people, and yielded too much in practice to its impulses and ideas. But the principle of doing nothing except with and by the people, while its leader, is the only one which in times of popular revolution can save the laws; and all who cut themselves adrift from the people will in the end ruin themselves and perhaps the people too. Besides, Danton has the precious quality never to be found in ordinary men. He neither hates nor fears enlightenment, talent, or virtue.

In France most people seem now to agree with Condorcet, if we may judge by the streets called after Danton's name, the statue erected to him at Arcis, and the school books dealt out to French boys. In England, where no life of him has yet been written, the old legend still lingers, though modified to some extent by Carlyle and later writers, and evil indeed it is. ' Danton devised and organised the hellish massacres of September' says one of his most recent critics, who also repeats other charges against him long ago disproved. 'It was,' says a writer in the Spectator of November 27, 1897, 'Danton's suspicion of an aristocratic plot which caused the September massacres '—a less direct but hardly less damaging verdict. Even a friendlier critic, Mr. Morse Stephens, avers that 'the greatest blot of his administration was his indifference during the massacres in the prisons, for his power could have stopped them at once. But he regarded these massacres as an advantage to France.'

In the face of such and so many other accusations no wonder that it seems hard not to believe some of them to be true. But the further proof is sought the more elusive it becomes. Levasseur said that Danton painted himself in his speeches, and no surer antidote to instilled prejudice can be imagined than those speeches when read along with their context in the Moniteur. This book is based mainly on his speeches. In quoting his actual words the first person is used ; for the gist of what he said, the third. It should be borne in mind that he was badly reported, partly because he was a rapid speaker, partly because it often did not suit the wire-pullers of the journals that he should be reported well.

Of the principal writers on the Revolution in whose pages he figures Taine is incoherent, self-contradictory, and prone to present as evidence unsifted gossip. Michelet also, in his noble history, has relied a good deal on oral information, which it is impossible for his readers to test. Louis Blanc is an insidious partisan of Robespierre. Mignet is too meagre. Thiers too often draws a bow at a venture to be trusted, masterly though his method is. Carlyle, with the intuition of genius, had not the facts before him now available. To form an adequate estimate of the man it is necessary to turn to specialists like M. Bougeart and M. Robinet, the latter of whom in his ' Danton : Mémoire sur sa Vie Privée,' his ' Danton, Emigré,' his ' Procès des Dantonistes,' and in certain passages of his ' Le Mouvement Religieux à Paris pendant la Révolution,' has devoted his life to vindication of Danton's good name. Next to them I am most indebted to Mortimer-Ternaux, whose history, though one-sided and anti-Dantonist, is a mine of information and delightful reading ; to M. Sorel's ' L'Europe et la Révolution Française ;' to M. Claretie's ' Camille Desmoulins ;' to M. Dubost's ' Une Page d'Histoire ' and his ' Danton et la Politique Contemporaine ;' to M. Aulard's ' Études et Leçons sur la Révolution Française ' and his ' Danton ;' to G. Lenox's ' Danton ;' and to the recent edition of Arthur Young's 'Travels' by Miss Betham-Edwards, who has kindly furnished the photographs reproduced in these pages.   The English History which I have found most useful is Mr. Morse Stephens' 'French Revolution,' unfortunately unconcluded.   His 'Orators of the French Revolution,' with its numerous little biographies, has been very helpful.

For quotations from Danton's speeches other than those reported in the Moniteur, and for notices in contemporary journals, I have mainly relied on M. Bougeart's 'Danton.' References to other authorities—historians, essayists, memoir-writers, &c.—do not call for special mention.

Jan. 14, 1899.

CONTENTS

CHAPTER V

1791

CHAPTER VI

1791—*continued*

CHAPTER VII

1791—*continued*

CHAPTER VIII

1791—*continued*

CHAPTER IX

1792

CHAPTER X

1792—*continued*

CHAPTER XI

1792—*continued*

CHAPTER XII

1792—*continued*

CHAPTER XIII

1792—*continued*

CHAPTER XIV

1792—*continued*

CHAPTER XV

1793

CHAPTER XVI

1793—*continued*

CHAPTER XVII

1793—*continued*

CHAPTER XVIII

1793—*continued*

CHAPTER XIX

1793—*continued*

CHAPTER XX

1793—*continued*

CHAPTER XXI

1793—*continued*

CHAPTER XXII

1793—*continued*

CHAPTER XXIII

1793—*continuea*

CHAPTER XXVIII
1794, *March*

CHAPTER XXIX
1794, *April; the Trial*

CHAPTER XXX
Conclusion

ILLUSTRATIONS

'A hovel in Champagne'
TAINE, Eng. tr. i. 90.

1789	April . .	President of Cordeliers District. (?)
	July . .	At the Bastille. Palais Royal orator.
	September .	President of Cordeliers.
	October . .	President of Cordeliers. Urges them to go to Versailles.
	November .	President of Cordeliers. Heads their struggle with Commune for Mandat Impératif.
	December .	President of Cordeliers.
1790	January . .	Elected, by District, Commissioner to scrutinise arrests. Resists Marat's arrest. Member of Commune.
	March . .	President of Cordeliers. Prosecuted by Châtelet.
	April . .	President of Cordeliers. Advocates suppression of Châtelet.
	May or June .	Elected, by District, 'Assistant Notable.'
	June and July .	President of Cordeliers. Leads the district in its struggle against Bailly; against the subordination of Commune to Department; against the transformation of sixty Districts into forty-eight Sections
	August . .	Elected, by Section, 'Notable.'
	October . .	Elected, by Section, Member of the Electoral Assembly.
	November .	Elected Commandant of the Cordeliers Battalion of National Guard.
1791	January . .	Elected Administrator to Department.
	April . .	Resists King's departure to St. Cloud.
	July . .	The Champ de Mars affair.
	August . .	(about middle of.) In England.
	September 9 .	Returns to Paris on being again elected Member of Electoral Assembly. Attempt to arrest him. Not elected to Legislative Assembly.
	December .	Not elected Procureur, but is elected Assistant Procureur to Commune.
1792	January . .	Vice-President of Jacobins.
	August 10 .	Minister of Justice.
	September 6 .	Member of Convention. 21, Resigns Ministry. Acting Minister till October 9.
	October 10 .	President of Jacobins. 11, Member of Constitution-Committee. 18, Secretary to the Convention.
	December 1 .	First Mission to Belgium.
1793	January 14 .	Returns from Belgium. 31, Second Mission to Belgium.
	February 10–11	Wife dies. 24, He is in Paris.
	March 5 . .	Back in Brussels. 8, In Paris. 17, Mission to Dumouriez. 22, In Paris. 26, Placed on Committee of General Defence.
	April 7 . .	Placed on Committee of Public Safety.
	June 4 or 17 .	Second marriage. 10, Not on Second Committee of Public Safety. 25, President of Convention.
	August 26 .	Placed on Committee of Subsistence.
	October 12 .	Obtains leave of absence.
	November 22 .	First speech after return.
1794	April 5 . .	Executed.

SOME GENERAL EVENTS, 1789-1794

1789	*June 20* . .	Tennis Court oath.
	July 12 . .	Necker dismissed. 14, Bastille taken. 16, First Emigration begins.
	August 4 .	Renunciation of Feudal Privileges.
	October 3 .	Officers' Versailles Dinner. 5, March of Parisians to Versailles. 6, Second Emigration begins.
1790	July 14 . .	Federation Festival. Bastille Day.
	August 31 .	Nanci ' Massacre.'
1791	*June 20* . .	Flight to Varennes.
	July 17 . .	Champ de Mars ' Massacre.'
	August 25–7 .	Convention of Pilnitz.
	October 1 .	Legislative Assembly meets.
1792	February 7 .	Treaty of Pilnitz.
	June 20 . .	Mob gets into Tuileries.
	July 25 . .	Brunswick's Proclamation.
	August 10 .	Capture of Tuileries.
	September 2 .	Paris Massacres begin. 20, Valmy. 21, Convention meets.
	November 6 .	Jemmapes. 19, War of Propaganda avowed.
1793	January 21 .	Execution of King.
	February 1 .	War against England.
	March 18 .	Neerwinden.
	April 13 . .	War of Propaganda renounced.
	May 31–June 2	Overthrow of Girondins.
	July 13 . .	Murder of Marat.
	August 23 .	Levée en masse.
	September 8 .	Hondschoote.
	October 16 .	Wattignies. 16, Execution of Queen. 17, Cholet. 31, Execution of Girondins.
1794	March 24 .	Execution of Hébert.

LIFE OF DANTON

CHAPTER I[1]

GEORGES-JACQUES DANTON was born at Arcis-sur-Aube on
October 26, 1759, the year in which the French lost the battle
of Minden and Wolfe captured Quebec. The townsmen of
Arcis were noted for laborious industry and a stubborn spirit
of independence. Stocking-making and the pursuits of men
living by a navigable river were their main occupation.
Danton's father, Jacques, was an attorney. His mother's
name was Marie-Madeleine, and his sponsors were her father,
Georges Camut, a carpenter, and Marie, daughter of a surgeon
named Papillion.[2] His father died in 1762. In 1770 his
mother married a cotton manufacturer named Jean Recordain
(or Recordin), who proved a good husband to her and a good
father to her too vivacious boy. For the future hero of
insurrectionary Paris is said to have been somewhat of a rebel
as a child, and if the Rev. Patrick Maguire, in 'The Surest
Way to Heaven,' published in Belfast, 1871, is to be believed,

---

[1] The chief authorities for this chapter are Robinet's *Danton, Mémoire
sur sa Vie Privée*, edit. 1865, with its quotations from Béon, St. Albin,
and Despois ; and Bougeart's *Danton*, 1879.

[2] So printed by Bougeart. Query, *Papillon* ?

he was, even when in petticoats, well advanced on the surest way to hell.

Alas, the monster from his earliest infancy showed forth the seeds of the fatallest inclinations, *i.e.* an incurable indolence and a passionate love for gambling. He usually played at cards during the school hours, and the observing man who could have seen him, still in baby's clothes, ducking from morning to night in the Oobe (*sic*), or wrestling with dogs and pigs in the town gutters, might have foreseen clearly the frightful career of crime and debauchery which this unnatural creature was to follow.[1]

On better authority, however, we know that, though fonder of play than work, and in consequence not seldom a victim to the rod of his schoolmistress, he was a popular boy, generous and frank of disposition, and repaying the love of a most tender mother with passionate affection. In his combats with the animals mentioned by Mr. Maguire, he shared the tastes and only narrowly escaped the fate of the little Boileau. His censor, however, might have placed to his credit a love of water when chronicling his indifference to dirt. The distance to the Aube from the gutter was short, and not one of all his playmates sported in it oftener or was a bolder swimmer. Scarcely, in fact, had he recovered from his encounter with pigs when in some swimming exploit he was nearly drowned. A fever supervened, and then an attack of small-pox, which greatly disfigured his face. Its ugliness, however, was mainly due to yet other misadventures. Once, when as a baby he was being suckled by a cow, a bull interfered, and with its horn severely gashed his lip. When older, he is said, out of resentment, to have provoked an encounter with a second bull and to have come off conqueror, though this time at the expense of a mutilated nose. Hence a visage which graphic historians, after likening it to that of every savage beast in a menagerie, have apparently felt incapable of adequately describing without reference to monsters of classic fable, the most hideous being chosen as most appropriate,

---

[1] Lenox's *Danton*, p. 13.

even in defiance of incongruities of sex. It would not, perhaps, have been so extravagant had they suggested that but for this boyish escapade his looks might have less displeased the fastidious eyes of Mme. Roland, and that as a consequence the Girondin party might have proved less implacable and the course of the Revolution have been materially changed.

When he was eight years old, Danton was taken from the dame's school, where he had learnt little, and sent to one for older boys, where he learnt to play cards. The stakes were often cakes, and it was remembered that it was his wont to share such winnings with the loser. His next move was to an ecclesiastical boarding-school at Troyes, where, though more tractable, he was bored to death. 'If,' said he, 'I have to listen much longer to that bell, it will toll for my funeral.' Tradition says that at this school a boy could procure a measure of wine in exchange for a ticket which was presented at the buttery. Some boys were too poor to indulge in such luxuries. To these Danton liberally presented tickets. The evening before the holidays, the Superior, observing how many of these bore Danton's signature, amid his farewell speeches thus addressed him, 'You, my friend, may pride yourself on being the school's champion toper.' The other boys laughed, but Danton seems to have taken the master's unlucky irony or his schoolfellows' ingratitude to heart, for he told his mother that he would not go back to this school, where it is noteworthy that he was known by the nicknames 'Anti-Superior,' 'Republican.'

Not over-happy memories of such schooldays may have made Danton glad in later years to make boys with whom he was connected happier than he had been himself. His nephew, for whose education he made himself responsible, never forgot his kindness. 'He used often,' he writes, 'to send for me, especially when he had friends to dinner, and nothing can obliterate from my memory his goodness to me and his affection for his own mother and mine. As he pressed them to his heart I have seen tears of happiness fall from his eyes.' The friends alluded to were Camille Desmoulins, who would frolic with the child by the hour, Delacroix, Robespierre, &c. ; and these dinners to which a young schoolboy was invited were no doubt some of the 'orgies' at which his uncle was charged, by detractors, as sapient as the Superior of the seminary, with wasting his own money and that of the State.

The following year he was sent to another school at Troyes, where he carried off some prizes, and gained some knowledge of the classics. His class was always eager to hear his themes read, because they were sure to contain something original and striking; and in declamation he distinguished himself still more. But, as at his previous school, it was for insubordination that he was best known. One of the professors wished to avenge himself on a pupil for some slight by caning him. The offender, whose nominal crime was not knowing his lesson, was eighteen years old, and his class, led by Danton, protested, and protested successfully, against his being so humiliated. The same professor announced, as the subject for a theme, Louis XVI.'s coming coronation at Rheims. 'Thoroughly to master one's subject,' said Danton, 'one must see it with one's own eyes. I should like to see how they make a king.' So, telling only some of his friends among the boys, who lent him money for his journey, he set off for Rheims without asking his master's leave, and, passing by Arcis without visiting his family, was present in the cathedral when the young king, with his hand on the Bible, swore to reign according to law and for the good of the nation.

On his return, and when his schoolfellows crowded round to hear his story, he had little to tell of the ceremony and the gorgeous decorations, but graphically described the setting at liberty of a number of birds in the cathedral, with the comment, 'Pretty liberty that, to flutter between four walls without a crumb to eat or a straw for a nest.' The courtiers, too, with their 'Le Roi est mort ! Vive le Roi !' struck him as a set of chattering magpies. The truant's return was naturally followed by a scene with the schoolmaster.

But the boy won his pardon by the brilliance of his 'theme,' and, after carrying off all the honours on the next prize-day, left school in a blaze of triumph.

Two careers were now open to him—the Church and the Bar. His uncle urged him to the former, but he emphatically avowed his preference for the latter, and after a period in his life of which practically nothing seems to be known—during which, however, he must have been studying for his profession—we find him at Paris in 1780. He was then in his twenty-first year, and might have called on his stepfather to render an account of the property left him by his father. But M. Recordain was in embarrassed circumstances, and Danton placed all he had at his disposal—an act of generosity which he characteristically denominated 'setting his affairs in order,' as with a heart light as his purse, he prepared to leave Arcis. It is said that he travelled in the carrier's cart and that the proprietor wished to carry him for nothing. At Paris he at first took up his quarters at the Black Horse Inn in the Rue Geoffroy Lasnier. Afterwards he moved to the Rue des Mauvaises Paroles, in the parish of Saint Germain l'Auxerrois, thence to the rue de la Tisseranderie, and finally to the Rue des Cordeliers, Cour du Commerce.

He was soon engaged as clerk by a solicitor named Vinot for his board and lodging. Vinot is said to have shied at his handwriting, but, noticing the young applicant's self-possession, to have closed the bargain. Danton worked hard, and occupied his leisure hours in tennis, fencing, and, above all, in swimming, delighting to practise his strength and skill in the Seine. More than once he saved a friend from drowning. From his bathing-place could be seen the towers of the Bastille, and one day he was heard to ejaculate, 'Those strong walls overhead blind and stifle me. When shall we see them pulled down? I would wield a pick with a will if the chance came.'

Though tall, powerfully built, and muscular, Danton does not seem to have been constitutionally strong, and, while serving his time as clerk, had a long illness, which he utilised by reading the Encyclopædia, and such authors as Voltaire, Rousseau, Beccaria, and Montesquieu. After reading Montesquieu's 'L'Esprit des Lois' he exclaimed, 'What a new horizon opens before me! I am only vexed to find that a writer who carries you to such heights and so far was President of a Law Court.' 'Buffon's Natural History' became so familiar to him that he could say whole pages by heart. Corneille was his favourite poet, and he also read Tasso, Ariosto, and Dante. He even wrote poetry himself. It is an instructive example of the mendacity which has dogged his life that he was long said to be grossly ignorant and illiterate, when, as a matter of fact, he possessed a well-stocked library, and could read in the original the masterpieces of ancient Rome as well as those of Italy and England. He could, in fact, do more than translate. His brother *avocats* at his installation mischievously challenged him to compose an address on the existing relations between the law and the moral and political state of France. Danton did not flinch, and in scholarly periods astonished his audience by a scathing denunciation of despotism and a prophecy of the impending revolution.

It was at Rheims that Danton was called to the Bar, but he soon returned to Paris, and in 1785, pleading for a shepherd against his lord, gained his suit for the former and fame for himself. His address to the court was printed, and he was warmly congratulated by, among others, the well-known publicist, Linguet. In this case, as in others, Danton showed that he was by nature, as at school he was by name, 'Anti-Superior,' pleading by choice for the poor against the rich, and not seldom returning his fees.

But his profession was not one favourable to independence and was distasteful to him. In a conversation with his old declamation-master, who had come from Troyes to Paris, he is reported to have denounced the parasitic and obsequious attitude of the Bar to solicitors and the Bench, and to have concluded with words that might well have fallen from the

Danton of 1792 : ' As for me, barbarian that I am, I confess I cannot put up with all these servilities of civilisation.   I confess that I am by temperament unable to swallow so much humble pie.   I am stifled by such an atmosphere.   My lungs need a purer air to breathe.'

If his professional income was before his marriage small, Danton lived thriftily, a cup of coffee and a game of dominoes after a dinner at some eating-house being only occasionally varied by a visit to the Théâtre-Français.   The café he frequented most was the Café de l'École, of good repute, and much used by men of the law.   The proprietor's name was Charpentier, who was a *bourgeois* of position, holding the office of *Contrôleur des fermes*.   Danton fell in love with his daughter Antoinette-Gabrielle, and she with him.   Her parents, after due inquiry, agreed to the marriage, and gave their daughter a dowry of 20,000 francs, stipulating only that their son-in-law should look out for a source of income less precarious than poor clients' fees.   In June 1787 he was accordingly married, and some account of his circumstances then and afterwards will not be out of place here.   In the preceding March he had become by purchase Avocat aux Conseils du Roi, and as such, till the abolition of the office in 1791, received from 75,000 to 90,000 francs, or at the rate of 750*l*. to 900*l*. a year.

· The Avocats aux Conseils du Roi were seventy-three in number, and at the head of their profession.   To be enrolled among them it was necessary to produce testimonials to character, to have practised at the Bar, to have passed a searching examination, and to have become acquainted with almost every branch of law.   They were subject to strict discipline.   Their practice lay chiefly in the Chancellor's Court, where they had priority before all other advocates, and were of the highest importance and dignity.   They were constantly in contact with men in authority, acquiring thus a training in statesmanship and legislation.   Their close connection with royalty, or the representative of royalty, was

signified in the motto, *solis fas cernere solem*, and it is possible
that it was out of complaisance to fashion that Danton at this
time signed himself d'Anton, just as we read in Mme.
Roland's Memoirs of another young man prefixing the 'de'
to his name on becoming teacher to the pages at Versailles.[1]

Danton's assured position is shown by his having been
offered the Chancellor's Secretaryship by M. de Barentin, who
was Keeper of the Seals 1788–1789. One historian [2] even says
that the Court proposed to make him himself Keeper of the
Seals, but that he refused. We know that his business was
such as to necessitate his keeping two clerks,[3] and Courtois de
l'Aube describes him as full of work, and, at the time he wrote,
engaged on suits involving upwards of 12,000,000 francs.
Even apart from his professional income he was not penniless,
having inherited from his father, in real property only,
20,000 francs, while, in order to enable him to borrow a
portion of the purchase-money of his office, his relations had
become his security for 90,000 francs. Subsequently his
income must have been considerably greater. He was elected
Administrator to the Department of Paris, January 31, 1791,
and in the same year Joint Deputy to the Procureur Syndic of
the Commune, a post worth 240*l.* per annum. In 1792 he was

---

[1] Part III. Section 1.   About this 'de' which has been made a subject
of derisive comment, Danton felt, we may hope, what Béranger afterwards
sang :

> 'Eh quoi ! j'apprends que l'on critique
> Le *de* qui précède mon nom.
> Êtes-vous de noblesse antique ?
> Moi, noble ? oh, vraiment, messieurs, non.
> Non, d'aucune chevalerie
> Je n'ai le brevet sur vélin ;
> Je ne sais qu'aimer ma patrie.
> Je suis vilain et très-vilain . . .
> > Je suis vilain
> > Vilain, vilain.'

[2] A. F. Desodoards quoted by Lenox, p. 28.

[3] Mme. Roland's Appeal to Impartial Posterity, *My Second Arrest*
(Eng. tr. 1795).

DANTON'S MOTHER.

for a short time Minister of Justice, and in the Convention was in receipt of 18 francs a day as deputy, besides whatever extra payments he received when on mission.   And though in 1791 the office which he purchased prior to his marriage was abolished, he purchased, with the sum given as compensation and other funds, land worth between 80,000 and 90,000 francs. This, with some 5,000 francs personalty, was all he left to his children after he 'had had in his hands the treasure of two nations.'

But small though the estate thus purchased was, it cost him dear.   Courtois names it as the main source of the swarm of rumours prejudicial to his name.   He himself was stung by them out of his usual indifference to what was said about him. When taking office under the Commune of Paris in 1791 he scornfully said that the property he had recently purchased had, in spite of its modest proportions, been 'exaggerated by malice into enormous estates bought for him by imaginary agents of England and Prussia.'   And in 1793, after his famous outburst at the Jacobin Club, 'Has my face a free man's look? Am I no more the companion of your dangers, the friend you have embraced, your sworn ally till death?   Have I not been the mark of persecution without end?' he went on, 'You will be amazed when I prove to you that the huge fortune fabricated for me by men who are your enemies as much as mine is in reality the modest property I have always possessed.   I challenge proof of the smallest criminality.   Try what anyone may, it will be in vain.   The people shall see no shuffling on my part.   You shall judge me in its presence.   I will no more tear out a page of my history than you will the pages of yours, which are destined to immortalise the annals of freedom.'

The proofs Danton challenged were not forthcoming.   He had plenty of money for his frugal household, for hospitality to friends, for congenial generosity to his nephew, his good mother (who was his constant guest), his nurse (to whom he left a pension), and for an occasional day in the country, and a merry dinner.   But he did not save much; and well it was for him that he did not.   For at a time when charges of venality were scattered broadcast by and at everyone, when Royalists, Girondins, Jacobins—Mirabeau, Brissot, Isnard, Vergniaud, Guadet, Fauchet, Condorcet, Grégoire, Pétion, Delacroix, Desmoulins, Fabre d'Eglantine, Marat, Chaumette, Merlin of Thionville, Chabot, were all tarred with the same brush by their respective enemies, who often specified the exact price for which a man sold himself; when, in the Princesse de Lamballe's memoirs we are told to a franc the sum by which the Incorruptible himself was corrupted, a fortune left by Danton would never have been believed to have been amassed by fair means.[1] What webs of falsehood his enemies would have woven round him if they had found fit material we may guess from those which spider-like they spun out of their own bowels.   Mirabeau mentions his having been given 30,000 francs in March 1791. Lafayette says that his compensation for his office in 1791 was really a bribe of 90,000 francs from the Court.   Brissot, with Bertrand de Molleville, raises the sum to 300,000 francs, Brissot saying he had seen his receipt for it, though Lafayette says that Montmorin told Danton it was burnt.   And if every charge were taken as true, the total of his illicit gains would amount to two million francs and more.   Two years after he was in receipt of a very considerable income, he was, according to Mme. Roland, 'a wretched advocate more burdened with debts than causes, whose wife said she could not have kept house without the help of a guinea a week from her father.'

Lafayette's charge is precise.   Had he himself published his venomous accusations he would possibly have been less positive.[2]   But little did he and his congeners dream that the day would come when every detail of Danton's indemnification for his avocatship as well as of its acquisition would be brought to light, to Danton's honour and their shame.   The fact was that while Lafayette supposed him to be bribed by Mirabeau,

---

[1] The Duke of Brunswick was said to have been bribed to evacuate France by the proceeds of the robbery of the Garde-Meuble ! (S. iii. 96.)

[2] Cf. *Mémoires*, iii. 84, and iv. Avertissement (edit. 1837).

Mirábeau considered him the creature of Lafayette, and they and Brissot repeated every gutter-story till perhaps they even came to believe them, involving themselves thereby in hopeless absurdities and self-contradiction. Proof they had none, unless the assertion of Brissot, which clashes with Lafayette's in two points, is proof. But Brissot was a needy man himself, charged with accepting bribes—one of 6,000 francs a month, and for other service 300,000 francs down. He was author of the axiom that property is a theft,[1] was charged with the theft of other people's property,[2] and, by Peltier, with being himself Montmorin's murderer. No one would believe Peltier, but the lines he quotes are suggestive :

> Haine de philosophe est un feu qui dévore :
> Haine de Gazetier est cent fois pis encore.

Moreover, if Brissot could have shamed Danton, why did he not do so when they were enemies, and during the death-struggle of the Girondins and the Mountain? Such proof as has come to hand since Lafayette's day has been all against Lafayette, and Louis Blanc, who in one edition most relied on him when assailing Danton's reputation, was forced in another to admit that he had been leaning on a broken reed.

We who know that not one scrap of evidence against Danton was ever found in the iron cupboard, or the King's desk, or the secret accounts of Montmorin, or those of the Intendant of the civil list, Laporte, inventoried by Danton's enemies, the Girondins, and printed by order of the Convention ; that no evidence of his venality was produced at his trial ; that in Paris he lived in a small unpretentious house in a side-street ; that the country houses—modest enough, as one may still judge from engravings of that at Sèvres—which he was said to have kept up, were the property, first one, then the other, of his father-in-law ; that he himself, at his trial,

---

[1] Claretie's *Œuvres de C. Desmoulins*, i. 254.

[2] Bourgoing's *Hist. Dipl. de l'Europe*, Part I. p. 433, and Carlyle, *Fr. Rev.* ii. 94 (edit. 1871).

summoned as a witness in his behalf the landlord at whose house his 'orgies' were said to have been held, and that the Court would not let the witness be called ; that at a time of incessant surveillance over, and preternatural suspicion of, rich men, orgies which could have swallowed up two million francs, even if otherwise credible, would have been impossible for a popular leader, would, in fact, have brought him post-haste to the guillotine ; that the lists of proprietors of the theatre in which he is said to have speculated do not contain his name ; that no estate purchased for him by an agent was ever inherited by his family or has otherwise been accounted for ; and that the whole of the fortune he left at his death was some three or four thousand pounds, may confidently pronounce Danton Not Guilty of charges as rancorous as they are unproved, and appreciate his own words to Courtois, 'I shouldn't know how to spend 50,000 livres prudently if I had them. The fear of misusing such a sum, even more than of having Hébert and his gang at my heels, would hinder me from dreaming of its acquisition.'[1]

[1] See Appendix A, ' Danton's Income.'

CHAPTER II

REASONS FOR BECOMING A POLITICIAN—CAUSES OF THE REVOLUTION
—MISERY OF THE PEOPLE—TAXATION—PENAL CODE—FEUDAL
BURDENS—CONDUCT OF ARISTOCRACY—ROYAL EXTRAVAGANCE

IF Danton were not the needy adventurer of legend it may
still seem surprising that when well-to-do and happily married
he should have voluntarily launched out of so quiet a haven
into the stormy sea of politics. But it would have been far
more surprising if he had not done so.[1] He was, as his
boyhood shows, a born politician, a born orator, and of a
temperament which, while equal to immense effort at a crisis,
was indisposed to humdrum drudgery. Moreover, in that
stormy decade during which he came to Paris, to be young
and able and not a politician was almost impossible. Stupid,
indeed, is the criticism which can account only by dishonest
motives for such a career as his at such a time. It needed a
far less keen vision to foresee the coming decomposition of
society, and far less consciousness of ability to make him aspire
to preside over its reorganisation. For though it has been
said that no man can name the causes of the Revolution, that
they are countless, old as the world, beginning at the remotest
eras of history [2]—reflections true in a sense of all great
historical events—from a less nebulous point of view never
were causes more certainly known or susceptible of more exact

---

[1] St. Albin says that Danton proposed to M. de Barentin a plan of
reform in which the King was to play the part of chief reformer. *Homme.
d'État*, p. 32.

[2] Lewes's *Robespierre*, ed. 1849, p. 62.

definition. A people rebels when it is misgoverned or starves. The French people were both starved and misgoverned. The writings of Voltaire and Beaumarchais killed many superstitions. The writings of Rousseau created many yearnings. The Encyclopædia was the entrance gate to an avenue of far-reaching thought. The example of America may have stimulated some theorists. The imbecility of the Court surpassed the hopes of its most sanguine enemies. But each of these factors in the Revolution, and all of them put together, might not improbably have failed to revolutionise France if it had not been for the profound misery and degradation of the French people.[1]

In 1709 a curé entered in his parish register, 'I certify to all those whom it may concern that all the persons who are named in this parish register have died of famine, with the exception of M. Descrots and his daughter;' and adds, 'The people have been eating dead carrion for a fortnight past; there is no corn, and women have smothered their children for dread of having to feed them.'[2] In 1739 D'Argenson says, 'The men are dying as thick as flies, and the living are eating grass.' In ten years the population diminished one third. The people were already full of rage. 'When,' says D'Argenson, 'the people no longer fear anything, they are everything. All these materials are combustible.' At the time of Danton's marriage there was no change for the better.[3] All over France land was going out of cultivation. The high-roads were deserted. You might go on one thirty miles from Paris and not meet a diligence or a carriage. The fields, where cultivated, were cultivated badly. The houses were often

---

[1] 'Il n'est personne qui n'avoue que la Nation a été préparée à la Révolution par le sentiment de ses maux bien plus que par le progrès des lumières.'—Mirabeau (quoted by M. E. Champion in his *La France d'après les Cahiers de* 1789).

[2] 'Famine de 1709 dans le val de la Loire,' quoted by M. Claretie (*Camille Desmoulins et les Dantonistes*), p. 40. Cf. *La France d'après les Cahiers*, pp. 221–2.

[3] Cf. Michelet, ii. 2. 'Dès le mois de mai (1789) la famine avait chassé des populations entières les poussant l'une sur l'autre.'

without glazed windows. The castle you might see perched overhead on some rock would be kept garrisoned for the reception of prisoners sent by *lettres de cachet*. In Paris alone there were thirty prisons where you could be incarcerated without trial.[1] In six only of the twenty bastilles of France there were in 1775 three hundred prisoners. There were vast wastes, huge forests, and grand mansions. But the owners were absentees, squandering the rents, wrung from their serfs, in the luxury of towns. The wretched peasants shoeless, stockingless, living on bread that was bread only in name, were often hardly human to look upon. Women of 28 seemed like women of 70, being deformed and disfigured by incessant and grinding toil. Wages were incredibly low. Inns were often less clean than an English pigsty. Outside Paris and some of the larger towns a newspaper was a rare article. Yet everywhere was an ominous craving for news, and as a result a constant crop of monstrous rumour. The lazy swarm of monks was hated, and the tithes of the clergy, though less cruelly exacted than other dues, were a burden daily harder to be borne. For famine, never unknown, was becoming chronic.

And as if the people were not unhappy enough by reason of what their masters did not do, they were trebly tormented by what they did. Taxation was of the most crushing kind, and levied capriciously. The intendant was omnipotent, and he and his parasites harried the poor to gratify the rich. Many hundreds of farmers were annually ruined by the *corvées*— three hundred of them being reduced to beggary by the filling up of one vale in Lorraine. Enrolment for the militia was another scourge, which fell only on the third estate, for the nobility and clergy were exempt from it, as they were from the *corvée* and the *taille*.

The penal code was of merciless severity. Nearly 3,500 prisoners were sent every year to the galleys. Torture was still employed. Men were still broken on the wheel. Flogging

[1] Michelet, Introduction, *La Bastille*.

and branding were the common punishment for smuggling such necessaries as salt, and were inflicted on women as well as men. Peasants were forbidden to weed or hoe where there were young partridges, to use manure which might injure their flavour if they fed on corn so nourished, to mow before a certain time or take away stubble lest they should lack shelter. In one place mowing barley with a scythe was illegal, and punishable by a fine of 100 francs. In another it was illegal to keep a dog or cat.

The feudal fines and exactions were innumerable and their names untranslatable into English because in England they were unknown. 'What,' asks the writer [1] whose observations are here recapitulated, 'are these tortures of the peasantry in Bretagne which they call chevauchés, quintaines, soule, saut de poisson, baiser de mariées; chansons; transporte d'œuf sur une charrette; silence des grenouilles; corvée à miséricorde; milods; leide; couponage; cartelage; barage; fouage; maréchaussée; banvin; ban d'août; trousses; gelinage; civerage; taillabilité; vingtaine; sterlage; bordelage; minage; ban de vendanges; droit d'accapte?' [2] What, indeed? 'Horrible, hateful, monstrous, not to be told,' they were links in the chain which by road and river, and over every province of France, fettered all industry and turned human beings into savage beasts. For in addition to the ferocity of the penal code, its administration was infamous. 'Woe,' says our writer, 'to the man who could not conciliate favour by the beauty of a handsome wife or by other methods.'

. In shocking contrast to all this wretchedness was the cold-blooded insolence of the nobles and their impunity for all sorts of crime. In 1788, on the very eve of the Revolution, the Duc de Béthune's carriage ran over a girl in a Paris street. [3] Amid the shrieks of the child's mother he exclaimed, without getting out, 'Let the woman come to my house, she shall be

[1] Arthur Young.
[2] The words are given as in the original.
[3] Thiébault's *Memoirs* (Butler's tr.), i. 61.

paid for her loss.' In the preceding reign the Comte de Charolais amused himself with shooting some slaters at work on his property, laughing merrily as his victims rolled from the roof. This, however, was too much, even for Louis XV., and he warned the count that if he *committed any fresh offence* he would pardon anyone who killed him.[1]

How an attack on the King himself was punished the awful death of Damiens has branded on the memories of all readers of history. Less familiar are the details of another horror perpetrated on a man who had written some satirical lines on the King's mistress. Seized, when asleep, in the harbour of the Hague, in defiance of international law, he was immured beneath the sea-level of Mont St.-Michel for eight years in a stone hole, where he could neither sit, lie, nor stand naturally, the length of which was between four and five feet, the width four feet, the height three feet, where no light penetrated except for one hour in the twenty-four, and where he was incessantly assailed by rats. It has been conjectured that he sustained life by eating them. But at last they ate him, bit by bit, beginning with his toes. Modern writers who draw roseate pictures of Bastille drawing-rooms forget that a system under which such things are possible must be judged not by its least harsh manifestations at any given moment, but by its worst possibilities.[2]

And if brutalities of this sort were, in degree at least, probably exceptional, other of the nobles' misdeeds were flaunted by them in the streets every day. Haggard men muttered how, in the hour of national bankruptcy, and when deaths from hunger were common, one of the King's brothers, the Comte d'Artois—'a creature who would do anything under the influence of fear, a very dare-devil of cowardice'[3]— could spend 6,000,000 francs on a house and gardens,[3] and

<hr>

[1] Baron F. de Rothschild's *Personal Characteristics from French History*, p. 99.

[2] See *Cornhill Magazine*, 1896, p. 345.

[3] Thiébault *Memoirs*, vol. i.

could sponge on the King to the tune of 17,000,000 francs
more;[1] how another brother, 'Monsieur,' tampered with
assassins;[1] how the Cardinal de Rohan, type of many others
of the higher ecclesiastics, said it was impossible to live on an
income of less than a million and a half;[1] how year after year
the processions in the Longchamps Avenue grew more and
more extravagantly luxurious, till, escorted by their aristocratic
lovers, Phrynes rode there covered with jewels and little else;[1]
how Marie Antoinette bought St.-Cloud;[2] how the King
bought Rambouillet; and how such entries as 'à Madame,
500,000 livres' figured in the Royal Red Book at a time when
the Finance Minister was robbing the chests of hospitals to
fill the Royal exchequer. Louis XIV. had left as a legacy to
France 2½ milliards of debt;[2] 750 millions had been added to
it during seven years of the regency. But the Queen went on
gambling, the nobles went on scandalising even Paris, the tax-
gatherers went on squeezing blood from stones, and still the
people endured; and, but for what seemed the revolt of
nature herself against man's wickedness and folly, might have
endured still longer. The words in which an English poet
consecrated 'Carnage' a Frenchman might have more truly
used of 'Famine,' and hailed it as God's daughter. For at the
cost of infinite suffering it was yet, indirectly, the salvation of
France. Those who speak with horror of the 1,200 victims of
September would do well to bear in mind the appalling
amount of wrong and wretchedness which, though unrecorded
by newspapers and unexaggerated by loud-tongued pamphle-
teers, had gone on accumulating during those interminable
years which preceded the vengeance of one week. Well may
the sturdy English farmer,[3] who has been quoted, doubt the
wisdom of those who 'feel no compassion for the many
because they suffer in his eyes not individually but by millions;'
and conclude that 'he who chooses to be served by slaves and
by ill-treated slaves must know that he holds his property and

---

[1] Thiébault's *Memoirs*, vol. i.　　[2] Michelet, Introduction.
[3] Arthur Young.

life by a tenure far different from those who prefer the services of well-treated freemen ; and he who dines to the noise of groaning sufferers must not in the moment of insurrection complain that his daughters are ravished and then destroyed, and that his sons' throats are cut.'

What the Englishman had generalised during a tour of a few months, Danton had watched in detail from boyhood, and had treasured up in a heart which naturally rebelled against tyranny.   This was why it was inevitable that, being in Paris, he should embark on a political career.[1]

[1] ' Il n'est pas douteux non plus que l'insurrection avait de très-sérieuses excuses, que sous prétexte de droits peut-être légitimes à leur origine, les seigneurs et leurs agents avaient accumulé des fraudes impudentes, exercé une oppression lourde, et que le délire passager, dont ils furent les victimes, était provoqué par une interminable série d'iniquités ' (*La France d'après les Cahiers de* 1789, p. 154). 'Si Tocqueville et Taine les (cahiers) avaient étudiés comme il faut, ils auraient mieux compris la chute de l'ancien régime ' (*ibid.* p. 4).

CHAPTER III

1789

PRESIDENT OF THE CORDELIERS—CHAMPIONSHIP OF MARAT—THE CHÂTELET—THE BASTILLE—THE MARCH TO VERSAILLES—FIRST MENTION IN THE 'MONITEUR'—CHARGES OF ORLEANISM, OF ROYALISM—TESTIMONY OF THE CORDELIERS—STRUGGLES WITH THE COMMUNE

DANTON, we have seen, had on two occasions at least attracted the notice of his contemporaries by his eloquence, once in defending a client, and once at his installation as Avocat aux Conseils. Though we do not know it, we may reasonably infer that as he acquired confidence he exercised his natural powers frequently, and that it was owing to constant experience of his persuasive speech that the district of the Cordeliers elected him as its president in the spring of 1789.[1] That year might have been christened the Year of Newspapers if other things had not made it even more memorable. The liberty of the press had been decreed in August, and journal after journal sprang into existence, potent at the time and still not forgotten. Among them were the 'Patriote Français,' the 'Révolutions de Paris,' the 'Courrier de Brabant,' and, most famous of all, the 'Ami du Peuple.' But Danton had no newspaper and wrote in none. He was never a writer. And when so many

---

[1] Bougeart's *Danton*, p. 7. Though no proof of Bougeart's statement exists it cannot be set aside. Danton may have been the first informal chairman. Another sort of presidency—*à mortier*—in the mock parliaments of the Palais Royal, the following year, showed where his eloquence of the rougher and readier kind was practised and trained. Cf. *Homme d'État*, pp. 49-50.

active intelligences were stirring with their pens it is significant that not one of them should have been preferred before him in the place where, even more than in the Mother Society, the mother ideas of the Revolution were engendered. The mechanism of the Revolution was to be seen at work at the Jacobins. But that the motive force was drawn chiefly from the Cordeliers, we gather both from its enemies and its friends. 'It was,' says Fréron, 'the terror of the aristocracy and the refuge of all the oppressed of Paris,' and it was in the hope of disuniting it and cutting at the root of the vigour which it displayed under Danton's presidency, that the sixty districts were converted into forty-eight sections.[1] But the attempt failed, and the flame of patriotism was kept burning as brightly as ever in the Section Théâtre-Français.

Mercier's testimony from the opposite point of view is to the same effect. During Danton's life the two men had, it seems, been on tolerably familiar terms. Mercier in a chance conversation had been moved to begin a solemn exhortation with the words, 'You are ruining the Republic and France,' only to hear Danton's bantering ejaculation, 'The rabid man,' and such irreverence may have helped to embitter his pen.[2] Hence his abusive epithets 'client-hunting pettifogger with the fluency of the gutter and the logic of a thief.' But though our confidence in the acumen of his political post-mortem is not enhanced by the operator's maledictions, Mercier's estimate of the influence of the Cordeliers district is instructive. Every revolutionary crime was, according to him, sown there and grown there, and its president was the arch-fiend who scattered and watered the tares. Equally significant is his judgment that the first act in the demagogic drama was Danton's championship of Marat in the winter of 1789–90. The first warrant for Marat's arrest should have been, though it was not, executed on October 6. Though he escaped then, he was

---

[1] In June and July 1790 Danton strenuously opposed the change. 'Sixty democratic clubs' Aulard calls the districts. *Rév. Fr.* xxiv. 228.

[2] *Le Nouveau Paris*, c. 27.

arrested December 12 and was to have been rearrested January 22. Danton, though personally he did not like Marat, viewed his arrest as an attempt to stifle free speech and to bolster up sore-smitten regal tyranny by the municipal tyranny of Mayor Bailly. He spoke out boldly, therefore, in behalf of Marat, threatening to raise St.-Antoine in his defence. Marat affirms that 12,000 men, cavalry and infantry, were called out to catch him, and that the reason for such a grotesque display of force was that the authorities dreaded the resistance of the Cordeliers. They might well do so. That district named five commissioners, of whom its president was to be *ex officio* one, to protect any citizen from arrest unless with the committee's cognisance and assent. It called on the military force of the district to enforce its decree, in which it invited the other districts of Paris to co-operate. And it sent formal notice of the decree to the Châtelet and the National Assembly.[1]

The Châtelet was not slow in taking up so bold a challenge, and issued a warrant for Danton's arrest. His menacing language seemed doubly outrageous to the men of the robe as coming from the lips of one of their own order. But they had gone too far. The National Assembly's decree of August 23 had plainly forbidden interference with a citizen's free speech. Their action excited universal indignation, and the appeal of the Cordeliers to the National Assembly was universally approved. Meantime the case was also brought before the Assembly of the Commune. Though at that time by no means Dantonist, it incidentally testified through its president to the uprightness of Danton's career, giving the lie thereby to Mercier's insinuation that he was to be arrested for debt. But it prudently shrank from interference where legal means would suffice. Danton equally disclaimed any idea of resisting the National Assembly, and a manifesto of the Cordeliers was

---

[1] The Châtelet was the name of the Court of the Provost of Paris, so called after the fort where it was located. Rabaut de St. Etienne calls it 'one of the chief hopes of the monarchical party. *Hist. of Rev.* Eng. tr. 1792, p. 179.

issued which in politic terms said the same thing. The Châtelet had to recognise its mistake and for the time abandon the attack. But it did not forget, and we shall find a second onslaught on Danton in the following year.[1]

At the same time as this affair of Marat, and even prior to it, Danton had taken other parts in 'the demagogic drama' of 1789. He is said to have shared in the attack on the Bastille in July, and two days after its capture to have gone at the head of the men of his district and arrested its provisional governor. Camille Desmoulins records his share in the events of October 5-6. When tidings came to Paris of regiments concentrating at Versailles, of plots for spiriting the King away to Metz, of the fatal banquet at which the 'Austrian Woman' smiled on the bodyguard and their guests, as, 'flown with insolence and wine,' they trampled on the national cockade, it was Danton's voice that sounded the tocsin among the men of the Cordeliers, and he no doubt worded the manifesto with which they placarded Paris and demanded and headed the march to Versailles.

His name first appears in the 'Moniteur' on November 30, 1789. The Cordeliers district, at the instigation of its president, is noticed as insisting on the responsibility of deputies to their constituents and on their dismissal in case of contumacy. Doctrine so democratic at so early a date naturally provoked criticism and opposition. Danton, while not dissociating himself from the principle at issue, thought it necessary to disavow 'instigation,' saying that the whole assembly and not he only as president was responsible. He also disavowed the authorship of a characteristic decree of the district, in which he must have cordially concurred, enforcing a small poor-relief contri-

---

[1] In 1790 (April 20) Danton, as president of the Cordeliers district, retaliated on the Châtelet by signing an address having in view its suppression and the creation of a 'grand juré' in lieu of it to deal with charges of treason. This address, which was presented to the Assembly, contained the germs of the revolutionary tribunal of 1793, and was a manifestation of the tendencies which produced the High Court of Orleans in 1791. *Rév. Fr.* xxiv, 227.

bution from every member, and inviting the rich to supplement this contribution according to their means. On December 26 he headed a deputation of the Cordeliers to the Commune with reference to some informality in the commissions of the National Guard. The Commune at that time was not a favourable audience, and the reporter records its impatience at Danton's vivacity and superfluously vigorous oratorical gestures.[1]

From all this it is plain that by the end of 1789 Danton had become a power in Paris,[2] and as a corollary stories began to be circulated of his being in the pay of Orleans, in the pay of Mirabeau, in the pay of the Court. Lafayette relates how he frustrated a design of his to make the Duke of Orleans commandant of the French Guards, and so put the King in his power. This may have been true, but, if true, what Danton probably aimed at was the restoration to power of the people's friends, the French Guards, rather than the aggrandisement of Orleans. Lafayette, who charges him in one breath with Orleanism, and in the next with being bribed by the Court, prefaces with a 'probably' his supposition that Danton meant Orleans to replace Louis on August 10, 1792. 'Probably' he had no better ground for his assertions and prognostics than such garbage as this, ungrammatical and untranslatable into decent English, which came from one of his own adherents in 1790:

'En 1790, un agent du général, le sieur Estienne, écrivait: Je devons en conscience avertir les MM. de la nation que les égrefins dont le duc d'Orléans se servit pour faire ameuter le faubourg St. Antoine et brûler la maison de Réveillon, que les maquereaux et les chevaliers de manchette de ce prince, que ses gouines, Lameth, Barnave, Duport, Marat, Danton, font leur impossible pour afin de nous donner le change sur le compte de ce prince manqué, qu'ils mettent tout le monde en

---

[1] He spoke of Bailly as Monseigneur le Maire. Though he had to retract it, Aulard remarks that the 'plaisanterie, toute grossière qu'elle fût, résumait à merveille les griefs populaires.'—*Rév. Fr.* xxiv. 122.

[2] For minuter details of how this came about, see note at the end of the chapter.

ribotte pour nous empaumer, que ce sont encore eux qu'avons mis le feu aux étouppes entre les vainqueurs de la Bastille et les gardes françaises.'

Here we see Danton coupled with Lameth, Barnave, Duport, and Marat.   Louvet and Barbaroux, who brought the same charges against him in their memoirs, coupled him with Robespierre.   Finally, as if in a burlesque, Robespierre charged him with the crime imputed to himself by Louvet and Barbaroux.   That Danton, before the idea of a republic dawned on his mind—and no one thought seriously of a republic before the flight to Varennes—may have thought of using the rebellious whims of Orleans as a lever against the Court is probable enough, and he may even have imagined he could make a constitutional puppet out of him more easily than out of the stolid claimant to divine right, but there is no proof of it, and there is no shadow of proof that he took the money of Orleans, supposing that close-fisted intriguer ever to have shown a disposition to loose his purse-strings.   What is certain is that, whereas it would assuredly have been the Duke's policy to back up Danton if Danton had been his man, Danton and his district met with no such support in the 'Journal of the Friends of the Constitution,' edited by the Duke's secretary, Laclos.   But what seems conclusive is that in 1793, when Danton demanded that Orleans should be sent to the Revolutionary Tribunal, the Duke said not a word in retaliation, though Danton's reputation was at his mercy, if Lafayette's tales had been true.

As to Mirabeau's accusations, the words of a prostitute on another woman's purity would be as convincing.   'C'est un bois' rose only too readily to his cynical lips.   Venal intriguer himself, he scattered charges of venality right and left ; but while he was being paid Danton was being prosecuted, and the Court would never have countenanced the prosecution of a creature whom it paid.   It is curious, too, if Danton had been on such treacherous intimacy with Mirabeau as was imputed to him at his trial, that Mirabeau should allude to him as the

Court's enemy, and that not a word to incriminate him can be quoted from Mirabeau's adopted son, who came into possession of the family papers, nor from Mirabeau's friend, Dumont, who is not silent about Mirabeau's intimacy with Camille Desmoulins.   Anyone who thinks such considerations inconclusive, and that Danton was so artful an actor in the 'demagogic drama' as to treble the parts of Royalist, Orleanist, Democrat, in 1789, and fill his pockets at the same time from three treasuries, should at least weigh well the resolution passed with reference to yet other devices of the enemy by the men who knew him best, the members of the Cordeliers district, on December 11 of that year.

The General Assembly of the Cordeliers District, hearing that enemies of the State have calumniously disseminated stories against M. Danton—to wit, that he has illicitly tampered with their suffrage, and procured a unanimous vote for the prolongation of his presidency by bribes; considering that such calumnies are as injurious to the dignity of the Assembly and the rectitude of its members as to the loyal and indefatigable zeal of the President of their choice; considering that such rumours, however contemptible and unworthy of the Assembly, may, in circumstances so delicate, put weapons in the hands of the enemies of liberty,

Hereby declares (1) that the unanimous vote for continuing M. Danton's presidency is only the just reward of his courage, talents, and patriotism alike in his civic and his military capacity as evinced by the strongest and most striking proofs.

(2) That the gratitude of the Assembly to its beloved President, its highest esteem for his rare qualities, and its enthusiasm in recording its vote for his re-election are fatal to all insinuations of foul play.

(3) That the Assembly is proud to possess so stalwart a champion of liberty, and is happy in being able to give him reiterated proofs of its confidence.

(4) That the Assembly hereby orders that this resolution be communicated to the other fifty-nine districts of Paris,[1]

---

[1] As the democrat he was, and always remained, Danton had in 1789 waged a long war, the upshot of which was his own election to the

Commune and the assertion of the principle that representatives must obey their constituents' mandate.

The history of the struggle was this. In July 1789 the Electoral Assembly at the Hôtel de Ville invited the districts to choose two deputies apiece for the new Commune. These in their turn called on the sixty districts to choose five deputies apiece, and the 300 so elected sat as a provisional Commune till October 8, 1790. The Assembly of the Hôtel de Ville submitted this plan, while it was being executed, to the districts, and the Cordeliers, though they elected five deputies, protested against their hand being so forced. To emphasise their protest they laid certain injunctions on the five, and, when the Commune objected, retorted by making the injunctions imperative. Their resolution was signed by Danton as president, and the five were required to take an oath to carry it out. Two of the five, Peyrilhe and Crohard, took the oath. Three resigned. On the three, elected in place of them, coming to take their seats in the Commune, Peyrilhe and Crohard were questioned as to the oath. Peyrilhe would say nothing, and resigned. Crohard gloried in his district's action. The Commune quashed the election and, reinstating the old three members, expelled Crohard. Danton, on the ground that as long as the Commune was only provisional, the districts could impose any mandate they thought proper on their representatives, appealed to the Assembly, which finally decided that matters should stand as they had done on November 10. The five originally elected thus became once more representatives of the Cordeliers. Four, however, resigned, and three of those replacing them were probably the same men who replaced them before, so that Danton practically won the battle. He himself in the middle of January was elected representative of the district, but objections were raised against his admission, based on Lafayette's report of the Marat affair. The Cordeliers protested and the Commune gave way. It kept him, however, in the background as much as possible, though on one occasion he was member of a deputation appointed to thank the King for presenting the Commune with the royal bust. (*Rév. Fr.* xxiv. 113, and following pages.)

CHAPTER IV

1790

FRIENDSHIP WITH DESMOULINS—AS YET MONARCHIST—NOT ELECTED
TO MUNICIPAL COUNCIL—SPOKESMAN OF THE PEOPLE—TURNS
OUT MINISTERS—COMMANDANT IN NATIONAL GUARD—CONFRONTS
REACTIONARIES

THE year 1790 was probably the hopefullest of Danton's short life. The first child of his happy marriage was born in June. He signed the marriage contract of his friend, Camille Desmoulins, in December. They were already, perhaps, planning the two households of No. 1 Cour du Commerce, where Danton was to occupy the upper and Desmoulins the lower storey.[1]   The lately formed Cordeliers Club was close at

---

[1] Claretie's *Desmoulins*, pp. 181 and 199.   It is clear, however, from the 'Almanach Royal' referred to by M. Aulard, *Rév. Fr.* xxiv. 114, that Danton came to the Cour du Commerce in 1788, and we know that in March 1793 he occupied the *first* floor, while Lucile's language about the events of August 9-10, 1792, seems to show that the two families were then in separate though adjacent houses.   She says that she was in her apartment and Mme. Danton with her when 'nous entendîmes crier et pleurer dans la rue . . . et nous *partîmes pour aller chez Danton.*   On criait aux armes et chacun *y* courait.   Nous trouvâmes la porte de la cour du commerce fermée.' . . . 'Nous voulûmes entrer par chez le boulanger' (Bougeart, p. 67).   And in a curious letter written by her on the 10th (see Beaumont-Vassy's *Mémoires secrets du dix-neuvième siècle*, p. 29), she wrote to her mother : 'C'est de chez Danton que je t'écris,' which she would hardly have done if she and Danton lived on two floors in the same house.   Michelet, b. iv. c. vi. and b. xvi. c. iv. describes Desmoulins as living in the Rue de l'Ancienne Comédie on the second floor of a house in which Fréron occupied the first.   This street, close to the Cour du

hand.[1]   The two friends had their differences, and two years later Desmoulins described Danton to his father as 'a man who esteems me too much to extend to myself the hatred which he bears to my opinions.'   But each must have equally exulted as he saw abuse after abuse, privilege after privilege, of the old régime—*lettres de cachet*, arbitrary imprisonment, feudal dues, titular distinction, distinction of orders, religious disabilities, parliaments, serfage, game-monopolies, *corvées*—all swept away within the twelve months beginning November 1789. And how their eyes must have hailed the publication of the Red Book with items much relished by Desmoulins, such as a retiring pension of 1,700 livres to M. Ducrot for services as hairdresser to Mademoiselle d'Artois, who died at three years old, before she had any hair, and of 1,500 to Mademoiselle X. because she once washed the Dauphin's ruffles ! [2]

Yet Danton was a Monarchist still.   Those speculations in 'La France Libre,' in which, the day after the taking of the Bastille, Desmoulins originated the idea of a Republic, as he inaugurated the Revolution with the green cockade, were for Danton not as yet within the sphere of practical politics. On February 4 the national oath was renewed by the Assembly and the Municipality, and the ceremony seemed to him of happy omen.[3]   When the last official '*je le jure*' had been uttered at the Town Hall his voice arose declaring that the people would like to participate in the oath, which was accordingly administered to them by Bailly to the accom-

Commerce, was afterwards called the Rue des Fossés St.-Germain des Prés. The Municipal Register (Claretie's *Desmoulins*, p. 456) shows that in April 1794 Desmoulins was living in the Place du Théâtre Français.

[1] The exact date of its formation is not known, but it became the district-centre when, in order to strike a blow at the power of the sixty districts, which were so many 'democratic clubs' (*Rév. Fr.* xxiv. 228), they were replaced by forty-eight sections.   *Homme d'État*, p. 73.

[2] *Rév. de France et de Brabant*, No. 20, quoted by Claretie, *Desmoulins*, p. 42.

[3] He had been elected member of the Commune in January.

paniment of ringing cheers and rolling drums.   But what was this oath in which Danton proposed that the people should participate?   It was an oath of fidelity to the Nation, the Law, and the King; to the constitution decreed by the National Assembly and accepted by the King.   Writers who have taunted the subsequent assailants of royalty with violation of this oath would do well to mark the order of its terms. Fidelity is sworn, not to the King, the Law, and the Nation, but to the Nation, the Law, and the King;[1] not to the constitution granted by the King, but to the constitution which has been imposed on the King by the Assembly.   The English House of Commons in 1643 expelled Henry Marten for declaring it better that one family should be destroyed than many and not denying that he was alluding to the King and the King's children.   In September of the same year the two Houses swore to venture their lives to preserve and defend the King's majesty's person and authority.   But a year later the Independent leaders were discussing the deposition of Charles.   And why?   ' Providence and necessity, not design,' to quote Cromwell, 'had cast them upon' what even at the outbreak of the civil war no man dreamt of.   Cromwell's words are as applicable to the French Revolution as to the English. Lafayette relates that Danton once said to him, ' I am more Monarchist than you.'   He may have said so, and certainly may have said so honestly.   Everyone was Monarchist till the Monarchy committed suicide, and to a man with Danton's robust insight into actualities, a monarchy kept in leading strings by the enemies of the Revolution may well have seemed a monarchy only in name.   It was not therefore with perjured or hypocritical lips that Danton was spokesman for the people on February 4.

His conduct on this occasion, however, did not conciliate the more timid Parisians.   When Bailly was re-elected mayor in August, Danton could not obtain a place on the Muni-

---

[1] Cf. *Mémoires de Madame de Tourzel*, edit. 1884, i. 393.

cipal Council.[1] Nor was he one of the justices appointed the same month. It is for his assailants to consider whether these two rebuffs would have been likely if he had been backed by Court influence or the purse of Orleans. The people did not doubt him. On November 10 he was again their spokesman, and in a more important matter than that of February 4, appearing in the National Assembly to indict the Ministry on behalf of the Commune of Paris. He had, as Lafayette testifies, been the moving spirit of the Sections in drawing up this indictment. Its uncompromising terms, which Bailly— who, as mayor, was forced to introduce the deputation—could have little relished, and which evoked effervescent comments from the Abbé Maury, are noticeable now for two reasons:

1. They state in the abstract what afterwards took concrete shape in the creation of the Committee of Public Safety. 'When the National Assembly, by the decree which we expect from its wisdom, shall have completely destroyed the resources and hopes of the enemies of liberty, it will constitute the National High Court, and *when some stringent example shall teach ministers that responsibility is not nominal we shall perhaps at length see them submit to the will of the nation.'* 2. They boldly assert that the Paris Commune represents France. 'This Commune, composed of citizens who in some sort belong to the eighty-three departments '— (*Several members of the Right: ' That is not true'*)—'eager to fulfil, to the satisfaction of all good Frenchmen '—(*Several members of the Right: ' That's what we all are'*)—'our duties as first sentinels of the constitution,' &c.

The pretensions here advanced were countenanced by results. Two of the ministers assailed, the Marquis de la Tour du Pin, Minister for War, and the Archbishop of Bordeaux, Keeper of the Seals, were dismissed that month; Saint-Priest,

---

[1] He was elected by the Section Théâtre Français one of the ninety-six 'Notables' of the Council-General, but his election was quashed by the other Sections, and he was not chosen at the second election. *Rév. Fr.* xxiv. 231, 232.

Minister of the Interior, in the following January. Such was the outcome of what pictorial history calls 'the first apparition of this Medusa's head.' Four days later Danton was appointed Commandant of the Cordeliers battalion of National Guards.[1] The thought of his reception by Lafayette tickled Fréron. ' *Cela sera curieux*,' he wrote.

But though Danton could take a tolerably cheerful view of the political as well as the domestic horizon, there were threatening clouds in sight. The effects of the suppression of monastic establishments and the confiscation of church property were already ominous. The grievances of the army had come to a head at Nancy, and insubordination had apparently been quenched in blood. Reactionaries, clerical and aristocratic, took heart, and daily became more insolent. Spadassins swaggered about the streets of Paris till Spadassini-cides proved that two could play at the same game. Charles Lameth was forced into a duel, but the people retaliated by sacking the Hôtel de Castries. The strife of Frenchmen, though in this case dangerous to the Court, favourable to the people, could never give Danton pleasure. ' Excidat illa dies ævo ' was the sentiment of the Cordeliers—words as noble then as when uttered by the Chancellor de l'Hospital after the Day of St. Bartholomew.

Danton had shown in July that he personally was not to be cowed. In theatrical circles royalism was fashionable, and when at the desire of their guests from Marseilles the Corde-liers district asked for a representation of Chénier's tragedy, ' Charles IX.,' at the Théâtre Français, the management at first refused, on the plea of being forbidden by the authorities, and, though afterwards induced to consent, admitted a number of young dandies in order to create a disturbance. Danton seems to have met them more than half-way, putting on his hat at the

----

[1] M. Aulard, *Rév. Fr.* xxiv. 235, thinks he resigned at once, but Lafayette, *Mémoires*, iii. 64, uses the words ' *son* bataillon ' with reference to April 18, 1791, and M. Aulard admits that in any case Danton retained great influence in the battalion.

end of the first act apparently as a sign of defiance, and, if
Marat is to be credited, to show his contempt for a survival of
the servility of the old régime.

The incident would not be worth recording except as showing how 'the man of energy'—as Marat calls him—was in
small and great things alike steadily coming to be looked on
as the popular leader. In 1790, as Mirabeau's star waned, his
flamed higher. Mirabeau's hand had made the throne totter,
but he had not meant it to fall. It is very doubtful even if he
had lived that he could have saved it from Danton's strokes.
When he died there was no one, unless it was Lafayette, left
to guard it. And already Danton was measuring swords with
Lafayette.

CHAPTER V

1791

STRUGGLES WITH LAFAYETTE—LAFAYETTE'S CHARACTER—ADMINIS-
TRATOR TO THE DEPARTMENT—LETTER ACCEPTING APPOINT-
MENT—FIRST RECORDED APPEARANCE AT THE JACOBINS—
THWARTS KING'S JOURNEY TO ST. CLOUD

LAFAYETTE was contemptuously called by Mirabeau Grandison-
Cromwell. Some modern writers have forgotten that
Cromwell had not been rehabilitated in Mirabeau's time, and
that hypocrisy and cant were then recognised as parts of his
character. Mirabeau meant to sneer at Lafayette, but meant
something more. He certainly did not mean to attribute to
him such qualities as to-day would be associated with
Cromwell's name. What excited Mirabeau's scorn excited the
Queen's hatred. Those who think that because Lafayette
said a thing of Danton therefore it must be true, and that
because Danton may have said to Lafayette 'I am more
Monarchist than you,' therefore Danton was a cynical hypocrite, should note what Mirabeau thought of Lafayette in 1790.
His policy, he said,[1]

will always be to fear and flatter the people, to partake in its
errors from hypocrisy and self-interest; to support, whether
right or wrong, the most numerous party; to terrify the
Court by popular riots, which he himself has planned or has
inspired the fear of, in order to render himself necessary; to
prefer the public opinion of Paris to that of the rest of the
kingdom, because his strength does not come from the
provinces. The man, though no demagogue, will always be
dangerous to the royal power so long as the public opinion of

---

[1] See Morse Stephens' *Hist. of French Revolution*, i. 317.

Paris, of which he can be but the instrument, continues to be a law to him.

Mirabeau, in short, thought Lafayette to be a weak and vain hypocrite fundamentally actuated by selfish motives. Danton was of much the same opinion. Napoleon called him a 'noodle.' Jefferson said he had a 'canine appetite' for popularity and fame. Though we may discount somewhat Mirabeau's estimate as that of an enemy of wholly opposite temperament, it is plain that he was a vainglorious man, from boyhood bent on playing a showy part in the world, and returning from his petty though genuine success on the stage of American affairs with the conviction that he was to be the leading actor in the drama of the French Revolution. As experience disillusioned him he seems to have become spiteful as well as vain, and it is easy to conceive his disgust at finding that he, an aristocrat, a soldier with scars, a handsome cavalier, was outfaced and overborne by an ugly gowned civilian. He is said to have something to do with—he certainly must have welcomed—Danton's exclusion from the Municipality. But his satisfaction was to be brief. On January 31, 1791, Danton was appointed Administrator to the Department of Paris, *i.e.* he became one of the thirty-six members of its Council-General, an honourable if not lucrative position, and superior in dignity to that refused to him five months before. The party of Bailly and Lafayette groaned over his election, though in the Council his minority was almost a minority of one;[1] but by the Jacobins it was hailed as a heavy blow to municipal despotism.

It has been alleged that he owed his appointment to Mirabeau—Mirabeau, the supporter of the Veto and the King's right to declare war; Mirabeau 'suspect'; Mirabeau, whom Desmoulins' journal, in the next number but one to that

---

[1] Danton, according to Fréron, said : ' I have made no recruits among the Departmental donkeys ' (Bougeart, xxvii.), and is said to have attended only six meetings in 1791. *Rév. Française*, xxiv. 239.

which announced the appointment, reproached for ingratitude to Danton ! The supposition is preposterous. Danton might have helped Mirabeau, but could only have weakened himself by intrigue with a declining, discredited man.

This is the letter which Danton wrote to M. Cérutti, president of the Electoral Assembly, on his election :—

I beg you, Sir, to announce to the Electoral Assembly that I accept the duties to which it has been pleased to call me. The votes with which Liberty's true friends honour me cannot strengthen my sense of what I owe my country. To serve it is a debt renewed day by day and ever increasing with increased means of paying it. I may deceive myself, but I feel, by anticipation, confident that I shall not disappoint the hopes of those who have credited me with that fervour of enthusiastic patriotism without which one can have no share either in winning or securing freedom, and with that moderation necessary for reaping the harvest of our happy Revolution. Eager always to have as my enemies the last partisans of overthrown despotism, I care not for calumny. I have only one ambition—to add to the esteem of my fellow-citizens who have done me justice that of those well-meaning men who cannot be for ever blinded by baseless prejudice. But however opinion as to my public life may fluctuate, as I am convinced that it is for the interest of all that the people's supervision of its agents should be free from all restriction and all danger, even in the case of men who may not shrink from accusations as false as they are grave, I pledge myself to reply to detraction only by my acts, and to revenge myself only by giving stronger and stronger proofs of my attachment to the Nation, the Law and the King, and of my undying devotion to the maintenance of the Constitution.

Danton had now two footholds for resistance to the Bailly-Lafayette party. As member of the Departmental Council he had a hand in assessment of taxes, poor relief, hospitals, charities, education, agriculture, trade, sanitation, public security, and, finally, the service and employment of the National Guard. As commandant of the Cordeliers battalion of the National Guard he had armed friends on whom he could rely. There was an anti-Dantonist minority in it which tried to change its name, but the failure of the attempt only strengthened his position. It was not long before he had need of all his resources. Meanwhile his first recorded appearance at the Jacobins is to be noted as having taken place on March 31, when he put Collot d'Herbois into a great rage by sharply criticising his praise of a certain M. Bonne-Carrère.

The occasion of the collision between Lafayette and Danton was the King's attempt to leave Paris in order to perform the ceremonies of Easter at St. Cloud. Stories were in circulation of his slights to the clergy who had taken the constitutional oath, and he was suspected of hoping to receive the sacraments at St. Cloud from the cleaner hands of nonjurors. As a matter of fact he was afflicted by sore qualms of conscience. In assenting to the civil constitution of the clergy he felt he had committed heinous sin. He quite meant to set himself right with Heaven by breaking his oath as soon as possible; but meanwhile, as long as he kept it, was he fit to receive the sacraments? A curious but characteristic dilemma of this most unkingly of kings! So he consulted the Bishop of Clermont, confessing his scruples, and pleading in extenuation his purpose, as soon as he should fully recover his power, to restore the rights of the Church. The Bishop's answer, reeking though it did with episcopal unction, was not altogether such as bishops are wont to make to kings. It was eminently unconsoling. In plain though dulcet terms he told Louis that he ought to have braved martyrdom and that he ought not to receive the sacraments; and though beginning with an invocation 'of wisdom from above' he ended more practically by a candid exposition of the mundane reasons which dictated his advice. To avoid communicating in the parish church, and thereby rendering the scandal more scandalous, the King would have to communicate in his own chapel. But by this 'you will expose yourself to what you so prudently have at heart to avoid.'

The wretched King, unassisted by such cold comfort, thought he could turn the position by going to St. Cloud. Probably, too, he had other than spiritual tricks in his mind. The Parisian populace did not believe his purpose to be purely

devotional, though as such they decidedly disapproved of it.
They thought, not without good reason, that he meant to show
them a clean pair of heels.   Every morning since the autumn
of 1789 some of them had visited the Tuileries to make sure
with their own eyes that he was not gone.   And now, on
April 18, he was going.   When the royal carriage appeared in
the Place du Carrousel it was mobbed.   Lafayette was sent
for.   He was determined that the King should go ; the people
were determined he should not.   Bailly's entreaties were as
futile as his.

Danton was at the National Assembly when Talleyrand
called his colleagues of the Department into a room there
where Lafayette and Bailly had come urging that force should
be used to clear a passage for the King.   Their faces fell when
Danton entered, but, as they persisted in their demand, he
said : ' I have already subjected myself to arrest in my country's
service, but if I should be sent to the High Court for it I tell
you plainly I am going to denounce you to the people.   They
are clearly right.   You want to massacre them for obeying the
supreme law of the people's good.   Well, you must massacre
me too, for if I cannot thwart your mad proclamation of
martial law here I will run and resist it at the people's side.'
On Lafayette offering his resignation Danton said : ' Only a
coward quits his post in a time of peril.   Besides, the Department did not appoint you.   You must give in your resignation
to the forty-eight Sections which elected you General.
Kersaint seconded him equally hotly, and ' Mottié ' went off
in a towering rage.   Danton then ran to the Caserne de
l'Observance, the headquarters of the Cordeliers battalion, and
brought the force to the Carrousel.   It was a rough shock to
Lafayette's vanity to find that the National Guard, his children,
as he called them, his worshippers, as he believed them to be,
menaced him when he spoke of martial law, and cheered him
when he threatened to throw up his command.[1]

[1] See Robinet's *Le Mouvement Religieux à Paris pendant la Révolution*, i. 472 and following pages.

At last the King gave way. Then Danton went to the Departmental Office at the Palais de Justice, and a remonstrance to the King was drawn up, which he and Kersaint inspired and Sieyès and Talleyrand may have toned down. To Bertrand de Molleville it seemed the language of 'cannibals,' to Camille Desmoulins the words of a paladin of romance, the first perhaps ever addressed to a king in the style of a free people. In it the King was told that enemies of liberty were shedding hypocritical tears over religion and working upon his conscience for their own ends; that he should cease to favour the refractory, assure foreign nations he was king of a free people, dismiss evil counsellors, and choose a new Ministry. The Department also passed a resolution for the convocation of the Sections, that they might vote Aye or No to these two questions: 'Ought the King to be asked to go, as he had intended?' 'Ought he to be thanked for abstaining from going in order to avoid a riot?' This truly astonishing resolution—made more astonishing by the fact that the ex-duke and Laodicean revolutionist, Larochefoucauld, was Departmental President—was followed by a long-winded proclamation, in which we may be sure Danton had no share, exhorting the citizens after this fashion: 'People attribute to the King a design of severing himself from the nation, and so breaking his royal oath. Citizens, can you forget his probity? He is said to encourage the refractory priests. Have you forgotten he has sworn to maintain the Constitution?' &c.

The inanity of such platitudes, long drawn out like the lullaby of a loquacious nurse to a fractious baby, at first suggests irony; but it was clearly hoped that they would tranquillise Paris. One sentence, however, is memorable for something besides its absurdity: 'The citizens of Paris, who form only one section of the French people, can as such only act by addresses and petitions.' Considering that the people had just acted to much purpose by quite other agencies we can imagine their titters as they read; but this belittlement of Paris did not, we may be sure, provoke smiles. Like the Department, the

Municipality was eager to have its say, and, like the Department, warned the King against evil counsellors whose loyalty meant trickery, whose power was abuse of power, and whose fidelity was that of lazy drones to the hive's honey.

If we wonder at a Department blowing hot and cold, and a Municipal Bailly backing Lafayette one day and signing such an address the next, we must remember what historians have sometimes forgotten—first, that there must have been acute divisions in each body likely to account for much inconsistency; secondly, that men like Bailly, who dearly loved preaching, would like to lecture Louis, though disinclined to interfere with his liberty; and thirdly, that *ex officio* both Larochefoucauld and Bailly were bound often to appear to countenance what they really disapproved of. What is certain is that such men disapproved of Danton even more than of the King. Danton published his defiance of Lafayette and Lafayette's wish to fire on the people. The Department contradicted him, saying it had held two meetings on April 18, that Lafayette had made no such proposal at the first, which took place during the mob's meeting, and at which Danton was not present, and that he could not have proposed it at the second, when Danton was present, because the mob had already dispersed. But the words assumed to have been used by Danton at the Palais de Justice seem to have been really uttered in the room at the National Assembly. Camille Desmoulins, it is true, adds to a confusion of places not unnatural in such feverish moments by making Danton say he had spoken '*dans la tribune du départe-ment*,' but there can be no real doubt of the part played by his friend on this memorable day. Lafayette ludicrously pretends that he was in the Court's pay, and provoked the riot in order to give the King a pretext for posing before Europe as a prisoner. But though Lafayette might rage and the Department imagine a vain thing, those hours during which the King sat waiting in his carriage added a cubit to Danton's reputation in the eyes of the Parisians. Mirabeau had died on the 2nd. On the 18th Lafayette was shown to be a shadow. His resignation and subsequent withdrawal of it were equally useless, and Danton, from that day forward, was the foremost man of action in Paris —that is to say, in France.

He triumphed, in fact, all along the line. The feeble attempt of the Department to throw responsibility on the Sections was defeated by his inducing them to vote that it was not a subject for their deliberations. And the King who on the 19th indignantly told the Assembly he was still determined to go to St. Cloud, stayed at home, fearing for ' our good priests.' He even issued a manifesto to Europe, which he induced M. de Montmorin, in spite of his disgust and his proffered resignation, to sign, protesting that he was perfectly free when he was in fact a prisoner. and praising a Constitution which had robbed him of his throne.[1]

[1] B. de Molleville's *Annals of Fr. Rév.* tr. by Dallas, ch. xxxix.

CHAPTER VI

1791—*continued*

KING'S PLOTS—DENUNCIATIONS OF SIEYÈS AND LAFAYETTE—
CHARGES OF VENALITY—LAFAYETTE'S STORY ABOUT MONTMORIN
—BERTRAND DE MOLLEVILLE'S LETTER

COWARDLY though the King's proclamation seemed to Montmorin, it was not prompted by cowardice. It was a deliberate
attempt to throw dust in the people's eyes. At the very
moment it was written the King's chief embarrassment was
which to choose of plots for the overthrow of his lauded Constitution and for the re-enslavement of his free people. Should
he escape to Montmédy? Should he listen to Breteuil,
Montmorin, or Calonne? Or should he be guided to less
irredeemable issues by the Lameths? He himself hankered
after Montmédy. And had he manœuvred and dissimulated
only to get out of Paris much might have been forgiven him.
But the Montmorin plan was of more far-reaching villainy.[1]
It was to induce the Emperor, Prussia, Spain, Naples, and
Sardinia to declare war on France in order to create a pretext
for the King putting himself at the head of the army. The
Queen, by a refinement of treachery, was to stay in Paris and
make herself popular by sham appeals to the Emperor and the
King of Naples to withdraw from the coalition. The National
Guard was to be dissolved. A new Constitution was to be
voted. The King was to re-enter Paris once more indeed a
king.

To all this treachery the King was privy while the Assembly

---

[1] B. de Molleville's *Annals of the French Rev.* ch. xxxix.

were receiving his manifesto to Europe with rapturous cheers, and while the people were as yet not dreaming of a republic. But dissimulate as he might, something kept leaking out. The Moniteur published a letter practically revealing the Montmédy plot in outline.   Montmorin in a letter to the Assembly denied on his responsibility, on his head, on his honour, that the project ever existed, denying the charge as an injustice most injurious to the Royal Family.[1]   He is said not to have known of the Montmédy plot, but all the while he was himself at the bottom of another and a baser one with precisely the same object in view.   Again the Assembly broke out into vehement cheering as the jesuitical letter was read; for it was a royalist Assembly still.   Yet in a series of questions propounded to the King and Queen on behalf of the Comte d'Artois, to this one, ' In what state is the mind of the people ?   Have your Majesties in the Assembly any persons on whom you can rely ? ' we find this answer of the Queen : ' The mind of the people is detestable ; they are for no king. We have no person in the Assembly.   The only Deputy who made overtures to us is dead.'[2]

It is to be observed that she does not allude to Danton. He was not, it is true, in the Assembly ; but if he had been in the Court's pay is it conceivable she would not have mentioned him ?   Of his fast-increasing importance at this time there can be no doubt.   He summoned the Municipality before the Department for threatening to prosecute the Cordeliers Club, and the Department prohibited the prosecution. And in the new '*Journal des débats de la société des amis de la Constitution*,' where for the first time his speeches are properly reported, we find a fierce denunciation of Sieyès and Lafayette on June 20.   Sieyès, he said, was

priest to the core, who had defended tithes, opposed nationalisation of Church property, and tried to fetter the press. And now he was proposing two chambers.   Lafayette was his coadjutor and had proposed the same thing to himself a year

---

[1] B. de Molleville's *Annals of Fr. Rev.* ch. xxxix.   [2] *Ibid.* ch. xl.

before, trying to sap his patriotism by reminders how he had been ostracised by the Sections while Bailly was re-elected Mayor. Both of them were traitors, as everyone was who proposed disunion while the State was in the throes of a second birth. They wanted to remain nobles. France had a horror of nobles. Unity was what was necessary for the Revolutionary drama—unity of time, place, and action. The enemy was half beaten now his plots were unmasked, but there must be no false security. 'Do not forget that it is with a priest, and the priest Sieyès, you have to do.'

Perhaps Danton was speaking at the very hour when the King was starting on his fatal flight to Varennes, and if the idea of divided chambers shocked him we may judge how infuriated he was by the King's attempt to divide France. In fiercer tones than before he thundered at the Jacobins against Lafayette. The President had announced that Lafayette, Bailly, and the Ministers were coming to the meeting. 'If the traitors show themselves,' he said, 'I must speak. Willingly would I see two scaffolds prepared, and willingly would I die on one of them, if I do not prove to them face to face that their heads ought to roll at the feet of the nation against which they have never ceased to conspire.'

Turning to Lafayette on his entry he said : ' I am about to speak as if I were in the presence of God himself, and I would gladly brave death to say to your face, M. Lafayette, what I would say in the presence of Him who reads all hearts.'[1] He went on to speak of Lafayette's having tampered with him, of the scheme for two chambers— ' a torch of discord thrown, not, I think, without design, amid the eighty-three departments '; of the harshness shown to the rioters at Vincennes as contrasted with the leniency to the *chevaliers du poignard* ; of the King's Guard, that 21st of June, being the same grenadiers who had been his guard on the 18th of April, weeded only of the patriotic fourteen who had opposed his flight to St. Cloud ; and then, declaring that time was short and that all those

---

[1] *Révolutions de France et de Brabant*, quoted by Bougeart, p. 46.

present would eagerly listen to Lafayette's defence, he concluded—

You have waited to be reconciled with us till now—now,
when the people have a perfect right to take your life. You
have come for an asylum here—here, where all your friends,
your confidants, your journalists, your parasites, have gone on
declaring is the den of factionists, libèllers, robbers, regi-
cides. They will show themselves more generous than you—
these factionists, these assassins. They grant you asylum.
But answer me this : You swore the King should not go. You
made yourself surety for him. Choose one of two things.
Either you are a traitor who has betrayed his country or a dolt
to make yourself responsible for a man over whom you have no
hold. On the most favourable construction you have shown
yourself incapable of your command. I have nothing more to
say, but I have said enough to prove that while I despise
traitors I do not dread assassins.

A fierce, uncompromising speech, delivered, it must be remembered, immediately after the discovery of the King's
flight. And yet the man denounced so contemptuously as a
fool or a traitor, or a compound of both, could, if we can credit
him, have confounded his bold accuser with a word. Lafayette says that he knew that Montmorin had in his hands
Danton's receipt for a bribe of 90,000 francs from the Court,
that to mention it would have been to hand over Montmorin
to death, and that Danton counted on his silence. Lafayette,
in his rancour against Danton, forgot that he, posing always as
a precisian, convicted himself, if his story were true, of guilty
knowledge of the Court's bribery. Why should he screen
Montmorin ? He was bound to denounce him. And why
should denunciation have involved Montmorin's death ?
Could not Lafayette at the head of all the National Guards
have managed to get him out of the way ? Or did he per-
chance fear Danton's handful of Cordeliers ? But they would
have turned on Danton. It was Danton's life, not Montmorin's, that would have been in danger from the mob, if mob
violence were feared. In such circumstances it is Judas who

is punished first.   As to any other sort of death, the time was June 1791 : executions had not begun.

And the receipt.   How often do men give a receipt for bribes ?   And, if given, what became of it ?   Why was it never produced by Montmorin or the Court to ruin Danton when Danton was the Court's most energetic foe ?   Who ever held such a trump card without playing it ?   Lafayette says that Montmorin told Danton that it had been burnt.   That hardly tallies with what Bertrand de Molleville says ; but is such idiocy conceivable ?   Why should Danton get a man killed for having evidence against him when the evidence was destroyed ?   It is on a par with Lafayette's suggestion that Roland made away with documents in the iron cupboard damaging to Danton.[1]   Roland—Danton's enemy !   What would not the Girondins have given for papers incriminating Danton ?   The real reason why the receipt was not produced was because it never existed.   Lafayette should have spoken out and on the spot, at the Jacobins, or have for ever held his peace.   Lamer afterthought as a plea for silence was never resorted to by resentful vanity.

It is possible, however, that Lafayette did see some sort of receipt which he greedily assumed to be that of Danton, who never wrote a line, it should be remembered, if he could help it.   Bertrand de Molleville's unblushing narrative should be read in this connection.   He relates how he deliberately concocted a letter to Danton, full of falsehoods, by which he hoped to play upon his fears, and so help the King.   Let him speak for himself.

I made no scruple of employing falsehood in order to tame the fury of that monster (Danton).   On December 11 (1792) I sent him the following letter :—' You ought no longer to remain ignorant, sir, that among the papers entrusted to my care about the end of last June by the late M. de Montmorin, which I have brought to this country (England) with me, I find a note of different sums which you received from the funds for secret expenses of the Foreign Department.   The occasions on which

[1] *Mémoires*, ii. 435.

you received these sums, and the different dates, are specified,
as also the person who negotiated that affair.   Your connection
with this person is clearly proved by a letter in your own hand,
pinned to the note in question, which is entirely in the handwriting of M. de Montmorin.   I have not hitherto made any
use of those papers, but I warn you that they are joined to a
letter I have written to the president of the National Convention, which I send by this same courier enclosed to a confidential friend, with orders to send the letter to the president,
and to cause your *billet* and the note to be printed and placarded
in the corner of every street if you do not conduct yourself in
the King's affair as a man who has been so well paid ought to
do.   But if, on the contrary, you exert yourself to render him
the services which you have in your power, be assured they will
not pass unrewarded.   You need have no uneasiness with regard to this letter, as nobody shall know that I have written to
you.'—(Signed) 'BERTRAND.'

The truth of this matter was that M. de Montmorin had
communicated the affair to me, and showed me the papers, but
never gave them into my hands, as I had asserted to Danton,
who, knowing the intimacy in which I had been with M. de
Montmorin, could not doubt, after what I had written, of my
having them in my possession.

A remarkable letter !   A game of bluff cunningly played.
Now, if ever, Danton must flinch.   Eagerly we look for the
dénouement, which the very next words reveal with dramatic
brevity.   'I received no answer to my letter.'   Not one line !
M. de Molleville appears to think Danton wanting in common
politeness.   The 'monster' clearly had 'no uneasiness with
regard to this letter' in quite another sense than that attached
to those words by his correspondent.   'But,' adds M. de
Molleville,

I saw by the public papers that two days after that on which he
must have received it he caused himself to be deputed to the
Northern Army, and did not return to Paris till the day before
sentence was pronounced on the King.   He voted for death at
the *appel nominal*, but without supporting his opinion, as was
his custom, by reasoning or any discourse whatever.

As if Danton could have saved his head by going to the
Northern Army, supposing Paris to be placarded with proofs of

his treason !   But even so self-evident a reflection is unnecessary ; for none of the results attributed to the letter took place.
To the last M. de Molleville lies.   The King was sentenced on
the 17th.   Danton returned, not on the day before, but on the
14th.   On the 16th he spoke strenuously for putting the King
to death, and on giving his vote said : 'No compromise with
tyrants.   Kings are only struck at the head,' &c.

What candid reader will fail to see that every falsehood of
the knave testifies to Danton's innocence ?   But this is not all.
Elsewhere he tells us of an unnamed Court spy employed by
Montmorin to bribe Danton, and admits that he himself did
not trust the man.   Now, though neither Brissot nor Lafayette
is an unimpeachable witness, it is certainly curious that
Brissot should say he had seen Danton's receipt.   But surely
a probable solution of the mystery is to be found in these
naïve confessions of M. de Molleville.   The go-between,
evidently a thorough-paced rogue, found he had to produce
Danton's signature for payment received.   He could not get
it and he would not disgorge.   So he filched the money and
forged the name.   In any case Danton acted straightforwardly
throughout.   He repeated his charges against Lafayette the
next day at the Jacobins, challenging him to reply.   And when
Bertrand de Molleville thus carried one step further Lafayette's
'I could an I would,' Danton treated him as contemptuously
as he had treated Lafayette.[1]

[1] Levasseur (Bougeart, p. 55) writes of this affair : ' Le bruit de corruption dont se vante Bertrand de Molleville est parvenu jusqu'à la Convention.   La Montagne, Danton à sa tête, a demandé l'examen des pièces ;
cet examen a eu lieu, et les accusés ont été reconnus innocents.'

CHAPTER VII

1791—*continued*

THE Jacobins showed what they thought of Danton's attack on Lafayette by accepting Desmoulins' offer of 1,000 copies of his paper, in which it was chronicled, for distribution in the Department of the Moselle. Meantime Danton was flying at higher game. Till now he had been a monarchist. In 'La France Libre' published July 15, 1789, Desmoulins had argued that the only Government fit 'for men, for Frenchmen, and for the Frenchmen of this age' was that of America and Athens.

He therefore had sounded the first republican note, and he was proud of it. 'On July 12, 1789, there were perhaps not ten republicans in Paris,' he writes, 'and what covers the Old Cordeliers with glory is that they began such an enterprise as the Republic with such small means.' But the politics of Desmoulins were a pamphleteer's politics rather than a statesman's, and his republicanism rather a matter of sentiment than of deep-seated conviction. As he himself said : 'Our republicans were for the most part youths who, having been fed on Cicero at school, had conceived a passion for liberty.' Of such might Brissot be, and it illustrates the instability of Desmoulins to find him in 1792 reproaching that publicist with prematurely professing republicanism.[1] It was also in 1792 that Desmoulins wrote of Danton as 'a man who

---

[1] Claretie's *Desmoulins*, p. 180.

esteems me too much to extend to myself the hatred he bears to my opinions.'[1] What Desmoulins calls his 'opinions' Danton would have called his fitful likes and dislikes. He himself, more practical and opportunist, had up to the flight to Varennes forbidden himself 'to pronounce the word' republic. So had Robespierre.[2] In 1791 [3] he disclaimed any hostility to monarchies as such. Republic and monarchy were, he said, vague terms, apt to breed sects and sow dissension, and a State, if free, was republican even though a monarch were at the head of it. Danton had, no doubt, theorised less than Robespierre, his one guiding principle being that, monarchy or no monarchy, the people's will should be enforced. But republicanism was now in the air. On July 1 a prospectus of a journal called 'Le Républicain' had been posted at the entrance to the Assembly,[4] and with the flight to Varennes he found himself at the parting of the ways. He detested incompetence, and the King was incompetent. He knew there could be no solid government if it was being undermined by those in high places. And now it seemed clear that no faith could be placed either in the King or Lafayette. So when Robespierre, *à propos* of the flight to Varennes, besought the Jacobins to repel every proposition for a republic, and respect the decrees of the National Assembly, Danton replied: 'How could the Assembly take on itself to pronounce judgment when perhaps it would be reversed by that of the nation?'[5]

Robespierre might sit on the fence till August 1792. The Cordeliers Club made up its mind at once. It drew up an address to the Assembly containing the essence of Danton's policy, as no doubt it was the echo of his words.

We were slaves in 1789. We thought ourselves free in 1790. Legislators, you have assigned away the power of the nation you represent. You have invested Louis XVI. with unlimited authority. You have consecrated tyranny by con-

---

[1] Claretie's *Desmoulins*, p. 181.　　　[2] *Ibid.* p. 180.
[3] July 13, L. Blanc, b. vi. c. vi.　　　[4] Michelet, b. v. c. vi.
[5] *Procès*, p. 215.

stituting him an irremovable, inviolable, hereditary king. You have consecrated the slavery of the French by declaring France to be a monarchy. Good citizens have lamented it. There have been violent conflicts of opinion. But this was the law and we obeyed it. A healthier state of things we could only expect from the growth of intelligence and reason. This sham contract between a nation which surrenders all and an individual who gives nothing it seemed necessary to maintain, and till Louis XVI. showed himself an ungrateful traitor we could only thank ourselves for spoiling our own work. But times are changed. This sham connection between people and King exists no longer. Louis has abdicated. Henceforth he is nothing to us, nothing unless he becomes our enemy. We are as we were after the taking of the Bastille, free and without a king. Is it worth our while to name another ? This Society is of opinion that a nation ought to act either of itself directly or through officials removable and chosen by itself; that it is unreasonable that any one man in the State should possess such wealth, such prerogatives, as to be able to corrupt the administrative body. It is of opinion that no citizen of the State should be debarred from any State post, and that the more important the post the shorter should be the term of its occupation. Impressed with the truth and importance of these principles, it can no longer be blind to the fact that royalty, above all hereditary royalty, is incompatible with liberty. Such is its belief, for which it holds itself responsible to all Frenchmen. It foresees a host of antagonists. But was there no antagonism to the Declaration of Rights ? In any case this question is important enough to deserve the serious consideration of those who frame the laws. Once already the Revolution has miscarried owing to lingering regard for the phantom of royalty. That phantom has vanished. Therefore, without fear and without terror, let us do everything to prevent its resurrection. This Society would not, perhaps, have demanded the suppression of royalty so soon if the King, abiding by his oath, had regarded royalty as a duty; if the peoples, ever the dupes of this institution, so fatal to the human race, had not at length opened their eyes to the light; but to-day, when the King, free though he was to keep the crown, has of his own accord abdicated; to-day, when the voice of the nation has made itself heard ; to-day, when all citizens are disillusioned ; we make it our duty to act as the medium of its will by demanding the destruction at once and for ever of this scourge of liberty. You, legislators, have a striking warning before your eyes. Remember that after what has happened you cannot possibly inspire the people with any confidence in any functionary named king. Accordingly we conjure you by our common country either at once to declare that France is no more a monarchy, but that it is a republic, or at least to wait till all the primary assemblies have expressed their will on this momentous question before a second time plunging the fairest empire on earth into the chains and fetters of monarchy.

Whatever else may be thought of it, no one can deny the trenchant force of this manifesto,[1] so refreshingly free from the eternal classicalities of Desmoulins and the eternal abstractions of Robespierre. But it was not acceptable to the Jacobins. In answer to a speaker in that society, on June 23, Danton said :—

The individual declared King of the French, after having sworn to maintain the Constitution, has become a fugitive, and yet I hear someone say he has not forfeited his crown. But this individual declared King of the French has signed a paper whereby he declares he is going to seek means of destroying the Constitution. The National Assembly ought first to put forth the whole strength of the State to provide for its safety. It should then confront him with this paper. If he acknowledges it he is a criminal, unless we are to take him for an imbecile. It would be a dreadful spectacle to exhibit to the world if with the alternative of a criminal or an imbecile king we did not choose the latter. The royal individual being an imbecile can be no more king ; and what is necessary is not a regent but a commission of restraint, such commission not to be taken from the legislative body, but to consist of ten men chosen by electors, one from each department, to be changed, like members of the Legislature, every two years.

'*Ce n'est pas un régent qu'il faut.*' The words are important. If Danton had been in the pay of Orleans would he have used them ?

Soon afterwards, also at the Jacobins, he spoke as follows :—

I will briefly refute M. Anthoine. He said that the previous speaker was mistaken in alleging that the Constitution had not

---

[1] '*Où éclate tout le génie politique de Danton.*'—*Procès*, p. 211.
'*Où l'on ne peut guère méconnaître la main ou l'inspiration du président perpétuel.*'—*Homme d'État*, p. 79.

safeguarded royalty, seeing that it had decreed a regency. But M. Anthoine has not reflected that no judgment had then been pronounced on the King. Well, that being so, it is not a regent, but, royalty being now vacant, sequestration that is wanted.

He added a warning against appearing to distrust the National Assembly.

But ought we to be free from all apprehension? It is in my opinion, scandalous that the King has not been publicly examined, scandalous that commissioners should be appointed, who should wait in the royal ante-chamber and then be refused admission because 'we are in our bath.'

A man who spoke thus meant business. To Danton's matter-of-fact mind attempts to explain away the King's flight by the fiction of his having been kidnapped, or to ignore it on the pretext of his inviolability, or to draw a distinction between his personal and official inviolability, seemed, what they were, a farce. Timider or more pedantic men thought that by accepting the farce they might escape a tragedy. Bailly and the *bourgeoisie* were not for extreme measures. Lafayette, like Danton, may have thought Louis an imbecile, but Providence, he would reflect, had fully compensated France by providing it with the wisdom of Lafayette. Danton had logic on his side, but they had the law. So he appealed from them to the populace. The Departmental Council had been summoned by the National Assembly, on the news of the King's flight, to permanent session in the hall next its own—a fate-laden summons, followed, as it immediately was, by the request of the Sections also to sit permanently. As the members of the Council marched through the streets Danton harangued the people, denouncing traitors in Paris, attempts to stifle inquiry, the 'Austrian Committee at the Tuileries,' and declaring that the King would be a good riddance.[1] These thunder-charged clouds broke into flame on the Champ de Mars on July 17.

[1] Cf. Morse Stephens' *Fr. Rev.* i. 456.

CHAPTER VIII

1791—*continued*

THERE were from June 21 to July 17 three main currents of opinion in Paris. The Assembly as a whole was for Monarchy and Louis. The Jacobins as a whole were for Monarchy, but not for Louis. The Cordeliers as a whole were for a Republic. There were, too, in each cross-currents. In the Assembly Constitutionalists like the Lameths and Barnave were becoming more, and Robespierre less, Royalist. The Jacobins were divided against themselves, part of them seceding to the Feuillants, where the Lameths and Duport were leaders. Marat, at one with the Cordeliers group in deriding the farcical manœuvres of the Assembly, still expressed himself strongly in favour of constitutional royalty ;[1] royalty, however, to be tempered by dictatorship in time of need. Besides these groups and the offshoots from each there was an Orleanist party, though not with Orleans at its head. On June 26 he had, to the disgust of the extreme Royalists, renounced all pretensions to regency.[2]

The citizens of Paris were divided into two groups. The *bourgeoisie's* revolution was won. It was satisfied with its achievements, satisfied with having humiliated the King. Barnave successfully appealed now to its selfishness and

---

[1] Villiers' translation of Biré's *Diary f a Citizen of Paris,* i. 51.

[2] M. viii. 764.

jealous dread of the people below it. It disliked the Queen. It despised Louis. But it thought a king useful as a figure-head. Its strength lay in the National Guard. In opposition to the *bourgeoisie*—opposition ever growing more acute—was the populace. The institution of Sections had by no means fulfilled its object. Those that were democratic were leavening the lump. Danton stepped forward as their natural leader against the Assembly's intrigues and the complicity of Bailly and Lafayette. Bonneville, Fréron, Desmoulins were some of his supporters.

Events moved fast. Billaud-Varenne on July 1 proposed for discussion at the Jacobins the question·'which was the Government best for France, a Monarchy or a Republic.' Instantly he was frowned down by the president, and it was proposed that he should be expelled from the Society. But shortly afterwards another member declared that a Republic was inevitable, as the diet on which strong men throve best. And Brissot, at this time a great admirer of Danton, on July 2 wrote that republicanism was winning and must win, because truth wins ; that it was moving with a giant's strides, &c. On the 11th Voltaire's ashes were placed in the Panthéon. The car which had brought them to Paris had on its two sides the lines—

> ' *Si l'homme a des tyrans il les doit détrôner.*'
> ' *Si l'homme est né libre il doit se gouverner.*'[1]

The Assembly's evasion of the personal question as to the King exasperated the popular leaders more and more. On the 15th, at the Jacobins, Danton strenuously defended the right of petitioning for his dethronement, and that night Brissot and Laclos—Orleanist editor of the Jacobin journal—proceeded to settle the terms of a petition. Danton, it is said, was also present, but did not stay long. Probably he was for much more drastic terms than Brissot and Laclos. He left Brissot writing it and Laclos dozing. Laclos, when Brissot had finished, woke up, and after the words ' provide for replacing '

---

[1] M. ix. 107.

interpolated 'by all constitutional means,' thus adroitly leaving a door open for Orleans, his patron.

On the 16th Pétion came to read the petition, but found the Club deserted. The secession to the Feuillant Club had taken place. This symptom of reaction being temporarily in the ascendant had its counterpart in the streets, where passion ran high. Rotondo was bludgeoned and half killed, Fréron nearly met the same fate. In the Assembly, on the 13th, Vadier made a furious speech against the King. Frequent interruptions evinced the royalist bias of his audience. He deprecated them, saying, 'I am charged with speaking like Marat. It is very seldom I speak at all.' 'So much the better, sir, so much the better,' shouted his hearers. But on the 16th this same Vadier, with equal fervour, forswore a republic and all its works, this time winning for himself plaudits.

That day the petition was taken to the Champ de Mars, and Danton harangued the crowd from the altar there.[1] The words Laclos had inserted excited comment. The meeting was divided, but those who were for expunging the words carried the day. While it was being revised, another petition, protesting not only against Louis, but against any king, was drawn up by Peyre, Vachart, Robert, Demoy, and placed for signature the next day, Sunday, on the altar. In the riot that ensued three hundred were killed and wounded. Bailly and Lafayette succeeded in cowing the people for the time. But they were to take a terrible revenge in June and September 1792. The conquerors had mistaken for an *émeute* what was in reality a manifestation of the will of Paris emerging out of incoherence.

Some say that on the evening of the 16th Danton went to Fontenay-sur-Bois; others that he went next day. In either case it is a ridiculous supposition that he fled from cowardice. There seemed little to fear. The people on the 16th had applied for leave to meet on the 17th, and had been

---

[1] Erected (that the National Oath might be taken at it on July 14) in 1790. 'Un tertre que l'on avait pompeusement décoré du nom d'Autel de la Patrie.'—Laponneraye, *Hist. de la Rév. Fr.* i. ch. ii.

officially told they were not breaking the law in doing so. Sunday was a beautiful summer's day, and a few minutes before the fusillade the crowd was singing and dancing as at a fête. Danton, in his speech on the 16th, may have said all he had to say with regard to the second petition, which the crowd was bent on substituting for the first, and when next day's meeting was sanctioned have gone from Paris for the Sunday. If we knew what he said we should know why he went, but if he had feared for himself he would never have spoken at the altar in the morning. When he spoke of himself before his judges as 'one of the authors of the petition' he appears to have been alluding to the second petition.[1] Having had to do with the first he may not have cared overtly to father the second, knowing that Brissot and the other Jacobins were wavering, but he may have prompted it all the same. This would account for its being drawn up by such obscure men as three out of the four were, while Robert, the fourth, was an ardent Dantonist.

The authorities, at all events, had no doubt as to the advisability of punishing Danton's hostility. They at once issued a warrant for his arrest, though on some petty charge to which he alludes in his speech, soon to be quoted. He went quickly from Rosny, near Vincennes, to Fontenay, Arcis, and Troyes. Officers of the law were on his track at Arcis and Troyes. One of them being recognised at Arcis was nearly torn to pieces by the people. At Rosny his father-in-law's house was beset and his step-brother maltreated. He himself went to England, with results to be noticed hereafter, and only returned to Paris when a friendly president of the Tribunal of Cassation—Garran Coulin—had been appointed. Perhaps he was not in much danger outside the Department of Paris. But the Jacobins of Bar-sur-Aube wrote to him that

---

[1] These words are purposely left as in the first edition. But see note at the end of the chapter, where the whole question is discussed at length, with reasons for thinking that, while the general account given in the text is correct, it may have been the *first petition* to which he alludes.

if the people of Arcis would not safeguard him they would.
To this those of Arcis replied they would die to a man in his
defence. Another letter of theirs to the 'Patriote Français'
shows how dear he was to them. It speaks of him as a
citizen without reproach, a victim of unjust persecution, and a
worthy patriot. This might have come from personal friends.
But his name was now known through France. The Marseilles
Jacobins summoned the members of the mother society to be
answerable for his life and make their bodies a rampart for
him. Nor were their turgid words without a basis of reason.
He became a candidate for the Legislative Assembly which
met in October, and an attempt was made to arrest him in
the electoral convention. It was repulsed, and Danton
vigorously protested that the electoral body ought to be as in-
violate as the Assembly itself. But reaction was still too strong,
and in spite of Desmoulins' strenuous advocacy he was not
elected. Nor when he stood for the procureurship of the
Commune was he more successful. In December, however,
he was elected joint deputy-procureur, and on this occasion
delivered a memorable speech.[1]

It was not at one of the moments of his glory that a man
whose name must be for ever celebrated in the history of the
Revolution said he well knew that it was not far from the
Capitol to the Tarpeian Rock. And I, at almost the same
time, when excluded by a sort of plébiscite from this assembly,
to which a part of Paris had summoned me, answered those
who ascribed to the enfeebled energy of the citizens what was
merely an ephemeral aberration, that for an honest man it was

---

[1] In the *Patriote Français* of December 6 the following announcement,
dated December 5, occurs : 'Aujourd'hui les quarante-huit sections se
sont réunies pour procéder à l'élection du second substitut-adjoint du
procureur de la commune ; les suffrages des patriotes ont dû se porter sur
MM. Danton et Collot d'Herbois.' Danton went to England in the
middle of August and returned September 9. He had just been elected
by the Section Théâtre Français to the Electoral Assembly of Paris. The
question of his arrest was brought before the Constituent Assembly, but
its vote (Sept. 13) for a general amnesty made it unnecessary to come to
any decision. *Rév. Fr.* xxiv. 325, 326.

not far from what seemed ostracism to the highest functions of the State. Events have justified my belief. Public opinion, and not the short-lived cry of a short-lived faction, public opinion once formed formed for ever, which is based on realities impossible to be long concealed, which has no amnesty for traitors, which finally annuls the judgments of fools and the decrees of venal judges, this public opinion recalls me from retirement and the cultivation of my little farm. Humble though it is, and notoriously bought with the money I received for my suppressed avocatship, it has yet been magnified by calumny into vast estates paid for by mysterious agents of England and Prussia. My duty, gentlemen, is to take my seat among you because the friends of liberty and the Constitution so will it, a duty the more binding because at a moment when the country is threatened on all sides it is impossible to refuse a post which, like a sentinel's on outpost duty, may be one of peril. In embarking on the career thus opened to me I should not have addressed you now, after having disdained to say a word during all the Revolution in answer to innumerable calumnies, but should have let time and my conduct speak for me, if the functions to which I am about to devote myself had not wholly altered my position. As an individual I scorn the shafts aimed at me as I do the whistling of an idle wind. But I owe it to the people as their servant, if not to reply to every petty and contemptible accusation, at least to combat hand to hand anyone seeming to be sincere in his attacks.

Paris, like France, consists of three divisions. One hates all liberty, all equality, all constitutions, and deserves all the ills which would have crushed it as it would like to crush the nation. With it I hold no parley. My one wish is to fight it to the death. The second consists of the flower of the Revolution's ardent friends, coadjutors, and strongest mainstays. It has always wished me to be here. It needs no words of mine. Its judgment has been passed on me. I will never betray its trust. The third, as numerous as it is well meaning, is equally desirous of liberty, but dreads its storms. It does not hate its champions, whom it would second at a crisis, but it often condemns their energy, which it deems habitually out of place or dangerous. It is to citizens of this class, whom I respect even when they lend too ready an ear to the perfidious machinations of men hiding atrocious designs under the mask of moderation, to these, I say, I feel it my duty as a magistrate of the people frankly and solemnly to enunciate my political principles.

Nature has endowed me with an athletic form and liberty's rugged features. Happy in not being born of one of our old, privileged, and consequently emasculated orders, I am a self-made man with all my natural forces intact, though never for a moment ceasing, either in private life or the profession I have chosen, to show my ability to combine cool reason with a warm heart and strength of character. If in the springtide of our country's regeneration my love of my country has been an over-boiling passion ; if to avoid seeming weak I have allowed my-self to seem extravagant . . . . ; if, relying on my cause as the national cause, I have elected to incur a second judicial proscription based not on my imaginary participation in a petition of too tragic celebrity, but on some cock and bull story of pistols taken in my presence from a soldier's room on an ever memorable day —it is because I am accustomed to act in accordance with the eternal laws of justice, it is because I am incapable of continuing intimacies which are no longer honourable and associations with men who dare to apostatise from the faith in the people which they once proclaimed.

So much for my past life. Now, gentlemen, for the future. I have been appointed to help to maintain the Constitution and to execute the laws to which the nation has sworn. Well, I will keep my oath. I will fulfil my duty. I will to the utmost of my ability maintain the Constitution and only the Constitution, since so I shall at the same time defend equally liberty and the people. My predecessor said that in conferring office upon him the King gave a new proof of his attachment to the Constitution. With at least equal ardour the people in choosing me wills that Constitution. Therefore it has seconded the King's intentions. Are they not two eternal truths which we have uttered, he and I ? All history proves that never has a people under its own laws, under a constitutional monarchy, been the first to break the covenant. Nations never change or modify their Government unless driven to do so by outrageous oppression. Constitutional Monarchy may last for centuries longer than Despotic Monarchy has lasted. They are philosophers only in name who frame only systems for the destruction of empires. Vile flatterers of kings who tyrannise over and starve the people are surer causes of desire for another government than all the philanthropists who publish schemes of absolute liberty. The French nation with greater self-respect has not lost its greater generosity. Breaking its fetters it has preserved the Monarchy without fearing it, and without hating it has purged it of its taints. Royalty should respect a people in whom long oppression has not obliterated the inclination to be trustful, often too trustful. Let it hand over of its own accord to the law's vengeance all conspirators without exception, and all those lackeys of conspiracy who get kings to give them instalments of sham reactions to which they then want to rally, so to speak, a party on trust.

Let royalty at length show itself the loyal friend of liberty, its sovereign ; then it may be sure of lasting as long as the nation itself ; then it will be seen that the citizens who are only accused of exceeding the Constitution by the very men who clearly will not carry it into effect, that these citizens, whatever arbitrary theories they may have about liberty, do not seek to break the social pact ; that they do not wish, for the sake of something ideally better, to overthrow an order of things based on equality, justice, and liberty. Yes, gentlemen, I must repeat it : whatever my own ideal was, when the Constitution was being revised, as to things and persons, now the oath has been taken I would cry aloud for the death of him who should raise a sacrilegious hand against it, were he my brother, my friend, or my own son.

Such are my sentiments. The general will of the French people, as shown in its solemn adhesion to the Constitution, shall always be my supreme law. I have consecrated my whole life to the people, which will never again be attacked, be betrayed, with impunity, and will soon sweep all tyrants off the earth if they do not abandon the league they have formed against it. I will die, if necessary, in defence of its cause. My last prayers shall be in its behalf. It and it only deserves them. Its intelligence, its courage, have raised it from the depths of nothingness. The same intelligence and courage shall make it immortal.

To an English ear some of the periods of this speech have a too turgid and egotistic ring. It was evidently carefully prepared, and Danton excelled in impromptu oratory rather than in a set speech. But it was the fashion at the time to perorate, the fashion to be somewhat prodigal of, often very sincere, protestations of readiness to die for France, &c. To do Danton real justice all his speeches should be read, and it will be found that such egotism as occasionally crops up in them is infinitesimal in quantity, as it is inoffensive in quality, in comparison with the egotism of men like Robespierre.[1]   We must also take into consideration his nationality, the habits of his audience, and the moment at which he spoke.   He had been hunted by the law.   Stories were being spread broadcast to his discredit.   He was entering a body where such stories would find credence with not a few.   That accounts for the profusely personal and apologetic element in the speech, which, however it may violate canons of oratorical good taste, is certainly interesting.   How many times, for instance, when through the medium of foaming phrases we find him subsequently contriving to make an audience swallow some wholesome sedative, do we recall 'if to avoid seeming weak I have allowed myself to appear extravagant.'   But it is as a profession of faith, as a key to the whole of his political career, that it is really important.   It stamps him as an opportunist in the best sense of the word, as the practical statesman never averse to half a loaf if the alternative is no bread.   He had desired a republic ; he was content, sooner than enter on civil strife, with a constitutional king.   He will do his utmost for the Constitution *because* it is the people's will.   But all depends on that, and over and over again as he protests his devotion to the Constitution he reiterates the condition that it must not override the will of the people, with whom and for whom it is his sole ambition and immutable resolve to live and die.   Let the King be faithful to the Constitution and all will be well. Let him betray it—worst of all, let him call in the foreigner to overthrow it—and the people and their spokesman are *ipso facto* absolved from their oath.[2]

[1] But it is surely going too far to say as M. Aulard does : ' D'ordinaire Danton s'efface dans son discours.'

[2] A writer in the *Guardian*, May 3, 1899, misapprehending the views expressed in the preceding chapter, argued that the Cordeliers address was not due to Danton, that Danton at the time of the affair of the Champ de Mars was more Jacobin than Cordelier, that he had nothing to do with the second petition, that the Republic ' was never an idea ' with him, and that he carefully avoided giving the Republicans 'a false start' on the

Champ de Mars. The writer had neither noticed that Danton's 'opportunism' was insisted on in the text, nor the opportunist ending of the Cordeliers address. Danton was in July 1791 what he always was, in principle democrat, in practice opportunist, and the Cordeliers address, so far from being formulated republicanism, was likewise democratic and opportunist, praying the Assembly, as it did, either to declare a republic (a word, at the time, of most indefinite meaning) *or* to wait till the departments and the primary assemblies had declared their will. M. Robinet accurately describes this address as one 'où éclate tout le génie politique de Danton,' and ' où l'on ne peut guère méconnaître la main ou l'inspiration du président perpetuel.' Danton was wedded to no republican formula, but he was feeling his way to a republic, by which he meant ovemment by the people. The note of the address—democratic rather han republican—is characteristic, and exactly expresses his attitude— aggressive against the Assembly's royalism, aggressive against Louis, but unpledged as to what should replace him.

The argument of the writer in the *Guardian* is the argument developed in 1893 by M. Aulard in a series of articles in *La Révolution Française*. But I cannot help suspecting that it would have been modified if that admirable author had approached the subject somewhat less polemically. In attempting to confute Comte (with whose theories I am not concerned) and to prove that Danton was not the progenitor of the ' republican idea ' he seems to have been led to ignore the essentially democratic nature of Danton, to convict him of inconsistency where he was thoroughly consistent, and to misjudge the occurrences of the Champ de Mars.

To make this clear Danton's connection with the Cordeliers must be briefly recapitulated.

In July 1789 the Cordeliers district was already called ' The Republic of the Cordeliers ' (p. 116).' Danton was its leading man. He inspired it to march to Versailles. Bougeart says that he was its first president, and it is probable that if not formally he was so informally. In any case he was president in September. He conducted its war with the Commune about the Mandat Impératif; 'y joua,' says M. Aulard, ' le premier rôle ' (p. 140). In January 1790 it elected him to the Commune, and, though not then president, he was, says M. Aulard, ' plus que jamais meneur ' (p. 144). He was one of the five commissioners appointed then to scrutinise arrests, and, once more to quote M. Aulard, ' c'est au district des Cordeliers que s'exerça surtout son activité ' (p. 227). In April, as its president, he advocated the suppression of the Châtelet. In May or June he was elected by it Assistant-Notable to safeguard the rights of prisoners. Though a member of the Commune he conducted the district's war against Bailly in June and July. ' Le district des Cordeliers,' says M. Aulard, ' c'est Danton ' (p. 227). He inspired or signed its resolutions designed to

' The references are to the pages of tome xxiv. of *La Révolution Française* for 1893.

thwart the conversion of the districts into Sections, and, failing in the attempt, riposted by founding or concentrating the club of the Cordeliers, who 'se battirent contre le trône et l'autel, contre la politique constitutionnelle' (p. 229), and who invented the motto 'Liberty, Equality, Fraternity.' In August the district elected him a Notable, and in November the Commandant of its battalion of National Guards, he meanwhile having become a member of the Jacobins in September.

Here, then, we have an unbroken sequence of events which prove him to have been Cordelier to the core in 1790, one with his district in its policy, and the leader of its choice. Yet M. Aulard is of opinion that three months later it was no longer in the Cordeliers club or district that he exercised his authority, because he could only speak to Paris in the forum, whereas at the Jacobins he spoke to France (p. 240). He doubts his having anything to do with the Cordeliers demonstration against the fort of Vincennes in February 1791, and concludes that 'ces bruyants fanfaronnades n'étaient plus de son goût' (p. 240). He argues that Condorcet, not he, was the author of the republican idea when he advocated a National Convention and an Elective Council of Seven (p. 308), and that Condorcet at that time kept severely aloof from Danton. But what said Danton himself? 'Ce n'est pas un régent qu'il faut, c'est un conseil d'interdiction ; ce conseil ne peut être pris dans le corps législatif. Il faut que les départements s'assemblent, que chacun d'eux nomme un électeur qui nomme ensuite les dix ou douze membres qui devront composer ce conseil et qui seront changés, comme les membres de la législature, tous les deux ans.' In saying so he was merely echoing the Cordeliers address ; and the principle underlying his demand, that of the Cordeliers, and Condorcet's, is identical, *i.e.* democratic. To represent him as anti-Lafayette and not anti-Louis is to represent his minor as his major motive. His private quarrel with Lafayette no doubt embittered his language, but he assailed him as the outwork and buttress of royalism. When he cried on June 21 'Vos chefs sont des traîtres,' M. Aulard thinks that he was speaking of Lafayette. But he is said to have mentioned the King directly, and in any case it seems incredible that he did not include in 'Vos chefs' the man he was denouncing at the Jacobins as a criminal or imbecile. His attitude after the flight to Varennes was the natural and consistent development of his attitude towards the attempted flight to St. Cloud which he personally interfered to stop. On that occasion also he collided with Lafayette, and when taxed with calumniating him would not disown the spirit though he disclaimed responsibility for the letter of the incriminated placard, but his main attack was directed against the king on the board, not the knight. In short, he was Cordelier in April. There had been no sudden break in the continuity of his policy or friendships.

Nor was there any afterwards. M. Aulard (p. 240) says that '*sans parler de république* il essaie d'entraîner les Jacobins à une opposition plus vive contre la cour, de leur démontrer que de nouvelles journées populaires sont indispensables pour déjouer les intrigues de la contre-révolution,' and notes his words at the Jacobins, 'qu'il voit avec douleur qu'il faut un supplément de révolution' (p. 242); and his other words after Mirabeau's death, 'cette perte rendait encore plus pressant le besoin d'une autre législature' (p. 242).   After the flight to Varennes, M. Aulard shows how in Paris and the large towns ' il se forma un parti républicain' (p. 306), and how from June 21 to September 14 the government was practically a republic.   Is it conceivable that Danton was not one of that party? Surely M. Aulard must have forgotten his rallying-word in March 1794 to ' the men who first *spoke the word Republic and confronted Lafayette.*' Evidently Danton was unconscious of any such divorce from his past and his party as M. Aulard suggests.   And in August 1792, mentioning the Théâtre Français as, ' sous le nom de district des Cordeliers,' contributing so much to the revolution of 1789, and 'sous le nom de section de Marseille ' contributing so much to the revolution of 1792, he said : ' Vous me trouverez constamment et invariablement le même président de cette section ' (p. 482).'

No theory can weaken the force of such language, which M. Aulard himself emphasises, when he describes him as being at the time ' un démocrate exalté au milieu de modérés' (p. 484).   That, in fact, is the conclusion of the whole matter.   He was tentatively Republican in 1791. He was Democrat always, Cordelier always, from 1789 to 1794.

It remains to be seen what was his share in the two petitions.

The chief difficulty, however the petitions are regarded, is to reconcile what Danton said soon afterwards with what he said at his trial.   At the end of the year 1791 he spoke of his ' chimerical participation in a petition of too tragic celebrity.'   At his trial he said : ' I offer to prove that the petition in which I concurred had only pure intentions, that, as being one of its authors, I was menaced with assassination like the others, and that murderers were sent to my house to sacrifice me to the rage of the counter-revolutionaries.'   On the first occasion he seems to disown, on the other to boast of his share in a petition, and the words 'too tragic celebrity.' and ' assassination ' seem to point to its being the same petition, viz. the second, to which he refers.   I have come to the conclusion, however, that this may not be the case, and that the key to his speech at his trial is to be found in the words ' pure intentions.'   Robespierre and St. Just were charging him with having been ultra-revolutionary on July 15, 1791, in order to egg on the people to act, and furnish a pretext for a massacre.   Now Robespierre had opposed the first petition, according

---

' M. Aulard (*Études et Leçons sur la Révolution Française*, p. 122) exemplifies ' la haine immortelle contre la royauté' of the department of the *Aube*.

to his own account,[1] and Danton says in effect, ' In supporting the first petition I had no such treacherous intention.' But Robespierre and St. Just were also accusing him of Orleanism. ' No,' says Danton, ' I had nothing to do with the treacherous intention of Laclos.' M. Aulard argues that Laclos had nothing to do with the petition because he was not formally appointed to draw it up. This is not the only occasion in which M. Aulard seems to carry an honest habit of accepting nothing for which there is not evidence in black and white too far. Surely the argument is worth little. Laclos was undoubtedly the *proposer* of the petition. The committee to draw it up was appointed hastily during a tumultuous inroad of a mob at the Jacobins. There is no reason to doubt Brissot's testimony as to the share Laclos took in it. As to what took place on the Champ de Mars, there have and always will be *quot homines tot sententiæ.* Whether Danton read the second or the first petition, whether he signed the second or not, whether he did or did not harangue the crowd, and was or was not present at the massacre, can never probably be made absolutely certain. But all his previous and his subsequent history warrants our thinking that he was one of those behind who cried ' Forward ' rather than one of those before who cried ' Back.' One thing is certain. The Cordeliers were for the second petition, the Jacobins, or part of them, were not. Now, Danton, as we have seen, was trying to win over the Jacobins, and having run counter to some of them in signing the first petition, he did not wish still further to provoke them. Therefore very naturally he may not have signed the second petition. But his friend Robert drew it up, and even though i may have been written on the Champ de Mars, it is simply incredible that it could have been *improvised* there on the Sunday when its subject had been in everyone's thoughts since the miscarriage of the first petition the day before. M. Robinet says positively that it was drawn up '*chez Danton.*' It is certainly highly probable, nor was there anything unconstitutional or illegal in it (p. 321) to make Danton shrink. When M. Aulard lays so much stress on his not having signed it, he forgets that on other occasions he pursued precisely the same tactics. M. Aulard himself bears witness to this. With respect to the *émeute* of June 20, 1792, he says that Danton ' la laissa faire, il se tint à l'écart ' (p. 343). With respect to the ' terrible blow ' aimed at the throne by the Théâtre Français (*i.e.* the Cordeliers) in demanding the suppression of the État Major, he says : ' On remarquera que Danton n'a pas signé cet arrêté ' (p. 390). ' Il est cependant probable qu'il ne fut pas étranger à ce nouvel acte de guerre des ex-Cordeliers contre la cour, d'autant plus que cet acte n'est que la consequence naturelle ' of another Cordelier ' arrêté ' which he calls the charter of universal suffrage. And we cannot but recall Danton's attitude with regard to the placard denouncing Lafayette, and subsequently with

' à laquelle je m'opposai.'—*Procès,* p. 471. But cf. *Rev. Fr.* xxiv. p. 316.

regard to the popular manifestations against the Girondins at the end of May 1793. He was in short a democrat leading democrats, and 'toujours Cordelier,' in July 1791.

But how, then, are to be explained his words, 'J'ai préféré les dangers d'une seconde proscription judiciaire, fondée non pas même sur ma participation chimérique à une pétition trop tragiquement célèbre'? And of which petition was he speaking? Of the second. In talking of 'too tragically celebrated' he used a neutral phrase to which no one could take exception. But mark the 'même.' Surely that implies that there *would* have been plausible ground for prosecution if he had been prosecuted for participation, and though he went on to say 'chimérique' I believe he meant only that though plausible it could have rested only on guesswork. *He* knew, as his hearers did not, what had gone on between himself and Robert. If he had meant to deny indignantly having had anything to do with the petition he would have used very different language, whereas he was gliding over thin ice, and suggesting that bygones should be bygones on both sides. He had just alluded to the Revolution's ardent friends who wished him to be in office. By them he meant the Cordeliers. He had also alluded to men equally desirous of liberty but afraid of its storms. By them he meant the trimming Jacobins. Then he alluded to his own extravagance, to his over-boiling passion, to his having *elected* to incur a second judicial proscription, in addition, *i.e.* to that incurred in behalf of Marat. And in effect he says this : 'We have now agreed to a compromise. I accept and abide by it.' That is entirely consonant with his not having signed the second petition, though he inspired it, and his being then as always in principle Democrat, in practice Opportunist, and by tempera-ment and irrevocable ties *toujours Cordelier*.

CHAPTER IX

1792

EVENTS moved so swiftly in the Revolution that its months
seem in measure more than ordinary years. The compromise
which appeared a possibility in the winter of 1791 was, as both
sides saw, no longer a possibility in the spring of 1792. The
intervening months had been employed in mustering forces for
war instead of consolidating peace, and the pitched battle at
the Tuileries only ended what the skirmish in the Champ de
Mars began. The glory and gloom of a year never to be
effaced from French annals have alike been ascribed to Danton. But even if he had been the author of its shame as well
as its splendour France would have forgotten the September
massacres and remembered only by whom that year she was
'saved from Brunswick.' It opened ominously. Throughout
France famine reigned and panic, and the passions which
panic and famine always rouse. Foes without were combining
with foes within. Russia, really anxious for a war between the
Empire and France, that she might be free to work her will on
Poland, was profuse in expressions of sympathy with the emigrants, while inciting Austria and Prussia to help them with
the sword. Austria and Prussia, really hating each other with

a hatred destined to paralyse the invasion, had apparently at last come to terms. The threats uttered at Pilnitz had excited French fears and offended French pride.[1] The Constituent Assembly had been pacifically disposed. It had proclaimed its aversion to offensive war.[2] It had limited the army to 150,000 men,[3] afterwards supplemented by 97,000 volunteers. But the Legislative Assembly, though at first it avowed the same sentiments,[4] responded to menace by expediting the mobilisation of the volunteers,[5] by severer penalties against nonjuring priests,[6] by pronouncing sentence of death on emigrants continuing in arms, and by threatening the Emperor with war if he gave them aid. Then came the league between Prussia and Austria, the death of Marie Antoinette's wisest councillor, Leopold (March 1), followed in April by France's declaration of war.

How the war would be waged if the emigrants should guide it there was no doubt. History, which never fails to shudder at Marat's hyperboles, passes, as a rule, very lightly over the equally atrocious language of men whose programme was every whit as horrible as that of those who organised the September massacres, and subsequently established government by guillotine. 'Terror' was their avowed policy before it was the policy of Robespierre, just as the filth of the 'Actes des Apôtres' preceded, while escaping the odium of, the filth of 'Père Duchesne,' and as *noyades* of inconvenient negroes in pre-Revolutionary times failed to entail on Nantese Royalists the infamy of Carrier, who merely copied their methods and used their means.[7] The very term 'terror' may be said to come from the mint of the emigrants and their friends. *'Je crois nécessaire de frapper les Parisiens par la terreur.'*[8] *'La peur poussera cette Assemblée dans le sens ou elle va jusqu'à ce qu'une autre terreur la pousse dans le sens contraire. Soyez sûrs que*

---

[1] S. ii. 261–64; Bourgoing's *Hist. Dipl. de l'Europe*, Pt. I. 387.
[2] M. ix. 320.   [3] M. v. 416.   [4] S. ii. 311.
[5] M. x. 605.   [6] M. x. 191.
[7] Duhost's *Une Page d'Histoire*, p. 95.   [8] S. ii. 527.

ces gens-ci ne sont plus susceptibles d'autre sentiment que celui de la peur.' Invasion might involve an explosion, but '*la terreur y succéderait sûrement bientôt.'* [1] Such words recall many a page execrating the more famous '*en faisant peur.'* Yet they are Montmorin's, not Danton's, and the date of them is not August, but July. Mallet du Pan wrote that at Coblentz the sole talk was of hanging and extermination.[2] He himself was for 'no pernicious pity.' Mercy would be a crime against society.[3] The march on Paris was to be made '*en jetant partout la terreur et le désordre.'* [4] Mercy, Marie Antoinette's friend is never tired of the word. '*On ne peut écraser la Revolution que par la terreur,*' he wrote.[5] '*Ce ne seront ni une ni plusieurs batailles gagnées qui réduiront une nation laquelle ne peut être domptée qu'autant que l'on exterminera une grande portion de la partie active et la presque totalité de la partie dirigeante.*' And he went on to say that it was necessary to destroy this superb capital, *i.e.* Paris. Even the Queen did not go so far as this when she suggested to him the necessity of '*la crainte d'une punition prochaine.'* [6] The philosophy of such a programme was enunciated a couple of years later by Joseph de Maistre. The spirit of man, he thought, when it had gone astray, as in the Revolution, needed a blood-bath to regenerate it, '*ne peut être retrempée que dans le sang.'* [7] '*On dirait que le sang est l'engrais de cette plante qu'on appelle le génie.*' Others before De Maistre preached from the same text. 'This den of assassins must perish,' said a Minister of Sweden ; 'while France has a Paris it will have no king.' [8]

But the emigrants needed no stimulus. Had they been able they would have perpetrated all the Revolution's horrors unredeemed by one of the lasting benefits which it conferred on France. Their allies already loathed them. Brunswick cursed as he signed the abominable manifesto which bears his name

[1] S. ii. 491. [2] S. ii. 527. [3] S. iii. 3.
[4] S. iii. 333. [5] S. iii. 333. [6] S. ii. 491.
[7] S. iii. 479. [8] S. ii. 527.

'I would give my life not to have signed it,' he said.[1] Fersen thus describes their prelusive exploits in friendly territory : '*Ils ont fait des horreurs, pillé et ravagé tout dans le pays de Trèves.*'[2] The King of Prussia's secretary said of them : 'Young and old they seem to be the scum of the nation. Their words are atrocious. If one were to leave their fellow citizens to their vengeance France would soon be one monstrous cemetery.'[3]

In Paris the people could not know all these dissensions which foredoomed the invasion to failure, nor how much those emigrants were distrusted by the King, who yet shielded them, and how much hated by the Queen.[4] To them their enemies seemed at last to show a united front. They could not guess the subtleties with which Louis, in playing his double game, satisfied his conscience.[5] Nor if they had known it would they have appreciated the difference between the comparatively mild coercion invoked by Mallet du Pan[6] and the much more drastic suggestions of the King's much more intimate representative Breteuil.[7] Enough for them what they could see with their own eyes—famine ; plots of insurrection propagated by priests ; emigrants boasting of the agencies they had everywhere, and of the gibbets they would soon rear in Paris ; foreigners entering France ; a constitutional guard illegally tripled in number by the King, chosen almost exclusively from Royalists, and openly exulting at the news of the disasters to French arms. If such perils were to be weathered it could only be by promptly jettisoning traitors. The Constitutional Guard was suppressed. A volunteer camp was ordered to be formed outside the walls of Paris, and the troops of the line in Paris were ordered to the frontier.

Against the formation of the camp 8,000 National Guards petitioned, the petitioners, 'all under arms,'[8] defiling through an empty Assembly. For them it was to be a day of fatal memory

[1] S. ii. 510.   [2] S. iii. 3.   [3] S. iii. 3.
[4] M.-T. ii. 163, 164.   [5] Morse Stephens, *Fr. Rev.* ii. 74
[6] S. ii. 508, 509 ; Bourgoing's *Hist. Diplomatique*, Pt. ii. 144.
[7] S. ii. 509. Cf. Bourgoing, *Hist. Dipl.* Pt. i. 262, 427.
[8] Carlyle's *Fr. Rev.* ed. 1871, ii. 215.

but it encouraged the King.   He vetoed the camp.   He vetoed
the decrees against recalcitrant priests.   He had vetoed the
measure against the emigrants.   Roland lectured him and he
dismissed Roland.   He had long been credited with passive
connivance at the Queen's active complicity in the conspiracy
against the nation.   Even now she was felt to be the arch-con-
spirator.

> ‘ Madame Veto avait promis
>   De faire égorger tout Paris.’ [1]

So the people sang in the streets, and in June, little more than
half a year after the speech recorded in the previous chapter,
we find Danton demanding her expulsion from France.

Could Danton's demand have been executed and she had
been sent to Vienna, ‘ *avec tous les égards, les ménagements et la
sûreté qui lui sont dûs,*’ as he was careful to stipulate, France
might have been spared some horrors.[2]   But she would
neither save herself nor let others save her.   She was determined to fight, and she hoped, not without reason, to win.   It
is even possible that if she had had only the Girondin leaders
and not Danton to deal with she might have won.   Before this
we hear comparatively little of him in 1792, engrossed, as he
was, by his official duties.   But he had spoken at the Jacobins
on the all-important question of the war, and the manner as
well as the matter of the speech was characteristic.   Brissot is
complimented in it as ‘this vigorous athlete of liberty.’   His
Jacobin audience he captures with, ‘The destroying angel of
liberty will make the satellites of despotism fall, and the
clarions of war will sound.   But,’ and then after such rotund
tribute to those with whom the war was most popular, he proceeded to instil the necessity of caution, caution as to the time,
caution as to the men into whose hands the army was to be
entrusted.   And so he introduces his listeners gradually to what
practically were arguments against war.   Its champions, he
says, aimed at giving France an English Constitution, in the

----

[1] M.-T. ii. 93.   [2] Homme d Étal, p 302.

hope ere long of exchanging it for that of Constantinople. ' I am for war—it is indispensable—we are bound to have it, *but* —we ought to exhaust all means of staving it off.'

The speech reveals Danton's proficiency in the orator's art of keeping in touch with his audience, and leading it while seeming to be led. Incidentally he alludes to his official position in words showing that he clung still to the hope of avoiding civil war. 'However my own opinion may have been opposed to those who have hampered the Constitution, I now declare that I will only defend the people, will only terrify its enemies, with the club of reason and the sword of the law.' It was with other clubs and swords that the victory of August was to be won ; but much was to happen before August which Danton could not foresee. His attitude towards the war was dictated by doubts as to the motives of those who would direct it, not by any fear of the Austrians. He might have accepted it with misgivings, but he did not welcome it. Ultra-Royalists welcomed it as a desperate gambler welcomes double or quits, willing to stake all on the chance of regaining all.[1] The Girondins dreamt of it as a crusade abroad which would unite all patriots at home, and out of which they themselves should emerge covered with glory, 'masters of France, liberators of Europe, benefactors of humanity.'[2] Danton dreaded it as likely to render men like Lafayette more dangerous, and because the 'when' it should be made was not yet come. '*Mais, messieurs, QUAND devons-nous avoir la guerre ?*'

In both calculations he was correct. What he did not foresee was that the burden of the war was to rest on his own shoulders. But a shrewd observer had already said of him '*Il paraît que Danton jouerait désormais un grand rôle.*'[3] That rôle was forced on him. Little by little he had come to be looked on as the people's tribune, from whom more practical counsel was to be expected at a pinch than from the pontifical generalities and petty animosities of Robespierre, whose opposition to the war was as much opposition to

---

[1] M.-T. i. 32.   [2] S. ii. 314.   [3] S. ii. 321.

Brissot as anything else.   He had been, as we shall see hereafter, profoundly influenced by what he had observed in England
in 1791.   '*Il viendra*,' he said in the spring of 1792,
'*un temps où les baïonnettes n'éblouiront point les yeux des
citoyens, car en parcourant l'Angleterre on ne voit des baïonnettes que dans les lieux qu'habite le pouvoir exécutif de ce pays.*'
And though he had obtained only a one-sided view of English
politics he spoke after his visit with more weight than before.
Probably his communications with the English Opposition led
him, in common with Dumouriez, to hope to isolate Austria
by neutralising England and Prussia, for this would be in
keeping with his subsequent policy when in power.   Whether
he was unmasking the danger of war or the project of a military
guard for the Assembly, or pronouncing against the King
influencing the formation of the High Court, or against the
acceptation of royal bounty for the soldiers of Château Vieux
— though from the stage-foolery on the Champ de Mars in
their honour he kept aloof [1]—he was listened to as a man not
speaking often but with something practical always to say.
'Danton!   Danton!' cried the Jacobins one day when
Vergniaud, having to leave the chair, requested a substitute.
And shortly afterwards we find him defending Robespierre with
the air of the stronger man defending the weaker, a circumstance
which rankled, perhaps, in Robespierre's heart and was repaid
with murderous patronage a year later on the very same spot.[2]

It was, therefore, with consciousness of power that to meet
a triple danger he now made three demands.   To meet the
invasion, and at the same time nip any secret hopes which the
rich built on it, he proposed that these rich should bear the
burden of taxation.   To checkmate Court treachery he demanded the Queen's banishment.   To overawe Lafayette, whose
famous letter of June 16 was a declaration of war against the

[1] M. Stephens, *Fr. Rev.* ii. 62.

[2] On January 1, he had been made Vice-President at the Jacobins, and
it was rumoured that the King was thinking of making him Minister of
the Interior in a Jacobin Ministry.   *Rév. Fr.* xxiv. 342.

Jacobins, he proposed that he should be summoned to the bar of the Assembly. He would have nothing to do with the movement of June 20.[1] Aimless insults to individuals were not to his taste, and matters were not ripe for the larger issues of August 10. But every day it became clearer that if Louis remained on the throne France was lost. On June 13 Dumouriez had reported to the Assembly that the army was ill-armed, ill-clothed, ill-officered, and wretchedly supplied with horses and ammunition;[2] and in July that it was without instructions and without food.[3] Luckner had only 70,000 men to oppose to 200,000 of the enemy, and declared he would not answer for the Austrians not being in Paris in six weeks.[4] There were Royalist gatherings in the Cevennes.[5] The peasantry of the North and West were rising at the summons of the priests. Rumours of a republican secession of the South had been spread since April. Amid such national alarms Lafayette came on June 28 to demand the punishment of the sectional chiefs, an act which fully justified Danton's prevision and probably finally determined him to appeal to force. The Queen, had he but known it, was his best ally. 'Rather would I perish,' she said, 'than be saved by Lafayette,'[6] and by her besotted ingratitude to her last champion she made any *coup d'état* he might have meditated impossible, and sealed her own fate and that of the King. On July 3 Vergniaud in his greatest speech denounced the King's conspiracy with the foreigner.[7] On the 7th Pétion, Mayor of Paris, was, with the King's approval, suspended for his conduct on June 20.[8] On the 8th came news of the impending Royalist occupation of Jalès and the Château de Bannes.[9] On the 9th Brissot declaimed against the conspiracy to which the King, he said, was a party, and to which the weakness of the army was due.[10] On the 11th the

---

[1] M. Stephens, *Fr. Rev.* ii. 83.   [2] M. xii. 669.
[3] M.-T. ii. 82.   [4] M.-T. ii. 81.   [5] S. ii. 488.
[6] Morse Stephens, *Fr. Rev.* ii. 99. [7] M.-T. ii. 21. [8] M. xiii. 74.
[9] M.-T. ii. 51 says they were actually occupied then, but cf. M. xiii. 78, 123.   [10] M. xiii. 83.

Assembly, at the instigation of Danton's friend Hérault de Séchelles, declared the country in danger. This was no merely scenic appeal to sentiment. It meant that all National Guards were requisitioned, that in all parts of the country the constituted authorities must sit permanently, that everyone must send in a list of arms and ammunition in his possession, that everyone must wear the national cockade, and that display of any anti-national emblem was punishable with death.[1] On the 13th Pétion's suspension was annulled by the Assembly, and next day he was the hero of the Festival of the Federation. On the 14th Danton urged the Fédérés in Paris to swear not to leave the capital till liberty was established and the will of the departments about the Executive Power declared.[2] On the 17th the Fédérés responded by coming to the bar of the Assembly and demanding the suspension of Lafayette and the King.[3] On the 25th Thuriot, a Dantonist, carried in the Assembly a motion allowing the Sections to sit permanently and giving to each individual Section absolute freedom of petition.[4] That same day Brunswick signed the sinister proclamation which bears his name. On the 26th the first meeting of the Secret Directory of Insurrection was held ;[5] and when the Marseilles battalion arrived in Paris on the 30th only the details of the coming struggle remained to be arranged.

It is generally admitted that Danton was organiser in chief of August 10. He said so himself. His contemporaries, with the exception of Robespierre, said so too. '*Danton arrangea le* 10 *août et le château fut foudroyé,*' testifies Garat. '*Il avait fait le* 10 *août; il n'avait pas voulu nominalement le pouvoir,*' says Billaud-Varenne.[6] '*Dans l'intérieur de Paris Danton dirigeait les mouvements ; c'était à lui que se rattachaient les principaux chefs des insurgés; c'étaient ses ordres qu'ils exécutaient.*' Such is the emphatic language of the '*deux amis*

---

[1] M.-T. ii. 29. [2] *Procès*, p. 229. [3] *Ibid.* p. 229.
[4] M. xiii. 248 ; Morse Stephens, *Fr. Rev.* ii. 117 ; M.-T. ii. 197.
[5] G. de Cassagnac's *Hist. des Girondins*, b. x. sec. 4.
[6] *Procès*, p. 226.

de la Liberté.' The Cordeliers battalion, in which he was an officer and which contained his personal friends, was one of the four which did the fighting on the 10th.[1] On the 11th he alone of the leaders on the 10th was made a Minister. The Marseillais were the guests of his Section. The Communal decree of August 6, altering the guards at the Tuileries, and other points of importance, so as to prevent their being exclusively royalist,[2] the decree ordering ammunition to be given to the Marseillais and refused to Mandat,[3] the decree suppressing *corps d'élite* in the National Guard,[4] and such proposals as those for the reorganisation of the Staff, for punishing officers giving orders other than those emanating from the civic authorities, for distributing the artillery among the forty-eight Sections, must all have been within his cognisance as deputy-procureur. The Central Office . of the forty-eight Sections constituted in July, without which there would have been no 10th of August, was directly under the supervision and control of the procureur of the Commune.[4] The procureur was Manuel. His deputy was Danton. But which of the two was leader and which follower there can be no doubt, any more than that it was Danton who spurred on the vacillating Pétion. And on the eve of the combat it was to Danton, as we shall see, that people kept coming for orders. He was not, it is true, one of the five original chiefs of the Secret Directory of Insurrection. His official position made it more politic for him to act through subordinates. But he certainly attended one, and that the most important, of the three meetings which they held, viz. on August 10 between twelve and one o'clock A.M., and probably was at the other two. Camille Desmoulins was present at the second.[6] Once, in short, his resolution to appeal to force was taken he threw his whole energy into making success certain. To get rid of the Court was to him only a means to an end, viz. to get rid of the invaders, but that being

---

[1] *Procès*, p. 227. [2] M.-T. ii. 193. [3] *Procès*, p. 229.
[4] M.-T. ii. 194. [5] M.-T. ii. 135.
[6] G. de Cassagnac, *Hist. des Girondins*, b. x. sec. 4.

the first thing to do he did it with all his might. The
Girondins, on the other hand, began to waver when brought
face to face with the consequence of their own acts. They
had done their utmost to infuse vigour into the military
operations, and there Danton was with them. But they had
also done everything to humiliate Louis, and yet Vergniaud on
the 29th suggested to him to place himself in their hands.
Could Louis have stooped so low, their feeble hands could
never had laid the storm they had themselves raised.

Nor would Danton consent to any more compromise. To
him the Baiser de Lamourette of July 7 had seemed the Baiser
de Judas.[1] On the 30th a momentous resolution was adopted
by the Cordeliers, and signed by him as President, by which
‘passive’—that is, poor—‘citizens’ were summoned to enrol
themselves in the National Guard, of which only ‘active’
citizens had previously been members. On August 1 Carnot
carried a decree to the same effect in the Assembly.[2] The
purport of it was to add so many pikes to the strength of the
populace. For though the most populous of the Sections were
for the insurrection the wealthier ones were not, and it was
impossible to depend on all the battalions of the National
Guard. In all, in short, of the decisive steps taken before the
10th Danton’s hand is to be traced, and in the most decisive
of them it is clearly visible. ‘Cloudy Atlas of the whole,’
Mr. Carlyle calls him, a description only partly accurate,
though wholly picturesque. Atlas of the whole he was, and
Atlas of the Republic he remained during the first year of the
Convention, a year a history of which might well be headed
‘The Tribunate of Danton.’

---

[1] M.-T. ii. 36.   [2] Carnot the younger, for his elder brother.

CHAPTER X

1792—*continued*

KING'S FATUITY—PREPARATIONS FOR THE 10TH—PÉTION—EVENTS
OF THE 9TH AND 10TH -DANTON'S MOVEMENTS—DESPONDENCY
OF THE INSURGENTS—LUCILE'S JOURNAL—THE COUR DU COM-
MERCE—THE TUILERIES—MANDAT—THE KING'S CHARACTER—
AFTER THE COMBAT.

DURING the first days of August the King seemed bent on
playing into the Revolutionists' hands.   Perhaps nothing could
have convinced them that he did not sympathise with
Brunswick's proclamation, which was, in fact, only a cruder
and more violent version of his instructions to Mallet du Pan.

But after five days' silence he on August 3 sent a message
to the Assembly which it could not help regarding as the hypocritical plea of an accessory to a crime.   He threw doubts on
the authenticity of the proclamation, alluding to it in self-
excusing terms instead of with the passionate abhorrence
which it had roused in all patriotic hearts.[1]   Such abhorrence
his conscience would not permit him to feign.   Not a cheer
greeted his message,[2] and in a fiery outburst the Girondin
Isnard made a fierce attack on his conduct and motives, which
was followed by a petition from the Sections for his dethronement.   Danton was not one of those who signed it, but his
friends Legendre and Fabre d'Eglantine were, and we catch
his accents in 'We could have been content with the King's
suspension ; but the Constitution—the Constitution, which is
is ever on his lips—forbids it.   Therefore we invoke the

---

[1] M. xiii. 320.   [2] M.-T. ii. 167.

Constitution ourselves and demand that he be deposed."[1]
In the still Monarchical Assembly, which five days later was to
refuse to condemn Lafayette, indignation at the King's speech
had been chilled by the Sections' petition, and its passive
attitude increased the Revolutionists' anger and alarm.[2] On
the 4th the second meeting of the Secret Directory was held at
the Cadran Bleu, on the Boulevard du Temple, whence it was
adjourned to Anthoine's longing at Duplay's house in the Rue
St. Honoré, where also Robespierre lodged.[3] On this day
the general plan of insurrection was set forth by Camille
Desmoulins, but it did not take place that night because
Santerre was not ready, and because some preferred to wait
for the Assembly's decision as to the suspension of the King.[4]

The Mauconseil Section declared the throne vacant and
invited the other Sections to join it in announcing its declaration to the Assembly on August 5. Fourteen assented.
Sixteen opposed. Ten gave no sign.[5] The decision of the
other eight is not known. But the populous Sections were
with Mauconseil, and though the Assembly pronounced its
declaration illegal and the Departmental Directory ordered its
illegality to be proclaimed with the sound of the trumpet, the
Commune set at naught the order, and preparations for the
impending conflict went on openly and apace.[6]

In such crises the timider men who in times of order hold
sway efface themselves. Meetings are sparsely attended.
The bolder spirits vote and act. If their acts are afterwards
condemned those who stood aloof, though for that very reason
most blameworthy, are acquitted of all blame. Such was the
case now. Pétion's advice,[7] or possibly the jealousy of one
Section,[8] made the insurrection miss fire on August 5, and had
the propertied classes shown a united front Danton's task

[1] M.-T. ii. 172.   [2] *Ibid.* ii. 173.
[3] G. de Cassagnac, *Hist des Girondins*, b. x. sec. iv.
[4] *Bat. du* 10 *Août*, p. 246.
[5] M.-T. ii. 443.   [6] M.-T. ii. 180.
[7] M.-T. ii. 224.   [8] M.-T. ii. 182.

would have been rendered far more difficult than it was. But they stayed at home, and the Sections followed the lead of the men who knew their own minds and were not afraid to act.

The Secret Directory of Insurrection consisted of five men chosen by the Fédérés in Paris. These had added to themselves ten of the managers of the full-dress rehearsal of June 20.[1] This body, with Pétion's connivance, arranged that the representatives of the twenty-eight most revolutionary Sections should sit in the hall of the Hôtel de Ville. They were, therefore, in touch with the Old Communal Council, which sat in the next chamber, Pétion, the Mayor, being their secret ally, and Danton, the Assistant Procureur, their real chief. The Mauconseil Section had threatened that if the Assembly did not accept their petition the tocsin should be sounded at midnight, August 9.[2] The Section Quinze-vingts finally named the same time. That, therefore, was the hour fixed for insurrection.

Mandat, the commandant of the National Guard, made all preparations for the defence of the Tuileries. Westermann was chosen to lead the people to the assault. On the 9th Rœderer, the Departmental Procureur Syndic, wrote to Pétion requesting him to say what steps he had taken to prevent the tocsin being sounded, and suggesting that he should issue a warning to the citizens against disorder. This Pétion did, and it was read at certain of the Sections, which met about eight o'clock that evening, and must have considerably damped the revolutionary fervour of some of them. Mandat, commandant of the National Guard, also wrote to Pétion asking him to authorise various changes in the disposition of the troops. Between five and six o'clock Pétion went to the Assembly and gave it assurances that order would be maintained.[3] Rœderer took him thence to the Departmental Directory, and it was

---

[1] When the mob *first* got into the Tuileries.
[2] M.-T. ii. 181, and *Bul. du 10 Août*, p. 247.
[3] M.-T. ii. 222.

settled that the Departmental and Communal Councils should both hold permanent session.   Then Pétion went to the Hôtel de Ville and found there letters from Mandat pressing him to come to the Tuileries.

Pétion was a man of a vanity so prodigious that a reader of his self-revelations is at a loss to decide whether they are more odious or more ridiculous.   They excite more disgust than contempt in his account of the return from Varennes, more amazement than amusement when he was flying for his life in 1793.   Vanity had for him the force which higher instincts have for better balanced minds.   It was as a crown to the glory of his triumphal progress in the Berline, as a strong staff to him while limping painfully through the Valley of the Shadow ; for it enabled him to revel in the supposed passion excited in some female bosom by his form and countenance, whether his victim were a princess or a peasant.   On the present occasion it supplied, or rather reinforced, his courage, for physically he does not seem to have been a coward.   He afterwards with incredible frankness himself admitted, that when on this night all other men's minds were absorbed in terrible realities he was, as usual, posturing, so to speak, before a looking-glass.   '*Je désirais l'insurrection, mais je tremblais qu'elle ne réussît pas.*[2]   *Ma position était critique ; il fallait faire mon devoir de citoyen sans manquer à celui de magistrat. Il fallait conserver tous les dehors et ne point m'écarter des formes.*'   In other words, the dignity of this quintessence of all mayors demanded that he should lie decorously and handle a dagger only with a kid glove.   Even his false assurances to the Assembly and his hypocritical admonitions to the people were dictated rather by the vanity of the official than the politician's craft.   And now, when to enter the Tuileries was to enter the lion's den, it was, no doubt, vanity in arms that spurred him on.   In the Tuileries it had been grievously wounded by the King's curt ' *Taisez-vous* ' after June 20.   In the Tuileries he, Sergent, and Panis had been hooted, had, to

---

[1] M.-T. ii. 223.

quote a Monarchical historian, met with a reception '*plus que
brutal*'—nay, had experienced '*voies de fait très répréhensibles.*' [1]
Sergent no doubt, who had been actually knocked down,[2] had
borne this in mind when he handed the Marseillais their
cartridges. Too well were he and Panis to remember it in
September. Pétion must have remembered it too. As he
listened to the King's angry words and to the curses and
threats of the Royalists in the garden he must have consoled
himself with the thoughts of the morrow.[3] But his relief must
have been great when at 2 A.M. the Assembly sent for him
after he had been for nearly three hours in a most disagreeable
position. Merely reiterating his assurances to the Assembly,
he went straight to the Hôtel de Ville, leaving his luckless
coachman shivering on the box of his carriage at the Tuileries,
till between three and four o'clock in despair the man drove home.
At about six he tasted the first sweets of revenge in summoning Mandat, who had just cross-questioned him at the palace,
to be cross-questioned in his turn at the Hôtel de Ville.
Then, having with one hand helped the Revolution materially
and with the other seriously imperilled its chance of success,
he serenely welcomed at the Mairie the force sent by the Insurrectionary Commune to lock him up, and retired with his
Mayor's laurels, as he flattered himself, immaculate, only to re-
appear with something of the martyr's halo in their place.[4]
'*Ici le maire de Paris a manqué d'être assassiné dans la nuit du
9 au 10.*' So ran the legend on the flag which waved over the
conquered palace. Some men might be mourning over the
fall of an ancient monarchy. Others might be exulting in the
liberty won by a noble nation too long enslaved. But this
was the outward and visible sign of the Parisians' feelings.

---

[1] M.-T. i. 235, 237.　　　　[2] *Bat. du* 10 *Août*, p. 238.

[3] Condorcet (*Mém. de Condorcet sur la Révolution*, 1824, ii. 205) says
that after being closeted with Pétion from 11 till 12 o'clock the King came
out and said, ' Soyez tranquilles, messieurs ; monsieur le maire m'assure
que tout se pacifie.'

[4] For Pétion's defence that to appeal to force would have meant civil
war, see M. xiii. 375.

Almost might they be sooner pardoned for the massacres of September than for making such a posing ape their idol. 'He doubled the parts of Pontius Pilate and Judas,' says Mortimer-Ternaux, and his epigram is just.

It has been necessary to particularise Pétion's conduct in order to estimate properly the veracity of the Bulletin of the Revolutionary Tribunal, which makes Danton at his trial attribute to him a protagonist's part in the night's events.

Pétion, coming from the Commune, came to the Cordeliers Club, told us the tocsin would sound at midnight, and that the next day would be the tomb of royalty. He said that the Royalists had planned a night attack, but he had so managed matters that everything should be done in broad daylight and be over by midday, and that the patriots were sure to win.

But the independent notes of Topino-Lebrun tell a very different tale.

I was (said Danton) at the Cordeliers, though a delegate of the Commune. I said to the Minister Clavière, who came from the Commune, that we were going to proclaim the insurrection. After having arranged all the operations and the hour for the attack I lay down on my bed, like a soldier, having given orders that I should be called. I rose at one and went to the Commune, now become revolutionary. I delivered to his doom Mandat, who had orders to fire on the people. The Mayor was arrested and I remained there (*i.e.* at the Commune), according to the desire of the patriots.

There can be but little doubt which of these two versions is the correct one, the Bulletin's mendacious elevation of Pétion out of his actual service as decoy being a palpable attempt to detract from Danton's share in the 10th of August, and so lower him in the eyes of those to whom that day was sacred. His answer to the charge of having sneaked off to Arcis out of danger was similarly garbled, for similar reasons. But Topino-Lebrun again comes to our aid with Danton's real words:

'It was I who prepared the events of August 10, and I went to Arcis'—for Danton is a good son—'to spend three days, bid my mother good-bye, and regulate my affairs.'

How one poor woman's heart at Arcis would have ached could she have heard this answer, and how she would have attested its truth with her tears! For what he said about his expedition to Arcis was quite true. His presence there on the 6th, and its object, is proved by the legal document in which he made provision for his mother.

According to the Bulletin he also said,

I never left my Section except after giving word I should be apprised if anything fresh happened. I remained in my Section twelve hours on end, and came back at nine next day.

Now what was Danton doing on the night of the 9th and the morning of the 10th? It is difficult, or rather impossible, to specify with absolute certainty, hour by hour and act by act. If we take it that he was the soul of the insurrection we must also take it that its history is his, and that to relate the one is to relate the other. But by collating ascertained facts and comparing them with Topino-Lebrun's notes, with the Bulletin, with the diary of Lucile Desmoulins, and with other narratives, we may arrive at something more definite and in the main correct. If there are discrepancies in the evidence it is only to be expected. At such a crisis each narrator naturally makes small mistakes of time or place, especially when the narrative is written months afterwards, as Lucile Desmoulins' was. When guns are going off, or bells ringing, or persons are repeatedly entering and leaving a house amid great excitement the future recorder does not pull out his watch and time and note down precisely the quarter of an hour of such exits and entrances, nor is he able to be sure which was the first gun or the first bell. The result is a variety of perplexing details impossible to reconcile if we do not make some allowance for the looseness of expressions such as 'about midnight,' 'towards evening,' 'between eleven and twelve,' or even the apparently more exact 'half-past eleven,' 'a quarter to twelve'; for a quarter of an hour deducted from one story and added to another may make all the difference between a straightforward account and a tangle of contradictions.

Now, Danton was in Paris on July 30, as we have seen, and his action there of itself disproves Robespierre's impudent charge of poltroonery. On August 6th he was at Arcis, and his reason for going there is instructive. We, unable to see, as contemporaries saw, the state of things in August, and remembering only which side won, are apt to think of him and his friends as advancing to the destruction of a feeble monarchy with a tiger's leap, terrible, irresistible, confident. The exact opposite would be nearer the truth. Danton went to Arcis as a man who knew he might be dead a week later. ' *Si j'eusse été vaincu,*' he said, when all was over, '*je serais criminel. La cause de la liberté a triomphé.*' Barbaroux had poison in his pocket on the night of the 9th, in case of defeat. Fréron despaired of success. If the King's interviews with his confessor showed that he was in fear of the Revolutionists, so were they of him, or rather of the Queen. They thought the enemy would act on the offensive, and expected an attack on the 9th. Dr. Moore was told on the morning of the 10th that during the night 'false patrols were despatched all round under semblance of patrols of the National Guards to keep the peace, but in reality with the most hostile intentions against the citizens'; that this had been discovered and some of them had been killed. The Queen and her *entourage*, with the only real and the only really well-appointed soldiers in Paris fighting for them, with good officers, with plenty of cannon, with strong walls under shelter of which volleys of musketry could be poured on an exposed crowd, with the flower of the swordsmen of France to reinforce the Swiss, and with a total fighting force of several thousand men, were full of contempt for the undisciplined mob, and up to the very last eager to bring matters to an issue. Dr. Moore, writing on the 10th, says: 'All agree that the Swiss began hostilities by giving the first fire on the people'; and though he can see no motive which the Swiss could have for firing but self-defence, those who commanded the Swiss had other motives, and what 'all' said is likely to have been true.

The Sections, on the other hand, were irresolute and divided, and Pétion's hypocritical appeal divided them still more. Even on the morning of the 10th it was uncertain if they would rise. '*Le tocsin ne rend pas,*' they said at the Tuileries, in disappointment, perhaps, more than in relief. But in either case for a time it seemed as if it was true. All the doubts and fears of the moment are vividly reflected in Lucile's journal. She and her husband had been out of Paris, probably on some such errand as Danton. Probably, too, he returned the same day they did, viz. on the 8th. On the 9th they entertained some Marseillais at dinner. After dinner the company adjourned to Danton's lodgings. There his wife's mother sat weeping, and Lucile, though laughing hysterically, knew that her laughter must end that night in tears. And in fact that very night she wrote in her diary, 'What will become of us? I can endure no more. Camille, my poor Camille, what will become of you? I have no strength to breathe. This night, this fatal night! My God! if it is true that Thou hast any existence, save the men that are worthy of Thee! We want to be free. O God! the cost of it!'

While the rest of the company feared that the Sections might not rise, Danton was 'resolute.' The Passage de la Cour du Commerce, where he lived, was close to the Cordeliers Club, and when he said at his trial that he never left his Section for twelve hours he meant that he never left the Section Théâtre Français, which comprised the Cordeliers. As evening came on the two women went out to escort Mme. Charpentier home. The loveliness of the night tempted them to take a walk in the streets, which were pretty full of people. They retraced their steps and sat down at a café in the Place de l'Odéon. Some *sans-culottes* went by shouting 'Vive la Nation!' and then some cavalry, followed by a vast throng.

This frightened them, and, bidding Mme. Charpentier good-bye, they went back to Danton's house, where they found a number of people, and among them Fréron and Robert's wife. Danton was there too, and now 'agitated.' Lucile ran to Madame Robert and asked, 'Is the tocsin to be sounded?' and she answered, 'Yes, to-night.' Lucile whispered her fears to her husband, who said he would stay by Danton's side. Subsequently she heard he had exposed his life. Fréron was despondent, saying he was tired of life and longed to die. Then the men armed themselves and went out. Lucile looked out into the night. It was still and beautiful, and the moon shone on almost deserted streets. But in the Faubourg St. Germain, not far off, they were all illuminated, as Dr. Moore tells us, and if Lucile's gaze could have reached the Faubourg St. Antoine there too she would have seen lights in every window, and would have heard the tramp of patrols breaking at intervals the sinister silence. Danton, of whom Lucile curiously writes, '*Il ne sortit presque point,*' by which apparently she means that he only went to the Cordeliers Club and back, did not seem very anxious, and was going to lie down; but towards midnight several messengers came for him, and at last he went out for the Commune.

As twelve o'clock struck the first note of the tocsin sounded from the Cordeliers. St. Antoine answered, and bell after bell pealed through Paris the people's response to their leader's call. The women wept and listened. After a long time Danton came back, and, giving only vague answers to Madame Robert's frenzied inquiries for her husband, went to throw himself on his bed. But Lucile, in spite of Danton's attempt to lull their alarm, guessed that the people were going to the Tuileries, and said so amid her sobs to those who vainly tried to comfort her. Madame Robert could hear nothing of her husband, and vowed if he were killed she would poniard Danton, 'the rallying point of the insurrection,' with her own hand. '*Mais ce Danton, lui, si mon mari périt je suis femme à le poignarder.*' Desmoulins came back at one o'clock and at once fell asleep, his head on Lucile's shoulder. Did he go out again? Lucile does not say so, but it is perhaps implied by her saying he went to bed when it was broad daylight, *i.e.* about 5 A.M. Madame Danton, whom she had induced to come to her own lodging, lay down expecting to hear her husband was killed. Danton therefore, at all events, must have slept only a short time, and again have gone out. After the three had risen Camille left them, promising Lucile not to run into danger. The women breakfasted. No tidings of what was going on came, and they were reading the journal of the night before when suddenly they heard the roar of cannon. Gabrielle, Danton's wife, fainted, and Lucile, half fainting herself, tended her, while Jeannette, the cook, stood by ' bleating like a nanny goat,' and wanting to trounce a certain person who was throwing blame on Camille. Reviving a little, they attempted to go to Danton's house, but found the gate of the Cour du Commerce closed, and when they tried to effect a side entry through a baker's shop had the door slammed in their faces by the baker. At last they got in. Danton was absent, and for a considerable time they could get no news.

While such scenes were occurring in the humble households of Desmoulins and Danton, in the Tuileries too there was weary watching. Madame Elisabeth and the Queen were quite worn out when the noise of Pétion's departing carriage was heard. Madame Elisabeth ran to the window, and opening the shutter was amazed at the colouring of the heavens. 'Come, sister,' she cried, 'and look at the dawn.' An ominous outlook if they had faith in old proverbs ; for the sky was red as blood.

'Let us never glorify revolution,' ingeminates an eloquent writer in his essay on an English revolution. And who, as he reads the stories of this night, would not echo his refrain? Let us never glorify revolution. But nevertheless let us weigh revolutions in just scales, nor, out of pity for a losing side, traduce their great men. Whatever else is clear from Lucile's account, it is clear that Danton did not spend the night comfortably in bed and in that '*sommeil pesant*' at which his enemies have sneered.[1]

Another and circumstantial account of his movements is to be found in the '*Bataillon du Dix Août.*' According to its authors he went first, on the evening of the 9th, to the Church of St. André des Arcs, where his Section, of which he was president, held its meetings. This would be between eight and nine o'clock. Thence he went to the Cordeliers, where Camille, Robert, and Fréron followed him, and occupied the chair at their meeting for a short time. But he was mainly occupied in delivering stirring addresses to the Marseillais. At eleven o'clock it was reported at the Tuileries that he had told them they must not expect they were going to have a holiday promenade. At half-past eleven he had just finished speaking, when a shot in the Cour du Commerce was heard, and everyone cried, 'To arms! to arms!' The Marseillais formed ranks and marched to the Pont St. Michel, arriving there just after some delegates from the Section Mauconseil had reached the Pont Neuf. There stood the gun which (though in the hands of Mandat's troops!) was to be fired as a signal for the sounding of the tocsin. Mandat's officer, Wille, naturally refused to let the Marseillais pass; but when orders came from the Commune bidding him withdraw his battery his gunners obeyed in defiance of him. Then the alarm-gun was at last fired at a quarter to one, and the tocsin sounded, in the Lombard and Mauconseil Sections first, and afterwards all over Paris. Danton, who had gone home and thrown himself on his bed towards one o'clock, was summoned at one to the Hôtel de Ville, where the Insurrectionary Commune had just been proclaimed. There Manuel (procureur of the old Commune, which held session for some time simultaneously with the new one) signed the order for retiring Wille's battalion from the Pont Neuf. Danton charged himself with the transmission of the order, and having done so returned to the Hôtel de Ville and ordered back other troops who were barring

---

[1] G. de Cassagnac, *Hist. des Girondins*, b. xi. sec. v.

the march of the men of St. Antoine.   The next step was to summon Mandat before the Commune.

In several points this narrative clashes with Lucile's, but in others it elucidates hers.   It would be in one of the intervals between his visits to the Cordeliers that Danton first snatched some sleep in the Cour du Commerce.   In coming from St. André, for instance, he may have taken the Cour du Commerce on his way.   And whereas he had been 'resolute' early in the evening this narrative shows why he was 'agitated' later on; for besides the trouble of Madame Robert's anxiety and Fréron's dejection he had been haranguing the Marseillais to this effect :—

The people can no longer rely upon anyone but itself, for the Constitution is inadequate and the Assembly has acquitted Lafayette.   To absolve that traitor is to deliver us to him, to the enemies of France, to the sanguinary vengeance of the allied kings.   Your only chance, therefore, is to save yourselves. Quick, then, for this very night a sortie is to be made on the people by creatures in the Château, to massacre us before they quit Paris for Coblentz.   Save yourselves, therefore.   To arms ! to arms ! [1]

And, in addition to addressing the Marseillais, Danton had been settling with Westermann, Alexandre, Santerre, Moisson, and Garnier all the details of the march of the three columns which were to advance on the north of the Seine from St. Antoine, on the south from St. Marceau and the Cordeliers, upon the Tuileries ; St. Marceau to cross the river by the Pont Neuf or Pont Royal, the Marseillais by the Pont St. Michel and the Pont au Change.   St. Antoine was to take its orders from the Hôtel de Ville, but the headquarters of St. Marceau as well as of the Marseillais were the Cordeliers.

/From all this it seems certain that though we should be wrong in saying that August 10 was the work of any one man, Danton was then, as he had been since 1791, the chief man of the Sections, who more than anyone united them, cheered them,

---

[1] Cf. Alison's *French Rev.* i. 325, and *Bat. du 10 Aoôt*, p. 278.

organised them for the combat. Those in whose eyes all rebellions are crimes will so much the more execrate his name. But they can never affirm with Robespierre that he was a coward as well as rebel, and left his fellow rebels in the lurch.

With the summons sent by the old Commune to Mandat begins a fresh tangle of contradictory accounts, which might be easier to unravel if it had been possible subsequently to induce its secretary, Royer-Collard, to produce the minutes of the night's proceedings.[1] Mandat, after much hesitation, was persuaded by Rœderer to obey Pétion's summons, and reached the Hôtel de Ville about 5.30 A.M. There, after being interrogated by the council of the old Commune, he was dismissed, only to be seized by adherents of the Insurrectionary Commune, which, it must be remembered, was sitting in a room close to the old one, and was in collusion with some of its members. Huguenin was its president. According to Vilain d'Aubigny's narrative of what he was told by the citizen Dufraisse, it was Danton who with his own hands seized Mandat. How much of D'Aubigny's story is true, it is impossible to say. And here it may be remarked that any impartial writer who would examine carefully and adjudicate upon the credibility of the innumerable writers on the French Revolution would perform a more useful as it would be a more arduous task than that of writing many histories. Where every other man is accused of some crime by his neighbour it is hard indeed to pick and choose between them as authorities. D'Aubigny, for instance, was accused of robbery of the Garde-Meuble, but he was acquitted, and though the hour of the morning at which Dufraisse is said to have conversed with him is inexplicable there is certainly verisimilitude in his narrative.

Mandat, it alleges, went into the office of the General Staff, which was also in the Hôtel de Ville, after leaving the council-room of the Commune. There Danton followed him and summoned him before the new Commune. Mandat denied its legality, and said he would not appear before factious rebels,

---

[1] Hamel's *Robespierre*, b. viii. sec. xix.

nor would answer for his acts to any but honourable men ; whereat Danton sprang at his throat as he stood in the middle of his staff, saying, 'Traitor ! you will be forced to obey the Commune, which will save the people, whom you are betraying, and against whom you are conspiring with the tyrant,' and dragged him by the collar before the Insurrectionary Commune. To its members Mandat said in his defence that he had Pétion's order to repel force by force, but had left it behind him. This may have been true, though his not having it with him was suspicious ; but his interrogators merely sent to Pétion for confirmation of the assertion. This at least acquits Pétion of the charge of having got Mandat murdered, and the body thrown into the Seine, in order to destroy all trace of the written order. And the defence is superfluous, for Pétion would certainly have considered murder an indecorous act for a mayor. Mandat, however, had no orders from Pétion to beat the *rappel* or to increase the number of National Guards at the Tuileries, and had therefore disobeyed the law ;[1] and when suddenly his own order to attack the people in the rear on their march to the Tuileries was produced against him he was at once sent to the Communal prison, and not without reason.

Mandat was a gallant man. No one can read of his death without pitying him. But he had been on the popular side when an officer in the Gardes Françaises, and had been, in fact, like Lafayette, in very bad odour with the Court as a strong Constitutionalist. By the people he, like Lafayette, was now looked on as a renegade, and this order seemed to his judges an atrocity. It has been urged that when crushing an insurrection it matters little whether you do so by an attack in front, on the flanks, or in the rear. This, however, is a more specious than just argument. Along with and following any revolutionary body in Paris always went a crowd of unarmed men and women.[2] To charge them, or even the presumable combatants, with cavalry and infantry before a

---

[1] *Bat. du 10 Août*, p. 258 ; G. de Cassagnac, *Hist. des Girondins*, b. xii. sec. 2. [2] M.-T. i. 167.

shot was fired, or ever they had got near the Tuileries, might strategically be good tactics, but to the citizens spelt murder. At any rate, with the author of such an order in their hands, they would have been mere madmen to let him return to the Tuileries.

In Danton's eyes he was a dangerous traitor. When at his own trial Danton's accusers sought to prove his contra-revolutionary conduct on the 10th he replied, '*Je fis l'arrêt de mort de Mandat.*' What this means is not quite clear. After Mandat had been dismissed by the old Commune the Insurrectionary Commune, which consisted of commissioners chosen by certain of the Sections the previous evening, seized him, questioned him, appointed Santerre commander in his stead, and, on the fatal firing-order being produced, committed him to the Communal prison. They then turned out the old Commune, with the exception of Danton, Pétion, and Manuel, and took possession of their hall. There they decided on sending Mandat to the Abbaye prison. Danton in 1794 said, '*Je fis l'arrêt de mort de Mandat.*' By this he meant either, in the more colloquial sense of the phrase,[1] 'I doomed Mandat'— that is, by bringing him before the Insurrectionary Commune —or, less probably, though that is how it has been interpreted, 'I made out the warrant committing him to prison on a capital charge.' 'Sentence of death,'[2] of course, he had no power to pass. Mandat never reached the Abbaye, having been shot on the staircase of the Hôtel de Ville about seven o'clock. Pétion, according to pre-arrangement, was then confined to his own house, under guard. And about eight o'clock the first ranks of the Revolutionists were in the Carrousel.

In spite of Mandat's death the odds were still in favour of the King. But he was king only in name. It has been said picturesquely of the deaths of kings that 'their sunset paints all their sky, and we remember not how they bore their glorious

---

[1] Cf. M. iv. 312. It, xiii. 378, gives 'un mandat d'arrêt' in its account of what happened.

[2] So it is interpreted in *Taine*, Eng. tr. ii. 178.

burden, but with what grace they laid it down,' and it was certainly true of Louis. Till he entered the Temple everyone in Paris, whether Royalist or Revolutionist, seems to have despised him. When the Queen had urged him to put himself at the head of his army the Princesse de Lamballe says it was like speaking to a corpse.[1] On the day the Bastille was taken he made in his diary the entry, '*Rien.*' Even such a barber's block as Pétion looked on him with contempt. Pétion mentions the language used about him, before he set out to fetch him back from Varennes, at a meeting consisting of himself, Tray, Duport, Barnave, Maubourg, and Lafayette. '*Chacun disait que ce gros cochon-là était fort embarrassant.*' Maubourg afterwards spoke of him as '*une bête qui s'est laissé entraîner,*' Barnave as '*un imbécile,*' Pétion as of a face '*inanimée d'une manière vraiment désolante, et, à vrai dire, cette masse de chair est insensible.*' All sorts of stories were told to his discredit, chiefly, it would seem, in the upper circles of society. His boorishness as a bridegroom had moved his grandfather to indecent mirth, and Marie Antoinette, it was said, to more delicate raillery.[2] Young Montmorin, according to Gouverneur Morris, told M. de Trudaine that he was by nature cruel and base.[3]

An instance of his cruelty among others is that he used to spit and roast live cats. In riding with Madame de Flahaut I tell her that I could not believe such things. She tells me that when young he was guilty of such things ; that he is very brutal and nasty, which she attributes chiefly to a bad education. His brutality once led him so far, while Dauphin, as to beat his wife, for which he was exiled four days by his grandfather.[3]

Thiébault says that his laugh was loud and coarse, and more like that of a tipsy farmer than of a monarch, and relates how near

---

[1] *Secret Memoirs of the Royal Family of France from Journal, Letters, &c., of the Princess Lamballe*, ed. 1895, ii. 8.

[2] *Ibid.* i. 48, 49.

[3] *The Letters and Diary of Gouverneur Morris*, i. 431.

the Tuileries he saw a lady who had a pretty little spaniel
with her, which, before she noticed it, ran close up to the King.
Making a low curtsey, she called the dog back in haste ; but
as the animal turned to run to its mistress, the King, who had
a large cane in his hand, broke its back with a blow of his
cudgel.   Then, amid the screams and tears of the lady, and
as the poor little beast was breathing its last, the King,
delighted with his exploit, continued his walk, slouching
rather more than usual and laughing like any lout of a peasant.

This, Thiébault adds, was 'in keeping with the cuts of
his whip with which the King used to gratify any hairdressers
or priests who were unlucky enough to come in his way when
hunting.'   And this charge tallies with that of the Deputy
Peyssard, curé of Falleron: '*Ses premiers jeux furent des jeux
de sang, et sa brutalité croissant avec l'âge il se délectait à
l'assouvir sur tous les animaux qu'il rencontrait.*' [1]

In Gaston Maugras' biography of the Duc de Lauzun he
is thus depicted :—

At meals he ate grossly.   This is the programme of a
morning : At six o'clock the King rings and asks what there is
for breakfast.   'A fat fowl, Sir, and cutlets.'   'That is not
much ; I will have eggs with gravy.'   He himself superintends
the preparation, eats four cutlets, the fowl, six eggs *au jus*, and
a slice of bacon, drinking a bottle and a half of champagne ;
he then dresses, goes out hunting, and comes in with an
incredible appetite for dinner.[2]

He could always eat and always did eat in the direst
crises of his life.   Some writers have extolled the philosophy with
which, on his return from his examination by the Convention,
he begged a crust from Chaumette.   But with his habits he
must in reality have been ravenously hungry, for he had
breakfasted eight hours before.   In the Logographe box,
while the fight at the Tuileries was going on, he sucked a
peach.   '*Il mangeait,*' writes the mordant historian, '*pendant*

[1] M.-T. v. 535.
[2] *The Duc de Lauzun and the Court of Marie Antoinette*, Eng.
tr. p. 24.

qu'on mourut pour lui.' [1]   His suspicious gaolers in the Temple laid rude hands on the peaches and macaroons.   Yet his dinner there was not insufficient.   In November it consisted every day of four entrées, two roasts, four side dishes, three tarts, three dishes of fruit, a small decanter of Bordeaux and one of Malvoisie or Madeira, the wine being for him alone. Michèlet, who records this, also relates that after dinner his habit was to sleep 'for two hours in the midst of his family,' and that one who had seen him described him as short-sighted, vacant-looking, with a slouching, waddling walk, like a fat farmer. [2]   When he was brought back to the Tuileries from Varennes Camille Desmoulins says that his first words, more natural than royal, were, ' It's devilish hot,' and then, ' That was a —— journey.'   Afterwards, looking towards the National Guards who were present, he said, ' I have done a foolish thing, I acknowledge.   But must not I have my follies, like other people ?   Come, bring me a chicken.'   They brought the chicken, and Louis XVI. ate and drank with an appetite which would have done honour to the ' King of Cockayne.' [3]

His personal appearance was not calculated to arouse enthusiasm.

He was about five feet five inches high.   His physical structure was large and common-looking. . . . He had pale blue eyes, without the slightest expression, and a loud laugh which savoured of imbecility.   He was short-sighted ; his carriage was most awkward, and his whole appearance was that of a badly brought up rustic. . . . He ate like a pig and drank like a fish ; he scarcely ever left the table without being a little unsteady, and then his jokes with the one he wanted to entertain were somewhat gross. [4]

We might distrust this as coming from Barère, but he goes on to say that ' his judgment was clear, he meant well, and would

---

[1] Michelet, b. ix. c. vii.   [2] *Ibid.*

[3] *Révolutions de France et de Brabant*, No. 83, quoted in Claretie's *Desmoulins*, p. 171.

[4] *Memoirs of Barère*, translated by Payen-Payne.

have always done well if his disposition had been supported
by a true woman or a truly patriotic Minister.'

All this gossip, certainly malevolent, and much of it
perhaps untrue, ought, as any biographer of the much vilified
Danton would be the first to admit, to be most carefully
sifted before it could be accepted as a faithful portrait of
the King.　Here it is quoted because, whether false or true,
it equally evinces the small estimation in which he was
held, just as the stories about Danton prove how much he was
dreaded.[1]　And undoubtedly it tends to show how much it
was owing to his personal shortcomings, whether they were
his fault or his misfortune, that he lost his throne.　Even the

---

[1] This seems, though it has been denied to be, an accurate description
of the net result of Paris talk about the two men.　Danton assuredly was
' dreaded ' rather than ' held in small estimation.'　It rests with those who
think that Louis was not ' held in small estimation ' to investigate the
evidence against him, as Danton's defenders have investigated the evidence
against Danton.　To investigate it was not within the scope of this book.
But not to notice it was impossible, because it influenced history at the
time, and has lately been brought prominently before English readers in
books like Thiébault's *Memoirs*, which Mr. A. J. Butler has translated, and
the new edition of the Princess Lamballe's *Memoirs of the Royal Family*.
Nor because it may be termed malevolent can it be dismissed offhand as
a mass of lies.　Michelet makes mistakes, and his language about Louis is
certainly the reverse of benevolent, but anyone calling Michelet ' a liar '
would only stamp himself as one.　The *Nouvelle Biographie* calls attention
to the ' *droiture* ' and ' *sincérité de caractère* ' of Gouverneur Morris, whose
strongest remarks about Louis are not quoted in the text.　M. Aulard
testifies to the ' *véracité ingénue* ' of Thiébault, whose evidence as to
what he has *seen* has an importance altogether different from that of his
hearsay and opinions.　Barère was a liar, but his praise of Louis, above
mentioned, certainly makes his uncomplimentary remarks seem the more
credible.　Taine is ready enough to accept his evidence against revolutionists when he writes : ' Mendacious as Barère is, his testimony here may
be accepted.　I see no reason why he should state what is not true.'　The
Princesse de Lamballe was devoted to the royal family.　Yet her remark quoted above is by no means her only one pointing to the small
estimation in which the King was held, *e.g.* ' From the imperfect idea
which many of the persons in office entertained of the King's capacity, few of
them ever made any communication of importance but to the Queen,' i. 307.

most ardent Royalists could hardly conceal their shame at his demeanour at the Tuileries. If he had spoken one cheering word; if he had put himself at the head of his dauntless Swiss; if he had shown a spark of the spirit of his far more harmful Queen; if he had possessed one iota of the maleficent genius which that morning gleamed through Bonaparte's eyes,[1] then, even at the last moment, Danton's half-organised forces might have fared ill. But he came down to say his last word to his soldiers with his hair unpowdered and out of curl, his eyes red from sleep or tears, a dismal, slovenly figure which could only blurt out, 'Well, they're coming, it's said. I don't know what they want. My cause is that of good citizens. We'll put a good face on it, won't we?' and so on. No wonder that ' *Vive le roi !* ' in the court changed soon to ' *Vive la nation!* ' No wonder that Marie Antoinette exclaimed on his return, 'All is lost. The King has shown no energy, and such a parade has done more harm than good. '[2] And when, letting himself be guided by a man like Rœde.er, he quitted the Tuileries before a blow was struck, it is said that some of those he abandoned tore from their breasts their crosses of St. Louis and broke their swords.[3] ' *Le malheureux prince,*' says a fanatically Royalist writer, ' *ne considérait pas qu'en agissant ainsi il livrait la vie de ses braves soldats aux lâches assassins.*'[4] What enemy of the King could condemn him more severely than this apologist?

Of these 'assassins' Danton, say such writers, was ' *lâche* ' beyond others, because he took no share in the fight. They might as well talk of the cowardice of Carnot. But it is by no means certain that, in spite of all he had done during the evening and night, he was not in the ranks of the Cordeliers in the morning. He says that when Pétion was interned ' he remained there by the wish of the patriots.' By 'there,'

---

[1] Claretie's *Desmoulins*, p. 196, where Bonaparte is said to have looked on and muttered ' Est-ce bien là le dégel de la nation ?'

[2] L. Blanc, b. vii. c. xv.   [3] Michelet, b. vii. c. i.

[4] G. de Cassagnac, *Hist. des Girondins*, b. xi. sec. i.

however, must be understood 'at the Hôtel de Ville,' not the Mairie, which was some way off at the Palais de Justice. But he does not say how long he remained. He may have remained an hour or two, and then have gone to the Tuileries, where the fighting began at half-past ten. D'Aubigny says positively that he did so, that he left the Hôtel de Ville and rallied the columns after their first repulse. And we are told that an autograph letter of Camille Desmoulins has been seen in which it is mentioned that he and Danton took part in the combat.[1] Some colour to this is given by what Danton said at his trial. 'I know that on the 10th Westermann came out of the Tuileries covered with Royalist blood ; and as for me, that I said one would have been able to save the country with 17,000 'men disposed as I had suggested.' It is curious, too, that Louvet, spiteful though his intention is, should speak of him as strutting about with a big sabre at the head of the Marseillais after the victory, as if he had been the hero of the day. The Marseillais would surely have resented that, and the historian of the Terror, seeing the awkward construction which might be put on Louvet's indiscreet sneer, and more astutely choosing to represent Danton as absenting himself from the scene altogether, suggests with a fine air of impartiality that as regards Danton Louvet must be held 'suspect.' The best comment on Louvet's sarcasm and his critic's jesuitry, and what goes far to prove that Danton was, whether he was in the actual fighting or not, really the hero of the day, is that that night he was Minister of Justice.[2]

---

[1] Vallard's *Biographie de Danton*, quoted by Lenox (*Danton*), p. 107.

[2] And not only so, but was the first elected of the Ministers, with the right to sign for all departments of the Ministry till they were filled up. Aulard's *Recueil des Actes du Comité de Salut Public*, i. 2.

CHAPTER XI

1792—continued

To be called to the post of Minister at such a time was to be called to a post of peril. However fundamentally different may have been the tendencies of the Assembly and Commune, opposition to the Court as distinct from opposition to Monarchy had been ground hitherto common to both. But after the 10th of August other animosities instantly and inevitably came into play. To overthrow the Monarchy was arduous. To consolidate the Republic was far harder—was, in fact, to prove impossible. Flushed with success, the Insurrectionary Commune suspended all the Committees of Sections as well as the Departmental Directory, and showed complete independence of the Assembly.[1] The Assembly, in its turn, began to split up into groups, gradually but persistently to grow more implacable in the Convention. Voltairism, which was essentially anti-clerical, and Rousseauism, which was essentially anti-monarchical, could work to a certain point and to some purpose as destructive forces. But when schools of thought were transformed, as after the 10th, into political parties, when the Legislative Assembly's impotence finally demonstrated the Constituent Assembly's failure to engraft an English constitution on a society of such alien growth as that of France, when, in short, it was necessary to construct, and construct radically, neither Voltairists nor Rousseauists were equal to the task, having either no political programme or nothing but Utopias.[1] If the Republic were to be guided to maturity it must be by a man neither indifferent nor a dreamer, but content to aim at the possible, to accept facts, to lay the foundations of the social edifice without stopping to speculate on the ultimate shape of its roof and towers. This was what neither Girondins nor Robespierrists were content to do. This was what Danton attempted. But whereas his practical genius was welcomed, or at least used, by all as a rock of defence against external peril, at home his single strength could not stem the flood of intrigue and fanaticism by which it was eventually swept away. His strength and his weakness were both to be exemplified now. He could replenish the ranks. He could electrify the spirit of the soldiers. He could replace with victorious war what he rightly called the sham war—'*la guerre simulée*'—of Lafayette. He could 'save France from Brunswick.' But he could not save her from the massacres of September. The very moment he entered the Minister's bureau a counter-current against him set in. In spite of what he had done, and Robespierre had left undone, Robespierre on September 5 was elected before him member for Paris. He was on the eve of conflict with Marat ; and Sergent, Panis, and Billaud-Varenne were to go each his own way. Natural mediator between Commune and Assembly, he met with distrust in both, and had scarcely been a month in office when he had to protest against ' vain phantoms of dictatorship ' which hostile eyes pretended to see. Meanwhile, while steadily facing the sterner dangers looming ahead, it is characteristic of his nature to find him emitting something like a groan over the pettier drudgery of his new office. '*Le ministre de la justice annonce*' (August 20) '*que depuis le* 10 *il a expédié cent quatre-vingt-trois décrets.*'[2] What else he had

---

[1] Cf. Dubost's *Danton et la Politique Contemporaine, passim.*

[2] M. xiii. 479.

done, and was about to do, is connected inseparably with the famous massacres.

To understand those massacres it is above all else necessary to put oneself in the place of a Parisian of that time, to whom they seemed what they were, the direct consequence of August 10. We are apt to look on the Royal cause as lost and the Revolution as triumphant when Louis fled from the Tuileries to the Assembly. To the Parisian, and still more to the average Frenchman, with his hereditary fear of the Noblesse, the struggle seemed only begun and the Court a foe only scotched, not killed. So hopeless, in fact, seemed the outlook that the Executive was for abandoning Paris, and but for Danton's resistance would have done so.[1] Meanwhile all that month the air was filled with terrible rumours, hardly more terrifying, however, than the actual events. The invasion of France by the Prussians under Brunswick, by the Austrians under Clairfait; Frederick William's arrival at Luxembourg; the English Ambassador's recall; the desertion of Lafayette; the surrender of Longwy; the insurrection in La Vendée; Russia's menace of war; the discovery of letters purporting to convict the King of treason; the capture of Stenay; such were the thunderclaps of news which day after day sounded in the ears of Paris with more or less appalling import; and on September 1 a report came of the capture of Verdun.

As the surrender of Longwy had been followed by sentence of exile on forty thousand recalcitrant priests, so the reported capture of Verdun was followed by the massacres. We are told what the effect of the news was in a pamphlet entitled 'The Whole Truth on the Real Authors of the Events of September 2.'[2] A general cry,

---

[1] Cf. *Rév. Fr.* xxiv. 491-2. 'J'ai fait venir, dit-il, ma mère qui a soixante-dix ans; j'ai fait venir mes deux enfants. . . . Avant que les Prussiens entrent dans Paris, je veux que vingt mille flambeaux, en un instant, fassent de Paris un monceau de cendre.' Et se tournant vers Roland, il lui dit : 'Roland, garde-toi de parler de fuite, crains que le peuple ne t'écoute.'

[2] *The Reign of Terror*, pub. 1826, i. 424.

'Let us march against the enemy!' was heard throughout the city. 'But . . . our most cruel enemies are not at Verdun; they are here in the prisons.' Many individuals spread abroad this rumour, and others repeated it and gave it credence.[1] 'Our wives, our children will be left to the mercy of these wretches and will be immolated,' exclaimed some; while others rejoined, 'Let us strike before we depart—let us run to the prisons.' This dreadful cry, a fact which all impartial men will corroborate, was re-echoed at the same moment spontaneously and unanimously through all the streets and public squares and places where the inhabitants were assembled together and associated, even in the National Assembly itself.[2]

So too the Duchesse d'Angoulême relates that a municipal officer named Mathieu said to her father in the Temple, 'The emigrants are at Verdun; if they come we shall all be lost, but you shall be the first to perish.'

It was barely a month since Brunswick had proclaimed that if the Tuileries were assaulted, or the smallest outrage were offered to the King or Queen, Paris should be given over to military vengeance. And now the Tuileries had been assaulted. The King and Queen were prisoners in the Temple.

When I went into the street (writes Dr. Moore) people were hurrying up and down with rapid steps and anxious faces; groups were formed at every corner; one told in general that a courier had arrived with very bad news; another asserted that Verdun had been betrayed, like Longwy, and that the enemy were advancing; others shook their heads and said it was the traitors within Paris and not the declared enemies on the frontier that were to be feared.

And these people, agitated by such emotions, were men who were out of work, with nothing to do but sullenly watch events and listen to or swell the cry, ever growing more and more audible, of 'Blood for blood!'[3] For the sombre and imposing ceremonial of August 27, in memory of those slain on the 10th, had intensified the longing for revenge. Plots too were in all

---

[1] Not so Danton, cf. his 'de l'audace' speech later in this chapter.

[2] Cf. Thiébault's *Memoirs*, Eng. tr. i. 125.

[3] Michelet, b. vii. c. iii.

men's mouths—plots of the Court with the invaders ; of disguised priests thronging the city ;[1] of the prisoners to break out of their prisons ;[2] of the Duke of Brunswick with traitors in Paris, many in number and long in the pay of the Court ; of concealed leaders ready to take the command of concealed troops, who would set the Royal Family free and condemn to death all the patriots remaining in Paris.[3] The Royalists were said to be eagerly tracing on their maps each advance of the Prussians and to be gloating over the gibbets which the emigrants had ready for erection when once they were within the walls.[4] Some of the prisoners indulged in foolish threats and prophecies which alarmed the volunteers, who felt them a peril to their wives and families when they should be away with the army.[5] The King's health and that of the Prussians was drunk in costly wines by the inmates of the Abbaye carousing with their mistresses, and hungry men were incensed by seeing gaolers acting as valets,[6] and by rumours that they were paid by *assignats* forged in gaol.[7] The extraordinary acquittal of Montmorin—found guilty of assisting in plots the tendency of which was to kindle a civil war, but not guilty of an intention to do mischief—had made people think that justice was only to be had if they enforced it with their own hands. ' For several days before September 2,' says Moore, ' frequent mention was made of the indefensible delays of justice with regard to the trials of the prisoners.' Deputation after deputation threatened the Assembly. ' *Le peuple est las de n'être vengé ; craignez qu'il ne se fasse justice. Louis XVI et Antoinette voulaient du sang ; si avides du sang du peuple, qu'ils soient rassasiés en voyant couler celui de leurs infâmes satellites.*'[8] And this dangerous exasperation of the thirst for vengeance was still further inflamed

---

[1] Michelet, b. vii. c. iii.

[2] L. Blanc, b. viii. c. ii.

[3] Moore's *Journal*, i. 302.

[4] Michelet, b. vii. c. iii.

[5] Michelet, b. vii. c. iii.

[6] *Ibid.*

[7] L. Blanc, b. viii. c. ii.

[8] ' Je demande que Louis XVI et Marie Antoinette, si avides du sang du peuple, soient rassasiés en voyant couler celui de leurs infâmes satellites.'— M. xiii. 443.

by the affair of Jean Julien, a wretched carter whose seditious cries were taken for revelations of a concealed counter-revolutionary conspiracy. Surely, if panic begets cruelty, never was a town riper for cruelty than Paris was on September 2. Nor was this the worst. A Government fresh in harness and without cohesion, in all the disorder inevitable after the overthrow of an ancient régime, a Government merely provisional till the elections to the Conventions could be held, and divided against itself, could hardly be called a Government at all. Finally, the Assembly was at war with the Commune, and it was into the Commune's hands that the reality of power passed on August 10. In defying the Assembly the Commune summoned to its aid the grisly figure of Marat. One man and one only could have dominated disorder and defied Marat, the man who was a link between the Commune as its ex-deputy-procureur and the Assembly as its Minister of Justice. But even Danton could have succeeded only if the Assembly had thoroughly trusted and loyally supported him, whereas its jealousy of him was even greater than its dread of Marat.

How difficult the task would in any case have been may be gathered from the anti-Dantonist historian Mortimer-Ternaux [1] when he describes how the law provided for the gradual ascent of administrative authority from lower to higher, but failed to provide the higher with means of making itself obeyed by the lower, with results which even in October, when panic had quieted down, Barbaroux could say were still as follows :—

If this moment the tocsin sounded, what means would you have of repressing disorder or preventing crime ? The Power Executive ? It is *without any force*, and may be still exposed to warrants of arrest. The Department ? Its authority exists no longer. The Commune ? It consists for the most part of men whom you ought to prosecute. . . . The public force ? There is none. Good citizens ? They dare not.

The same historian in his account of the Municipal Organisation says : [2] 'As for the central power, it was nowhere to be

<hr>

[1] M.-T. i. 252. [2] *Ibid.* i. 345.

seen. In the constitution of the municipal as of the departmental administration it had no means of independent action.' The new *gendarmerie* had been created only in July 1792 'from the men of July 14 (1789), who had sided with the National Guard in the battle for freedom,' *i.e.* from the Gardes Françaises and the river-side populace, who had taken part in all the *émeutes.* As for the National Guard, its old battalions no longer existed.[1] They were replaced by the armed Sections, each quota being at the orders of each Sectional Committee. Though nominally the force so composed numbered 90,000 men, in reality there were not more than 4,500.[2] Moreover, as the flower of the youth of Paris went to the frontiers, those 4,500 were men rather desirous of disorder than of putting it down. And so some looked on and some took part in the massacres.[3]

Such were the real causes of the September massacres—the absence of any authority with physical force at its disposal, and fear—fear of the enemy without and within, and the inability of the Assembly to allay that fear, owing to its own fear of the Commune and of Danton.[4] As Napoleon said, they were '*dans les forces des choses et dans l'esprit des hommes.*' The best defence to be made for Paris is to be found in Brunswick's atrocious proclamation, which, more than anything perhaps, had propagated this panic fear. The slow-blooded Roland was moved to write in his Circular of August 27 : 'The people should recognise that, apart from its love of liberty, it must expect to suffer the most cruel vengeance if it shows any weakness before the wretches who have been brooding over it so long.' And how did the people interpret that vengeance ?

The whole of the inhabitants were to be conducted to the plains of St. Denis, where the men were to be decimated and

---

[1] M.-T. iv. 223.　　[2] *Ibid.* iv. 224.

[3] G. de Cassagnac, *Hist. Girondins,* b. xx. sec. ii.

[4] Perhaps, when it is remembered how the massacres began, another cause should be mentioned—viz. the intense feeling in Paris against priests. Cf. M.-T. iv. 391.

executed with impartiality on the spot, the most distinguished
patriots having been previously selected, who were to be
broken on the wheel; but the women and children were to be
spared, except forty or fifty fishwomen, who would undergo the
same death as the patriots.[1]

But who were patriots, who were not? In street and
square every man looked askance at his neighbour as he
passed, discovering in him an enemy. Revenge and policy
may have influenced the Committee of Surveillance in insti-
gating the people to murder, but the main cause of the
massacres, without which they would never have gone on for
nearly a week, was panic fear.

Of these massacres, of which the journalists, and among
them the Girondins Brissot[2] and Gorsas, were apologists, which
the National Guards would not stop, and which, if the actual
murderers were few, were witnessed by apathetic or applauding
crowds—'*une foule innombrable de femmes et d'hommes furieux*'[3]
—Paris as a city must bear the guilt, though in a less degree
than the Assembly and the Commune's Committee. Guilt it
was, for the butchery of helpless prisoners can never be other
than detestable, but there has been wholesale murder with less
to palliate it, which has moved history to less horror. A red
Terror is always judged more severely than a white,[4] and a
general who orders that no prisoners shall be left in the rear
(as at Austerlitz) may recount his order without a blush;
whereas Marat, who would have the volunteers leave no prisoners
behind in Paris, will be execrated for all time, though *salus
populi* would seem as specious a defence for the one atrocity

---

[1] Moore's *Journal*, i. 303.

[2] Biré's *Diary of a Citizen in Paris*, Eng. tr. ii. 161.

[3] St. Méard's *Mon Agonie*. Cf. Hue's *Last Years of Louis XVI.*, tr.
by Dallas, p. 400. M.-T. iii. 267, 280, 320, 480, and iv. 415. *The
Whole Truth on the Real Authors of Events of Sept.* 2. Moore's *Journal*,
i. 330. Common-sense teaches that the crowd of onlookers must have
been large, but it has been denied.

[4] Cf. S. iii. 314.

as the other.[1]   And whereas Marat fought with a halter round his neck, Thiébault did not.   But Paris was guilty and the Assembly was guiltier.   And why?   The part played by Danton during the three weeks after August 10 supplies the answer.

On the 10th a rebel, on the 11th he was Minister of Justice.   Then if ever he might have been expected to breathe nothing but fire and sword against men who, had they been conquerors, would assuredly have dealt him short shrift.   But what were his first words as Minister?   'Where justice comes into action popular vengeance should cease.[2]   In the presence of this Assembly I pledge myself to defend its members.   I will place myself at their head.   I answer for their safety.'   At their head !   Alas !   that was just what the Assembly could not endure.   And so justice did not come into action and popular vengeance did not cease.   To comprehend fully the boldness as well as the moderation of Danton's words it must be remembered that, as he himself said, he was Minister by title of cannon-shot, and that it was the Commune which had fired the guns.   When its Committee read those words in the Moniteur it must have felt like a runaway horse curbed in full career.   No doubt the speaker was from that hour suspected by its darker spirits.   We know, in fact, that the Burleys and Mucklewraths of the day considered him a backslider.[3]   But none the more credit did he gain in the Assembly, which, in spite of the efforts of Cambon and Vergniaud to strengthen the Executive, could not stomach his predominance. Yet only Danton could have held the Commune in check ; for, unless influenced by his personal ascendency, the Commune

---

[1] This sentence—or rather a reviewer's version of it, which is a very different thing—has been represented as an apology for the massacres !

[2] So in his Circular of August 18 he wrote : ' Que la justice des tribunaux commence, et la justice du peuple cessera.' *Homme d'État*, p. 112.   For summary of the Circular, see note at the end of the chapter.

[3] Cf. Michelet, b. vii. c. 6, ' les vagues dénonciations, dans lesquelles on essayait de l'envelopper,' and *Rév. Fr.* xxiv. 502.

cared neither for the orders of the Executive nor the Assembly's resolutions. With Robespierre as one of its most violent members its negative power was immense, and, positively, it was more powerful than the Assembly. The Assembly had yielded to it the nomination of the commander of the National Guards. It could issue warrants. It could arrest. It could imprison and release from prison. If the Executive wished to employ force it could do so only through its agency. And with such formidable power in its hands it echoed the voice of proletarian Paris furious, clamorous, demanding blood for blood. Many, perhaps the majority of it, would have stopped short of murder, and the orator Robespierre might be trusted not to act [1]; but the Committee, the terrible Committee of Surveillance, 'cet enragé de comité,' as Danton called it, which had Marat for its sentry and the police power at its disposal, had no mind to be robbed of its revenge.

What Danton could do he did. Where the people seemed to have just cause for indignation, as in the Montmorin affair, he appeased it by quashing the acquittal. And when furious deputations came to terrorise the Assembly, and the walls were placarded with denunciations of individual Deputies, his hand is to be traced in the proposal of his friend and confidant Delacroix to create a court-martial for trial of the Swiss prisoners.

A fierce cry for revenge had rung through Paris on August 10 as the dead were recognised by their relations, a cry which was to grow louder and louder till September. On the very evening of the 10th the Insurrectionary Commune, whose instincts were by no means all senseless or sanguinary, resolved that an extraordinary tribunal must be created to try those who had fired on the people.[2] No better expedient, perhaps, if we may judge from the scenes in the Assembly at the time, could have been devised for getting breathing-time in which to restore order, if the Assembly had only recognised

---

[1] Cf. his own admission, Hamel's *Robespierre*, b. viii. sec. xix.
[2] *Ibid.* b. viii. sec. xx.

that desperate diseases need desperate remedies. But not till
the 15th did it vote for the tribunal, on Chabot's proposal,
having meanwhile infuriated the Commune by attempting to
restore the balance of power between it and a new Departmental Directory.[1] And, though on the 17th Hérault announced what was to be its composition,[2] Brissot's maladroit
whittling at it and the week's delay made what might, if
frankly adopted by the Assembly, have appeased the people
and made it more tolerant, seem a too tardy and too feeble an
instrument of vengeance, and the Commune accordingly tried
to render it more terrible. Delacroix's proposal on the 11th
was induced by the threatening aspect of the people and was
meant to stave off an instant massacre. It was characteristic
of Danton, as students of his speeches soon recognise, to mask
a really merciful proposal under the semblance of severity.
Delacroix had himself gone on his knees in the Assembly to
induce the mob to spare certain of the Swiss, and the true
meaning of his proposal for a court-martial is shown by its
being superseded at the instance of the Commune by another
for the establishment of an Extraordinary Court with wider
powers. ' *Ces crimes*,' grumbled Robespierre, '*remontent bien
au delà*' (*i.e.* the 10th of August).[3] From the one court even
the Swiss might expect some mercy, from the other none.[4]

When, again, a proposal emanating from the Commune
was made to deprive the prisoners of what had hitherto been
regarded as a prisoner's sacred right, and make the same men
judges and jury in one, it was the Dantonist Thuriot who,
along with Choudieu, withstood the proposal in an admirable
speech, saying that though he loved the Revolution he would
sooner poniard himself than see it triumph by such means.
And on the 22nd Delacroix, then President of the Assembly,
sternly reprimanded a Communal deputation headed by
Robespierre for daring to assume the Assembly's functions in

<hr>

[1] Hamel's *Robespierre*, b. viii. sec. xxi.   [2] M. xiii. 444.
[3] M. xiii. 430.
[4] M.-T. iii. 29. M. xiii. 389-90. Hamel, viii. sec. xx.

suspending the Departmental Directory.[1] Delacroix imprudently reminded Robespierre of this on October 29, and
Robespierre never forgave him.[2]

On the 31st Delacroix took an even more uncompromising
tone. 'The formation of the Provisional Commune is,' he
said, 'contrary to existing laws,' and 'a rebel commune' is a
'scandal.'

The Commune, in short, wanted revenge. Danton and
his friends sought to regulate revenge by the action of a
responsible court, and to minimise it by swift execution.
Punishment they knew the people would exact. The quicker
it was the less terrible it would be. For a time they partially
succeeded. Delacroix as President of the Assembly answered
angry demands for the suppression of the Court of Orleans by
saying that the Assembly would never be coerced by threats or
danger. But then came the news of the surrender of Longwy,
and, like a spark to gunpowder, the cry so often fatal to
Frenchmen, 'We are betrayed!' 'All Paris is in an uproar,'
said Bertrand de Molleville's landlord to him, 'about that
cursed little town.' Forthwith Danton proposed the domiciliary
visits, perhaps to some extent influenced by that cry himself,
but as a necessary and perfectly justifiable measure of precaution, and none the less striving to quiet the panic, which
was fast becoming murderous. 'It is true,' he said on the
evening of August 28, 'that the enemy threatens France, but
all he has got as yet is Longwy. Your dangers are exaggerated.
The Assembly must show itself worthy of the nation.' The
majority of those arrested were at once released, but neither
arrests nor release could stay the panic which the Committee of
Surveillance fanned.

The rest of the Ministers wavered before the double danger.
At a conference of the Committee of General Defence and the
General Council, Servan, the War Minister, avowed that he
had no confidence in the armies, and that it was impossible to
prevent the Prussians capturing Paris. Then Danton rose,

　　　　[1] M. xiii. 509.　　　　　　　　　[2] M.-T. iii. 110.

and declaring that Paris represented France, and to abandon
Paris was to abandon the Revolution, he went on to say that
the Royalists were many, the Republicans few, that they were
between two fires—foes without and foes within—that the
Royalists undoubtedly met and corresponded with the Prussian
army, though where they met or who they were was not
known; that to disconcert these projects some measures were
necessary, and the Royalists must *be made to fear*.[1]   These are
the words which his libellers, who add that the words were
accompanied by 'a ferocious gesture,' pretend were provocative
to and a defence of the September massacres.   Surely it is
only necessary to read them to see that he·was speaking, not
of the Royalists under lock and key who were the victims on
September 2, but of the Royalists at large who were reported
to him as being in correspondence with the enemy.   Scant
mercy, no doubt, Danton would have shown to them.   But
for the prisoners already in hand what Danton wanted was not
massacre, but speedy trial.   In hours of revolution the losers
pay.   Danton meant them to pay as he would have paid himself if he had lost, and he voiced the ever·increasing impatience
of the people at the Assembly's inaction.   The longer the
debt was owing the more merciless would be its liquidation.
This was why on August 30 he wrote to the President of the
Assembly—

I am at a loss to conceive any reason for the delay in
putting into execution the two important decrees for suppressing the Royal Commissioners of Justice and for the mode of
replacing them.   From all sides I receive complaints and
protestations, and there is reason in them; for it is essential,
in order to cement the dominion of Liberty and Equality, that
the people should be given, as representatives of the Executive
at the tribunals, men in whom it has confidence.   For the
second time I appeal to the Assembly and implore it to order
that these decrees be carried into effect without delay.   My
own sense of patriotism as well as the voice of the people
renders it imperative that my sole study shall be to get the

---

[1] Thiers, *Rév. Fr.* c. vi.

laws enforced and to make it clear that it is no fault of mine
that those relative to the abolition of the old Commissioners
for the administration of justice and the appointment of new
ones have not been carried into execution.

Were these the words of a massacre-maker?   A cut-throat
does not prelude his spring on the victim by calling vigorously
for the police.

Again, the Commune,[1] which had doubled its members on
August 12, had reorganised itself on the 25th,[2] and after much
squabbling with the Assembly as to its constitution during the
month had been dissolved by it on August 30,[3] was, for all
that, the real master of Paris.   And as the Assembly had its
Executive so the Commune had its Committee of Surveillance
—Sergent, Panis, &c.—with Marat as its assessor.   Panis and
Sergent, though Members of the old Commune, had been
continued in their functions as Administrators of Police, and
were, in fact, the chiefs of the Committee of Surveillance.   As
such they exercised enormous power.   All Paris stood in awe
of them, and no man, says Mortimer-Ternaux, was great
enough to brave their vengeance.   To drive the Commune to
desperation was, as Danton knew, sheer madness—was to
embark on an internecine civil war.[4]   On August 29[5] it was
announced in the Assembly that the enemy was close to
Verdun – Verdun, some 120 miles, as the crow flies, from
Paris.   On the 30th came disquieting news from the Army of
the North.   In the Moniteur of September 1 was published,
with no detail of horror omitted, an account of the prospective
doom of the inhabitants of Paris as soon as the enemy should
be within its gates.   On the morning of September 2
Brunswick's summons to Verdun was read in the Assembly.
It would never do at this supreme crisis for Commune and
Assembly to come to blows.   Some middle course must be
found at any cost.   It is notable that Danton from August 29
kept aloof from the Commune, because, according to Michelet,

[1] M.-T. iii. 16.   [2] M.-T. iii. 148.   [3] M.-T. iii. 157.
[4] M.-T. iii. 208.   [5] M. xiii. 571.

he was sitting on the fence and doubtful whether Commune or Assembly would get the upper hand ; because, according to more virulent critics, he was, while planning the massacres seeking to hide his trail.   But the reasonable explanation consistent with all his words and acts is that he purposely marked his disapproval of '*cet enragé de Comité*'[1] and '*ce petit boute-feu qui gâte tout*'[2]—Marat—and his determination to act with the Assembly, while to render his opposition to the Commune as little exasperating as possible he again acted through a friend.   It was Thuriot who proposed to legalise the as yet illegal Commune of August 10, and to legalise and call into actual existence its hitherto nominal total of 288.[3]   This compromise tended (1) to appease the Commune in general, and (2) to weaken its Committee of Surveillance by increasing the strength of the Moderates, and by depriving the Committee of such popularity as the Assembly's opposition to it conferred. It was a well meant and able attempt, and the first result of it was one dear to Danton's heart, since the Commune's Council-General, which now felt itself secure, at once summoned the citizens to enrol themselves on the Champ de Mars.[4]   But it was too late.   The Assembly only passed Thuriot's resolutions towards one o'clock on September 2,[5] and the Committee of Surveillance had that day reconstituted itself, had prepared warrants for the arrest of Roland, Brissot and thirty other Deputies, and was, it seems too probable, arranging for the massacres in the prisons.[6]

No doubt Danton divined what the Assembly's vacillation would entail, and about one o'clock he made one last effort for order, one parting protest against panic.

It is, gentlemen (he said), gratifying to the Minister of a free people to have to announce to you that the country is on the way to safety.   Everywhere it is alert, astir, afire for battle.

[1] Mme. Roland's *Appel à l'Impartiale Postérité*, Pt. i. 111.
[2] Prudhomme's *Histoire Générale* &c., *Anecdotes sur les Factions*.
[3] M.-T. iii. 211.　　　　　　　　[4] M.-T. iii. 214.
[5] Michelet, b. vii. c. v.　　　　　　　[6] M.-T. iii. 216.

You know that Verdun is not yet in the enemy's hands. You know that the garrison has sworn to sacrifice the man who first utters the word 'Surrender.' Our people are on the way, some to the frontier, others to dig entrenchments, while the rest will defend our towns with their pikes. Paris is about to second these splendid efforts. The Commissioners of the Commune are going by solemn proclamation to invite citizens to arm themselves and march in the country's defence. This, gentlemen, is a moment when you may proclaim that the capital has deserved well of France. This is a moment when the National Assembly is about to turn itself into a War Committee. We demand your concurrence with us in directing this sublime movement of the people, by nominating Commissioners to second us in these great measures. We demand punishment of death against anyone refusing to serve or surrender arms. We demand that instructions shall be issued to the citizens which shall give method to their movements. We demand the despatch of couriers to all the departments, notifying them of the decrees you will have issued. The tocsin which is about to sound is no alarm-signal, but a summons to charge the foe. To conquer, gentlemen, we must dare, and dare, and dare, and so save France.[1]

It is hardly credible that this noble outburst of patriotism should be part of the evidence alleged as incriminating Danton 'in the massacres. The tocsin was the signal for murder. The enemy were the prisoners, and so on. He spoke '*avec un geste exterminateur*,' says Lacretelle. Surely only eyes purblind with malignity could so distort plain language. Let anyone turn to the Moniteur and he will see that Danton's words were suggested by, and only a more eloquent echo of, others just uttered in the Assembly. An hour or so before he spoke the Commune had sent a deputation saying the tocsin was about to be sounded, the alarm-gun fired, and the people summoned on the Champ de Mars to march against the enemy, and the Assembly had received it with loud applause. And subsequently the

---

[1] Danton's knowledge of English may have suggested to him Spenser's 'Be bolde, be bolde, and everywhere be bolde,' or Bacon's 'What first? boldness: What second and third? boldness.'

President had said 'cannon was long the ultimate resource of kings against peoples, now it must be that of the people against kings.' We may be sure that no man who heard Danton that day supposed him to be referring to any but the invading armies. His appeal was supplemented by the proposal of his friend Delacroix that anyone directly or indirectly refusing to execute or in any way hampering the orders given and measures taken by the Executive should be punished by death. This proposal, no doubt emanating from Danton, was meant to overawe the party of violence by strengthening the Ministers. But again the Assembly vacillated. It adjourned for four hours—four fatal hours—at the end of which the golden chance was gone. The Massacres had begun. In disgust, but not in despair, Danton hurried from the Assembly straight to the Champ de Mars, and there animated the crowd to enlist. If enlistment should divert attention from the prisoners so much the better. But in any case he was bent now on devoting himself to the object always nearest his heart and the burden of all his speeches, resistance to the foreigner. We can see now that enlistment, though it did not prevent the massacres, did probably prevent far worse. What if these volunteers had caught the contagion of assassination? '*La masse*,' says Michelet, '*des volontaires, dont personne ne savait le nombre, n'allait-elle pas se mettre en mouvement, livrer bataille aux prisons, puis à l'Assemblée peut-être, puis d'hôtel en hôtel aux aristocrates?*' And in October Dr. Moore writes: 'It is more difficult at present to execute any great atrocity than it was at the beginning of September, because a great number of profligate and idle fellows who were at that time in Paris have been sent to recruit the armies.' What Dr. Moore could observe in October after the event Danton had foreseen the month before.

But it is said that when once the massacres had begun it was Danton's special duty as Minister of Justice to suppress them. Such a notion is based on an entire misconception of the functions of the Minister of Justice. It might be almost as sensibly contended that it was the Lord Chancellor's business to suppress the Gordon riots. If there was a culprit it was Roland, not Danton. It was Roland whose business it was as Minister of the Interior to preserve the peace and security of the citizens and to see that the police discharged their functions. It is Madame Roland—evil genius of the Revolution, as Marie Antoinette was of the Monarchy—who, out of hatred of Danton more than out of love for her husband, has exonerated the latter at the expense of the former. But her husband's words answer her own. On September 3 he wrote—

Yesterday was a day on the events of which we should perhaps cast a veil. I know that the people, terrible in its vengeance, yet tempers it with a sort of justice, not indiscriminately immolating the objects of its fury, but directing it against those who have been too long spared by the sword of the law, and whose immediate death is demanded by the dangers of the hour. But I know that it is easy for wretched traitors to abuse such an effervescence. I know that we owe it to all France to declare that the Executive have been able neither to foresee nor to prevent these excesses.

A more illuminating account of the massacres was never penned. It was written by Roland to screen himself, and it seems to have quite escaped his wife's notice that *a fortiori* it screened Danton. But in trying to blacken his reputation she unconsciously testifies to his greatness. For if Danton was the culprit it could only be by virtue of his commanding personality overshadowing the technical responsibility of Roland. As to Roland's technical responsibility there can be no doubt. When the *émeute* of June 20, 1792, was imminent, and measures to prevent it were being discussed, the Departmental Directory came into collision with the Mayor, Pétion. Issuing orders to the commandant of the National Guard they reported the whole matter to the Minister of the Interior. The Mayor, the Directory, the Minister of the Interior, were therefore concerned in the matter. The Minister of Justice was not.

In point of fact, however, neither Danton nor Roland could prevent the massacres.[1] It may seem almost incredible that for nearly a week wholesale murders need have gone on unchecked. But the incredible is the truth. You may influence an Assembly by words. But when you come to action you must dispose of men. Now even Roland had no force at his disposal. All he could do could only be done *through the Commune*, and the Executive of the Commune was paying the murderers their wages. 'An imposing armed force,' says Prudhomme, 'would have been necessary and might have easily been found if the Commune had not been directress of the crime.' Some of the National Guards when summoned would not obey.[2] Some of them went on quietly drilling within earshot of the victims' cries.[3] Some of them were among the murderers. Practically they were the only force available, and therefore, by their inaction, they kept the ring while the murders went on. Many of them, Royalists or semi-Royalists before August 10, were, no doubt, doubly anxious to do nothing to render their new-fledged patriotism suspicious. It is to be noted, too, that the elections to the Convention showed that the people were indifferent to, or approved of, the massacres, for two days after the Versailles massacre they elected Sergent and Panis.

As for Danton, after his famous speech on September 2, he appeared no more in the Assembly till the morning sitting of the 7th, if indeed he appeared in person then. It is a curious and at first sight a suspicious fact. But on September 7 he notified to the Assembly a merciful order, which he had issued, manifestly calculated to save life and repress violence, viz. that any person arrested near Paris should be, in view of current events, detained where arrested, *i.e.* not be brought to Paris.[4] Such and similar business would occupy some of his time, and on September 3 he presided at a Council. The elections, too, were in progress. But how was he mainly occupied? We are

<hr>

[1] Cf. M.-T. i. 252.
[2] Jourdan's *Declaration.*
[3] *Rév. Fr.* xxv. 18.
[4] M. xiii. 644

prone to think solely of the massacres on those days. But the Assembly and the majority of the citizens were thinking of something else too. Suppose a German army had captured Bristol and were marching on London, having sworn to hand it over, when taken, to fire and sword. Suppose the Commander-in-Chief to have declared that London could not be defended, and that all the city were a scene of wild confusion, that the civic authorities and the House of Commons were at loggerheads, that both bodies were sitting permanently day and night, that constant councils were being held in the Guildhall and the rooms of Ministers, that arms were so scarce that every gift of a gun seemed a godsend, yet that from 500 to 2,000 volunteers were being armed and hurried off every day to the army.[1] Suppose that friends of the Germans, ready to join them and praying for their success, were in the London gaols, and the mob broke into the gaols and murdered their inmates. Would all our Ministers think first or most of saving the prisoners' lives, or would they be likely to leave their fate to those ordinarily responsible and think first and most of saving London? In after-days, when the invasion-panic was forgotten and the murders had grown redder and redder in men's memories, people would wonder at the passive callousness of those Ministers. And yet they would have had much else to do which at the time seemed even more urgently imperative. What Danton was doing was, with all the energy that was in him, inducing the citizens to enlist, equipping them, sending them off in batches to the front, and reporting to the Assembly. And, what is more, he was acting by the Assembly's express orders. On the 3rd Gensonné proposed and the Assembly ordered that the Executive should report at once on the measures taken for hurrying off troops to the camps and fortifying the heights round Paris. The safety of the inhabitants of Paris, on the other hand, was expressly left by Gensonné's resolution in the hands of the Mayor and the other Municipal Authorities. Danton therefore was doing his duty,

[1] S. iii. 31.

and he did it in such a fashion that even his bitterest assailants have been unable to refuse him some grudging gratitude.

If instead of such action, and trusting to his personal influence, he had, as one historian suggests he should have done, gone into the streets with a flag in his hand, he would in behalf of his bitter enemies have lost a popularity essential to the main work he had in hand, and without saving anyone else's life might have lost his own. Lafayette's experiences were too well known to him. On an occasion when the popular frenzy was far less, and at a time when respect for authority was far greater, and Lafayette's authority especially was at its height, Bertrand de Molleville relates how 'he harangued, but his rhetoric was in vain. The feeble voice of this popular general was everywhere drowned by that of the sovereign people, who in this insurrection . . . . truly thought that they were performing the most sacred of duties.' So it would have been now. When the procureur of the Commune —Manuel—interfered with the mob we are told that his life was in danger.[1] So was the Abbé Fauchet's. Prudhomme says that the murderers seemed disposed to massacre anyone who should show any inclination to try and stop their executions, and he puts into Camille Desmoulins' mouth precisely the same opinion. Lamartine too says that Maillard, who of all men might have been supposed to interfere with least risk, endangered his own life in doing so.[2]

Now, suspicion had already breathed on Danton's name. A rumour spread through Paris that the Commune had declared the Executive to have forfeited the confidence of the nation,[3] and a violent altercation took place between him and Marat[4] when the latter was going to arrest Roland—Roland

---

[1] For Manuel's conduct cf. Beaumarchais' account of his incarceration. Hue's *Louis XVI.* (Eng. tr. 1806), p. 409. M. xiii. 603.

[2] *History of Girondins*, xxv. sec. xiii. (Bohn).

[3] Michelet, b. vii. c. v. Mme. Roland's *Appel*, Pt. i. 109, 'ils répliquèrent . . . que tous ces ministres étoient de —— traîtres.'

[4] Of whom writes Michelet: 'Massacrer la Législative, c'est son texte ordinaire.'—*Fr. Rév.* b. vii. c. vii.

not, be it noted, a Royalist nor a prisoner, but a Minister by virtue of the 10th of August. All, therefore, that Danton could do he had done in his own way. If he had failed it was not his fault. All now possible was to rescue individual prisoners through the agency of their Sections. It is known that some lives were spared by his intervention, and no personal enemy of his is said to have lost his life.[1] When his enemy Duport's life was threatened he, because this particular case fell under his special jurisdiction as Minister of Justice, interfered resolutely, and in defiance of the Commune, in his behalf. Historians who cannot ignore such facts may prate about the inconsistency of human nature, but a Royalist and a sharp-tongued enemy, Royer-Collard, read his man better. 'This Danton,' said a friend to him, 'seems, however, to have had a generous heart.' 'A magnanimous one, sir, that is the right word,' answered Royer-Collard.

Englishmen who may be inclined to pronounce offhand that if there had been a will there would have been a way to coerce the Paris riots might with advantage read an account from a French source of the Birmingham riots of 1791, when from Thursday till Sunday night the rioters were in possession of the town, burning houses and committing all sorts of excesses, which continued in the surrounding country some time longer.

En vain les magistrats et les principaux habitants se concertèrent le lendemain (Friday) pour le retour de l'ordre, ils manquaient de force armée pour en imposer à ces scélérats, que leurs mesures de prudence et les exhortations ne firent qu'irriter, de sorte qu'ils continuèrent les mêmes excès pendant tout le vendredi et la nuit suivante. . . . On a remarqué dans les chefs de cette insurrection le plus grand sang-froid, tandis que les exécuteurs de leurs ordres étaient presque tous ivres.[2]

---

[1] This has been made a reproach to him. 'If he interfered for some why not for all? if he interfered it was because he knew beforehand,' &c. But *everyone* knew beforehand that there was danger, and interference was only possible through the Sections, which would not have interfered for all. He also saved L'Homond, Barthélemy, and Magerie.

[2] Robinet's *Danton, Émigré*, p. 66.

Danton's Circular of August 18.

In his Circular to the Tribunals, August 18, Danton wrote as a man fresh from the conflict and from the combatant's point of view. He spoke of the plot in the Tuileries and how it had ended in the destruction of the *chevaliers du poignard* and the Swiss by the 'sacred and ever-memorable insurrection' of Paris, which was unanimous as France would be on hearing the news; of Mandat's treachery ending in his death; of the destruction of a libellous and hireling press; of the provisional Commune having been sanctioned by the Assembly; of the change of Ministers and the personnel of government; of the King's imprisonment; of his own accession to office 'through breach in the Tuileries walls and by ultimate argument of cannon;' of his steadfast adherence to his Cordeliers principles of July 14, 1789; of his determination to maintain law, order, national unity, the splendour of the State, the prosperity of the people and 'not an impossible equality of property, but of right and content.' He affirms that the liberty won at the taking of the Bastille might have been bloodlessly consolidated in six months; that no decemvirs were needed, for Mably and Rousseau — 'immortal beacon-lights for legislation' — with Locke, Montesquieu, and Franklin, would have been ample guides; but that those in power willed otherwise, and priests and tribunals had conspired against the people. He exhorts the officials to whom it is addressed to make known Lafayette's proscription, forthcoming proofs of the venality of the press, the King's subsidies to traitors and projected *coup d'état*, the perfidious conduct of the troops in firing on the people when fraternising with them, and the consequent fight and victory, and he bids them, if they have been misled by ignorance, to open their eyes now to the truth and enlighten others, and to enforce the sword of the law against traitors and enemies of the State. 'Let the Courts begin to enforce justice and the people will cease enforcing it for themselves.'—*Homme d'État*, p. 109.

CHAPTER XII

1792—*continued*

How comes it, then, that on Danton's name has been heaped
so much obloquy? It is because Royalists, Girondins, and
Robespierrists united to libel the man with whose robust
common-sense their narrow fanaticisms clashed. But as long
as he lived the last two at least were, practically, dumb. Yet
the question of the massacres were raised in the Assembly more
than once. On September 25, in the Convention, some of its
members and the Commune were accused specifically. Danton
spoke and launched out against Marat, ending with the challenge, 'If anyone has any accusation to bring against me let
him get up and make it.'[1] The Assembly cheered him and no
man took up his challenge ; but when Marat rose some of the
Girondins must have hoped their enemy's hour was come, for
Marat feared no one and never minced his words,[2] and he was
smarting under Danton's attack. But Marat simply avowed
his own responsibility and said not a word incriminating Danton.
Again in the following March Danton spoke.

Since they have dared to speak of those days of blood which
every good citizen has mourned, I, for my part, will say this :
that if there had been a tribunal, then none of that blood would
have been shed by the people who have been unmercifully reproached with it. I will say, and every eye-witness of those

____

[1] M. xiv. 41.   [2] Cf. Moore's *Journal*, ii. 264.

dreadful events will say so too, that no human power was in condition to dam the tide of popular vengeance.   Let us profit by the errors of our predecessors.

This time too the Convention applauded, and the tongues of Danton's enemies—and they were many and eloquent and bitter tongues—did not stir.   The Girondins were silent because they had no evidence.   As for the Robespierrists, the only fault they had to allege against him was his '*modérantisme*' and weakness.   His real accuser is Madame Roland.

I looked (she writes) at this repulsive and horrible face, and though I felt I ought not to judge a man on hearsay and that I knew nothing against him, that in such times the most respectable man must have one reputation with one party, another with another, and, in short, that I ought to distrust appearances, I could not associate an honest man with such a countenance. I have never seen anything so absolutely the incarnation of brutal passion and astounding audacity half veiled under an appearance of immense joviality and an affectation of great *bonhomie*.   Often have I pictured to myself Danton, dagger in hand, hounding on with voice and gesture a band of assassins more cowardly and less savage than himself.

Madame Roland was no mean portrait-painter.   But whose portrait are we promptest to recognise here?   Surely that of the woman who had pet names—Antinoüs, Nisus, Euryalus— for her favourites, who found relief from Danton's ugliness in the faces of handsome Barbaroux, handsome Buzot, and who, as the historian of the Terror records,[1] at one and the same time drove her poor husband to despair and ruined the Girondin party by coldly informing him that she had ceased to love him and loved another man in his place.   Yet this is the woman who has inoculated history with its horror of Danton, who had specially offended her by saying that the nation needed Ministers who were not in leading-strings to their wives.[2]   Her vivacious spite,[3] transfigured and consecrated by her courage

---

[1] v. 146.   [2] M.-T. iv. 74.

[3] It is impossible to forget her words on the evening of June 20, 1792, when she heard how the mob had insulted the Queen: ' *Que j'aurais voulu voir sa longue humiliation!*'—Biré's *Légendes Révolutionnaires*, p. 118.

on the scaffold, has been taken as gospel, and the falsehoods to which she gave form in her prison seem as though they would never die.

Perhaps the charge which has created most prejudice against Danton is that he countersigned and sent to the Departments the atrocious apology for the massacres drawn up by the Maratists in the Commune. It is sufficient to say of this charge, which, however, thanks to Madame Roland and M. Bertrand de Molleville, is still repeated, that it has long since been disproved. The circular was examined, and found to have no countersignature at all. What a comment it is on the judgment of history on Danton that, though the most prejudicial charge against him has been thus dissipated, its effects none the less continue ! But calumny had a second string to its bow. The circular, it was alleged, at any rate was forwarded in Danton's official letters. Yet no proof of this is vouchsafed, and even if it were true it is obvious that any clerk might have been bribed to insert it surreptitiously. This is no forced supposition. Roland complained to the Convention of a circular of the Commune being enclosed in a cover directed and franked by Pétion of which Pétion denied all knowledge.[1] But there is other evidence than supposition. When Danton attacked Marat and declared himself innocent of the blood of September what a retort it would have been if Marat could have said, ' Why, you sent off my circular,' much more if he could have said, ' Why, you countersigned my circular.' And Marat would certainly have never hesitated to make the retort if he had been able. In short, the secondary charge is as devoid of proof as the primary one, and if proved would have but little force.

Lafayette has charged Danton with getting Montmorin murdered in the massacres, because Montmorin knew something to his discredit,[2] and some writers have confused two men

---

[1] M.-T. iv. 284. For abuse of the Assembly's ' contre-seing ' or ' frank,' cf. M. iii. 674.

[2] *Mémoires*, iv. 329.

of the same name.   The Marquis de Montmorin, massacred on September 3, had been brought before the Criminal Tribunal and acquitted—we have seen on what grounds—and Danton had quashed the acquittal.   But it was the Comte de Montmorin, ex-Minister of Foreign Affairs, who was supposed to know things discreditable to Danton.   *He* was denounced by the Girondins, and having been, on the report of Lasource, committed for trial on September 2, was massacred the same day.   There is nothing to show that Danton had anything whatever to do with his fate.   Lafayette says that Danton had given Montmorin a receipt for a bribe, that Montmorin had 'imprudently' told Danton the receipt was burnt, and that Danton had him massacred.   He seems not to have seen that with the disappearance of the receipt any special motive for massacring the owner would have disappeared too.

As Danton was said to have murdered Montmorin to prevent Montmorin's revelations, so to prevent Duport's revelations he is said to have defied the Committee of Surveillance and saved Duport.   Proof of Duport's knowing anything damaging to him there is none.   But the affair is remarkable as showing how resolutely Danton asserted the authority of his special office when it was encroached on by the Commune. Duport was arrested by order of the Commune and brought to Nemours.   Had he been brought to Paris he would certainly have lost his life.   Danton ordered the Nemours magistracy to retain him.   The Committee of Surveillance protested and issued counter-orders.   Instantly Danton sent instructions that no orders but his own were to be obeyed, and to this firm intervention Duport—Danton's enemy—owed his life.

Even the monster supposed to commit murder and dispense mercy from one and the same motive might have been expected to earn a modicum of credit for his championship of Roland, the 'old fox' whom he cordially disliked, against Marat at the height of Marat's power.   At all events one might have expected some to be given to him by Roland's wife, even if her conjugal affection be estimated at Mortimer-Ternaux's valuation as an out-of-door affair kept for public display. But no, Danton was too ugly, and Madame Roland notices the affair only to suggest several ugly motives, either of which she asserts may have actuated him, while she leaves her readers to make their choice. What is to be said of a woman who under such circumstances can only repay good offices by insinuations of bad faith ?

Something like an insinuation is another of the charges associated with Madame Roland of which much has been made. In her *Appel à l'Impartiale Postérité* is a note in the handwriting, it is said, of her friend Bosc, but according to the editor copied from her manuscript. In this note of somewhat ambiguous parentage Grandpré, in fulfilment of his duty to report to Roland the state of the prisons, is related to have found the prisoners in a great state of apprehension, and after releasing some of them to have awaited the exit of Ministers from the Council held on September 2. It broke up at 11 P.M., and Grandpré, apparently unaware that the massacres were going on, spoke to Danton, who happened to come out first, and told him of the alarm of the prisoners and of the inefficacy of Roland's demand for an armed force, adding that it was Danton's duty to do something ; upon which Danton, plagued by such an untoward declaration, cried out in his bellowing tone (*avec sa voix beuglante*), and with *an appropriate gesture,* ' The prisoners be damned ! let them look to themselves,' and passed on. To render the exact malediction ascribed to him one would have to resort to English not to be found in dictionaries, and no tale of him would seem to have been thought complete without its introduction. But though we may wonder at a lady, even from impressionist ardour, reproducing it, we ought not to grudge her such verisimilitude as it may lend to her narrative, since it seems to have been on the lips of contemporary Frenchmen of every class, from the lowest to Princes of the Blood, and, if we may trust some accounts, on the lips of the son of St. Louis himself. Madame Roland in fact uses it in her own letters.[1] We cannot, however, help noting that to this 'perpetual' expletive is appended that 'appropriate gesture' of which we have heard before. And an even odder point about the story is that though the words were uttered 'in the presence of twenty persons,' and persons who 'shuddered at such rude language from a Minister of Justice,' none of the twenty shudderers seem to have reported it to Danton's enemies, though treasuring it up as specially suited for a lady's ears. But 'neither the Royalists nor Prud-homme mention it, nor any memoirs except Madame Roland's own.'[2]

Again, it is clear, from Grandpré having to report to Roland, that Roland was the responsible man. If Roland could not get troops how could Danton? It is the old story over again of Madame Roland paying an unintentional tribute to Danton's ascendency in a dramatic fib meant to exculpate her husband. But in an undramatic form, in a form not shuddered at by the twenty hearers, Danton may, it is likely enough, have said something which to an artist of such skill as Madame Roland would have made her embellishments easy. Throw in the expletive even, and what does it come to? Danton had just left the Council at which all the perils of the hour, internal and external, had been anxiously discussed. He was going to carry out the measures which had commended themselves as wisest. And up comes this buttonholer, this secretary of another Minister, his enemy, pestering him with that Minister's business. And what a Minister! With Servan, the War Minister, Danton could confer, and at his trial he said half his time was spent at the War Office. But how could he interfere with the wooden-headed Minister of the Interior? The two men were antipathetic. So he may have brushed Grandpré aside with a 'Go to — Roland; the prisoners are not my business.' If anyone should say that this is only con-jecture let him consider whether it is less probable than that

---

[1] Letter to Bosc, July 26, 1789. Cf. Moore's *Journal*, ii. 18.
[2] Dubost's *Une Page d'Histoire*, p. 121.

if twenty persons heard the other version the only person to report it should be Madame Roland. The fact is that Madame Roland's stories about Danton (written at the rate of three hundred pages in twenty-two days) have the same elements of improbability as Mrs. Pipchin's story of the bull, and Paul Dombey's criticism is all they are worth.

As the above tale of a scene witnessed by twenty persons, but recorded only by one, is believed on the authority of Madame Roland, or rather on the authority of a note in Madame Roland's Memoirs, so the story of another scene equally public is believed on the authority of Prudhomme, or rather of information imparted to Prudhomme secondhand. The day is September 3; the scene, Danton's official residence. Danton is presiding over a meeting of the Ministers, and—the ogre—is arrayed in a scarlet robe.[1] All the Ministers are present. So is the President of the Assembly, Delacroix, and the Assembly's secretaries and the presidents of the forty-eight sections—altogether an assemblage of over a hundred persons. Terror is on every face but one, and that Danton's. He alone remains firm. A number of great measures are resolved upon, all of his initiative. Outside, the massacres are going on. Towards the close of the meeting Mandar, vice-president of the Temple Section—'*personnage*' according to Hamel,[2] '*assez peu digne de confiance*'—interrogates Danton. 'Are all measures for external defence settled?' 'Yes.' 'Let us, then, see to Paris, assemble all the troops, and dividing ourselves, all who are here, into as many sets as there are places where massacres are in progress, either by haranguing the mob or getting together all the force we can, stop this bloodshed.' The audience show interest, but many are entirely taken up with anxiety about the great measures just determined on. Then Danton gives him a cold look ('*froidement regardant*' here does duty for '*un geste approprié*') and says, '*Sieds-toi, c'était nécessaire.*'

[1] *Histoire Générale* &c. v. 124.
[2] viii. sec. xxx.

The words *c'était nécessaire* are perhaps ambiguous. 'It couldn't be helped' is how the English version of the *Biographie Moderne* (1811) translates them. But it is not a question of words so much as of the whole story. Would such a story, if the facts of it were true, have been kept secret by the hundred persons, many of them Danton's foes, present at the council? Secret from Madame Roland, for instance, secret from all those future members of the Convention who were so soon to be challenged by Danton for evidence against him? Yet Madame Roland makes no mention of the story. And those members whose own ears must, if it were true, have provided them with such evidence neither produced it themselves nor imparted it to others. Moreover, what Danton is represented as frowning down Mandar for proposing was actually done by the Executive of which he was a member! It did order the National Guards to be called out. And both the Assembly and the General Council of the Commune did send commissioners to try and stop the murders. Prudhomme, in short, has overshot his mark, sensation-monger that he was by nature and by trade. The above is a specimen of his 'Crimes of the Revolution.' But the author was in other times and with other manners author also of 'Crimes of the Queens of France,' 'Crimes of all Kings, Popes, &c.'—in intention at least—for with advertisements of books so named he placarded the walls in the days before he had found salvation. Danton was a striking personality. Anything about him, especially malignant gossip—as grateful to large societies as to small— would be good copy. How much of the story Mandar contributed, and how much Prudhomme, no man can say, but we may safely affirm that, though its words are strong, it is 'a tale of little meaning.'

Another of Prudhomme's stage-play scenes must be examined. In his journal of September 2 he had spoken of the massacres as 'the justice of the people.' Times changed, and with them M. Prudhomme, and he felt it necessary to explain these exceedingly awkward words away.

At 2.30 P.M. on September 2 (he accordingly writes)[1] I called on the Minister of Justice and said, 'I come as a patriot to demand the meaning of this alarm-cannon, this tocsin, and the arrival in Paris of the Prussians.' 'Be tranquil,' said Danton, 'old friend of liberty; 'tis the tocsin of victory.' 'But,' said I, 'they talk of cutting throats.' 'Yes,' said he; 'we were all to have our throats cut to-night—the best patriots first.' 'All that,' I answered, 'strikes me as rather imaginary; but pray what means for preventing such a plot are in contemplation?' 'Means!' said he, 'the people, warned in time, wishes to give all the criminals in prison their deserts, with its own hands.' 'I was horror-stricken at this speech, and just then, Camille Desmoulins coming in, Danton said to him, 'Here's Prudhomme come to ask me what's on foot.' Then Camille said to Danton, 'Oh, you haven't told him that the innocent won't be confused with the guilty? Everyone claimed by his Section will get off.' I replied, 'It seems to me less violent measures might be taken, &c.' To which Danton, 'All moderation is useless; the people's rage is at its height. It would be positively dangerous to stop it. When its first rage is sated we may make it listen to reason.' 'But,' said I, 'supposing the Assembly and the authorities paraded Paris and harangued the people?' 'No, no,' replied Camille, 'it would be too dangerous, for the people in its first anger would be capable of slaughtering its dearest friends.' I went away overwhelmed with grief. As I passed the dining-room I saw the wives of Camille, Danton, Fabre d'Eglantine, and others at table. I didn't know what to think. Everything induced me to believe that in fact it was impossible to check the popular fury at the news of a plot of the aristocrats and their friends. Finally I was reassured by the public manifestation of joy at the acquittal of certain prisoners and by the spectacle of Sombreuil borne in triumph with his daughter, and many similar things. I went back to my colleagues, and after six hours' deliberation determined to head our column 'Justice of the People,' by which was meant solely such acts of generosity.

A very pretty story this of the old friend of liberty, but one that smacks of the footlights throughout. How sage, how virtuous he is, how sublimely impartial in his headlines. Readers who remember how, according to him, the French

[1] *Hist. Générale* &c. iv. 90.

Revolution was an English plot, how Marat was England's agent, how he had a conference with Pitt in a London eating-house ('*fait que nous attestons*'), the very words of the former being quoted,[1] how after the capture of the Tuileries he describes the mob as cutting the soldiers up and eating broiled Swiss cutlets ('*des côtelettes de Suisses passées au feu*'),[2] &c. &c., will be very slow to take literally this graphic interview of a renegade trying to escape from an inconvenient past.

Danton made a stirring speech in the Assembly between one and two o'clock, according to Michelet, but, as his words were with regard to the tocsin '*va sonner*,' and, according to Dr. Moore, the tocsin sounded at one o'clock, probably he spoke a little before that hour. Between one and two o'clock he went to the Champ de Mars.[3] From the Champ de Mars he went to a Council of Ministers or home. He must have been worn out by such a morning's work, and if Prudhomme as he asserts, saw him at half-past two must have been a remarkably short time in the Champ de Mars, and taken a remarkably short time over his dinner. But granting Prudhomme saw him, what modicum of truth can we discern in his narrative? First, it is to be observed that Prudhomme does not hint at Danton having *organised* the massacres, and as a hostile witness his omission of the charge is very important. Secondly, minus an inveterate interviewer's embellishments, there is nothing incriminating in what Danton said. Prudhomme knew and all Paris knew, and had for some time known, just as well as Danton, that the prisoners were being threatened by the people. Prudhomme knew and all Paris knew that there were rumours of aristocratic plots against the people. Prudhomme knew and Danton knew that these alarms had reached their maximum that morning—the morning after the capture of Verdun had been announced and the morning of the day on which it was actually taken. 'The

[1] *Hist. Générale* &c. iv. 160.   [2] *Ibid.* iv. 68.

[3] Before doing so, according to Robespierre, he himself ordered the tocsin to be sounded. *Rév. Fr.* xxiv. 498.

alarm,' says Dr. Moore, writing that morning, 'is increased by the circumstantial account' that 'a great number of persons of influence have given assurance of their being ready to join the invading army.' What that army was believed to have in store for Paris we know, and the threats of Brunswick almost justified the credulity, of which the instant effect was to 'fill many people with disquietude and increase the general alarm.' Danton, some writers suggest, though without the smallest proof or probability, spread such rumours. Prudhomme, while posturing as a suggester of remedies, actually admits coming away convinced there was nothing to be done. Danton knew there was nothing to be done. He may have said so then, for he said so afterwards. Or Prudhomme may have invented the whole story, basing it on Danton's subsequent words and on a hint supplied by Peltier's *Tableau de Paris*. For Peltier represents Brissot coming to Danton on the 4th, as Prudhomme says he himself did on the 2nd, and raising the question of the innocent being mixed up with the guilty just as it was raised in Prudhomme's story. Peltier, however, makes Danton, who, according to him, was sole authoriser and organiser of the massacres, say that the innocent would not perish, because he had made out the lists with his own hands.[1] The character of Peltier's statements, 'gross as a mountain, open, palpable,' would have been familiar to Prudhomme, but he may have thought that with a little bowdlerising and botching they would do very well for him.

Another anti-Dantonist legend is to be found in Prudhomme which is conspicuous by its absence from the pages of Peltier and Madame Roland, Prudhomme, however, here being rather copyist or adapter than concocter. A batch of prisoners had been brought to Versailles on their way to Paris—treacherously, as some writers maintain, and that they might be murdered there. When they entered Versailles, Alquier, president of the Department of Seine-et-Oise, went to Paris and demanded that Danton should take prompt measures to defeat the

---

[1] *Tableau de Paris*, ii. 379.

sinister intention of the people of Versailles.[1] 'But,' said Danton brusquely ('*brusquement*' this time, not '*froidement*'), 'what's that to you? Mind your own business.' 'But, sir, the laws make us answerable for their safety.' 'What's that to you?' again said Danton. 'Well, give me an order.' 'Sir,' said Danton, striding up and down, 'don't meddle in the matter. The people will have revenge.'

Very dramatic, no doubt, like the other Prudhomme stories, but open to similar suspicions, for neither Peltier nor Madame Roland mentions it, and to the same fatal objection that Roland, not Danton, was the man to whom Alquier, supposing he took his ride of nine or ten miles from Versailles when the peril was so imminent, and when he was deserting his post to do so, should have gone. Alquier is said to have had Robespierre's knack of disappearing at a crisis, and it has been suggested that this story was his way of accounting for his absence at the critical moment from Versailles. And it is curious that Dr. Moore should have been told by a 'gentleman of character' and 'veracity' that, coming from Paris to Versailles that day, he observed nothing 'which gave him a suspicion of such an event.'[2] However that may be, it seems clear that instead of going to the proper Minister, Roland, to go to Danton, who had neither orders to give nor troops at his disposal, and who was then at war with the Commune, would have been so gratuitously circuitous a way of procuring instantaneous help that either the whole tale is an invention trumped up to suit altered tastes or so distorted by malice, caused by some rebuff administered by Danton, as to be in effect an invention.

Such a conclusion is endorsed by considerations of common sense. Lamartine admits that the mayor of Versailles 'took every precaution that humanity and prudence could suggest,' and that the escort numbered 2,000 men with cannon.[3] Now,

---

[1] *Hist. Générale*, iv. 182.

[2] *Journal*, i. 442. M. Thénard, in *Rev. Fr.* xxiv. 363, says that Alquier was not at Versailles at all from September 2 to September 12.

[3] Hue's *Louis XVI.* p. 408, Eng. tr.

supposing Danton to be the proper person to give orders, what orders did the mayor who thoroughly did his duty need? And the escort of 2,000 men with cannon—if ready to do their duty, were they not numerous enough? If not, where could Danton have got men in Paris who would not have sided with them sooner than their prisoners? The escort, it should be added, is said to have been paid by Roland.[1] But, like a sequel to some novel of Dumas, there is a sequel to this tale. The day after the Versailles massacre Danton, so it runs, from the windows of the Minister of Justice harangued men who had come from that town, and said, 'He who thanks you does so not as Minister of Justice, but as Minister of the Revolution.' But who is the author of the story? Would Prudhomme have left off at Part I.? Would not Peltier and Madame Roland have rolled it as a sweet morsel on their tongues? Yet neither of them mentions it, nor the 'Two Friends of Liberty,' nor any contemporary journalist. Mortimer-Ternaux mentions it and seizes on it for, what is comparatively rare in his history, open and violent abuse of Danton, whose reputation he generally assails more insidiously. But he confutes himself. Danton he describes as conniving '*dans l'ombre*' and '*le chef secret des assassins.*' Well, but if that were true, if he was indeed a villain working in the dark, what possible motive could he have had for parading his villainy in the streets when his end was achieved and he had nothing to gain by it? Many have thought Danton a knave, but no one ever called him a fool, and no folly could have been more gratuitous than his, if, when the reaction against the massacres was beginning, he had used these words in the sense attributed to them. The words themselves may have been used; but to whom, and in what sense? Michelet says there

---

[1] He gave Fournier what M. Aulard terms 'un certificat d'honorabilité.' *Rév. Fr.* xxv. 36. For this see M.-T. iii. 595, where it will be seen that he speaks of Fournier's *zèle et patriotisme.* For the payment, see M.-T. iii. 598. Cf. for a similar proceeding G. de Cassagnac's *Hist. des Girondins*, c. xiv. 6.

were 6,000 discontented, angry men in Versailles clamouring for the war. Lamartine says that the men to whom Danton spoke went to him to demand arms to go to the frontier. What Danton said, if he said anything, amounted, no doubt, to this : 'As Minister of Justice I cannot thank you for yesterday's work. As Minister of the Revolution I do thank you for volunteering.' Not only is this a natural thing to have said—for how could he tell who of the crowd had actually had a hand in the murders ?—but it is in keeping with all Danton's speeches, the keynote of which always is, Before all things, " Resistance to the enemy." '

Peltier says that Danton prepared the lists of prisoners for the massacres. But, like Prudhomme, he supplies the answer to his own calumnies. Danton, he says, '*s'est fait donner les listes dès le 27.*'[1] What if he did? Though Roland was responsible for the prisons it was Danton who proposed the domiciliary visits, and on the next day but one the domiciliary visits began, whereupon Peltier remarks, ' *Voilà donc les prisons comblées . . . . les couvents, les séminaires sont remplis . . . . il arrivait à chaque instant de nouvelles victimes.*' Now, besides those before in the prisons, great numbers had been incarcerated since August 10, and Danton, knowing what an influx of prisoners there would be on the 29th, may have very likely sent to see what were the numbers in each prison on the 27th. But this common-sense precaution is distorted by Peltier into cold-blooded proscription by an assassin. There is some evidence too not only that[2] 'many guilty persons paid for real crimes with their lives,' but that those murdered after production of the lists were condemned not because their names were down in those lists, but because of the charges on which they had been imprisoned.[3]

<hr>

[1] Peltier, *Tableau de Paris*, ii. 224. Cf. M.-T. iii. 632, where one, Chantrot, is quoted as defending himself by saying he had read out the list at La Force because he was a lawyer, which seems to show that the murderers did not know who were on the lists beforehand.

[2] *The Whole Truth on the Real Authors of Sept. 2.*

[3] L. Blanc, b. viii. c. ii.

These, then, are the main accusations on which Danton has been found guilty of the September massacres. They are the accusations of enemies, of renegades, of men without character. They teem with improbabilities and self-contradictions. They are wholly inconsistent with the tone of Danton's speeches and the tenour of his acts. They were not made to the Assembly by those who would have been only too eager to make them if they had had evidence. Their whole force is cumulative, and each examined by itself is found to be flimsy or absurd. They are based mostly on town talk such as might make up queer chapters in the biographies of some of our own contemporary political personages, did such things in England now find their way into print. They are, in short, to quote Danton's own protest, '*un tas de petites histoires, fort bien imaginées, et qui ne laissent pas que d'obtenir créance dans l'esprit des faibles ou de ceux qui se laissent trop aisément prévenir.*' Finally, it is affirmed that at the trial of Septembrisers in 1796 'Danton's name was not mentioned by accusers, accused, or witnesses.'[1]

---

[1] Gronlund's *Ça Ira*, p. 89. Cf. Robinet's *Vie Privée*, p. 192. M. Aulard (*Rév. Fr.* xxv. 36) seems to think that Gillet did inculpate Danton, whom he defends. But no '*evidence*' of Gillet's is mentioned as M. Aulard infers. Cf. M.-T. iii. 391, where he alludes to a '*letter*,' but without even saying if he had seen it himself.

Taine (*Durand's Translation*, ii. 212) tells the following story about Danton which it may be well to notice here. According to him, the Duc de Chartres came to Paris September 22 or 23, 1792, and went to Servan's house to ask a favour. Servan refused, but Danton, who was present, told the Duc to come to him next day, and in conversation said to him: 'You have one fault, you talk too much. You have been in Paris twenty-four hours and already you have repeatedly criticised the affair of September. I know this. I have been informed of it.'

'But,' said the Duc, 'that was a massacre, how can one help calling it horrible?'

'I did it,' replied Danton. 'The Parisians are all so many —— ——. A river of blood had to flow between them and the *émigrés*. You are too young to understand these matters. Return to the army: it is the only place nowadays for a young man like you and of your rank. You have a future before you; but, mind you keep your mouth shut.'

'Keep your mouth shut!' Strange advice to come from a man with the words 'I did it' still on his lips, from a man, too, still practically Minister, and at a moment when reaction against the massacres was growing apace. And what a confidant to choose! We who believe that other people 'did it' look at once for M. Taine's authority. '*The person*' he says, 'who gives me the following had it from the King'! A story so guaranteed, with its monstrous attribution to Danton of the belief which no one, he least of all men, in Paris could have held, viz. that the *émigrés* were popular with the Parisians, would need no further notice, except as an object-lesson how a welter of gossip may be churned into history. For M. Taine apparently did not know that in other fashion it is told by Beaulieu. Only by him it is dated October not September, and Danton, after a different exordium, gives a different reason for his deeds, viz. '·I fairly terrified the mob of Paris ready to shout "Vivent les Prussiens!"' and ends with a sort of prophecy that the Duc would one day be King, and with the hint of a thief—not repentant—that he should then expect a *quid pro quo*. (See Biré's *Diary of a Citizen of Paris*, translated by Villiers, i. 194.)

Side by side with the above another story of M. Taine's should be noted. The eldest Lameth, an *émigré* in Switzerland, came back '*about a month before the King's death*' to try and save him; 'went straight to Danton's house, found him 'in a bath-tub,' told him he was a villain, but not so bad as to denounce his visitor; then had a friendly chat with him, in the course of which Danton offered to save the King for the sum of a million with which to buy votes, adding that though he would save him he must *vote* for his death. So Lameth tried to get the money, but— Pitt (!) refused it.

'Pitt' in this story, 'I fairly terrified' in the other, what familiar and suggestive words! Again we look for M. Taine's authority. 'I have the account,' he says, 'from M. . . . . who had it from Count Theodore de Lameth's own lips' (iii. 135).

'The person,' 'M. . . . .' So M. Taine concocts history. Is the story worth criticism? If so the criticism need be but short. Danton 'about a month' before the King's death (January 21) was *in Belgium*, had gone there December 1, and did not return to Paris till January 14. Cf., for Taine's description of Danton's house at Arcis (i. 90) as 'a hovel,' the photogravure of it later on.

Von Sybel (*Hist. of Fr. Rev.* tr. by Perry, b. iv. c. iii.) writes : 'In a circular to all the communes of the empire it was announced that the People had destroyed a portion of the imprisoned conspirators by an act of necessary justice, and all "fellow citizens, brethren, and friends" were called on to imitate in their respective districts this urgent measure of political salvation. To increase its weight this circular was countersigned by the ·Minister of Justice, Danton, and distributed in numerous copies through his bureaux.   Danton, however, was not satisfied with this ; to increase the effect *he added a manifesto of his own* in these emphatic words : "Once more, citizens, to arms ! let the whole of France bristle with pikes, bayonets, cannons, and daggers ; in the towns let the blood of all.' aitors be the first sacrifice offered to liberty, that when we march against the enemy we may leave no one behind who can trouble us."'   Then in a foot-note Von Sybel adds : 'The letter of the Committee has been frequently published, but *this circular of Danton is only found as far as we know* in Blon(*sic*)dier-Langlois *from the archives* of Angers.   It has escaped even the industry of Ternaux.'

It is to be observed (1) that in saying with regard to the first circular 'To increase its weight this circular was countersigned by the Minister of Justice, Danton,' Von Sybel says just what he says about the second—viz. 'To increase the effect he added a manifesto of his own.'   Now, the fact that his first charge has been disproved—Danton not having countersigned the first circular—at once throws suspicion on his second charge, and it will be found that the superior industry which he vaunts consists in en-grafting on a misstatement of Blordier-Langlois, which he has not examined, an additional and aggravated misstatement which Blordier-Langlois does not make.   As, however, he used the words 'from the archives of Angers' it seemed necessary to examine those archives.   I could not go there myself, and only recently, through the great courtesy of M. Charavay (whose name is well known in connection with valuable historical research), was enabled first to obtain a facsimile of Danton's handwriting and afterwards the services of a Paris expert to compare it with the documents at Angers.   Alas ! when he got there the cupboard was bare.   There is not a word in the register about a manifesto countersigned by Danton.

Before the expert's opinion of the mare's nest, of which Von Sybel so complacently announces himself to be the sole discoverer and showman, is read, let us see what Blordier-Langlois says, and what weight attaches to it.

1. He does say that incendiary placards countersigned by Danton were sent from Paris to Angers.

2. He does give as the words of placard No. 4 the words quoted by Von Sybel.

3. He says that the Council-General of the Commune of Angers resolved (September 24) to send the facts to the Convention, ' considérant que l'envoi s'est fait à la connaissance du ministre *ou à son insu* ; que dans le premier cas, le citoyen Danton doit être dénoncé à l'Assemblée Nationale ; que, dans le second, il se fait dans ses bureaux un abus bien étrange du contre-seing.'

Now, as to 1, it will be found from the extracts appended from the register that nothing is said about the *placards* being countersigned by Danton ; that, on the contrary, the Council, which (cf. M. xvi. 576) was

Girondin in its opinions, at once suspected 'un abus du contre-seing,' and that Von Sybel's 'own manifesto' ·countersigned by Danton,' turns out to be Danton's printed official ' frank ' to *envelopes*, which the Council had no difficulty in supposing to have been obtained *à son insu*.' (Cf. for this M.-T. iv. 284 and M. iii. 674.)

2. As to the words of No. 4, Blordier-Langlois does not say how he obtained them, but introduces them with '*On lisait*.' Taking them for granted, however, they are merely a *réchauffé* of the first circular—a squib after a rocket, if sent early in the month—and we know who were the authors of the first circular. Presumably, however, the placard came just before complaint was made about it. If so, it came when a strong reaction against the massacres had set in, and when it would have been the height of folly in Danton—who was disavowing them in the Convention—to send such a placard or get it sent by anyone else, when he had everything to lose by doing so.

3. The Council's account of the facts was forwarded to the Convention— *i.e.*, I presume, either to the Minister of the Interior or to the President. Roland was Minister of the Interior. If there had been any real handle against Danton would he have failed to use it? The President was Pétion. If we turn to the debate of January 21, 1793, we shall see what a godsend anything seriously implicating Danton would have been to him even if he had hushed it up in September 1792.

On the whole, I conclude that No. 4 was a variant of the circular of the Committee of Surveillance—the work of some Paris journalist, a Maratist—who deliberately tried to make it appear to come from Danton. (Query? Was *Fabre d'Eglantine* at the bottom of an ' *abus du contre-seing*'?)

I. Letter of Expert

J'ai cherché 1° aux archives départmentales, 2° à la Bibliothèque de la ville d'Angers, 3° aux archives municipales (à l'hôtel de ville), et nulle part je n'ai pu trouver la trace de ces envois. Je me suis fait montrer le registre des délibérations du conseil général de la commune d'Angers, et à la date du 25 septembre j'ai trouvé la délibération signalée par Blordier-Langlois. Cette délibération est précieuse pour vous parcequ'elle donne le signalement de l'imprimé et de l'enveloppe qui servait à l'envoi. Il est bien certain qu'elle ne pouvait être écrite par Danton. J'ai copié le passage du registre et vous l'adresse sous ce pli. L'enveloppe était en partie imprimée et l'on remplissait les vides à la main. Il est dit que l'enveloppe portait la signature du contre-seing de Danton, mais il est expliqué que c'est la signature imprimée ; c'est ce nous appelons une griffe. Il n'y avait donc pas d'expertise d'écriture à faire, au cas où j'aurais pu retrouver les enveloppes, car de la description donnée par le procès-verbal, il s'ensuit bien clairement que les enveloppes étaient preparées d'avance et qu'on y apposait le *contre-seing imprimé* de Danton. Il est bien certain que les enveloppes ne portaient pas l'écriture de Danton.

II. Extracts from the Register of the Council-General of the Commune of Angers

Copie du registre des délibérations du conseil général de la Commune d'Angers (fragments, feuillets 47 (verso), 48 et 49) :

' L'officier municipal président, en l'absence du maire, a présenté à l'assemblée les nos. 4, 6, 7, 8, 9, 10, et 11 d'un imprimé portant pour titre : *Compte rendu au peuple souverain*, de l'imprimerie de P.-J. Duplain, libraire, cour du Commerce. Il a dit que ces numéros avaient été affichés en cette ville. . . , Un citoyen dans son indignation avait déchiré le no. 4 et lui avait apporté des fragments.

' Le président du Club des Amis de la Liberté de cette ville lui avait remis les 6 autres numéros, ainsi que 5 enveloppes dont deux, *empreintes* de l'ancien cachet du ministre de la justice, portant une adresse écrite à la main, ainsi conçue : *Aux amis de la Constitution à Angers* et contre-signée Danton et renfermant une lettre imprimée sans autre signature que celle-ci : *Les vrais amis de l'Égalité.*'

(Suit la citation d'un fragment du journal.)

' La seconde enveloppe avec cette adresse imprimée : *Aux citoyens composant la Société des Amis de la Constitution*—en caractères romains ; *Angers*—en imprimé ; *département*—en caractères à la main ; *de Maine et Loire*, avec le contre-seing de Danton, *en imprimé.*'

' Les 3 autres enveloppes avec les mêmes adresses et contre-seings imprimés et parfaitement semblables à celle précédemment décrite, fors le cachet qui, sur ces 3 dernières, est le nouveau du ministre de la justice.'

Suivent les citations—le procès-verbal à été envoyé à la Convention.

CHAPTER XIII

1792—*continued*

THE CONVENTION—SPEECH RESIGNING OFFICE—GIRONDIN AGITATION FOR GUARD—APPARITION OF MARAT—DANTON'S APPEAL FOR UNITY—THE ROLANDS—DANTON'S ACCOUNTS—ELECTED SECRETARY—DANTON'S OPINION OF MARAT—APPEALS AGAIN FOR UNITY—AGAINST LAWYER-JUDGES AND REDUCING PAY OF PRIESTS—FOR RELIEVING VICTIMS OF MAISON DE SECOURS—LIBERTY OF THE PRESS.

THE Convention met on September 21. Danton had to decide whether he would be Minister or Deputy. The Rolands charged him with wishing to be both. He soon made up his mind. Charged with seeking dictatorship, he replied by resigning the Ministry of Justice. His reasons, offered when the session was only an hour or two old, are best stated in his own words :

Before expressing my opinion of what ought to be the Assembly's first act, I ask to be allowed to resign the office entrusted to me by its predecessor. I received it to the accompaniment of the guns with which our fellow-citizens overthrew despotism. Now, when our armies (*Dumouriez'*, *Kellermann's*) have effected a junction, when the junction of the people's representatives is also effected, I am no longer bound by my previous functions. I am only the mandatory of the people, and as such I am going to address you. You have been invited to take certain oaths (*as to their motives as legislators*), and in truth you ought, ere entering on the vast career opening before you, to make to the people a solemn declaration of the sentiments and principles by which you will be guided in your work. There can be only one Constitution—that accepted, chapter and verse, by the majority of the primary assemblies. That is what you must proclaim to the people.

Fabulous dictatorships, imaginary triumvirates, and all such bugbears invented to alarm the people would then vanish, since the Constitution will contain nothing to which the people has not given its assent. This you should announce first, and then another thing of equal importance for liberty and order. Hitherto the people have been stirred up because it was necessary to rouse them against tyrants. It is necessary now that the law should be as terrible to anyone who would do it despite as the people have been in overthrowing tyranny; should, in order that the people may have nothing to desiderate, punish all criminals. Some excellent citizens have apparently entertained the idea that some fervid friends of liberty might, by carrying principles to excess, injure social order. Well, let us abjure all excess in this hall; let us proclaim that all property, territorial, personal, industrial, shall remain secure. Finally, let us never forget that we have to re-examine, to reconstruct everything, that the Declaration of Rights itself is not immaculate, and must needs be revised by a people really free.[1]

The Convention passed a decree in accordance with what the voice of detraction, ' affingens vitia virtutibus vicina,' calls this ' crafty speech.' To juster minds it will surely seem in the highest degree unselfish, statesmanlike, and wise. And it will seem even wiser and more statesmanlike to those who read the frothy inanities of previous speakers—of Manuel, for instance, his late superior, with his '*il faut voir ici une assemblée de philosophes occupés à préparer le bonheur du monde.*' An assembly of philosophers, engendered by revolution and baptised in blood ! Men of Manuel's stamp—and they formed, perhaps, the majority of his audience—must have shivered as under a douche of cold water at Danton's assertion of the rights of law and property, and as he laid his hand upon their sacred ark, the Declaration of Rights. But there were abler men who should have hailed his moderation and hastened to co-operate with him, but did not. Envy, hatred, and malice were in full swing in Madame Roland's *salon*, and now that Valmy had been fought and won, and those who had been for flying from

---

[1] Condorcet, previously hostile to Danton, was won over by this speech. *Rév. Fr.* xxv. 134.

Paris a month before felt safer, they thought they could afford to be rid of the man who had been useful as '*le levain qui fait lever la pâte*.'[1]   On September 24 his right to vote in the Assembly was disputed, because his successor in the Ministry was not yet appointed.   But he replied that he was only acting Minister, and that as the elect of the people he could not be deprived of his right to vote, and when Philippeaux proposed that he should be appointed Minister provisionally he refused.[2] As acting Minister he used his opportunities to some purpose, as we shall see hereafter, but it was as member for Paris that he strove to hold the balance between unallayed passions.[3]

Roland—'*ce vieillard rogue et morose habitué aux paperasseries de l'ancien régime,*' as Mortimer-Ternaux calls him—and the mouthpiece of his meddlesome wife's mischievous rhetoric, on the 23rd made a report to the Assembly on the state of France, in which, with side-thrusts at the Commune, he first introduced what was soon the burning question of a Conventional Guard.   On the 24th Buzot took the same line with less circumlocution.   'Can anyone,' he said, 'fancy our becoming slaves to certain Deputies of Paris?' winding up with resolutions which that same night the Jacobins styled the 'signal for civil war.'   '*Je crains le despotisme de Paris,*' said Lasource on the 25th; '*il faut que Paris soit réduit à un vingt-troisième d'influence, comme chacun des autres départements.*'   A madman's speech at such a moment, and one to bear bitter fruit. Scorning generalities, Rebecqui denounced Robespierre by name, and after Robespierre had demonstrated his own virtue Barbaroux furiously accused the Commune, threatening it with the fresh band on their way to Paris from Marseilles.

Then at the challenge of Cambon rose a figure at sight of which a shudder of horror went through the Assembly, many

---

[1] M.-T. iii. 132.   [2] M. xiv. 76–77.

[3] After his resignation he received several marks of honour.   On October 10 he was elected President of the Jacobins, on the 11th Member of the Constitution Committee, and on the 18th Secretary of the Convention.   *Rév. Fr.* xxv. 145.

of whom, perhaps, had till that day never seen Marat in the flesh.   Marat denied point-blank the accusation brought against Robespierre, saying that both he and Danton had invariably disapproved of any tribunate, triumvirate, or dictatorship. 'If anyone is guilty,' he said, 'I am the man,' and went on to explain his policy at length. Vergniaud voiced the majority's abhorrence of the speaker, and Boileau produced another quotation from Marat's journal of that day.[1] It is a celebrated passage, which should be read elsewhere than in Mortimer-Ternaux, who omits essential words.   A dictatorship those words certainly do not *recommend.* They seem rather a prophecy that, unless the people compel the Assembly to act, things must end in dictatorship after fifty years of anarchy.[2]   The Assembly, however, was as indignant then as the historian afterwards, and shouted, '*A l'Abbaye!*' But the impenitent Marat continued his speech, ending with, '*Eh bien, je resterai parmi vous pour braver vos fureurs.*'

Such was the tone and temper of the men between whom Danton essayed to hold the balance.   He spoke in the debate, and, it must be observed, before Marat's exculpation of him, and this is what he said :—

It is an auspicious day for the nation and the French republic which brings us to fraternal explanations.   If there are criminals, if there exists any man so ill-minded as to desire to dominate the people's representatives despotically, let him be unmasked, let his head fall.   There are rumours of dictatorships and triumvirates.   Such charges should not be

---

[1] This journal was called *Journal de la République Française,* and its motto was ' Ut redeat miseris abeat fortuna superbis.' Bax's *Marat,* p. 63.

[2] M. xiv. 51.   Even if the words '50 *ans d'anarchie vous attendent et vous n'en sortirez que par un dictateur vrai patriote et homme d'État*' be taken, as the Assembly took them, to mean ' Your only means of escape is a dictatorship,' they do not *recommend* it, but mention it as a *pis aller* if the people do not force the Convention to hurry on with the Constitution.   In his journal, that very day, Marat wrote ' *consacrer mes lumières à la nouvelle constitution qui sera donnée à la France, tel est l'objet de ce journal.*'

vague and indefinite. Let the man who makes them give his name. I would do so myself were the charge to involve the death of my best friend. The members for Paris ought not to be charged collectively. I shall not attempt to answer for each of them. I am responsible for no one, shall speak for no one but myself. I am ready to recapitulate to you all my public career. For three years I did all that I felt it my duty to do in the cause of liberty. As Minister I used all the vigour in me to the utmost. To the Council I brought all the zeal and energy of a citizen glowing with love for his country. If there is anyone who can accuse me in this respect let him rise and speak. There is, it is true, among the Deputies of Paris a man whose opinions are to those of the Republican party what those of Royou are to the aristocrats—Marat. I have been long, too long, charged with being the author of this man's writings. I take you, President, as my witness. Your President, I say, read the threatening letter addressed to me by Marat. He witnessed our altercation at the Mairie. But I attribute his outbreaks to the persecutions he has endured. The cellars in which he has been cooped up have ulcerated his spirit. . . . It is very true that excellent citizens have allowed themselves to carry republicanism to excess. It cannot be denied. But no one has a right to accuse a group of members of the excesses of the individuals who compose it. As for me, I do not belong to Paris. I belong by birth to a Department towards which my eyes always turn fondly, but not one of us belongs to this or that Department, but to all France. Leaving personalities, therefore, let us consider what is the interest of the State. A strong law to put down conspiracies against liberty is undeniably necessary. Well, let us pass such a law, a law making advocacy of a triumvirate or dictatorship punishable with death. But while laying firmly the foundations of equality let us crush out the spirit of faction, which can only end in ruin. It is alleged that there are men among us who would like to dismember France. Let us dispel fantasies so monstrous by making advocacy of them punishable with death. France must be an indivisible whole. The men of Marseilles stretch out hands to the men of Dunkirk. I demand, therefore, the death-penalty against anyone attempting to destroy the unity of France, and I propose that the Convention should lay down, as the basis of the Government it is to constitute, unity of representation, unity of executive. Such concord is sacred. To hear of it will make the Austrian tremble. Achieve it, and your enemies are no more.

The juxtaposition of the words 'excellent citizens' with the mention of Marat has evoked animadversion less reasonable than eager. Danton was a rapid speaker, and it is notable that after what he said about Marat he paused, as the text of the Moniteur evinces. His words, therefore, were comprehensive, and comprised all floating charges of ultra-republicanism to which he had alluded. Expediency, he may have thought, dictated an amnesty for all, not excluding Marat, for though he looked on him as a wolf it was as a wolf who had been hunted by hounds; but he dissociates himself from him unmistakably.

He did so still more emphatically a month later, and was vituperated for doing so in the 'Révolutions de Paris.'[1] Marat himself, though he had genuine respect for Danton, began to croak against him in October,[2] and Brissot, once his ardent admirer, lifted up his heel against him in November.[3] But he would not be moved from the course he had marked out for himself. For all cases where republicanism clashed with reaction he had one regimen, speedy execution of stern law in the people's behalf, to prevent it taking the law into its own hands. '*Il faut faire justice au peuple pour qu'il ne la fasse pas lui-même.*' 'Let the law be terrible and order will be restored. Prove that you wish law to reign, but prove also you wish the good of the people, and *above all spare the blood of Frenchmen.*'

The charge of aiming at a dictatorship having broken down, an attempt was made to discredit Danton's honesty in dealing with State money. Roland, smarting under Danton's sarcasm, that if he was to be invited to remain Minister provisionally Madame Roland should be included in the invitation, did what he could to damage him obliquely. His wife was even more bitter than himself. Danton had previously been a frequent visitor at her house, but before the end of August had ceased

[1] No. 173 quoted by M.-T. iv. 319.

[2] Bougeart, p. 155, quoting *L'Ami du Peuple.*

[3] Bougeart, p. 172, quoting the *Patriote Français*, No. 1,205.

to call there. Madame Roland suggests that Danton may have guessed that she could sometimes wield a pen—a very significant suggestion. The coolness naturally developed when he became Roland's equal as Minister, Minister by grace of cannon-shot, not of Madame Roland. Henceforth she and her friends were implacable. In vain Danton said he was ready with his accounts and offered to meet any charge. In vain he protested that the expenditure of secret-service money must be, by its very nature, secret, but that he had accounted for such expenditure to the Council. The Council being asked whether this was true, answered in the affirmative. Madame Roland says he never gave any accounts to the Convention at all, and thinks she disposes of Danton's reply as to secret-service money and the Council's 'Yes' by saying they were afraid to say 'No.'

Now, the account which, according to Madame Roland, was never given to the Convention exists in black and white. M. Aulard discovered and has printed it in full.[1] To the same author is due an exhaustive analysis of the secret-service money question, used by the Rolandist picadores so tormentingly at the time, and so persistently by historians ever after. On November 7 the Executive Council presented to the Assembly a report for the first time published by M. Aulard. According to this report the Ministers of Justice and War, when both were leaving office, offered to state to the Provisional Council Executive on October 6 how they stood with regard to the secret-service fund assigned to each by the Council on September 3. Both furnished details of its expenditure, along with receipts and accounts which each member present had the opportunity of inspecting. The report was signed by the only Ministers qualified to sign—Lebrun, Clavière, Monge, who added that it was deliberately and in accordance with precedent that no entry of this expenditure had been made in the register. This, the common-sense of the matter, was expressed also by that rigid economist Cambon, who, though he had found fault with

[1] 'Les Comptes de Danton' in *Études et Leçons sur la Rév. Fr.*

Danton for unnecessarily spending money on pikes, and for too lavish gratuities, said that to account for secret-service money publicly was neither necessary nor required by law. M. Aulard points out the insignificance of the total sum expended on secret service by Danton—164,690 livres—compared with the amount of work rendered for it and the results obtained, and this at a time when, as Danton said, he was '*autant l'adjutant du ministre de la guerre que ministre de la justice*,' and when the Assembly's *mot d'ordre* was, ' *N'épargnez rien ; prodiguez l'argent, s'il le faut, pour ranimer la confiance et donner l'impulsion à la France entière.*'. On the day that he used these words he was elected Secretary of the Convention. But though Danton's defence was perfect these incessant attacks injured him, made people think that there must be fire where there was so much smoke, and laid the foundation, no doubt, of many stinging stories.

Nevertheless on October 29 he again pleaded for concord. Roland—or rather Madame Roland—had addressed to the Convention a long-winded report full of severe reflections on the Commune and containing a philippic against Marat.[1] The question at issue was whether this report should be circulated in the Departments. Passion ran high, and Robespierre was singled out for special attack by Barbaroux and Louvet. Danton, to whom Marat's attacks on Dumouriez during the month must have seemed outrageous—for as president he had welcomed Dumouriez to the Jacobins—began his speech by lamenting the atmosphere of mistrust in which the Convention was enfolded, and said it was high time it should be swept away. 'I own,' he went on, 'to the Convention and the whole nation that for Marat as an individual I have no liking. To speak frankly, I know his disposition by experience. Not only is it violent and perverse, but unsocial.' He went on to disavow on his own part all factions, to admit the good motives that might have dictated the report, but to remind the Convention how it contrasted with that of another Minister—Garat—and to point out that

---

[1] Which the *Moniteur* strangely does not print till Nov. 10.

no monarchy had ever been overthrown without some good citizens suffering, and that if in the hour of passion there had been vindictive revenge on the part of individuals there had been marvellous achievements on the part of the community. Roland had mistaken petty and miserable intrigues for vast conspiracies. If there were men aspiring to a dictatorship or triumvirate let them be named. There should be full and complete inquiry, and the Convention should proceed against anyone held guilty. To speak of a 'Robespierre faction' seemed to him the language of prejudice or bad citizenship. He had brought no accusation against other people, and was ready to answer any brought against himself. What was wanted was a thoroughgoing inquiry, so that good citizens wishing only what was straightforward and above-board, both as to men and affairs, might know whether there was anyone it was their duty to hate, or whether they could co-operate like brothers in what must assuredly be the Convention's sublime career.

Many who listened thought themselves wiser men and better patriots than Danton. But though in their hearts they despised his counsel and would have none of his reproof, and though the gulf between parties continued to grow wider and wider, his personal authority was great and ubiquitous at the end of the year, and on December 1 he was sent to Belgium as Commissioner. But before his foreign policy is considered some other examples of his good sense and moderation deserve mention.

In an earlier chapter the disgraceful administration of justice under the Monarchy has been recorded. The reform of the courts coming under consideration, Danton spoke strongly of their composition ('*il y a parmi les juges actuels un grand nombre de procureurs et même d'huissiers*'), of their monarchical professions and prejudices, of their merely superficial acquaintance with law, amounting only to a jargon of chicanery, and of the people's well-founded distrust of them ; but too sweeping changes he thought premature, and only argued against choosing judges exclusively from lawyers. The Convention agreed with him, and ruled that they should be chosen from all citizens, whether lawyers or not.

Cambon proposed to reduce the pay of priests, a most dangerous project at such a time. Danton pleaded for postponement of the general question and for punishing only refractory priests by diminution of salary. His ideal was that there should be no State-paid Church, but he regarded it as an ideal realisable only when enlightenment and knowledge had penetrated the cottage. Till then to abolish salaries, and so deprive the people of their priests, was, he held, cruel.

A man with whom fortune has dealt hardly, looks forward to happiness hereafter. When he sees a rich man giving the rein to all his tastes, gratifying all his desires, while the merest necessaries perforce limit his own, then he believes, and it is a consoling thought, that in a future life his joy will be multiplied in proportion to his privations here. . . . It is barbarous, it is a crime against the nation, to rob the people of men in whom it can still find some consolation. I should think, therefore, that it would be useful if the Convention were to issue a manifesto to persuade the people that it wishes to destroy nothing, but to perfect everything, and that if it coerces fanaticism it is only out of its wish for liberty of religious opinion.

All fanaticism displeased Danton. In this case he came into collision with the fanaticism of the economist. And he did so again on the question of a State loan to the Municipality to provide for cashing small notes issued by a bankrupt company called the ' *Maison de Secours*.' Cambon was theoretically right. But Danton held that it was owing to the remissness of the Legislative Assembly in checking jobbery that such gambling had been made possible, and that the urgent necessity of the moment ought to override the general axiom that the State was not called upon to take private debts on its own shoulders. Whether he was in this contention right or wrong, it is another instance of his invariable tendency to take into consideration existing circumstances, and to prefer expediency to hard-and-fast rule.

On October 15 Manuel proposed that the people's sanction of a republican form of government should be obtained.[1]

[1] M. xiv. 222.

Danton's common-sense at once saw what a source of anxiety such a resolution must prove ; and he replied by showing how they had already agreed that the Constitution should be sub-mitted to the people's approval as a whole, and how meantime provisional law must necessarily be accepted as absolute.

When the liberty of the Press was under discussion Danton made no speech, but he hit off the feeling of its champions by an exclamation which was loudly applauded, ' *La liberté de la presse ou la mort !*'   It was his last utterance in the Convention that year.

CHAPTER XIV

1792—*continued*

Danton's foreign policy — intrigues of allies — policy of Dumouriez—Talleyrand—proposed english alliance — belgium—holland—belgian parties—dumouriez in paris—danton on national frontiers—mission to belgium

THE successes of Valmy and Jemmapes were, as far as they were due to the French themselves, owing to the heroic spirit infused into Paris by Danton's speeches, and into France by the Commissioners of his choice, to the energy with which he acted as 'adjutant to the Minister of War,' to his refusal to quit Paris when the other Ministers were for flight, and to the choice of Dumouriez as general.[1] We have now to examine his foreign policy during the remainder of 1792.

Never was the field of foreign politics more beset with snares and ambushes than when he entered into it. Seldom has history contained a more sordid chapter than that of the invasion.   That invasion was, nominally, the crusade of knights errant to aid an *émigré* chivalry in behalf of a martyr king.[2] In reality its motives were on a level with those of the *agioteurs* of the '*Maison de Secours.*' Every kind of diplomatic trickery

---

[1] Danton guided the diplomacy which facilitated the evacuation of French territory, and it is a tradition that when, Sept. 26, Lebrun threatened the King of Prussia and spoke with scorn of diplomacy, he was merely talking to the gallery, having been persuaded by Danton to go on diplomatising all the same. But dysentery and dissensions among themselves were the real reasons why the allies retreated. The see-saw of negotiations, for which each side alternately evinced more eagerness, is described minutely by Sorel.

[2] S. ii. 559.

was played in it. Not a player but had a card up his sleeve.
In comparison with other interests not one of them cared one
straw for Louis.[1] Russia, loudest in stimulating others to an
onset which she had no intention to share, coveted Poland.[2]
Prussia coveted Poland too,[3] but was, above all, determined
that, whatever Austria got, she would get as much herself.
Austria also, with an eye on Poland, coveted Bavaria.[4] Both
Austria and Prussia hoped, before Valmy, to carve a slice out
of France.[5] England, when much against the grain she was at
last drawn into the struggle, fought not for the enhaloed Queen
of Burke's rhetoric, but for maintaining the closure of the
Scheldt.[6]

Into an arena where so many conflicting interests were
pushed so unscrupulously, Danton, resolute to increase 'the
splendour of the Republic' as he was to consolidate the demo-
cracy, came somewhat handicapped. He was no hoary
schemer versed in ' the paperasseries of the old régime.' He
was young and of bourgeois origin, and his name where known
to kings was one of loathing. But he was not wholly
unequipped. He could write and speak English. He had
visited England. In associating with Talleyrand and Dumouriez he had acquired an insight into two of the acutest
brains in France. The long contest with the Court had made
him familiar with much intrigue. But above all he had natural
sagacity and knew how to profit by his own mistakes. The
authority he had acquired was also in his favour. He remained
acting Minister till October 11, though he resigned on September 21 ; and such had been his ascendency that he continued
to influence foreign politics when he ceased to be a Minister.[7]
For his colleagues had all been second-rate men—good clerks,
like Servan and Lebrun ; less good, like Roland, Monge, and

---

[1] S. ii. 557-8 and iii. 130, 317, 318, 321.   [2] S. iii. 45, 136.
[3] S. iii. 131, 316, 443.   [4] S. iii. 131, 315.
[5] S. iii. 329, 498 9, 563.
[6] S. iii. 219, 225. M. Stephens, ii. 205. Bourgoing's *Hist. Dipl.*
pt. ii. 299-301.   [7] S. iii. 77, 247. M. xiv. 171.

Clavière. Though Roland might fume and Madame Roland backbite and thwart him, he was the Ministry's first man. '*Il n'y a ici qu'un homme, c'est Danton*,' said Dumouriez.[1] 'If I were to say " No " to him he would have me hanged,'[2] said good-humoured Monge. Servan, eager for the efficiency of the army and the expulsion of the invaders, recognised that for these objects at least he could have no abler auxiliary. When Dumouriez was trying to get himself appointed Commander-in-Chief it was to Danton that he wrote : '*Pesez tout cela dans votre sagesse, brave Danton ; chargez-vous de me faire des réponses précises, des oui ou des non.*'[3] When Servan resigned, Lebrun became the most important Minister, and Lebrun was the disciple of Dumouriez when the policy of Dumouriez and Danton was in the main identical, that policy being, in brief, to detach Prussia from Austria, to play off Turkey against Russia, to secure the friendship, or at least the neutrality, of England, Sweden, and Denmark, and to meet any other Power, hostile to France, in arms.[4] To carry out this policy Dumouriez, whom however Danton intended to watch,[5] was on August 18 appointed commander of the Army of the North in lieu of Lafayette.

After August 10 there was naturally a panic among the agents of foreign Courts in Paris.[6] Danton did his best to reassure them, knowing that otherwise the new Government could hope for no recognition from the Powers. He used the secret-service money at his disposal freely, and he availed himself of the good offices of Hérault de Séchelles, whose birth and social connections made him useful, and of Talleyrand, who became the chief medium of his policy in England.[7] It was Talleyrand who drew up a circular to foreign Governments which was an apology for the 10th of August. This he was the more eager to do as his republicanism was considered anything but flawless, and when, later on, such suspicions took definite shape, Danton,

---

[1] Lenox, 165.   [2] S. iii. 13.   [3] S. iii. 65.
[4] S. iii. 16.   [5] S. iii. 25.   [6] S. iii. 14.
[7] S. iii. 14, 15, 393.

it is conjectured, wrote a letter defending him in the Moniteur signed 'D.,' or at least got it written by a subordinate of the Foreign Office named Ducher. He was, in fact, responsible for Talleyrand as far as the charge of 'emigration' went, for he had signed his passport. Danton had himself, as we have seen, in 1791 visited England, where he had a half-brother, who wrote letters to him in English, or such English as is represented by 'your much affectionate and patriote brother.'[1] He was intimate with Thomas Paine and Thomas Christie, by whom he was introduced to other politicians in sympathy with the Republic. When Noël, whom Danton apparently distrusted, was sent as agent of the Council to England he was joined there by Danton's relative Mergez.

Noël's letters have significance as showing that he looked on Danton as really the man in authority, but Danton relied most on Talleyrand, who shared his views as to England, and may have imbibed them from him. For their acquaintance dated from January 1791, when they were colleagues in the Department of Paris; and whereas Danton went to England that year, Talleyrand's first informal mission was from January to March 1792. He was badly received at Court, where the Queen turned her back on him, but he was welcomed at Lansdowne House,[2] and his easy manners and wit did something to soften preconceived prejudices against the Republic. He was sanguine enough to fancy he could by concert with the Opposition get Pitt ousted from power, and, though Grenville's frigid words were little to build on, was confident that in any case England would remain neutral.[3] When he returned to France in the spring of 1792 he came with two fixed ideas, that an English alliance was France's best policy, and that if England could not be allured she must be alarmed into such an alliance by a display of the naval strength of France. Delessart, the French Minister, had repelled the suggestion as more likely to issue in war than alliance, but Danton's ideas were substantially the same, though he and Talleyrand probably approved, as

[1] Robinet's *Danton, Émigré*, p. 5. [2] S. ii. 388. [3] S. ii. 392.

they may have inspired, the wiser views at first entertained by
the Convention, of peace and non-intervention.[1]   These views
reappeared in Talleyrand's memoir of November 25 on the
foreign relations of France, and in the memorable speech of
Danton in April 1793, in which he renounced the doctrine of
propaganda.   But no doubt they were counsels of perfection
in the eyes of both men, impracticable at the end of 1792 ;
secondary to, though not incompatible with, the main trend
of their policy—an English alliance ; and only so far influencing them as to make them agree that conciliation should be
tried first.   Talleyrand was sent back to England in September 1792 with this object.   Noël was there already with instructions to offer, in return for an English loan, the cession
of Tobago, abstention from opposition should England seize
Spain's colonies in South America, and an undertaking not to
encourage revolution in Holland.[2]   Holland, in fact, might, it
was hoped, along with England and Prussia, become the ally of
France.[3]

The French agents were, like Danton, misled as to the real
strength and sentiments of the English Opposition.   The fall
of the Bastille had electrified many Englishmen, as it had many
men in all countries of Europe.   But sympathy with republicanism in England was only skin deep—an affair of literary
sentiment and emotional poetry, as Marat had seen when he
said, ' *Nous n'avons pour nous en Angleterre que les philosophes.*'[4]
It was more than counterbalanced by the royal family's imprisonment in the Temple and the King's death.   It was finally
extinguished by the French designs on Holland.

For Delessart was right in thinking that England, if alarmed,
would be alarmed into war.   Danton, however, did not despair
of an alliance in the end, and it is alleged that the Duke of
Bedford came to Paris to see him in April 1793,[5] and that
when he was at Arcis he was in communication with the

---

[1] Robinet's *Danton, Émigré*, p. 257.   [2] S. iii. 19.
[3] S. iii. 82.   [4] S. iii. 281.
[5] Robinet's *Danton, Émigré*, 96–7.

Duke of York. It is, moreover, noticeable that when the
Convention, on November 19, 1792, proclaimed the war of
propaganda, he was not one of the speakers, and that as the
Girondins had been the prime instigators of war at all, so they
were mainly responsible for converting it into a war of propaganda.[1] In September he had expressly stated how far he
would go in dictating their forms of government to neighbour
ing nations, and it was only to this point : ' *Vous n'aurez pas
de roi.*'[2] And in October a similar indifference to sentimental
republicanism was shown in the speech in which he said he
would only respect the neutrality and independence of Geneva
as long as the occupation of her territory could be safely
avoided.[3] But when, so to speak, he determined to swallow
the war of propaganda he swallowed it whole, bent on utilising
to the uttermost even misdirected enthusiasm.[4] And therefore
when enlightened as to the disaffection of Belgium he still advocated its incorporation with France.

There can be no doubt that the French party in Belgium
was at first numerous and hearty, as it continued to be in the
great town of Liège. But the oppressive conduct of French
officials produced a reaction, and the majority of the people
awoke to the consciousness that they had hated Austria more
than they had loved France. Danton had good grounds for
crediting at first their desire for incorporation. Afterwards he
would feel that to quit Belgium was to hand over the French
party to their adversaries and leave Belgium an open door for
an invader of France. On the other hand it was an open door for
a French invader of Holland. And when the die was cast,
when the French were in Belgium and England would not
listen to the voice of the charmer, he thought that to invade
Holland would strike such a blow at English commerce as

---

[1] S. ii. 360–5. Cf. Mallet du Pan's *Considerations on the Nature of
the French Revolution*, Eng. tr. 1793, p. 53, where he says that he had
seen a letter of Brissot's in which were the words ' We must set fire to the
four corners of Europe : in that alone is our safety.'

[2] M. xiv. 71.   [3] M. xiv. 231.   [4] S. iii. 146.

might disgust England with Tory rule and bring in an Opposition ready to make terms with the Republic.[1]

Prenons la Hollande (he said) *et Carthage est détruite, et l'Angleterre ne peut vivre que par la liberté. . . . Conquérons la Hollande, ranimons en Angleterre le parti républicain, faisons marcher la France, et nous irons glorieux à la postérité. . . . Que la Hollande soit envahie, que la Belgique soit libre, que la commerce d'Angleterre soit ruinée, que les amis de la liberté triomphent dans cette contrée.*

In this policy he was at one with Dumouriez, and this was why, in defiance of Marat, he supported Dumouriez to the very eve of the treason which finally confounded his own plans. But though at one in their main policy they were not at one as to the proper treatment of Belgium. Dumouriez was actuated by personal ambition. As early as August, while Servan, with of course Danton's complete assent, was peremptorily insisting on his making the defence of Paris his first object, he was quoting Rome's aggressive policy against Hannibal,[2] and eager to invade Belgium. He was never republican, certainly never proselytisingly republican, at heart. A Belgian republic in alliance with France was sufficient for him. To intrigue for, and still more to enforce, incorporation was distasteful to him, and, as he thought, impolitic. He regarded matters more dispassionately, because more detached from Paris influences, than Danton. Danton had swallowed the war of propaganda whole. If it was to be waged it should be waged thoroughly. Yet he was not for abstract equity first, but for what was expedient, not for Belgium first, but for France.

'*J'aime tous les hommes, j'aime particulièrement tous les hommes libres, mais j'aime mieux les hommes libres de la France que tous les hommes de l'univers,*' were his friend Robert's words, but they might have been his own.[3]

Such sentiments, indefensible on high moral grounds, have nevertheless been, *mutatis mutandis*, those of most men famous as patriots, and, as we have seen, Danton had strong

---

[1] S. iii. 272.   [2] S. iii. 26.   [3] Robinet's *Danton, Émigré*, 173.

reasons for judging the incorporation of Belgium equitable. After the battle of Jemmapes (November 6) Belgium was split up into three factions—the aristocratic and clerical partisans of Austria, those who wished for a Belgian Republic, and those who wished for incorporation with France. The two latter were represented respectively in the provisional municipal administrations and in the Jacobin clubs. On December 4 Barère, President of the Assembly, in answer to a Brussels deputation, said that France had made no conquest in Belgium, except that of Belgian hearts, and that Belgium might choose any government it liked. But Danton was not then in Paris. He had been sent to Belgium on December 1, generally to see with his own eyes what was going on, and specially to adjudicate between the Treasury agents and Dumouriez.[1] His observations led him to quite other conclusions than those expressed in Barère's flowers of speech. Belgium, he could not help feeling, was territory conquered from Austria by the sword of Dumouriez. Only a portion of the inhabitants was friendly. On the other hand, the French army was in a state of utter destitution, half-starving, half-clothed, without pay. Belgium, it was clear, could not receive without giving. He sent off Camus to Paris to explain the situation, and Cambon expounded it to the Assembly. The remedy he proposed was, in brief, ' *Guerre aux châteaux, paix aux chaumières* '—in other words, to seize on the property of the clergy and aristocracy, to suppress feudal imposts, to make *assignats* current in the country, and to convoke the primary assemblies for election of judges and provisional administrations. Belgium, in short, was to be enfranchised, but with an enfranchisement wholly French.

The Assembly decreed what Cambon desired. It had taken it exactly a month to discover the costliness of wars of propaganda, and though its practice compared with its professions appeared beggarly the decree was not so harsh as it seemed. What made it intolerable to the Belgians was the

---

[1] Bougeart, p. 182.

M

swarm of commissioners sent for its execution. These were not the Convention's commissioners, Danton, Camus, &c.,[1] who had to exercise a general supervision in military matters as well as civil, but thirty commissioners sent by the executive.[2] But · for their misconduct or fanaticism even so sweeping a decree might have been tolerated. It was wrecked by the way in which it was carried out, and by the squabbles of Dumouriez with the Thirty and with the War Minister Pache.

Dumouriez was not a man to relish interference, but when he went to Paris at the end of December it was not to grumble at Danton. His letter to the Convention alluded respectfully to Danton's Commission, and he knew well that Danton would, by whatever means, do his best to render the army efficient. He · had no liking, it is true, for the war of propaganda. He had expressed disapproval of, and he would not execute, the decree of December 15, which was the result of Cambon's speech.[3] He had even talked of resigning his command. But he had not resigned, and if only he had been given means to conduct the war effectually he might have remained republican. Pache, however, he could not tolerate, and even when Pache was dismissed he was galled and irritated in Belgium by the Thirty, most of whom, he said, were 'tyrannical dolts carrying out their functions like brutes.'[4] He had been in Paris most of January.[5] During the last fortnight Danton was there too, and he and Dumouriez must frequently have met.[6] Now, if Dumouriez is to be trusted, everyone to whom he talked disapproved of the decree of December 15, which, it should be observed, had been passed in Danton's absence.[7] And it is quite possible that even then Danton had misgivings as to what he nevertheless had made up his mind to swallow whole. However that may be,

---

[1] M.-T. vi. 141.

[2] M.-T. v. 77, vi. 168.

[3] M. xiv. 755–6.

[4] M.-T. vi. 168.

[5] M. xv. 18. M.-T. vi. 147.

[6] Bougeart, p. 183. M. xvi. 22.

[7] M.-T. vi. 168.

the decree, introducing as it did the whole French apparatus of sequestration, confiscation, *assignats*, &c., violently inflamed party feeling in Belgium. Most of the administrations protested against it. The clubs gave it a rapturous welcome. Dumouriez, irritated at seeing his own authority diminished by the Thirty, sided against the clubs.[1] It soon became clear that the real question to be decided was incorporation with France, for which Spa and Theux voted at once, and Liège and all its neighbourhood soon after.[2]

When Dumouriez came from Paris he may have been already revolving in his mind what later on issued in treason. But, though still discontented, he had gained something by his visit. Pache was dismissed. The army was to be re-organised. He was to invade Holland. For the present, therefore, he trusted to Fortune's favours and hastened to Holland with the more satisfaction that so he got away from the irritating Thirty.

Danton meanwhile, on January 31, had made his famous speech on the natural boundaries of France, at a time, it must be noted, when the allies were beginning their reconquest of Belgium, and war with England and Holland had become inevitable. He said he spoke in the name of all the Commissioners and in the name of all Belgian patriots in demanding the incorporation of Belgium, reminding the Convention that this had already been predetermined on December 15. He appealed not to the enthusiasm of his hearers, but their good sense ; for in inviting their friends in Belgium to organise they had practically promised to accept any proposal for incorporation coming from them when organised, and that very day there was a letter from Liège making the proposal. 'The limits of France,' he continued, 'are defined by Nature.'

We shall reach them at the ocean, the Rhine, the Alps, and the Pyrenees. We are threatened with kings. You have thrown down the gauntlet to them, and it is the head of a king, the presage of their own doom. Let us now think only of

---

[1] M.-T. vi. 137.   [2] M.-T. vi. 138.

developing all our forces ; let us send commissioners into every commune in the Republic, demanding men and arms ; let us launch all France against the enemy. As for Belgium, the husbandmen and workmen desire incorporation. They are ripe for liberty and worthy of being united with France by indissoluble bonds.

And he added that to get rid of incendiary priests and seditious aristocrats they had only to decree and enforce French law.

The Assembly passed decrees in accordance with Danton's advice, and he, with Delacroix, Camus, and Gossuin, afterwards joined by Merlin of Douai, and Treilhard, was sent to Belgium to superintend the convocation of the primary assemblies which were to vote on the subject of incorporation. The primary assemblies voted in favour of it, and it has been alleged that they did so under compulsion. But in view of the excited state of parties it is hard to see how order could have been ensured without the presence of soldiers. Nor can previous petitions against incorporation be considered proof that it was unpopular with the primary assemblies. It is likely that Danton had good reason for his allegation that the workmen generally were in its favour, and that it was pillage, and sacrilege, and experience of *assignats* which afterwards made it so unpopular.

He had still better reason for his doctrine of natural frontiers elsewhere. A genuine welcome was given to the French in Savoy ;[1] and along the Rhine, where the princelings were detested, the Declaration of the Rights of Man acted, it was said, like the sound of Joshua's trumpet, so that the towns were taken without any fighting.[2] Even when the conquered became, like the Belgians, alive to the thorns there were in the trees of Liberty, they were less restive than the Belgians, as having more to gain from their new masters and less of national spirit to resent their sway.[3] We can, then, understand how to Danton's practical eye his new programme seemed merely a curtailment of Utopian aspirations within

[1] S. iii. 115.   [2] S. iii. 97, 101.   [3] S. iii. 176.

reasonable limits. He was returning to, not receding further from, the wiser policy which he was to reassert more explicitly in April, and this speech came half-way between his declarations then and those of the previous autumn. Therefore, though it seems a far cry from a war of propaganda to a war for natural frontiers, it seems unreasonable to represent him as a cynic throwing aside the mask of moderation and resorting to 'the brute force which was his most congenial weapon.'

CHAPTER XV

1793

For the sake of continuity Danton's speech of January 31 has been noticed in the previous chapter. But he had come back to Paris on January 14, and much else had happened there during the fortnight of his stay. His first act was to speak and vote for the King's execution. Not having had a voice in the debates of the 14th, he did not take part in the voting on the 15th, but he was for no half-measures, as the Girondins were, who voted for death because, like Pilate, they were willing to please the people. Danton condemned him as a traitor guilty of the worst form of treason—alliance with foreigners against his own subjects. Traitors of lower rank were executed; why not he? '*Celui qui a été l'âme de ces complots mérite-t-il une exception ?*' [1] Poor Louis was quite incapable of being the soul of anything. The soul of the plots had been his wife. But he had been privy to them. He was the rallying-point of invasion and rebellion. On the 17th, even while the votes which decided his doom were being counted, Vergniaud, the President, announced an ill-timed letter·from the 'Minister of Spain,' begging for a respite in order that he might obtain the King of Spain's intervention. Vergniaud should have said that the letter was from the Spanish Chargé d'Affaires.[2] The Assembly, it seems, understood it to come from the Spanish Government. Danton at once rose, saying he was astounded

---

[1] M. xv. 183.　　　　　　[2] M. xv. 227.

at the impudence of any Power daring to attempt to influence
their votes, and that if everyone thought as he did they would
for this, and this alone, vote at once for war with Spain.
'*Rejetez, rejetez, citoyens, toute proposition honteuse. Point de
transaction avec la tyrannie.*'

When he had given his vote just before, '*Point de transaction*' was in his mind.

Je ne suis point (he said) *de cette foule d'hommes d'État qui
ignorent qu'on ne compose point avec les tyrans, qui ignorent qu'on
ne frappe les rois qu'à la tête, qui ignorent qu'on ne doit rien
attendre de ceux de l'Europe que par la force de nos armes. Je
vote pour la mort du tyran.*

Till the end of time different men will think differently of the
King and of his judges; but those who condemn Danton must
condemn Cromwell too.

When Danton used the word 'tyrant' it was at a time when
classical terms and allusions were on every man's tongue, and
he used it not in its now more familiar but in its original
sense of a sovereign over-riding law. When he spoke of
'*hommes d'État*' he was alluding to the Girondins. While he
had been inspecting the condition of the Belgian army and
fostering the movement for incorporation—had been, that is to
say, engrossed in matters of high policy—the Rolandists were
charging him with amassing wealth partly by embezzlement in
Belgium,[1] partly by burglary in Paris.[2] And on the 20th there
was a recrudescence of recriminations concerning the massacres
of September. Kersaint resigned his seat, saying he could no
longer sit with assassins like Marat, as a contrast to whom he
pointed to the shining light of Pétion.[3] And the Girondin
Gensonné expressed an opinion that 'in punishing the tyrant
Louis' the work had been only half done, and would be

---

[1] Cf. Appendix B, Charge of Malversation in Belgium.

[2] *Vie Privée*, 144. Mme. Roland charged him with robbery of the
Garde-Meuble.

[3] M. xv. 255.

completed only by the punishment of the 'cannibals' of September. Tallien retorted by counter-insinuations.

That evening Lepelletier was assassinated for having voted for the King's death, and next day Thuriot fiercely assailed Pétion as a hypocrite who tried to lay his own guilt at other men's doors. Bréard demanded domiciliary visits to discover the plot of which Lepelletier was the victim. No one had named Danton, but he knew what was in the air, and when Pétion had expressed his amazement at being supposed to be anything short of immaculate he delivered one of his most famous speeches. After a tribute to Lepelletier and a contemptuous remark that the previous speaker was a weak man whom he had always known as such, and who '*peut s'expliquer sur mon compte comme il jugera convenable*,' he added

that Pétion would have done better if he had been more explicit about men who had shown themselves better servants of the State than himself; and, with respect to the terrible massacres which had been used as a party-weapon for embittering the Departments against Paris, if he had stated plainly that no . human power could have arrested what was the fury of a people, and, though terrible and lamentable, was induced by remissness in bringing criminals to justice. A frank and thorough examination of the whole question would have checked a flood of calumny and perhaps saved the Republic from worse misfortune.

Therefore (he proceeded) I challenge you who knew me as Minister to say if I have not always been the advocate of concord. I call you, Pétion, you Brissot, I call all of you as my witnesses, for at last I am tired of these misunderstandings : I call all of you, I say, that I may no longer be misunderstood. For months I have run the risk of silence, but, since I have to specify others by name, I am resolved there shall be no more mystery about myself. Be you yourselves my judges. Have I not always shown deference to the old man now Minister of the Interior? Did I not constantly warn you of, did not you constantly agree with me about the fatal acerbity of his temper at the time when at the centre of the Republic it was desirable, it was indispensable that a man whose functions were in some sort those of a Consul should yet be of a disposition to conciliate, to appease, when violent controversies were certain to result from so violent a convulsion? What I said you said too. But, and this is why I blame you, you did not say so openly. Roland, whose good intentions I do not impugn, but of whose nature I mean to speak plainly, Roland, I say, thinks everyone a scoundrel and an enemy of his country who is not in love with his own thoughts and opinions. I call on you, dear fellow citizens, on you, Lanthenas, so intimate with Roland, and therefore so unimpeachable a witness, to mark what I say. I demand his deposition, and I base my demand not on calumny but on the judgment of his own friends. I demand in the interest of the Republic that Roland cease to be Minister. Consider if I am likely to say so out of revenge. I appeal to you, citizens, have I ever replied to calumny? Roland, I know, misconstrued me, but what I wish is the good of the Republic, and not needing, I do not seek, revenge. And how can you discredit me when I call Roland's closest friends as witnesses? Roland, because in a too memorable crisis he was indicted, because he feared arrest, has ever since then seen Paris through black spectacles. In his indiscriminate terror he became incapable of discriminating at all, till in his delusions he dreamt that our mighty tree of liberty, which binds together the foundations of the Republic with its roots, would be over- thrown. From that hour he could not restrain his rancour against Paris, Paris, whose existence is inseparable from that of the Republic. For Paris belongs to all the Departments, Paris is the focus of all enlightenment, and every Department con- tributes to it a ray. This is Roland's great error, his great blunder, his great fault, that out of rancour he has helped to stir up the Departments against Paris. I myself will remind him of what he has used against me as an accusation. When he spoke of a Departmental Guard[1] to me I said: 'It is repugnant to all principle, but it is a foregone conclusion, and you will carry it. What then? No sooner has it taken up its abode in Paris than it will take the tone of the people, for the people's sole passion is for liberty.' Well, citizens, do you doubt that now? Are not the Fédérés of the Departments and the citizens of Paris of one mind? No man doubts it, not even you, Roland's friends. Many citizens were deluded, and they see it now; but who deluded them? I say with sorrow that it was Roland. For proof you have only to turn to one of your committees. It was Roland who circulated pamphlets based on the muddy idea in which his own mind wallowed that Paris wished to domineer over France.

[1] To safeguard the Convention.

He went on to disapprove of domiciliary visits, but to suggest the reconstitution of the Committee of General Security, with extended powers, and, on suspicion of conspiracy, with the right of entry to any house should two-thirds of the Committee think it expedient, a characteristically sensible modification of Bréard's proposition. Then turning to what he said were higher matters, he adjured all parties

to devote their energies to prosecution of the war with Europe instead of the war among themselves. It must be waged ungrudgingly, unparsimoniously. '*Il faut, pour économiser le sang des hommes, leurs sueurs.*' The soldiers were bravest of the brave. Tell them to go to Vienna or drop on the road, and their answer would be, ' Vienna or death.' But the army must be reorganised ; nor ought they to rely on the genius of any one man. The nation was greater than they were. The genius of the people was the people itself. All that was wanted was wisdom in its legislators and a light hand on the reins of a noble nation.

Lastly he spoke of Pache—circumspectly, for Pache had friends among his own friends, but yet uncompromisingly, as a man without initiative or that eagle eye necessary to one in so terribly onerous a post as Minister of War. And he proposed that someone else should divide his functions.

Dumouriez, if Lamartine may be believed, had advised the Girondins to come to terms with Danton. Surely some of them, even though only for a moment, must have repented of not taking his advice as they listened to this speech, a damning indictment if it was sincere and a masterpiece of hypocrisy if it was not.

CHAPTER XVI

1793—*continued*

SECOND MISSION TO BELGIUM—DEATH OF WIFE—OUTLOOK ABROAD—
SPEECHES ON MARCH 8, 10, AND 11—RESPECT FOR PROPERTY—
DEBTORS—RIOTS IN PARIS—DANTON DEFENDS DUMOURIEZ AND
DEPRECATES FACTION—REVOLUTIONARY TRIBUNAL—PROPOSAL TO
STRENGTHEN THE EXECUTIVE—DANTON ABJURES OFFICE

TILL summoned home by the death of his wife, who died on
the night of February 10-11, Danton was in Belgium. On
the 24th he was in Paris attending to the removal of the
official seals which had been placed on the property in his
house at her death. But he was in Belgium again on March 5,
and signed a decree that day in Brussels.[1] He had been
engaged at first in superintending the convocation of the
primary Assemblies, but when news of the reverses at Maestricht
and Liège arrived he and his colleagues issued orders for
reinforcing the army by levies of the newly incorporated
Belgians, and then, Delacroix and he having done all that was
possible on the spot, hastened back to Paris.

It was a gloomy home-coming, and not merely for personal
reasons. The King's death, which it had been thought might
obliterate factions, had in fact given them for the first time
free play. On the other hand it had exasperated foreign
Courts. All the objects of French diplomacy seemed to have
miscarried. The attempts—persisted in to the verge of infatua-
tion—to detach Prussia from Austria, to detach Austria from
Prussia,[2] to obtain the goodwill of Genoa at the expense of

---

[1] M. xv. 665.   [2] S. iii. 22, 297, and *passim*.

Sardinia, of Sardinia at the expense of Genoa,[1] of England at the expense of Spain, had failed.[2]   So had the revolutionary propaganda essayed in Spanish towns.[3]   Belgium and the Rhenish towns had been alienated by ill-usage.[4]   The friendship of Sweden and Turkey was more of a shadow than a substance.   The second partition of Poland had been settled two days after the execution of Louis, and Prussia had promised Russia to make no separate peace with France.[5] Dumouriez had been unable to cross the Meuse;[6] Miranda had been checked at Maestricht.   Liège was reoccupied by the Austrians.   The armies were dispirited and disorganised, not yet having felt the effects of the decree for incorporating volunteers with regulars, destined afterwards to produce great results.   France was at war with Austria, Prussia, England, Holland, Sardinia, and Spain.   And just as what Lafayette might do was uppermost in men's minds at the beginning of the previous August, so now at the beginning of March the treason of the infinitely more dangerous soldier Dumouriez threatened to give the staggering Republic its mortal blow.

Now too, as in August, when men's hearts were failing them for fear, Danton remained undaunted, and for the second time infused his own spirit into the nation.   Fondly attached to his wife, he was at first broken-hearted at her death, and is even said to have exhumed her body in order to see her face once more.[7]   But in the public cause he suppressed his

[1] S. iii. 295.   [2] S. iii. 20.   [3] S. iii. 300.
[4] S. iii. 282, 339.   [5] S. iii. 317.   [6] S. iii. 337.
[7] Robinet, *Homme d'État*, p. 133, discredits the story.

A Letter from Danton to his Wife.

'Le courier qui m'a apporté ta lettre, ma chère Gabrielle, part dans la minutte et je nai qun instant pour te faire connaitre le plaisir que jai eprouvé en recevant de tes nouvelles ; noublie pas de surveiller lenvoy de mes arbres a Arcis et dengager ton peré a presser larrangement de mon logement dans sa maison de Sevres ; embrasse mille fois mon petit Danton dis lui que son papa tachera de netre plus long temps a Dada.

'DANTON.'

For this letter I am indebted to the courtesy of MM. Charavay.

private grief, and on March 8, 10, and 11 he made a succession
of great speeches on the imminence of the danger and the
spirit in which it should be met. Robespierre also spoke on
the 8th and the 10th, and his speeches are an instructive
contrast. In all misfortunes and reverses the great 'delator'
can trace only one hand—the aristocrat's—and for remedy can
suggest nothing but suspicion, inquisition, arrest. Patriotism
with him is a detective's vigilance, and to be victorious the army
needs only to be better policed. Not that, like Marat, he
suspected Dumouriez. '*Quant à Dumouriez*,' he said, '*j'ai
confiance à lui.*'[1] And he went on to give his reasons—the
reasons for a constable's confidence in a ticket-of-leave man—
'because the invasion of Holland was his own plan three
months ago, because he is so closely bound to the success of
our arms by his personal interests and his military reputation.'

Danton as well as Robespierre had his doubts of Dumouriez,
but by instinct he expresses himself more nobly, and with a
nobler inference.

With a general's genius Dumouriez unites the art of
inspiring and cheering the soldier. We have heard the army
even in the hour of defeat calling for him with loud cries.
History will judge his talents, his passions, his faults. But one
thing is certain—that his interest is in the splendour of the
Republic. If we support him, if we send an army to aid him,
he will soon make our enemies repent of their past successes.

He said this in the first of his speeches, after some letters from
Dumouriez had been read in the Assembly. The necessity of
reinforcing the army was its keynote.

Only danger could evoke the full energy of Frenchmen
Recruiting was well enough, but what was wanted was
volunteers, the volunteers of 1792, the volunteers of Paris.
Paris must rekindle the blaze she lighted then, and do it at
once, without a moment's delay. Commissioners must visit
every Section that very night ('*ce soir*'), and call out its
members to enlist, to fly to the defence of Belgium, in
redemption of liberty and their oaths to their country. It was

[1] M. xv. 674.

not the generals but themselves who were to blame in having promised reinforcements never sent. In 1792 the enemy had begun by victories. But those victories had roused the nation. So now let it be again, and let the Commissioners be appointed that very hour ('*à l'instant*').

The subsequent reports of the Commissioners showed how efficacious had been the results of their mission.

On the 9th he proposed the release of all who were imprisoned for debt, to give them the chance of volunteering. After a fling at Burke, whom he called the Abbé Maury of the English Parliament, he said that

the propertied class must not take fright at his proposal. Whatever extravagances individuals might have countenanced the nation would always respect the rights of property. But if the poor were to respect the rich the rich must respect the poor. Even on lower grounds the lender would not suffer by his proposal. Now when he could imprison a debtor he was less cautious in his loans. It was not, however, on mercenary considerations but in accordance with eternal laws and the rights of humanity that misfortune should not be punished as a crime.

In so speaking Danton was in advance of his age.

The next day riots broke out in Paris in connection with,[1] if not wholly in consequence of, disastrous rumours from Belgium and of alleged atrocities of the enemy in Liège. Danton's speech of the 10th was in effect an answer to that of Robespierre, and in its first and last sentences was so undis-guisedly.

What has been said to you about the general situation is true, but at the present moment we are less concerned with the causes of our disasters than with the remedies. When I see a house ablaze I don't attend to the rascals running off with the furniture : I put out the fire. What I wish to impress on you, now you have heard Dumouriez' letters read, is that if you would save the Republic you have not a moment to lose. The plan of Dumouriez was worthy of his genius. I am bound to

---

[1] Biré's *Diary of a Citizen in Paris,* i. 365. M. xv. 678–9.

say so, and more emphatically now than lately. He warned us three months ago that the difficulties in its way would be doubled if we were afraid to execute it in winter. We are to blame. Let us make amends. Let us march to his aid. Dumouriez only needs men. France has men in millions. Our enemies are making desperate efforts. Pitt spares nothing, because he has everything to lose. Our seizure of Holland means the destruction of Carthage, and England to live must live for liberty. Let the chains of Holland be broken by our conquest, and the commercial aristocracy of England will of its own accord rebel against a Government which has dragged it into a war of despots against a free people.[1] Despatch your commissioners, then, at once. Sustain them energetically. Send them off this evening, this very night, with this message to the rich. 'Either the aristocracy of Europe must pay our debt or you. All the people can give is its blood. It gives it lavishly. Be you lavish with your miserable gold.' I brush aside all party passion. The only passion dear to me is the public good. In a terrible crisis, when the enemy was at our gates, I said : 'Your disputes are despicable. I know no enemy but one. You weary me with your personal recriminations when you should be striving for the safety of the State. I abjure you all as traitors to the country. All of you are equally to blame.' And I said : 'Reputation ! What do I care for my reputation ?   Blighted be my name so France be free.' Why haggle about the loss this or that party will sustain by commissioners being chosen from its ranks ? Scorn such fears. Think only of disseminating your energy through France. The post of honour is his who proclaims to the people that the terrible debt under which it staggers shall be paid by the enemy or the rich. We are in cruel straits, with our dis-credited currency and starving workmen. We want a radical cure. On, then ! let us conquer Holland, reanimate English republicans, move all France to the war, and so win imperish-able glory. Be worthy of your noble destiny. No recrimina-tions, no quarrels, and the country is saved.

Commissioners might procure volunteers, but Danton knew well that a strong central authority was necessary if France was to emerge safely from the war. Scarcely had he spoken when

[1] This was Bonaparte's dream also, *Maître de Londres il se fût élevé un parti très-puissant contre l'Oligarchie.* S. iii. 345.

Stengel, one of the generals whom Robespierre had assailed, was again denounced, and Danton, to shield him from a fanatical prosecution for treason, proposed his being summoned to appear at the bar of the Assembly.

While these perpetual accusations of treason were being bandied about there was proportionate disquietude in Paris, the people of which were in a mood which at any moment reverses might render murderous. The establishment of an extraordinary criminal tribunal without appeal had been proposed on the 9th. Lanjuinais hotly denounced it. Brissot said that, for his part, he preferred anarchy to such despotic rule, and ironically expressed his gratitude for every moment of life vouchsafed to him by his opponents. Vergniaud vowed that his party would die rather than submit to an inquisition worse than that of Venice. Danton had already, as we have seen, spoken twice. But when the question was settled, and the Assembly had just adjourned, he again sprang to the tribunal, with the words, 'Summon all good citizens not to move.' An orator's ascendency has seldom been more strikingly illustrated than on this occasion, when everyone at once resumed his seat, and amid profound silence he went on—

What! citizens, at a moment when our position is so critical that if, as is possible, Miranda is beaten Dumouriez must capitulate, can you separate without taking the great measures absolutely necessary for our salvation? I am aware that judicial steps must be taken against the contra-revolutionary party. They are boldly rearing their heads again, everywhere offering provocation, though everywhere they have been beaten, stupid enough to think themselves in a majority because respectable citizens remain quiet at home and the artisan is engaged at his work, and sure to draw on themselves the vengeance of the people if you do not snatch them from it yourselves.

To understand this and what follows we have to remember that there had been riots on the 8th and the 9th, and on the very day this speech was delivered, the 10th. Their origin is somewhat obscure. They were headed by worthless men

like Varlet and Fournier, who may have been actuated by love
of notoriety, by hatred of Brissot, by hope of plunder ; or they
may have been secretly excited or abetted by Royalist agents.[1]
What is certain is that Billaud-Varenne and Marat denounced
the leaders,[2] that Vergniaud and Danton and Barère and Isnard
alike attributed them to the aristocracy, and that the Commissioners who, on Danton's proposition, had been sent to rouse
the Sections reported that the people were eager to enlist but
demanded a court to punish the contra-revolutionists.[3]   Clearly
the situation closely resembled that of September.   Now, as
then, had come the news of military disasters—of the evacuation of Aix-la-Chapelle and Liège and the raising of the siege
of Maestricht.   The mob laid the blame on the Girondin Convention now, as it did on the Royalist Assembly then.   There
was a Committee of Surveillance now of Varlets and Fourniers,
as there had been then of Sergents and Marats.   And there
was a growing belief in the treason of Dumouriez.   Danton's
policy now was what it had been then.   To prevent murder
he advocated a new Revolutionary Tribunal which should
prevent mob-violence by depriving it of a cry.   There is a
story told by one of the Lanjuinais family that at this point
in his speech the Deputy Lanjuinais interjected the word
' September,' and that it cowed Danton.[4]   Nothing about this
is to be found in the Moniteur, which curiously does report
two days later a similar interruption when *Marat* was speaking.[5]
We may, therefore, discard the story as that of a bragging
Breton.   Cowed in any case Danton was not.   He spoke
without pausing or any halt in his argument, and with scornful
indignation, sitting down amid a thunder of applause.   And it
seems clear that his heart was not so much set on the Tribunal
—which, however, he thought necessary—as on vigorous prosecution of the war and strengthening the Executive by permitting
its members to be chosen from the Convention.   He had not
been the first to mention the Tribunal, nor was the resolution

---

[1] L. Blanc, ix. 2.   [2] M. xv. 694.   [3] M. xv. 665.
[4] Biré's *Diary of a Citizen in Paris*, i. 351.   [5] M. xv. 694.

for it in its final shape proposed by him, but by the Girondin Isnard, and it is said that when it was passed the Girondins exulted openly, saying that by means of it they hoped to bring the Dantons, Robespierres, and Marats to justice.[1] Probably not one man in the Assembly had less thought of utilising the Tribunal for personal vengeance than Danton. He seems to have hoped that, by coupling together in his speech the two propositions for a Tribunal and for strengthening the Executive, he might get them carried together. But whereas party hatred or fear procured the establishment of the Tribunal, party jealousy got the more salutary measure adjourned.

The ground being thus cleared, the rest of his speech becomes intelligible.

Nothing is harder to define than a political crime. But if it is so easy to punish private and so hard to get at political crime, surely some law other than the ordinary law is necessary to overawe rebels and reach the guilty. This is a point where the public safety requires wide means and terrible measures. I can see no half-way between the ordinary law and a revolutionary tribunal. History attests the truth of this, and, since insolent reference has been made in this Assembly to those sanguinary days for which every good citizen has mourned, I, for my part, will aver that if a tribunal had then existed the people so often cruelly reproached with those days would not have imbrued them in blood ; I will aver, and I shall have the assent of every witness of those dreadful events, that no human power was in condition to dam the flood of national vengeance. Let us profit by the errors of our predecessors. Let us do what the Legislative Assembly neglected to do. Let us organise a tribunal, if not well—for that is impossible—as least badly as we may, that the sword of the law may descend on the heads of all our enemies.

Then he proceeded to urge the reorganisation of the Ministry.

Monge, for instance, good citizen that he was, was incompetent to manage the navy. What was wanted was a

---

[1] Biré's *Diary of a Citizen in Paris*, i. 361.

large and instant expenditure of money and men, and to ensure a proper return Ministers were wanted constantly in touch with the Assembly, which would have to answer, it should never forget, to the people for its blood and treasure. Let the existing distress grow greater, and who would be able to arrest their fury! Let them at this very sitting organise the Tribunal and reorganise the Executive, so as to render it more efficient and energetic. Let them attend to his arguments and despise the insults offered to him. Let Commissioners set out at once to electrify the Departments, and stifle all regret, at being in their absence unable to support good or resist bad legislation, by the consciousness of doing their duty to the country. This, then, in brief, was his programme: to-night organisation of the Tribunal, organisation of the Executive; to-morrow the nation's call to arms, to-morrow the departure of the Commissioners. All France must rise, must arm, must march. Holland must be invaded. Belgium must be free. The commerce of England must be ruined, and her party of liberty triumph. Everywhere victorious, the Republic in arms must bring liberty and happiness to all peoples and expiate the wrongs of the world.

Though Danton neither originated nor worded the resolution for a Tribunal his powerful advocacy no doubt went far to secure its adoption. For this, a year later, he is said to have implored pardon from God and man. If so, it was not the conception but the abuse of it that he regretted, as a man might repent having begotten a son grown into a monster. It is hard to see what sounder counsel he could have given if all the circumstances of the hour are fully weighed. And it is instructive to observe that men like Vergniaud were as bitterly hostile to Ministers being members as they were to the Tribunal.

Quelques patriotes (said Vergniaud) *dont je respecte la probité ont pu d'abord ne voir ni danger ni violation des principes dans l'élection qui serait faite des ministres au sein de l'Assemblée ; mais bientôt tous se sont réunis à l'opinion contraire, et la Convention a échappé à l'unanimité au danger qui l'avait menacée.*

'Whose probity I respect' is a notable testimony to a man against whom such charges were brought as were brought against Danton by the Rolandists. Vergniaud, indeed, of whom Madame Roland wrote '*Je n'aime pas Vergniaud*,' was more like Danton in subordinating faction to patriotism than most of his party. But blind jealousies influenced him here. Danton knew he had little chance of getting his wish carried out, and after the failure of his adroit attempt to get it passed on the 10th he was careful, when he returned to the subject on the 11th, to say that he proposed no definite resolution, but merely sought to elicit the Assembly's opinion. How earnestly, however, and disinterestedly he strove for it may be gathered from a *résumé* of his speech that day, on the resignation of the War Minister, Beurnonville.

Though I think strongly that the Convention ought to and must choose Ministers anywhere, even from its own members, entirely at its discretion, I at the same time swear by our country that I myself will never accept office as Minister while I have the honour to be member of the Convention. I say so not out of false modesty, for I think I am worth as much as my neighbours ; and I hope none of my colleagues will follow my example, for I hold it indisputable that unless you reserve the power of choosing from them at your discretion you will do the State grievous injury. Surely everyone must see the necessity of greater cohesion, directer relations, closer connection between the Executive which has to defend our liberty against all Europe and you who have the supreme legislative power and the Republic's outworks in your charge. . . . If personally I decline to serve, it is because I think I can act more usefully as whip and spur of the Revolution, and because I retain thereby the power of denouncing any Minister's incompetence or bad faith. Therefore let all of us feel sure that most of us— nay, all—have patriotic intentions. Let no personal mistrust block the way, since we all aim at one object. I at least will asperse no one. I am, not from conscientiousness, but constitutionally, free from malice. Hatred is foreign to my nature. I have no need of it, and so even those who have professed to hate me cannot doubt my sincerity.

Danton was wrong here. The Girondin Girey-Dupré, commenting on this speech, said that everybody knew that he

wanted to be Minister, and that to hear him swear by his
country was like hearing an atheist swear by his God.   Robespierre too, wincing under the lash, retorted in the same debate,
' I see no merit, I own, in declining the dangerous and difficult
office of Minister.   I judge a refusal to result from preference
and interest rather than principle.'

CHAPTER XVII

1793—*continued*

TREASON OF DUMOURIEZ—DANTON DEFENDS HIS CONDUCT AND DEPLORES FACTION

On March 14, less than a week after Danton, Robespierre, and even Marat [1] had expressed confidence in Dumouriez, came that general's famous letter of the 12th, which was practically a denunciation and a defiance of the Convention. Bréard, President of the Convention, took it to the Committee of General Defence, which decided that Bréard should not read it to the Assembly, but that Danton and Delacroix should at once go to Dumouriez and induce him to retract. Various historians state variously the date of the day on which they set out. On the 19th they reached Brussels, and on the 20th met Dumouriez at Louvain in the evening. [2] They were unable to see him before, because they came 'during the combat,' by which words Delacroix seems to refer to skirmishes after the battle of Neerwinden, Dumouriez having fought and lost that battle on the 18th. We shall find Danton referring to the same thing on April 1, when he speaks of 'rallying the fugitives.' The conference lasted till 3 A.M. on the 21st.

Danton's movements afterwards have never yet been intelligibly related. We may, however, by comparing Delacroix's letters with Danton's words, conclude that this is what happened: From Louvain he went to Brussels with Delacroix, and about midnight—that is, on the morning of the 22nd [3]—set out for

---

[1] M. xv. 693.　　　　　[2] M.-T. vi. 304.
[3] M.-T. vi. 323.

Paris, and, travelling post haste, arrived there at eight or nine o'clock (for he mentions both hours) at night.   In speaking on April 1 he, by mistake, said he came back on Friday, the 29th. It was clearly a mistake, because he had spoken in the Convention on the 27th and 28th.

He must have come back laden with anxiety.   It is true Dumouriez had been induced to write a short note to the President of the Convention, begging him not to prejudge his previous letter, but wait for further explanations.   But though Danton could not know what was coming he must have suspected much, and he knew that it might go hard with himself, who had so lately championed Dumouriez, if there should be a rupture between the Convention and the army.   And in Paris there were already loud clamours for the General's recall.   He could only silently watch events, hoping for the best, waiting to hear from Delacroix, and attending to his duties as member of the Committee of General Defence, which was reorganised immediately after news of Neerwinden, and of which he was appointed a member on the 26th.

Meanwhile the Rolandists were busy circulating reports to his discredit, and the outbreak in La Vendée, partly the work of the priests, but mainly provoked by the conscription, had assumed proportions alarming to his party, but encouraging the hopes of the Royalists.   On the 27th a Girondin Deputy asked for lists of names recommended to Ministers by members of the Assembly for appointments, saying that the practice was contrary to the law.   Danton rose, partly to answer this, partly to urge more activity on the part of the Convention, and partly to assert his own patriotism.   He said that

the law was obsolete and in a revolutionary Government absurd ; that he had recommended none but excellent patriots ; that if he could only serve his country he cared nothing for the idle gossip about himself ; that what was wanted was energy, yet the Tribunal was as yet a dead letter ; that the people were ready to rise as one man, but only if the Convention itself ceased to be supine ; that the enemies of the Revolution were at work in the Departments, and that in Paris allusions to the national reverses were received with applause at the theatres ; that every grown-up man should be armed with a pike at the public expense, and that the Convention should identify itself with the people instead of keeping it at arm's length. No man with a spark of the flame of liberty in his heart should stand aloof from the people, who were the fathers, not the children, of the Assembly.

In this speech, not one of his best, occur two of his ‘all-too-gigantic’ figures.

A nation in revolution is like boiling bronze regenerating itself in the crucible. The Statue of Liberty is not yet moulded. The metal is bubbling over. Watch the furnace, or you will all be burnt. . . . Marseilles has declared itself the Mountain of the Republic. It will expand, this mountain ; it will roll down the rocks of liberty, and the enemies of liberty will be annihilated.

It contains also two interesting bits of history.

After the 10th of August it was I—for there are times when a man must speak of himself—it was I who brought the Executive Council, the Sectional Councils, the Municipality, the Commune, the Legislative Committees to meet amicably at the Mairie. We were a numerous assembly. We concerted the measures which were indispensable, and they were laid before the people by the Commissioners of Sections. The people applauded and we supported them, and the result was victory.

Roland wrote to Dumouriez, who himself showed Delacroix and me the letter, ‘You must league with us in crushing this Parisian faction, especially this Danton.’

Roland next day wrote to deny that he had ‘formed any kind of league which he durst not avow,’[1] and to demand proofs, but the form of his denial is suspicious.

At the conclusion of Danton's speech Robespierre called for the production of all the original correspondence on the operations in Belgium. Then Cambon announced that the letter of Dumouriez, which had not been read to the Convention (though, of course, it was not a secret in Paris, as any

[1] M. xv. 815.

Deputy might attend the meetings of the Committee of General
Defence), had been printed in Belgium, and, blaming its suppression, demanded information.   On the 30th taunting voices
in the Assembly called for Danton's accounts, for the balance-
sheet of the secret-service money, and for a full narrative of
what he had done in Belgium.   Danton, on this, rose and
said

that, as new letters had reached the Committee, the explanation which, in accordance with Cambon's demand, the Convention had ordered had better be postponed till the next day,
when the Ministers could lay a comprehensive report on the
whole question before the Assembly ; that personally he was
eager to enter into a full explanation.   It was high time that
everything was known about Belgium, the generals there, the
Commissioners, the army.   Prudential reasons had compelled
the Commissioners to mark time, so to speak, but at last they
would defend themselves against the consequent obloquy to
which they had been exposed.   As for himself, he welcomed
the opportunity of defending his advocacy of Belgian incorporation, of reinforcing the army, of frankly confessing
reverses, and of supporting Dumouriez, whose talents as a
general had made him indispensable, though his politics were
wrong.   As for his letter, common prudence dictated its suppression, lest there should be wholesale desertion on the part
of officers, and the enemy should be able to seize the strong
places.   He asked for neither grace nor favour.   He had done
his duty then, as on August 10.   He was perfectly ready to
present his accounts, though he had presented them already.
While he had been actively at work in the service of the State
other men had been traducing him in Paris.   Now was the
time for them to step into the open, where he courted every
enquiry, every accusation, where he would categorically answer
all questions.   He had never used one stroke of a pen to
defend himself, but ever since the beginning of the Revolution he had been painted in the most odious colours.   Let
those who charged him with ambition and embezzlement speak
up boldly now, or for the future be silent.   Let Roland confront him there.   All these miserable suspicions should be set
at rest for ever as soon as everything could be verified by the
papers presented by the Ministers.   Some men were demanding his head.   It was on his shoulders still, and would stay
there.   Let each of them, as Nature had endowed him, strive

for the good of the Republic, not the gratification of petty passions.

A portion of his speech must be presented entire.

So prepare to be as frank as I am—frank-men even in your hatred, frank in your passions. All these discussions may even now, perhaps, profit the State. Our ills spring from our dissensions. Well, let us make a clean breast of them all. For how comes it that one half of this Assembly treats the other as conspirators, that one half thinks the other wishes to have it massacred? There was a time for passion. Unhappily that is in the course of Nature. But the hour is come for a complete understanding, that everyone may judge himself according to his own conscience. Let it be known, then, whether you are two factions in one body, an Assembly full of reciprocal jealousy, or whether you are united to save the country. Do you long for reconciliation? Then with one accord concur in those strict and strong measures demanded by the people against the treasons of which it has so long been victim. Tell the people the truth. Arm them. Armies on the frontiers are not enough. We want at the centre of the Republic one main column which may facilitate war abroad by confronting the enemy at home.

It was very soon to be made plain how the factions of the Assembly would respond to this appeal.

CHAPTER XVIII

1793—*continued*

DANTON REBUTS GIRONDIN CHARGES—SPEECH OF LASOURCE—SCENE
IN THE CONVENTION—DANTON'S REJOINDER — LEVASSEUR'S DE-
SCRIPTION OF THE SCENE

DUMOURIEZ was summoned on March 30 to appear before the
Assembly.   A report proving his treason was laid before it on
April 1.   When it had been read, Pénières, a Girondin member
of the Committee of General Defence, said that on its being
settled to suppress for the time the letter of Dumouriez Danton
declared that if Dumouriez did not retract he would himself
denounce him, but when he came back did not go either to
the Assembly or the Committee.   He now demanded why
Danton had not kept his promise.   The historian of the Terror
has made the same demand, adding that Danton 'lied impudently' in saying he did not return till Friday the 29th.   It
has been shown already that Danton, having spoken in the
Assembly on March 27 and 28, could not possibly have told
the Assembly on April 1 that he had not returned till the 29th.
Even on April 1 he could not have so hoped to befool his
listeners.   He said Friday the 29th instead of Friday the 22nd
accidentally, as no doubt everybody who heard him understood
at once.   We have also seen why Danton did not go to the
Assembly after the 22nd.   He was waiting to hear from
Delacroix, whom he had left in Belgium.   He was still hoping
against hope that it might be possible to avoid coming to
extremities with Dumouriez.   And on the 26th he was elected
member of the Committee of General Defence.   This will

clear up much of what followed in one of the most dramatic scenes which ever occurred in a representative assembly.

Danton, in answer to Pénières, said

that having arrived at 9 o'clock P.M. (*he mentions no date here*) he did not go to the Committee (*implying evidently that it was too late and he was too tired, as well he might be after being in a post chaise some twenty-one hours consecutively*; but next day he did go to the Committee (*Pénières had said he did not*), told it of the insolent language Dumouriez was using, and recommended the immediate publication of the whole affair, so that everyone present must have understood that he thought Dumouriez ought to be arrested at once. He and the other Commissioners had done their best to thwart Dumouriez by advocating the incorporation of Belgium, which he resisted, and by accusing him—they who were charged with defending him—of the reverses in Belgium. He had called Dumouriez' plan superb. So it was, and if it had succeeded Dumouriez might have remained loyal. In any case England would have been humbled and Holland conquered. Dumouriez had been led on to treason by members of that Assembly. A commission should be appointed to unmask the criminals, and it would then be seen that everything the Commissioners had done had been done with the Convention's approval. To undo the past a Committee of War should be at once named to improvise another army of 50,000 men; the other Commissioners should be recalled from Belgium; and the Executive Council should lay before the Assembly an exact account of what they had done in Belgium. To arrest Dumouriez at the head of his army would have been to disorganise the army. The Commissioners had no force at their disposal, and not having any badge to denote their having semi-civil, semi-military functions, would have had no sufficient authority in the eyes of the soldiers. No general would, or, if he would, could, have arrested Dumouriez when fighting was going on every two leagues. He made himself personally responsible for all the acts of the Commission, certain that so far from his head falling on the block it would be a Medusa's head to strike terror into all aristocrats.

The Girondin Lasource then rose and in a plausible speech gave his version of the facts.

How could Danton say no general would arrest Dumouriez

when he had said that the army was so republican that if it
read in the papers of his being arraigned for treason it would
itself bring him to the bar of the Assembly? When Robespierre proposed inquiry into Dumouriez' conduct Danton
opposed it, yet now he said that he told the Committee there
was nothing more to be hoped from Dumouriez.

Maure here interrupted that it had been proposed to send
(the Girondin) Gensonné, as being all-powerful with Dumouriez,
to concert measures with him.

Lasource, in continuation, said that Dumouriez

wished to restore monarchy. To do so he must be at the head
of an army. Who ensured this? Danton. To make the plot
succeed it must be popular, and be worked conjointly in Belgium
and Paris. So Delacroix gave himself popular airs in Belgium,
while Danton came to Paris 'to adopt measures of defence,'
and going to the Committee said not a word about what was
going on.

Danton : *'That's a falsehood !'*
Several voices : *'A falsehood !'*
Lasource—

When asked to say why he had quitted Belgium Danton's
reply was not to the point. And why did he still stay in Paris,
not having resigned his post as Commissioner? To make the
plot succeed it was necessary to depreciate the Convention.
This was why Danton had upbraided it with inactivity and
threatened an insurrection. To abase the Convention was to
exalt Dumouriez. That was what Danton did. To foster the
plot it was useful to exaggerate the national danger, so as to
alarm the timid or provoke an outbreak of the people, which
Dumouriez might be called in to quell. Danton and Delacroix
acted accordingly.

Then Lasource added that he seconded Danton's demand
for a Commission and proposed the arrest of Philippe Égalité
and sentence of death on anyone aspiring to royalty or dictatorship (i.e. *Orleans and Danton*). The Girondin Biroteau
interposed here, charging Fabre d'Eglantine, 'whom all the
world knows as Danton's intimate friend,' with having said, at

the Committee of General Defence, that he was in favour of a king. Biroteau added that Fabre d'Eglantine had only been induced to declare himself by being told that opinion was free and that anything said at the meeting was said under the pledge of secresy. He appears to have been unconscious of anything dishonourable in these revelations, which were received with cries of ''That is a lie!' and with an outburst from Danton: 'It is infamous. You, the King's champions, want to saddle me with your own crimes.' Biroteau was proceeding to quote, as he alleged, Fabre's very words, when Delmas intervened, declaring that such a discussion was ill-timed and that they had better await the results of the Committee proposed by Lasource. This was agreed to, but Danton called on Cambon to say what he knew about the 100,000 crowns sent 'to Danton and Delacroix,' and about their conduct in the matter of the incorporation of Belgium. He was interrupted by shouts of 'Let it be referred to the Committee,' and this also was agreed to. But as he sat down the whole of the Extreme Left rose and recalled him to the tribune. Danton sprang to it amid thunders of applause from the galleries and a great part of the Assembly. The President, putting on his hat and demanding silence, left it to the Assembly to decide whether Danton should speak or not. Amid tumultuous cries for and against his claim Lasource begged that Danton might be heard, and by a very large majority the Assembly decided in his favour.

While Lasource had been delivering his oration Danton sat motionless in his seat, curling his lip contemptuously, with a look of wrath and scorn. On reaching the tribune his first words were the key to the whole speech. Turning to the Mountain he told them, amid fierce interruptions,

that they had judged more wisely than he in blaming him for temporising with the Right, who blindly or basely had conspired to save the King and yet were so insolent as to assume the attitude of denunciators.

Then he explained:

that he had come back at 8 P.M., Friday, the 29th, twenty-four hours later than some of his colleagues supposed, they being under the impression that he set out immediately his fellow Commissioners in Belgium had come to a decision.

By this he meant, as has been explained already, that he did not set out from Louvain at 3 A.M. on the 21st, but from Brussels in the small hours of the morning of the 22nd. Previously he had named nine o'clock as the hour and had not mentioned any date. Evidently the slip was due to the agitation under which he was labouring. If it had not been so obviously a mistake and he had 'lied impudently,' scores of tongues would have convicted him on the spot.

He went on to say

that he was too tired to go to the Committee that night, but so far from holding his tongue, as Lasource alleged, he went there next day and denounced Dumouriez, proposing that he should be arrested ; that Camus, whom no one would suspect of being a partisan of his, had said neither more nor less than himself, and his report to the Convention was precisely like his own.

Appealing to some of his audience, who knew the facts, if these assertions were true, he was answered by cries of 'Yes, yes ;' and then he went on to say

that it was quite true he had declared that the army would arrest Dumouriez if he had been arraigned in Paris ; but when Lasource asked, 'Why, then, did you not arrest him ?' he replied, ' Because at that time he was *not* arraigned in Paris.' As for the prudent, the necessary suppression of the letter and his return to Dumouriez, it was he who had proposed that Guadet and Gensonné, friends of Dumouriez, should go, in order that both parties, not one, should be represented, and that Dumouriez might be convinced of their unanimity in refusing to be dictated to by one man. He could quote the very words he used. ' *Ou nous le guérirons momentanément ou nous le garrotterons.*' He had withstood the financial and personal projects of Dumouriez, who, the Girondin journal had said, would never mingle his laurels with the cypresses of September. As to the money he had received, he appealed to Cambon (*who rose and corroborated what Danton had said*). Lasource said he had abased the Convention. Abase it ! Who had done more to uphold its dignity than he, who had been respectful even to his enemies there? (*Here there were cries of ' Just now, for instance,' meaning that he had occupied the tribune.*) Just now! well, that was true; he admitted the charge; but why for once had he abandoned his usual moderation? Because incessant provocation had at last worn out his patience. Lasource had attacked Delacroix. Delacroix was his friend, and he was attacked because he had broken away from federalist ideas and would not join the conspiracy to spare the King. (*Here someone cried, ' Don't talk so much. Answer.'*) Answer! Answer what? He had already shown that his report and that of Camus were identical, that if Dumouriez was not brought bound hand and foot to the Convention he individually was not to blame, but Camus and the Commissioners as a body, who could only act collectively, and who did not arrest him simply because it was impossible. It was the Girondins, the men who sought to arm the Departments against Paris, who were the friends of Dumouriez (Marat: '*And those little suppers of theirs !*'), who had consorted with him at clandestine suppers in Paris (Marat: ' *Lasource, Lasource was at them. Oh, I will unmask all the traitors !*'); but he had nothing to fear from Dumouriez, whom he defied to produce one single line incriminating him in any way, whereas the federalists—(*Cries of ' Name them !'*) (Marat, to the Right; *No ; you shall not succeed in murdering the country !*') —did they wish him to name whom he meant? (*Cries of ' Yes, yes.'*) Let them listen, then. (Marat: '*Listen !*') Did they want one word that would serve for all? (*Cries of ' Yes, yes.'*) Well, he declared that there could no more be any truce between the patriots of the Mountain and the dastards who dared to traduce them as aiming at tyranny when they had themselves wished to spare the tyrant's life. Lasource had merely repeated once more the stale charges of the old fox Roland, who, poor old man, so lost his head that he thought everyone was seeking his life, even Pache, Pache whom he himself had made Minister ! How stupid to try and embroil Marseilles with the Mountain, the Departments with Paris, the people with the Jacobins, and to say that the same men could serve two masters, Orleans and the Mountain ! How stupid to suppose that the rebel against the Revolutionary Tribunal would coalesce with its author; the supporter of Three Estates in Belgium with the scourge of its aristocrats ; the calumniator of the Commissioners with the man who pro-

posed the Commission ; the reviler of the volunteers with him
at whose voice they volunteered !

After again demanding that the inquiry to be held
should be thorough, and into the acts of the Rolandists
as well as his own, he concluded with these words to the
' Mountain ' :—

No more compromise with them.   See to it, you who have
never known how to profit as you ought by your political
position !   Claim at last what is your due.   You see by the
situation I am now in how necessary it is to be firm, and to
declare war against your enemies, whoever they may be.   We
must form an unconquerable phalanx.   It is not you, friends
of the popular societies and the people, who wish for a king.
It is you who must eradicate that craze from those who
intrigued to save the tyrant now dead.   My goal is the
Republic.   Let us make for it side by side, and see which of
us, we or our detractors, will reach that at which he aims.   I
have proved that, far from being an accomplice of Dumouriez,
he accused us in so many words of enforcing the incorporation
of Belgium at the sword's point, that he publicly threatened
to arrest us, that it was impossible for Delacroix and myself,
apart from our colleagues, to arrest him at the head of his
army.   I have replied to every charge.   I have done so to the
satisfaction of every man of sense and honour.   And now I
demand that the Committee of Six, which you have just
appointed, inquire not only into the acts of those who have
calumniated you, who have intrigued against the unity of the
Republic, but also of the men who sought to spare the tyrant,
and, finally, of all criminals whose aim has been to ruin
liberty, and we shall see whether I have any fear of my
accusers.   My stronghold is reason.   I will issue from it with
truth for my artillery, and I will crush the wretches who would
incriminate me into dust.

The scene has been described by an eye-witness who was
by no means an indiscriminate admirer of Danton, and his
account is for this reason valuable as well as picturesque.

I shall never forget the moment when Lasource began his
amazing accusation of Danton.   While with captious arguments
he was labouring to metamorphose this formidable champion
of the Mountain into a secret partisan of Dumouriez ; while he

was piling up forced deductions to lend a semblance of substance to his indictment, and piecing together all the parts of this flimsy scaffolding with unconcealed self-complacency, Danton, motionless on his bench, kept curling his lip with an expression of contempt which was habitual to him and inspired a sort of fear. His look evinced at once disdain and anger. His attitude was in contrast to the workings of his face, and in this strange mixture of calm and agitation you could see he only refrained from interrupting his adversary because he would be so easy to answer and so certain to be overwhelmed. But when Lasource had ended and Danton was hurrying along our rows to the tribune, he pointed at the Right as he passed, and said in a low voice, 'The scoundrels, they would saddle us with their crimes.' It was easy to see that his impetuous eloquence, long pent up, was about to burst all barriers, and that our enemy would have cause to tremble. And in fact his speech was a declaration of war rather than an apology. His Stentor-voice pealed through the Assembly like an alarm-gun summoning the soldier to the breach. From that moment he abandoned those conciliatory tactics which he had thought to be for the interest of the State, and, convinced at last that the Girondins would never unite with him to save the liberty he held so dear, he declared plainly that it should be saved without them. Many a time had he refused to pick up the gauntlet flung to him day after day in the Assembly. At last he had accepted the challenge, and stepping into the arena for the first time armed at all points, he was about to show the Right that the overthrow of such an athlete would not be a painless achievement. After his vigorous outset Danton spoke more than two hours, answering his accuser charge by charge. His reply was ready, and of overwhelming logic and energy. He demonstrated that Dumouriez had reserved all his hatred for the Mountain, all his regard for the Right; that it was from the Mountain that the first shafts of suspicion had been launched at Roland's old colleague, only on that memorable 12th of March to be repelled by the Right as treasonable weapons. In short, after tracking Lasource through all his premisses and all his deductions in turn, he pulverised all of them alike. . . . After his defence he took the offensive. To judge of the whole effect produced by this eloquent improvisation it must be remembered that till then Danton had sought to act as mediator between the two parties in the Assembly; that though sitting at the top of the Mountain he was, in a way, chief of the Plain ; that he had often rebuked our passion, had combated Robespierre's suspiciousness, and had maintained that, instead of waging war on the Girondins, they ought to be constrained to second us and co-operate with us for the good of the nation. Only a few days before this onslaught of Lasource, Danton had had a conference with the leading men of the Right, at which it was agreed to act in concord and concentrate all efforts for the conquest of the invaders and the confusion of the aristocracy.

We all of us loved Danton, but most of us thought him mistaken in trying to reunite the Girondins and the Mountain. Most of us, it is true, had consented to be led by him to the fusion on which he seemed to build such hopes, but it was more by way of an experiment in which we had small belief than from conviction it would succeed, as Danton promised us. So when this impassioned speaker, stupidly provoked by one of the skirmishers of the other side, made so powerful a reply to so impudent an attack, when he declared such un-compromising war on men with whom we had long ago seen it was impossible to be at peace, when he, so to speak, burned his boats to deprive himself of any chance of changing his mind, we were transported with a sort of electric enthusiasm ; we looked at Danton's unexpected resolution as the signal of certain victory. As soon as he left the tribune a great number of Deputies ran to embrace him, and the hall rang with cheer after cheer. However, here the incident ended. Lasource having made no formal motion the Convention simply resumed business. But if Danton's oration had no immediate result it had an immense influence on men's minds. We felt sure of the future, and the Girondins no longer seemed formidable now he had determined to fight. The acquisition of him was in our eyes worth an army.

CHAPTER XIX

1793—*continued*

'PLUS de trêve, Plus de composition.' This seemed to be
indeed throwing away the scabbard—the voice of 'the strongest
and the fiercest spirit' of the Assembly, 'now fiercer by
despair,' declaring irrevocably, 'My sentence is for open war.'
But though henceforward Danton's demeanour to the Right
was never what it had been before, his 'fierceness' was
that of an impetuous, not a revengeful nature, and if his
hand could have averted them there would have been no
proscriptions.   On the very day of his speech Dumouriez
had arrested the Convention's Commissioners,[1] and in view
of the common danger he again appealed for concord, inter-
posing as peacemaker on April 4, after a scene of altercation provoked by a speech by Marat. '*Rapprochons-nous,
rapprochons fraternellement*,' he cried, '*il y va du salut de
tous.*'[2]

None the less did he prepare for the coming struggle. On
the 5th he proposed the formation of an armed and paid body
of *sans-culottes* to keep aristocratic citizens 'sous la pique,' and
the regulation of the price of bread by the rate of workmen's
wages, any loss to the vendor to be made good by the rich.
The abstract defensibility of this enlistment of physical force,

---

[1] M.-T. vi. 351.   [2] M. xvi. 57.

and of this rough and ready poor law, is open to criticism, but there can be no doubt of their efficacy in identifying the people with the revolutionary party; nor did he conceal his object. 'By this decree alone,' he said, 'you will ensure means of subsistence to the people without wounding its self-respect, and will attach it to the Revolution.' When the Army of the North was in retreat, when the Rolandists were stirring up the Departments, when La Vendée was in flames, there was no choice left. The people must be 'attached to the Revolution,' or the cause of the Revolution was lost.

Never, in fact, had it been in greater peril than when on the 7th Danton's name was announced as one of the newly appointed Committee of Public Safety. This famous Committee, nominally proposed by Isnard, as Reporter of the Committee of General Defence, was really due to Danton, who, also a member of that Committee, must have had much to do with the verbal definition of its powers. What it signified as to the past was the failure of Government by the Convention—that is, by its Girondin majority. What it heralded was government by Danton, who, as he had stemmed the tide of disaster in 1792, now stood in the breach again, and laid the foundation of the system by which the military reverses of the next two months were to be changed into the victories of September. The Girondins suspected then, but no one would assert now, that Danton aimed at becoming a Dictator. He had no such personal ambition. But the logic of events had taught him that there must be a responsible Executive; that 'a Republic, while proscribing dictators and triumvirs, had none the less the power, as it was indeed its duty, to create an authority which would be feared.' This was the policy which Danton advocated, at first in vain, in the Convention. It took concrete form in the Committee of Public Safety. He looked on it not as desirable in itself, but as a necessity—just as he had regarded the Revolutionary Tribunal, not as a good institution, but as the 'least bad' one possible.

While this great engine was being forged violent alterca-

tions went on in the Assembly.   On the 10th Pétion proposed
that the authors of a petition demanding Roland's arraignment
and using dictatorial language to the Convention should be
sent before the Revolutionary Tribunal.   Danton rose to a
point of order, and as he dashed towards the rostrum a
number of Deputies from each party followed him, almost
coming to blows.   'You are a set of scoundrels,' cried
Danton.   'Down with the Dictator!' retorted his antagonists.   At last Pétion was allowed to proceed, though a few
minutes later David grotesquely showed how electric the air
was by suddenly, on Pétion's using the word '*scélérats*,'
stepping solemnly into the middle of the hall and saying, 'I
offer my life and my conduct for examination.'   'You are
not in possession of the House, Pétion is,' curtly remarked
Thuriot, the President.   Pétion then introduced that perpetual
bone of contention, the name of Marat, who, he said, was an
Orleanist, and, far worse, was allowed to occupy the rostrum
far oftener than a certain 'man noted for his probity and
principles' whom Pétion did not name, though he clearly
thought him 'as pretty a piece of flesh as any in Messina.'
'*Que dira-t-on dans les départements?*' he said before he sat
down—words which, even from lips no longer looked on as
reverend, must have seemed grave and ominous.

Danton on another occasion pleaded for the utmost possible
latitude being allowed to the wording of a petition as being at
once dignified and more politic.   He now declared

that it was only natural that there should be feverish efferves-
cences among the people when they saw the Assembly
perpetually a gladiatorial arena.   Pétion's proposal was frivolous.   Petitions more or less exaggerated were presented every
day.   The wisdom of the Assembly was to take a hint from
such exaggerations.   If they reached the point of illegality there
were laws and tribunals to which those who thought it their duty
might appeal.   What a sea the Assembly would embark on if
it prosecuted them all itself!   It ought to be thinking how to
conquer the Austrians, how to pacify La Vendée, how to frame
a Constitution, and not to allow its time to be wasted on these
pitiful squabbles.

Two days later, on the 12th, Guadet, in answering Robespierre, taunted Danton with being at the Opera with Dumouriez, and attempted to work on Robespierre's jealousy by saying Danton only counted him 'third' among his agents. Danton rejoined that Guadet was at the Opera too, and that he would prove Guadet's criminality.

By such petty strategy the Girondins played into the hands of their enemies, and they were still worse advised in choosing this particular moment for measuring swords with Marat. Marat had expressed confidence in Dumouriez just before his treason, but on previous occasions he had denounced him, and the people, judging him as they might a weather-prophet, remembered only his true and forgot his false predictions. He was, therefore, never more formidable than now. Pétion had charged him with being an Orleanist. Guadet clinched the accusation by saying Dumouriez was an Orleanist, and the instrument in a plot of which Orleans was chief. Then he read out an extract from one of Marat's manifestos accusing the Right of treason. Marat sprang up, and beginning his speech with '*Pourquoi ce vain batelage, et à quoi bon?*' declared that the accusation was true. The Assembly were about to vote whether he should be sent before the Revolutionary Tribunal or not, when Danton rose. He began by referring to the original denunciation of Orleans by Robespierre, out of which all these counter-accusations had sprung, saying

it would have been better if he had refrained from saying anything he could not prove. The main question seemed to be an Orleanist plot. This plot had till now seemed to him a chimera, but he began to think there must be some truth in it. Marat was at least a member of the Convention and entitled to fair play. He was accused by Pétion and Guadet, and he was their accuser, but they agreed in incriminating Orleans. Let Orleans, then, be sent before the Tribunal. That was the first thing to be done. And let a price be put on the heads of the royal *émigrés.*

Here someone asked : ' But what would be the fate of our Commissioners whom Dumouriez arrested ? '

Their Commissioners (he answered) were worthy of the nation and of the Convention. They would face their fate like Regulus. As for Marat, it was only just that his case should be first referred to a Committee, and not decided in the Assembly, so many members of which were away on missions. Marat had no intention of running away.

While all these charges of Orleanism were being bandied about no one accused Danton, as Marat was accused, openly and directly, nor can language less like that of an Orleanist partisan be conceived than the above, while to use it, if he had been in the pay of Orleans, would have been to court an unscrupulous man's revenge. In tracing Danton's career from day to day we are perpetually confronted with this entire lack of contemporary evidence, when evidence would have been so greedily welcomed, for charges brought against him at his trial and after he was dead. Lasource's elaborate parade of evidence had dissolved into the thinnest of smoke. And now, while Marat was a target for the shafts of the Right, Danton went unscathed.

Marat's trial, acquittal, and triumphant reappearance in the Assembly, amid an escort of boisterous partisans, elicited from Danton a characteristic speech to the effect 'that everyone must hail the acquittal of a member of the Convention, that it was proper to allow his escort to pass through the Assembly, *but*—they must now go away and leave the Deputies to their work.' Thus almost in a breath he emphasised the humiliation of the Girondins and his own instinctive tact as a popular tribune. This occurred on the 24th.

Meanwhile on the 13th he made his famous retractation of the doctrine of propaganda, as will be noticed in a subsequent chapter,[1] and on the 19th expressed some noble sentiments on religious freedom. Once more, and evidently with unfeigned pleasure, holding conciliatory language to the Girondins, he said :

Nothing could be of better omen for our country's good than

[1] M. xvi. 128, 143.

our present attitude. We have seemed divided, but the moment we consider the happiness of our fellow creatures we are all united. Vergniaud has just uttered some great and eternal truths.

He went on to say

that a declaration of tolerance was no longer necessary, as it was in the time of the Constituent Assembly, when the reign of intolerance was only just over ; that the sacred right of a man to adore the Divinity of his choice was in no danger, for human reason could not retrograde, nor would the people believe it was not free to worship as it pleased because it saw no express permission graven on the table of the law. The people, when not led astray, invariably recognised that anyone intervening between itself and its God was an impostor.

On the 27th he vindicated the principle of the rich paying the expenses of poorer volunteers, pointing to the example of the Department of Hérault, and arguing

that it was for the good of the rich themselves, for their contributions constituted an insurance against invasion. Paris wealth and Paris luxury must also pay. It was a sponge that must be squeezed. There would be pleasure in making the domestic enemy pay for the foreign war. Paris would call on her capitalists, would give her sons to quell the civil strife in La Vendée. And for that purpose he demanded the enrolment of 20,000 men.

On May 8 he returned to the same theme.

It was a truth graven in history and the human heart that a nation when in revolution or civil war was no less formidable to a foreign foe. All France was astir. Twelve thousand troops of the line were marching for La Vendée, and the gaps thus created were being filled by volunteers. But while using force they would do well to take example by the Emperor in Belgium, and use clemency, freely offering pardon to all rebels who would anticipate the use of force by submission, and inflicting the most rigorous penalties only on those originating or propagating rebellion. In Paris commissioners must go to each Section in order to assess the rich and enrol the poor ; and any Section not furnishing within three days its proper contingent should be made to draw its men by lot. As for the richer Sections, the sum squeezed from each of these sponges should not belong to one Section, but to all.

On the 10th he controverted a fantastic scheme of Isnard for decreeing, previous to the Constitution, a '*pacte social.*'

The Constitution (he said) was itself the 'pacte social,' and, when once accepted by the people, imperishable.   But as that day the Deputies were holding session for the first time in the palace of despots it would be a fine opportunity for laying the foundation-stone of the Constitution by declaring anew that the Government of France was republican, and then discussing some elementary inferences therefrom, viz. that the Executive be elected by the people, and that as a counterpoise to its power a national tribunal be created, with jurisdiction over all officials when quitting office.

Little but the foundation-stone of which Danton spoke was to be laid by the members of the Assembly as constituted on the 10th.   For the next fortnight he was silent.   He was watching with sorrow the ever-increasing violence of the extremists on both sides of the Assembly, among whom Marat was always foremost, and when he spoke again on the 24th the struggle had become one for life or death.

CHAPTER XX

1793—*continued*

GIRONDIN THREATS — COMMITTEE OF TWELVE — ISNARD — DANTON'S SPEECH—ARREST OF HÉBERT—ISNARD'S FOLLY—DANTON'S REPLY AND THREAT OF RESISTANCE—PLOTS AND COUNTERPLOTS—GARAT —DANTON'S SPEECH — SUPPRESSION AND RE-ESTABLISHMENT OF COMMITTEE OF TWELVE—INSURRECTION — OVERTHROW OF THE GIRONDINS

WHILE the Convention was engaged in discussing the articles of the new Constitution its time had been taken up by incessant deputations, either from the Commune attempting to influence its decisions or from Sections favouring the Right or the Left, or from Bordeaux fiercely denouncing the party of Marat.   Marat's triumph had been followed by a reaction, and crowds had collected in the streets to the cry of 'Down with the Anarchists!'[1]   Irritated by this, he became more and more outrageous, but not one whit more so than the Girondin Press or some of the Girondin Deputies, led by the acrimonious Guadet.[2]   The Right declared they went in fear of their lives in Paris.   The Left retorted that those who whined had not received a scratch, that the only attempts at assassination had been made on their own Deputies, and that there was a plot to coerce Paris by an armed force from the Departments.[3]   The Girondin leaders were rash enough to lend colour to such assertions by their threats.   'The men of Bordeaux will come to Paris if the Convention is menaced,' said Guadet; and he proposed first that the Convention should adjourn to Versailles,

---

[1] M.-T. vii. 215, 241.   [2] M. xvi. 415, 421-2.   M.-T. vii. 216, 225.
[3] M.-T. vii. 226.

and then that another Convention should meet at Bourges, in case the existing Convention should be dissolved. 'If,' said Vergniaud, 'threats and outrages force us to withdraw, the Department which sent me here will have nothing more in common with a town which has done despite to the representatives of the nation.' And from a great part of the Assembly rose cries of 'So say we.' And afterwards he said: 'None of us will die without being revenged. Our Departments are up, and the conspirators know it.'

On the 18th of May it was agreed to appoint a Committee of Twelve to inquire into plots against the Convention. That same day a woman of the people outraged the decorum of the Assembly by trying to drag out a young man from one of the seats allotted to citizens from the country.[1] The President, Isnard, discerned in this a new plan of the French aristocracy, Pitt, England, and Austria for destroying liberty !

Ah ! (he wailed),[2] could you but open my heart you would see my love for France, and should I be immolated on this chair my last sigh would be for her, and my last words, 'O God, pardon my assassins—they are misled—but save the liberty of my country.' Yes ; the people are being misled, being urged to insurrection, and this insurrection will begin with the women. The murder of several members of this Assembly, and its dissolution, is desired. The English will make a descent and join in overthrowing the Revolution.

This speech was received with applause from a large part of the Assembly ! What hope could there be for a party which had a babbler of this sort as one of its foremost members, and could cheer him for seeing, in the descent of a Jacobin Amazon on a country bumpkin, the descent of an English fleet on the French coasts? Yet one chance more they had of showing tact and prudence when two days later they found themselves in a majority on the Committee of Twelve. On the 22nd that chance was lost. Rabaut-Pommier that day proposed that all towns of over 50,000 inhabitants should be

<hr>

[1] M. xvi. 420.　　　　　　　　　　[2] M.-T, vii. 239.

split up into several municipalities, and he was supported by Buzot, who hated Paris—at which of course the motion was aimed—with all his heart.[1] 'You might as well,' said Collot d'Herbois, for once not ranting, 'argue that a ship because it is bigger than another wants a number of helms.'

This mistimed and maladroit provocation to a city already half in insurrection was ill calculated to procure a good reception for the measures of the Committee of Twelve. The first article was as follows: 'The National Convention entrusts to good citizens the public treasure, the representatives of the nation, and the town of Paris.' On this Danton observed 'that it was absurd to create a new law for the protection of the Convention, since the existing laws were ample for the purpose.' Taking up the same position as Isnard, that the only danger was from 'the aristocracy'—a bugbear phrase resorted to by each party alternately when it wished to avoid naming the foe really designated—he argued

that the vast number of good citizens in a big town like Paris could easily overawe any assailants of the representatives of the nation. It had been an insult to Paris to propose a Departmental Guard, and they should beware lest the creation of a committee to inquire into Paris plots should create a demand for one to inquire into plots to spread disaffection in the Departments.

Such grim irony did not deter the Committee of Twelve from assuming the offensive, in spite of the strong opposition of such men as Rabaut, Fonfrède, and Garat, by arresting Hébert, the deputy-procureur of the Commune. The Commune at once sent a deputation to protest angrily. Isnard, again President, again signalised himself by the insanity of his language, language never forgotten, never forgiven,[2] which alienated from his party the *bourgeois* citizens in the coming struggle and was instrumental in bringing many of his friends to the block. 'If Paris should ever do despite to the representative body, I tell you, in the name of all France,

<hr>

[1] M.-T. vii. 211.   [2] M.-T. vii. 330, 342.

Paris would be annihilated. Someone would have to search the banks of the Seine to see if Paris ever existed.'

No words could have been used which Danton would have more resented. He hastened to answer Isnard.[1]

What a picture to paint, Paris devastated by the Departments ! The words of a President should be healing words. France could rely on Paris never deviating from the path it had always trod, and on its never replacing the old tyranny by a new one. The representative body had to steer its way between two reefs. Perfection could not be expected in a party. If in the popular party there were criminals the people would punish them ; but if a choice had to be made between one of two evils the license of liberty was preferable to a recrudescence of slavery. If there had been no men of action, if the people had never had recourse to violence, there would have been no Revolution, and that the men of the Mountain should never forget. He had no wish to irritate anyone. He felt himself too strong in reason for that. Nor should his opponents try to irritate the Departments against Paris. Paris outrage the National Assembly ! Paris, that immense city which every day drew from the nation fresh life, violate the sacred ark entrusted to it ! No ; Paris was the Revolution's lover, and for the sacrifices she had made for liberty Paris deserved to be clasped to every Frenchman's heart. The nation would know what to think of the proposal to remove the Convention to another town. Go where it would its passions would go with it. But, in spite of all their dissensions, France, still recognising Paris as the proper centre for its representatives, would know how to save itself.

Two days after this speech, the 27th, a deputation from one of the Sections came to protest against the arrest of its president and secretary by the Committee of Twelve, an act, they said, recalling the time of *lettres de cachet*.[2] Isnard snubbed them in a speech bristling with provocations to the leaders of the Mountain, and Robespierre claimed, but was refused, the right to criticise it. A violent scene ensued, and Danton said : ' Such shamelessness becomes intolerable. We

---

[1] M. xvi. 483.　　　　　[2] M. xvi. 491.

will resist.' The Right demanded that the threat should be entered on the minutes of the proceedings.

I demand that myself (said Danton). I declare before the Convention and before all France that if you persist in keeping in irons citizens only presumably guilty, whose sole crime is excess of patriotism, if you perpetually refuse to those wishing to defend them their right of speech, I declare, I say, that if there are a hundred good citizens in this hall we will resist. I declare, and I will sign my declaration, that the refusal to hear Robespierre is dastardly tyranny.

And he ended with : 'I protest against your despotism, against your tyranny. The French people will judge between us.'

Isnard had much to answer for. How much Thuriot said a little later, reminding the Assembly 'that Isnard was the man who had declared Jesus Christ to be Commander-in-Chief of the rebels in La Vendée, and denouncing Isnard as an incendiary rather than a maintainer of order, at a time when connivance with disorder meant complicity with the threatening movements of the foreign enemy.' This was the true Dantonist note, and, though Danton neither could nor wished to sever himself from the Mountain, anyone reading his speeches side by side with the furious words and insults scattered about by other men on both sides will recognise that mere personalities were never to his taste, and that he was always fighting for a principle or a policy.

The air of Paris was now full of rumours of plots—plots to crown the Dauphin, to punish all Deputies who had not voted for the King's death, to assassinate all except certain Deputies of the Mountain. On the other hand Marat's detective instincts unearthed meetings at the house of Valazé, which were attended by men like Brissot, Gensonné, Buzot, Barbaroux, Guadet;[1] and Valazé was compelled to own he had addressed to them the following summons : *'En armes à la Convention à dix heures précises du matin : je vous somme d'avertir le plus grand nombre possible de vos collègues. Couard qui ne se trouve*

[1] M.-T. vii. 254.

pas.' Danton, having to choose, as he had said, between two
evils, preferred the 'excesses of liberty' to those of 'slavery';
but he would have steered clear of all excess had he been able.
It was his friend Legendre who proposed on the 23rd that the
Convention should make all presidents of Sections and clubs
responsible for propositions of a lawless kind, unless they
called the proposers to order and handed them over to the
police. But when the Dantonists would have thrown water
on the flames Isnard and Marat poured oil. The battle still
raged inside the Assembly, and outside there was a mob of
citizens and a battalion sent by the Committee of Twelve to
hold it in check. Garat, Minister of the Interior, was announced,
and with him Pache, the Mayor. Garat made a long speech
which completely justified the line taken by Danton and
Thuriot, took exception to the acts of the Committee of
Twelve, acquitted Hébert as far as his acts in the Commune
went, and assured the Assembly that the mob outside were
less in number than the troops.

Garat, if a weak, was an honourable man, and it is impossible to disregard his evidence, even if there were no other to
show that the Girondins were themselves as much to blame as
anyone for the civil war. Danton's conduct is shown by the
appeal he addressed to Garat.

This thunder (he said) will, I flatter myself, clear the
air. . . . I did not know the Minister of the Interior. I had
no connection with him. I call on him to declare—and it
concerns me now, when a Deputy (Brissot) has made a sanguinary onslaught on me, now, when the money I received for a
post is exaggerated into a huge fortune—

Here he was interrupted by cries of:

'Don't talk about yourself and your squabble with Brissot.'
'I mention that,' he replied, 'because the Committee of
Public Safety has been accused of favouring the disturbances
in Paris.'

Other cries arose :
'We don't say so.'

You do not like to hear the truth, you friends of order. May your conduct make it clear who are the friends of anarchy ! I appeal, I repeat, to the Minister to say whether I have not over and over again gone to his house to press him to allay these agitations, to unite the Departments, to put an end to the prejudice instilled into them against Paris.   I call on him to say if I have not implored him to pacify rancour, if I have not said, ' I would not have you flatter either party, but preach the union of both.'   There are people who cannot live without a grievance.   I am not of that sort.   I am by nature impulsive, but I am not vindictive.   I call on him to say if he has not come to the conclusion that the pretended friends of order have been the cause of all these contentions, and the most far-going citizens the best friends of order and peace.

While Danton was speaking deputations continued to come demanding the suppression of the Committee of Twelve.   Now if ever at the crisis of their fate the Girondins might have been expected to show vigilance and resolution ; but, though it was still early, one by one they slipped away and went to bed. Isnard had left the chair.   Hérault de Séchelles took his place. Delacroix proposed the suppression of the Committee of Twelve and the release of Hébert.   Both resolutions were carried by the Left, and the House rose at midnight, May 27.[1]   That night the Girondins may be said to have dug their own graves.   One desperate effort to retrieve the position was indeed made next day.   The suppression of the Committee of Twelve was annulled, and the Right seemed again masters of the field of battle.   But it was a last, a Pyrrhic victory.   Danton's language presaged their fate.

It is time for the people to cease limiting itself to defensive war, and to take the offensive against the party of the Moderates. . . . It is time for us to coalesce against the plots of all who wish to destroy the Republic. . . . Paris will always be the terror of the enemies of liberty ; and its Sections, on the great days when the people shall form again in their thousands, will always annihilate these wretched Feuillants, those dastardly Moderates who triumph only for the moment.

[1] M. xvi. 500.

It is said that some of the Girondin leaders at last saw their folly and made overtures to Danton.[1] But it was too late. 'They do not trust me,' he said. Further forbearance might have ruined him and could not have saved them. All the 29th and most of the 30th the Sections made preparations for insurrection. On the 30th a friend of Danton's, Rousselin, headed a deputation demanding that the Committee of Twelve should be again suppressed.[2] This, of course, was a constitutional proceeding and justified by events. Even some of the Right had refused to vote with their party when it reversed the suppression of the Committee. Nor did the Committee of Public Safety, on which Danton sat, countenance unconstitutional movements. At midnight it summoned the mayor and the Minister of the Interior to answer for the state of Paris,[3] and Pache assured them that order would be maintained and no disrespect shown to the Assembly. But the conspirators who had met in the old episcopal palace, l'Évêché, ordered the tocsin to be sounded and the gates closed, and at 6 A.M. on the 31st[4] went to the hall of the Commune, ousted the members of it, who were all, or most of them, merely simulating resistance, and then reinstalled Pache, Chaumette, Hébert, and their friends. Much the same comedy was played in the Departmental Council.[5] Then, to complete the parody of August 10, Hanriot was appointed Commander of the National Guards, and received warrants for the arrest of Roland, Clavière, Lebrun, and others.

Meanwhile the Convention had assembled at 6 A.M.[6] Garat came there and recommended as a measure of pacification the suppression of the Committee of Twelve. After him appeared Deputies from the Department, who informed the Assembly that the insurrection was only a 'moral' insurrection. Then came Pache with reassurances, followed by a letter from the officer at the Pont Neuf,

---

[1] M.-T. vii. 297.　　　　　[2] M. xvi. 522.
[3] M. xvi. 523. M.-T. vii. 314.　　[4] M.-T. vii. 315.
[5] M.-T. vii. 3:9.　　　　　[6] M. xvi. 523.

reporting that Hanriot had ordered the alarm-gun to be fired. A hot dispute began at once, silenced for a moment by the ominous roar of the gun. Vergniaud then argued that the question of the Committee should be adjourned till next day, but that Hanriot should be summoned at once. Danton, in opposing him, urged

that the question of the Committee was beyond doubt the most pressing one. It had imprisoned men harshly. He neither accused nor defended it, but the Assembly, on the report of Garat, a man of amiable, impartial nature, had released one of the prisoners. Therefore he demanded not its suppression, but its dissolution. It had been created not for its own purposes but for theirs. If guilty, a terrible example must be made of it as a warning to all who dared refuse respect to the people even when revolutionary to excess. The cannon had thundered, but if it was only a warning— too grim indeed, too clamorous—that all citizens should insist on a striking example being made, Paris had deserved well of the country. His remarks were not addressed to those imbeciles who could only express their own passions, but to men endowed with some political capacity, and he told them that their aim should be to rescue the people from its own rage. The Committee had been so mad as to make fresh arrests. He demanded its dissolution and an inquiry into the conduct of its separate members. They had, in his opinion, been actuated by private animosities. The representatives of the nation should turn to good use the exuberance which bad citizens depicted as so sinister. If any really dangerous men wished to prolong disturbances after justice had been done Paris itself would thrust them back into nothingness. First let them dissolve the Committee, then summon Hanriot.

Those to whom these counsels of Danton may seem hypocritical or in a bad sense demagogic should remember that Vergniaud a little later declared that that day would be a proof how Paris had loved liberty, that order reigned everywhere, that the Sections had deserved well of the country, and should *be invited* to exercise the same surveillance till every plot was unmasked.

It was finally on the proposition of Barère, as spokesman

of the Committee of Public Safety, that the Committee of
Twelve was abolished, and the Assembly also voted two
livres pay *per diem* to all workmen remaining in arms till
order was restored.　And so, at half-past nine on the last
day of May, the long war between the Girondins and the
Mountain seemed ended.　Both had been violent, both
unscrupulous.　But the Girondins had been weak as well as
violent, and lax where their enemies were vigilant.　The
triumph of the Mountain was the survival of the politically
fittest at that time and under those conditions.　Danton had
not raised but had striven to lull the whirlwind.　Failing in
that, he meant to rule it,

CHAPTER XXI

1793—*continued*

MAY 31 had dawned amid universal apprehension. In the afternoon Section confronted Section in arms, and a cannonade and pitched battle in the streets seemed imminent. It closed amid universal embraces and cries of 'Vive la République!' The popular demands were apparently satisfied by the suppression of the Committee of Twelve. The Committee of Safety had procured this concession to the demands of the Commune, but it had taken no notice of the cry for arresting twenty-two of the Right, and to reassure the *bourgeois* element in Paris it procured also the Convention's decree that the force at the command of the Department should be ready to be called out at a moment's notice.[1] It had, in short, acted on Danton's principle of restraining the people from outrage by backing up its reasonable demands, and on June 1 it proposed that a proclamation should be issued, consisting of congratulations on the peaceful termination of the struggle with the Committee of Twelve, of salves to the dignity of the Convention, and of exhortations against intestine discord at a time of national danger.

But the extremists on both sides rose on June 1 in a different frame of mind from that in which they went to bed on May 31, and were each disinclined to listen to the voice of

[1] M.-T. vii. 145.

the charmer. Shame, and relief at not having been arrested, emboldened the Girondins. Anger at being balked of half their revenge actuated the fiercer of the Sections. One of them framed a resolution on the night of the 31st condemning its own leaders—not merely the new Commune but l'Évêché itself—for gross neglect of duty,[1] and demanding the election of a more stalwart revolutionary Committee—this too in spite of the Commune's attempted arrest of Roland. On the other hand, the Girondins professed to believe that Paris disapproved of the movement of the day before, which was the work of only a few conspirators, and cavilled at the Committee of Safety's proclamation.[2] Lasource proposed an amendment ending thus : 'The Convention is on the watch. It will take measures dooming conspirators to shame, contempt, and death ;' on which Barère, who had the Committee of Safety's proclamation in charge, remarked sensibly : 'If I wished to sound the tocsin I should adopt the amendment of Lasource ; if I wished to rally all the Departments to Paris, the address of the Committee.'[3]

The Commune had met at 6 A.M., four hours before the Convention.[4] Certain of its members, Henry and Cavaignac among them, were specially told off to report to it hour by hour what went on in the Convention.[5] Its first act in the early morning was to arrest Madame Roland; its next, to draw up an address to the Sections, which, like that of the Committee of Safety, was self-congratulatory and pacific in its tone. By ten o'clock it had become more bellicose, and withdrew the address for further consideration.[6] At ten the Convention met, and the Commune, informed of its proceedings by Henry and Cavaignac, resolved between one and three o'clock [7] on more drastic measures, listening to the counsels of its *enragés* members, led by Varlet, and turning a deaf ear to one who must have hardly known himself in the character of

[1] M.-T. vii. 358.   [2] M.-T. vii. 363.   [3] M.-T. vii. 366.
[4] M. xvi. 541.   M.-T. vii. 358.   [5] M.-T. vii. 323, 367.
[6] M. xvi. 542.   [7] M. xvi. 542.

'Moderate'—Hébert.   By three o'clock these measures were shaped into a new address to be sent to the Assembly that evening.[1]   Then the Commune adjourned till five.

On its reassembling the address was read over and a deputation of twelve appointed to take it.   But before they started it was announced that the Convention had risen at six o'clock.[2]   Just then Pache came in and said that he, with Marat, had interviewed the Committee of Safety and found it unequivocally anxious for order, and that it had promised to summon the Convention to meet again that evening.[3]   For such a decision there was much to be said.   The Convention had purposely risen at six o'clock in order to avoid receiving the address.[4]   This was a poor trick to play in such circumstances, and especially calculated to disgust a man like Danton. It infuriated Marat.   He urged the people to go themselves with the address and not come away till it was conceded. Probably the Committee of Safety got wind of this counsel, which was a breach of faith on Marat's part, because its promise had been coupled with 'unequivocal' stipulations for order, whereas his words were a direct incitement to disorder. In any case it did not fulfil its promise.[5]   But at the sound of the tocsin about one hundred members came to the Assembly at nine o'clock.[6]   Immediately afterwards came the deputation from the Commune with its address.   The helpless Convention practically threw itself on the mercy of the Committee of Safety by declaring that in three days it should report on the best means of defending the Republic at home and abroad, and on the cases of the members denounced by the Commune, the Commune to lay before it all evidence.   At half-past twelve the session ended.   But the session of the Commune did not end.   Enraged at the Convention's dilatory tactics, it spent all that night in mustering its force of *sans-culottes* and arranging for their pay and subsistence next day.   Its General

[1] M. xvi. 542.   [2] *Ibid.*   M.-T. vii. 367.
[3] M. xvi. 542.   [4] M.-T. vii. 367.
[5] M.-T. vii. 373.   [6] *Ibid.*

Council met at nine in the morning, and at once proceeded to draw up an ultimatum.[1] The Convention met an hour later.

No stranger spectacle has ever, perhaps, been presented by a great city than that of Paris on this Sunday, June 2, 1793. The extraordinary system of balanced authority resulting from the revolt against Monarchy had culminated in practical anarchy. Paris was in presence of the Convention, the Comité de Salut, the Executive Ministry, the Commune, the Central Revolutionary Council. The Convention, nominally supreme, had devolved all responsibility on the Committee of Safety. The Committee of Safety's sole power might almost be said to consist in Danton's personal influence with the revolutionary party. Two of the Ministers were actually under arrest, yet permitted to carry on their official functions provisionally, Clavière till June 13 and Lebrun till the 21st. The Commune was divided against itself, Chaumette tearing his hair and protesting against the ultra-revolutionary measures of the Central Council as contra-revolutionary. And that Central Council had also its less extreme and its more extreme members. The only point of union, in fact, was hostility to the Girondin Twenty-two. They were foredoomed by Isnard's madness. There was a sort of tacit compact between the *bourgeoisie* and the mob that if there were no pillage, and no second 2nd of September, the obnoxious Deputies were to be got rid of.

Danton was in much the same position and acted much in the same way as in September. It is absurd, as he said himself, to suspect him of any desire to humiliate the Convention. The most glorious moments of his life had been within its precincts. To this day he is known by the name of '*le grand conventionnel*,' a name indicating where now was the centre of his fame and strength. Nor did he desire revenge on the Twenty-two. But between their own half-rash, half-craven fatuities, and the relentless rancour of the Ultras, he

<hr>

[1] M.-T. vii. 378-80.

instinctively steered a middle course. As in September, so now the situation in Paris was dominated by events on the frontiers. This very morning of June 2 came tidings after tidings of disaster or alarm from La Vendée, from Finistère, from Lozère, from Cantal, from Lyons. Nothing seemed more certain than that if street-fighting once began in Paris it would end only in the entry of the allies and the dismemberment of France. Amid all this fury of party it was of that larger danger that he thought most. To save France he might have even sacrificed his friends. To shield his bitter enemies at the peril of France would have been, in his eyes, criminal lunacy So, as the only possible compromise, he acquiesced in the Committee of Safety's suggestion that the Twenty-two should 'voluntarily' resign their seats. He may have even proposed it, for his repeated offers and acts of self-effacement show the too sanguine faith he placed in magnanimous example. On this very occasion Garat had proposed at the Committee of Safety that the most bitter opponents on both sides in the Convention should offer to leave it in order to promote peace. Danton started up, with his eyes full of tears, and said : 'I will go to the Convention and propose it, and offer to go, myself first, to Bordeaux as a hostage for the arrested members.' In the Convention, however, the idea leaked out before anyone made the offer from the rostrum, and Robespierre covered it with ridicule as a snare laid against the Republic.[1] The offer was actually made, however, by Danton and all the other members of the Committee of Safety on the 6th.[2] But Robespierre spoke against it. Pétion and Barbaroux wrote against its acceptance, and it came to nothing.[3] To Marat the Committee's suggestion did not commend itself. With more logic than wisdom he contended that accused conspirators ought not to be invited to pose as martyrs. '*C'est à moi*' (he said), '*vrai martyr de la liberté, à me dévouer*' !

While the suggestion was being discussed the crowd outside grew more threatening. Delacroix, Danton's friend,

----

[1] M. xvi. 592.　　[2] M. xvi. 585-6.　　[3] M. xvi. 587.

protested against its violence, and Danton said that the
Committee of Safety would 'avenge vigorously the national
majesty, now being outraged.'   Delacroix then obtained a vote
from the Convention ordering the armed men intruding themselves into the Assembly to quit its precincts.   The order was
taken to Hanriot, who sent back a flat refusal, couched, it is
alleged, in brutal terms.   At last the frightened and wearied
Assembly decreed the arrest of all except two of the members
of the Committee of Twelve, of the Ministers Lebrun and
Clavière, and of twenty-two members of the Right.[1]

Meanwhile the Committee of Safety had sent for Pache
and Hanriot.   All, or almost all, its members were distressed
at the day's events.[2]   Cambon charged Bouchotte with
connivance.   'Minister of War,' he said, 'we are not blind.
I see very well that your subordinates have had a hand in all
this.'   Delacroix appeared embarrassed, as a man who has won
without winning much glory.   Danton seemed uneasy and
ashamed.   When Pache came he brought with him two of the
Insurrectional Committee, who declared its readiness to
resign the powers given it by the Sections.   This was accepted.
But Hanriot did not come.   He sent an aide-de-camp, and his
disrespect indicated the impotence, materially, of the Committee
of Safety.   All the physical force of Paris was, as Garat says,
enlisted on the side of the insurrection.   No doubt Danton
was ashamed of some of the occurrences of the day.   But he
was not ashamed of or sorry for its net results.   There had
been no bloodshed.   He said in September that Hanriot,
'with eyes vomiting saltpetre,' had prevented the sacrifice of
30,000 lives.   But the majority which any day might have
reimposed some Committee of Twelve was broken up.   He
was free to replace the two ejected Ministers by his own
friends.   We may discredit St. Just, on the one hand, who
charged him with having demanded Hanriot's head, and
Barère, on the other, who said he wrote with his own hand in

[1] M.-T. vii. 418.

[2] See Garat's account in his *Mémoires sur la Révolution*.

the committee-room of Public Safety the petition which the
Commune sent to the Convention on May 31.   There was
nothing to tempt him to the one step or the other.   He
approved of the insurrection just so far as it checkmated an
arbitrary majority.   His speeches in the Convention no doubt
inspired and encouraged those who brought it about.   He
considered, with another national leader of our own day, that
'a true revolutionary movement should partake both of a
constitutional and an illegal character.   It should be an open
and a secret organisation, using the Constitution for its own
purposes, but also taking advantage of its secret combinations.'[1]
He took one course in the Convention, l'Évêché another in
the streets.   It seems improbable that they had in common
anything except a common foe.

[1] B. O'Brien's *Life of Parnell*.

CHAPTER XXII

1793—*continued*

IN the middle of all these stormy scenes Danton married his
second wife, Mademoiselle Sophie Gély.[1] There is a story
that his first wife had recommended the marriage. Other
stories represent her successor as the owner of a pretty face,
and of aristocratic leanings, who, after her husband's execution,
was ashamed of his name.[2] Still other stories represent him as
so 'molten down in mere uxoriousness' as to have lost energy
for public affairs. Whatever else may be true, that at least is
false. Never in all his life was he more energetic. He was on
the Committee of Safety and on the Constitution Committee.
This meant that in these early days of June he had to work
day and night. On the 10th eager demands were made for
the draft of the new Constitution. Thuriot pleaded for one
more hour, saying, '*Le comité a passé la nuit à l'achèvement
de son travail.*' As member of the Committee of Safety he
had to attend to the report on the arrest of the members, to
the disturbances in the Departments, and to all the letters from
arrested Deputies, which, with other matters innumerable, the
Convention placed in the Committee's hands. Thus on June

---

[1] June 17 or June 4. *Homme d'État*, p. 133.

[2] Villiaumé, however, *Hist. de la Rév. Fr.* b. xvi., says that she retained a profound respect for Danton's memory.

3 we find the Convention adopting the Committee's schemes for the formation of a company of national artillery in every Department, for sending three companies from Paris to the Pyrenees, for sending Robert Lindet to Lyons, for indemnifying the people of Nantes for loss inflicted by the rebels, and so on. Of an easy, indolent disposition, and averse to drudgery, Danton could display enormous energy at a crisis. He did so now. He was still chief Tribune of Paris, and he controlled the foreign policy of France.

The Committee of Safety dated from April 7. As the supreme executive power, with secret-service money at its disposal, it was responsible only to the Convention. And as it deliberated in secret it was to a great extent responsible only nominally. There were other influential men in it, such as Cambon, Barère, Robert Lindet, and Delacroix. Cambon and Lindet were concerned with finance and home affairs, Delacroix and Delmas with the war, Danton and Barère with foreign affairs. But Danton was indubitably its ruling spirit. He sat in it for three months, and for that space it may be said, roughly, that he governed France. A detailed description of events at Paris in April and May was indispensable in order to comprehend his position and character, but it is time now to see what was his policy in the wider sphere which he had already occupied for two months.

The revolt of La Vendée was perhaps his first anxiety. The people there had originally favoured the Revolution.[1] The suppression of the old taxes and the militia filled them with enthusiasm. But they were attached to their priests, who during 1791 and 1792, sowed discontent and disaffection at nocturnal meetings into which Royalist agents gradually insinuated themselves.[2] After Jemmapes was won they were disgusted by the propagandist war. New imposts took the place of old taxes, and when the conscription was being enforced in March 1793 the storm broke. It was never really

---

[1] S. iii. 374.　　　[2] S. iii. 375.

a Royalist, and only partly a religious, movement. Its main-spring was disinclination to military service on the frontier. Of the Royalist element in it Danton had experience when he was Minister of Justice. Informed by spies of the details of La Rouarie's conspiracy, he ordered him to be arrested, and, though La Rouarie himself died, the papers he left behind were, in March 1793, dug up in a garden by Morillon, whom Danton had set to watch the movement.[1] Thanks to his vigilance, therefore, the Committee of Safety was, as far as La Vendée was concerned, forearmed. There could be no two policies there. It was in rebellion, and the rebellion had to be put down. So had the Girondin resistance now hatching in the south and north. These two were simple if disagreeable problems to be solved. What made the situation of France well-nigh desperate was their coincidence with the disastrous state of the armies. That of Dumouriez was in retreat, dis-organised, suspicious of its officers, without supplies.[2] The armies of the Rhine were in a similar condition. The army of the Moselle numbered only 25,000 men. And now in June, when between sixty and seventy Departments were in revolt against the Government,[3] when Marseilles, Lyons, Toulon, Montpellier, Bordeaux, Nantes were all in arms, and the allies were advancing on the eastern frontiers, the Paris Government seemed shrivelling up in a girdle of fire. To save it Danton resorted to two expedients, public disavowal of the war of propaganda and the *levée en masse.* The second of these measures he had conceived gradually. '*Il faut dire à la France entière, si vous ne volez pas au secours,*' &c., he said on March 8 ; '*Marchons t.us,*' on the 10th ; '*Que dira donc ce peuple ? Car il est prêt à se lever en masse,*' on the 27th ; '*La France entière va s'ébranler,*' on May 8.

His subsequent declarations, after he had quitted the Committee, were merely repetitions of the same idea. '*Il faut que la nation entière marche,*' he said on August 1. He devised

---

[1] Lenox's *Danton,* c. 14.   [2] S. iii. 373.

[3] Meillan, quoted by Lenox, p. 223, says 72.

the idea. His voice instilled it into the Convention. And though the conscripts who were the fruit of it did not win Hondschoote [1] or Wattignies it nevertheless contributed to those victories by ' its powerful moral effect, the soldiers feeling that the whole nation was its rear-guard.' [2] It transformed France into an armed camp. It made the revolt of La Vendée hopeless. It saved the Republic.

His other expedient, though less imposingly efficient, re-entitled France to the comity of nations. Selfishness had prompted intrigues with her hitherto, but she could not but be regarded by foreign Governments as a rabid wild animal while she proclaimed universal war. Danton had not been a week on the Committee when he reduced her pretensions to reasonable limits. These were his words on April 13 :—

It is time that the National Convention should make it known to Europe that France knows how to combine with republican virtues statesmanship. In a moment of enthusiasm you passed a decree, the motive of which was certainly noble, since you bound yourselves to protect nations resisting their tyrants. This decree would logically imply an obligation to assist an insurrection in China. . . . Let us pass a resolution that we will not meddle with our neighbours' affairs, but that anyone proposing to treat with other nations which refuse to acknowledge the Republic shall be punished with death.

The severity of the last sentence meant nothing. It was merely a rhetorical artifice so constantly resorted to by Danton for silver-coating the main thesis which many of his audience would find so unpalatable. Among them was Robespierre, who had just advocated the more sweeping sentence of ' death on anyone proposing to treat with the enemy,' and who on the 24th attempted to reinvolve the Assembly in a hazier atmosphere by declaring all men citizens of one State. But in Robespierre's eyes the Revolution was only in its infancy. The reign of the Saints and of one arch-Saint was to be its final outcome. To end it prematurely would be to nip nascent

---

[1] M.-T. viii. 366.   [2] Michelet, b. xiii. c. ii.

'virtue' in the bud. Danton, on the contrary, had learnt much from the popular reaction against France in Belgium and on the Rhine, from the revolt against conscription in La Vendée, from the danger to the Republic which a military adventurer like Dumouriez might threaten. He wished 'to arrest anarchy, to reconstitute the State, to convert the Rights of Man into a reality and the Republic into a government, to procure peace, to give security to industry.'[1] *Hâtons-nous, mes amis,'* he said, *' hâtons-nous de terminer la Révolution. Ceux qui font les révolutions trop longues ne sont pas ceux qui en jouissent.'*

In order to procure peace he thought he must procure allies. It is impossible to lay a finger on this or that negotiation and say he prompted it. But in April Lebrun, the Foreign Minister, became merely his subordinate, and in June was under arrest, and Deforgues, his successor, was Danton's protégé.[2] . So that all the foreign policy of France was in his hands. What that policy was is to be found in an instruction to representatives on mission issued in May 1793.[3] They were to demand from foreign Courts as essentials, recognition of the Republic, non-interference in the government of France, abandonment of the *émigrés,* and, in the case of Austria, surrender of the Commissioners seized by Dumouriez. They were to bear in mind that the Republic was intended to resume its old proportions, though for the present compelled by prudence to occupy certain territories. It would attempt a rectification of frontier by indemnities or exchange. It would oppose Austria's exchanging Belgium for Bavaria, but would not oppose the creation of a species of stadtholderate. It would not consent to the partition of Poland, but hoped active intervention might be avoided. It would not restore Savoy and Nice, but would compensate Piedmont by means of a redistribution of the Estates of the Pope, who was to be left simple Bishop of Rome. Lastly, in spite of the bitter hostility of England, attempts were to be made to come to terms.

[1] S. iii. 383-4.   [2] S. iii. 425.

[3] S. iii. 395.

To attain these ends it was hoped that Sweden, Denmark, and Turkey might be induced to form an alliance with the Republic, and that some members of the coalition might, by skilful diplomacy and the lavish use of secret-service money, be induced to withdraw. Alliance with Turkey proved as visionary as Polish freedom or friendship with England. Sweden, however, preserved a benevolent neutrality, and the old suspicious jealousy between Prussia and Austria was rekindled. To carry on this diplomatic campaign a crowd of agents was despatched to the capitals of Europe,[1] and their efforts might have been more positively successful but for the jealousies of the Paris factions, which rendered foreign Courts dubious whether agreements would be binding.

Danton, moreover, was hampered by his own past. His true character was beginning to be known even to foreigners. '*J'ai entendu,*' wrote Baron d'Esebeck, '*tellement vanter votre justice et votre humanité que je me jette dans vos bras.*'[2] And under the same impression the friends of Marie Antoinette hoped to stir him to save her from the guillotine.[3] But though '*l'amour de l'ordre, de la justice et de l'humanité*' were '*les véritables sentiments de son cœur,*' and '*il voulait garder toute sa popularité pour ramener avec l'adresse le peuple au respect du sang et des lois,*' he was still forced by the exigencies of his position to appear '*barbare pour garder toute sa popularité,*'[4] to be, as Gambetta afterwards said was necessary to govern the French, 'violent in language' while 'moderate in acts,' and it was hard to believe that the same man was in earnest in hoping for peace even with Austria,[5] who still breathed nothing but defiance to the invader and had so long seemed to be the incarnation of the militant genius of France.

Such incredulity was not lessened by the vigour infused by the Committee of Safety into the armies, which when it was appointed, and necessarily for a considerable time afterwards, were thoroughly demoralised. The Army of the Pyrenees was

[1] S. iii. 417.   [2] S. iii. 422.   [3] S. iii. 423.
[4] Garat's *Mémoires*, p. 192.   [5] S. iii. 425.

beaten by the Spaniards. The Army of Italy was disorganised. The army of Dumouriez was in retreat. One general, Keller-mann, was under a cloud ; another, Biron, was suspected and transferred to the West; another, Dampierre, was killed in action. The officers of the Army of the North were of doubtful loyalty. To restore discipline, to prevent treason, to infuse fresh spirit into the soldiers, Commissioners were sent to all the armies. They were on the whole able and strong men who did their work well. Gradually, as the effects of the Commit-tee's sway became felt, the troops recovered confidence, and out of their ranks sprang men like Hoche and Pichegru and the great captains of Napoleon.

In all this work of restoration Danton shared, and over and above this he roused France to the *levée en masse*, without which it might have been all to no purpose. He was no longer in office when the ebb of defeat became the flow of conquest, but as in 1792 so in 1793, to him more than any man the turn of the tide was due.

CHAPTER XXIII

1793—*continued*

ALIENS—ILLITERATE VOTERS—SPEECH IN CONVENTION—VIEWS ON
WHOLESALE PUNISHMENT, OFFENSIVE WAR, RIGHT OF SPEECH—
ATTACKED AT THE JACOBINS—NOT RE-ELECTED ON COMMITTEE
OF SAFETY—DESMOULINS ATTACKS THE COMMITTEE—DANTON'S
LOYALTY TO IT—ITS DIFFICULTIES—CUSTINE—DANTON PROPOSES
A PROVISIONAL GOVERNMENT—DEFENDS GARAT—OPPOSES INDIS-
CRIMINATE ARREST—ON CONSCRIPTION, REQUISITION, DESERTERS

THE Constitution which its framers were so eager to hurry into,
existence as all-important for the pacification of the country
became by the irony of circumstance almost at the outset a
dead letter,[1] though acceptance or non-acceptance of it was a
convenient shibboleth for testing the loyalty of the Departments.
Till rebellion was quelled the one thing needful was by any
means, constitutional or unconstitutional, '*diriger Paris sur la
Vendée,*' '*former une armée centrale de réserve pour rétablir la
paix intérieure.*' But Danton, knowing the importance of
keeping a cheerful countenance, was careful to assume that
France as a whole was with Paris.   In pursuance of his previous
assertions 'that all the Departments execrated dastardly
Moderatism' he refused to accept the intrigues of a portion of
Bordeaux as representing the whole city, or admit that the
nation would embark on civil war for a few Deputies.   And
with his usual common-sense he would not assent to a panic-
stricken proposal for the banishment of aliens.   'Alien

---

[1] It was actually suspended, on St. Just's proposal, Oct. 10.

intriguers should be banished,' he said, 'but it would be un-wise to impoverish their own population and commerce. There were aliens settled and domiciled in France better patriots than numbers of Frenchmen born.'

Equally sensible was the way he cut the knot as to the mode in which illiterate citizens should vote in the primary assemblies. 'What was wanted was free expression of opinion. Let every man vote as he pleased, orally or by signing his name, the rich man being empowered to write, the poor man to speak.' This has been condemned as an anarchical proposal, but short of modern ballot-box devices how better could he have reconciled conflicting opinions ?

On June 13 he made one of those inspiring appeals to the Assembly which, on the principle that

> The word that moves a nation's heart
> Is in itself a deed,

made his friends think 'the acquisition of him worth an army.'

We are at this moment laying the real foundation of French liberty by giving France a republican Constitution. At the birth of anything great it is with political as with physical bodies, they are threatened with imminent dissolution. Storms surround us. The thunder rolls. But out of its explosions shall emerge the work which will be the glory of the French nation. Remember, citizens, what happened at the time of Lafayette's conspiracy. We seemed in the same position as to-day—patriots everywhere trampled on, everywhere proscribed, menaced with the greatest ills, in perils such as seem the inevitable lot of men who engender liberty. Lafayette and his faction were soon unmasked. To-day new enemies of the people have betrayed themselves, fugitives as they are with false names, false descriptions, false passports. This Brissot, this corypheus of the patricidal gang which is about to be extinguished, who boasted of his bravery and his poverty while he accused me of rolling in riches, is now only a wretch unable to escape the sword of the law, and already condemned to arrest by the people as a conspirator. They talk of the insurrection in Paris causing movements in the Departments. I declare before the universe that what happened there will be the glory of our superb city. I proclaim before France that but for the guns, but for the insurrection of the 31st of May, the conspirators would have triumphed, would have been our masters. On our heads be the guilt of that insurrection. I invoked it myself when I said that if there were in the Convention another hundred like me we would resist oppression, we would found liberty on a basis which nothing could destroy. Remember that you have been told that the agitation in the Departments only arose after the events in Paris. On the contrary, there is documentary proof that the Departments issued a circular inciting to federation and combination before the 31st. What remained for us to do? To identify ourselves with the people of Paris, with all good citizens ; to tell the story of what had taken place. You know that I more than any man have been threatened with bayonets pointed at my breast. You know that I have sheltered at my own peril men who thought themselves in danger. But it was not the people of Paris who had any design on the liberty of their representatives. They assumed an attitude worthy of them. They rose in insurrection.   Be not alarmed at the manifestos of the Departments calumniating Paris. They are the work of a handful of intriguers, not of the citizens. Remember that others like them supported the Tyrant against Paris. Paris is the centre where everything converges. Paris will be the focus in which all rays of French patriotism will concentrate, and it will shrivel with them all our enemies. I appeal for a loyal understanding about this insurrection, which has had such happy results. The people see that the men accused of wishing to gorge themselves with their blood have done more in the last eight days for their good than the Convention, tormented by intriguers, has been able to do ever since it came into existence. Those are the results which you must make patent to the men of the Departments. They are honest men ; they will applaud your wise measures. The criminals in flight have spread terror everywhere they have gone. They have exaggerated everything, magnified everything. But the re-action of the people when undeceived will be all the stronger, and they will avenge themselves on their deceivers. As to the question now before us, I am of opinion that measures must be taken in all the Departments. Twenty-four hours' grace should be given to all officials who may have been misled ; to those who mislead them, none. In Departments where patriot communes are struggling with an official aristocracy

these officials should be displaced and true republicans placed
in their room. Finally I appeal for a declaration by the
Convention that there would have been an end of liberty if
there had been no insurrection on May 31.

Citizens, no weakness ! Make this solemn declaration to
the French people : that this horde of scoundrels which desired
the restoration of the nobles had no desire for a Constitution.
Bid them choose between this faction and the Mountain.
Say to Frenchmen : ' Resume your indefeasible rights. Range
yourselves round the Convention. Prepare to accept the
Constitution about to be offered to you, the Constitution
which, as I have said already, is a battery to rain on the
enemy bullet-showers which will destroy them all. Prepare an
army, but an army against the enemy in La Vendée. Stifle
the rebellion there and you will have peace.' When once the
people are informed of this last phase of our revolution they
will no more allow themselves to be beguiled ; they will listen
no more to calumnies against a city which engendered liberty,
which will triumph with liberty, and with liberty will be
immortal.

But though he blew a trumpet-blast of this kind when he
meant to encourage his own party and overawe any waverers
of the Plain he continued to draw a distinction between
masses and individuals, insisting that punishment should
always, if possible, be confined to the latter. When it was
proposed to treat as traitors two battalions of the Gironde
which had expressed a wish to go home from the army, he
argued that it was not the battalions but a few seditious
members of them that should be punished, and that the
Minister of War should be left to deal with the case ; that it
was unwise to denounce whole battalions or to declare whole
Departments rebels. And he proposed that every primary
assembly should send two armed men to Paris to form a
central army of reserve—a shrewd mode of raising troops and
obtaining hostages at one stroke.

Equally shrewd were the views he expressed in the debates
on the Constitution with regard to offensive war and
declaration of war.

Offensive wars they renounced, but when a neighbouring nation was making preparations for war, taking aim, so to speak, it would be absurd to abstain from firing first, from occupying the territory of others for a time, or from taking any measures dictated by self-preservation and not lust of empire.

As to declaring war,

it would be suicidal to forbid the Executive taking preliminary steps of precaution, and even at once attacking another nation assuming the offensive, but that ought not to prevent the people being convoked to decide on continuing or ending the war.

When Marat was assassinated, and Fauchet was denounced as Charlotte Corday's accomplice at the Jacobins, Danton, while expressing his own opinion of the man, urged that he should be allowed to speak before being condemned. This may have been considered by his enemies as one sign of many showing that he was becoming a 'Moderate,' and mutterings began to be heard at the Jacobins, where jealousy of the Convention was rife, that he was keeping aloof too much from their meetings. At last, on it being publicly stated that he had recommended a suspected person to the Minister of Marine, he thought it necessary to defend himself. After explaining the facts of the case he said—

The necessary result of my being chained to the Committee of Safety is that men with their own petty interests to serve have been let loose against me, circulating a quantity of small scandal absolutely without foundation, which finds credence only with the weak-minded or those who lend too ready an ear to it.[1]

A few weeks later, on an attack being made upon the Commissioners of the Convention, he told the Club 'that it should only present itself to the Convention to proclaim something important and novel which would result in useful discussion and salutary legislation.'[2]

[1] *Journal de la Montagne* quoted by Bougeart, p. 268.
[2] *Ibid.* Bougeart, p. 285.

This was subsequent to the reconstitution of the Committee of Public Safety on July 10. Danton on that day was not re-elected. The proposal for reconstitution was made by a member not named by the Moniteur, but it was supported in a bitter speech by Camille Desmoulins, who charged the Committee with gross incapacity. Camille Desmoulins was by nature disputatious. Politics interested him mainly as sub-ject-matter for logomachy. He liked to lecture other people—a friend, perhaps, by choice—was hardly happy when not wrangling, and was addicted to cramming his sense of infalli-bility, inspired by his own pamphlets, down his neighbour's throat. But he would hardly have assailed Danton personally, and may have even thought that if the pack were shuffled it would leave his friend with a better hand. It was, in fact, elicited from him afterwards that, as his manner was, he had been making a personal retort under cover of a patriot's anxiety, and was in reality assailing an individual member of the Committee—Delmas—one of the two members whose special duty it was to attend to the army and the war. Danton, moreover, newly married, and for months immersed in harassing toil, may have preferred a less onerous dignity in prospect and have let it be known he did not seek re-election. For, as Marat said, '*ses inclinations naturelles l'emportent loin de toute idée de domination.*'[1] Or, again, those who were angry at Camille's speech may have revenged themselves on his friend in concert with those levelling Jacobins who bore Danton a grudge. But if so, and if they thought he was assuming airs of superiority, why did they not prevent his election to the presidency of the Assembly on the 25th?[2]

In any case Danton neither showed any resentment nor changed his tone in the Convention. He knew, if Camille did not, the enormous difficulties with which the Committee had to contend, difficulties not to be surmounted in a month or two, and not the more easy to surmount while incessant reports were being required from it by the Convention. The

<hr>

[1] Bougeart, p. 265.   [2] M. xvii. 234.

revolt of the great southern towns, Marseilles, Lyons, Bordeaux, Montpellier, Grenoble, Toulon; of Caen and Evreux in the north; the capture of Saumur and Angers by the Royalists in the west; of Condé, Mayence, and Valenciennes by the allies; victories of the Spanish invaders and of the Prince of Orange; the siege of Dunkirk; the Girondin General Wimpfen's threat that he would visit Paris with 60,000 men, were perils all of which confronted the Committee during June and July. And at the end of July, Custine, general of the Army of the North, who had obtained leave to come to Paris, was accused of treason. Danton did not join in the gossiping charges brought against him, but he said it was plain something must be done at once, for the Army of the North must have a general, and that the Minister of War and the Committee ought immediately to examine into the charges.

Such an event, occurring at a crisis so momentous, was probably the immediate cause of his speech on August 1, in which he advocated the increase of the Committee's power. After saying that 'there would be no success till, remembering that the Committee was the fruit of freedom and what good work it had already done, they developed its capabilities to the maximum,' he proceeded thus :—

This Coburg who is marching into your territory is doing the Republic excellent service. What happened last year is repeating itself to-day. The same dangers menace us. But the people—for it has accepted the Constitution—is as vigorous as ever; I swear it by the sublime enthusiasm we have just witnessed. By this very act of acceptation it has bound itself to burst forth in its whole volume against the enemy. Therefore let us make war like lions. Why do we not institute a provisional Government to second by powerful measures the national energy ? [1]

He went on to protest

that he himself would not enter a Committee with such extended powers, preferring to remain independent and in a position to

----

[1] M. xvii. 295.

spur on the Government unceasingly. But if they heeded him they would turn the Committee into a provisional Government and the Ministers into its subordinates, its head clerks ; would supply it lavishly with funds, for a vast expenditure in the cause of liberty would be merely money put out at interest, and without a host of agents they would be unable to contend against Pitt on equal terms; would therefore place 50,000,000 francs at the Committee's absolute disposal, yes, to be expended if it. thought fit, on a single day; would, as soon as the harvest was over, muster the whole nation, of which the enemy had only as yet seen the advanced guard, which was chafing at inaction, which longed to hear the tocsin summoning it to arms ; would order returns to be made of all grain in the country and all arms ; and would allot to the Committee 100,000,000 francs more for guns and muskets and pikes ; and in every town of any size not an anvil should be struck but in forging weapons of war. They were at least rid of intriguers now, and the enemy could no longer, like Dumouriez, boast that half the Convention was at his beck. The people had faith in them and they should be worthy of its confidence, for if their weakness stood in its way it would save itself and they would be disgraced for ever.

In advocating a vast expenditure Danton preached what he had practised, having on June 2 sent Deforgues to see if a golden salve of 250,000 francs would heal the eruption in Calvados,[1] and on some members now declining pecuniary responsibility he added

that public men must not fear calumny, that while solemnly pledging himself never to be a member of the Committee which he was suggesting he had not shrunk from such responsibility in 1792, when singly he supplied the momentum which sent the nation to the frontiers, and when he had said, ‘ Let them calumniate me. What does it matter? Though my name should be disgraced I will save liberty ’; but that the 50,000,000 francs might be deposited at the national treasury and drawn from only by order of the committee.

This speech produced a great sensation in the Assembly, but Robespierre opposed it and Danton's proposals were referred

[1] Michelet, b. xii. c. i.

to the Committee of Safety for consideration.   The idea, however, rapidly took root.   Within a fortnight the Committee had
accepted the 50 millions from which it shrank on the 1st, and
its autocracy practically dates from that day.[1]

On August 5 Danton left the Chair to interpose generously
and successfully in behalf of Garat, Minister of the Interior,
who, having been arrested and summoned to the bar of the
House, was assailed by Collot d'Herbois.[2]   As the rescued
Minister passed by the Chair, Danton whispered to him, 'Write
a perfectly simple circular.   Throw your literary production
into the fire.   Reserve all that for history.'   The incident is
illustrative of the character of the two men, and Danton's
estimate of Garat, '*Il aime la Révolution*,' '*il a montré de la
faiblesse*,' has been endorsed by history.

On the 12th he again interfered on the side of moderation.
A Deputy belonging to the six thousand members of the
Primary Assemblies, who had come to Paris for the national
fête, called on the Assembly to decree a *levée en masse*, and at
the same time seize all suspects, enrol them, send them to the
frontiers, and there place them in the forefront of the battle.
In his usual fashion when about to attenuate too Draconic
proposals Danton began with some generalities to which no
Draco could take exception.

The Deputies have just suggested 'terror' towards the
enemy within our gates.   Shall we disappoint them?   No!
No amnesty for any traitor !   Honest men do not favour knaves.
Let us signalise the people's vengeance by summary punishment of domestic traitors, but let us try and turn this memorable day to account.   You have been told that the *levée en
masse* is wanted ; and so assuredly it is, but it should be made
in an orderly way.

He went on to suggest that the Deputies of the Primary
Assemblies should, each man of them, incite twenty others to
come in arms and enlist, that they should be invested with
authority to make inventories of arms, food, and munitions of

---

[1] Michelet, b. xiii. c. i.   [2] M. xvii. 304.

war, to enrol forty thousand recruits for the armies of the North, and to announce the Constitution to the enemy by cannon-shot. And he felt sure, he said, that the Deputies, of whose energy he had seen many proofs, would swear to rouse their fellow citizens to action when they went home.

The enthusiasm with which this sagacious appeal was received pledged each Deputy to a missionary zeal for the conscription. Taking advantage of it the orator insinuated counsels of moderation. He demanded

the arrest of all persons suspected—*justly*—but this should be done more circumspectly than hitherto, when, instead of seizing great criminals, real conspirators, men who were less than insignificant were arrested. It would never do to send them to the armies, where they would be more dangerous than useful. Let them be confined and kept as hostages.

In this characteristic speech he advocated moderation, but for men shirking their share of the war's burdens either in purse or person he had no indulgence. Of the rich he said—

If the tyrants were getting the better of us we should surpass them in daring, should devastate French soil before they could traverse it, and the rich, vile egotists that they are, would be the first victims of the people's wrath. You, who hear me, report what I say to the rich men of your communes. Say to them, 'What are you hoping for?' See what would happen if France were overrun. On the most favourable supposition you would have an imbecile's regency, a minor's rule, the ambition of foreign Powers, the partition of the land, eating up your property ; you would lose more as serfs than by all the sacrifices you could make to maintain yourselves free.

And then he insisted on the agents of the Primary Assemblies being authorised to enforce conscription and requisitions vigorously.

For soldiers wishing to quit the service when every man was wanted he advocated not the blind sentence proposed against the men of Bordeaux, but still stern severity.

Any citizen deserting the flag before someone has been found to take his place should be punished with death.

Equally stern was the view he took of the conduct of the merchant-princes of Marseilles, who had

exulted in the abasement of their priests and nobles in the hope of getting fat on their wealth, and had then basely turned against the Revolution, to which they owed that wealth. They should be treated like those priests and nobles and pay the penalty of their treason with confiscation or death.

Having said so much to urge on the *levée en masse*, he warned the Committee to beware

of its being abused or misused. It should be regulated methodically, and men should not be concentrated unless where they could be properly organised. By all means have numbers, but only efficient numbers, directed to points where they were imperatively needed; not a mere herd which it might be impossible to equip, to feed, or to employ properly. But, lest enthusiasm should be damped by delay, instant measures should be taken for the proper provision of a force amply sufficient for all contingencies,

CHAPTER XXIV

1793—continued

DISINTERESTEDNESS OF DANTON DAMAGING TO HIM—EFFECTS OF
MARAT'S MURDER AND CAPTURE OF TOULON—SCARCITY IN PARIS—
DANTON'S ISOLATION—GARAT'S INTERVIEW WITH HIM—THE MAXI-
MUM—'SANS-CULOTTE' ARMY—DANTON'S SPEECH—HE SUPPORTS
COMMITTEE OF SAFETY—HIS SPEECH ON THE WAR IN LA VENDÉE
—HÉBERT—ILLNESS—RETIREMENT TO ARCIS

THOUGH the Revolutionary Tribunal was only, as Danton
said, the 'least bad' remedy, when France was honeycombed
with Royalist and Girondin disaffection, it was beyond all
doubt efficacious, having, in fact, all the force of a civilian
court-martial. Equally efficacious for the national defence
was the *levée en masse*, the dictatorship of the Committee of
Safety, and, taken as a whole, the missions of members of the
Convention to the armies. If the speeches quoted in previous
chapters prove anything, it is that it was always for France
Danton was thinking as he urged these measures, and not for
himself. He might flatter Paris, he might parley with men he
disliked, he might court popularity, but it was for public not
personal ends.

Such disinterested patriotism placed him at a terrible dis-
advantage amid the bitter rivalries and selfish ambitions by
which he was surrounded in September. He had come into
collision with Robespierre, and, worse offence still in Robespierre's eyes, he had shielded him with his own popularity.
He had come into collision with the Hébertists, who professed
to look on him as a 'Moderate.' He was suspected, and on
good grounds, of being opposed to the execution of the
Girondins. He was suspected on slenderer evidence of wishing

to spare Marie Antoinette.[1] At the very moment when his policy seemed on the verge of success two events occurred which robbed him of the power to control the vast engine which he had set in motion, the stupid murder of Marat on July 12 and the betrayal of Toulon to the English in August. His most insidious peril arose out of the '*terra incognita au delà de Marat.*' Marat had always admired Danton, and when their formidable leader had fallen, the rest of the pack with whom he himself, had he lived, would have had to fight, sprang at once at the nobler quarry. Marat's murder, too, begat murder, sealing the fate of the Girondins and the Queen, and reawakening all the worst passions of the Revolution.

On the other hand, the capture of Toulon revived the hopes of the Royalists. They could not conceal their transports. They sang derisive songs about the *levée en masse* and applauded anti-revolutionary sentiments at the theatre.[2] They formed plots to rescue the Queen.[3] And, rashest of all schemes, they essayed to 'royalise' the lowest of the mob, to overthrow by means of the people the people's leaders. There seems to have been considerable scarcity of food in Paris, a scarcity exaggerated and manipulated by Royalist agents. Trading on such genuine distress as was produced in many poor families by the absence of their bread-winners at the war, they raised a cry for the 'bread of the King.'[4] Discontent was fanned by the Hébertist press, which was at this time a great power in Paris, the paper most read by the mob being the 'Père Duchesne.' It began to attack Danton. To be confronted by the social spectre at Paris while there was civil war in the Departments was a terrible misfortune. Whether owing to real or manufactured discontent, Robespierre for the moment seemed 'suspect,' and Chaumette was insulted in the streets.[5] The mob invaded the Commune. The Commune in its turn in

---

[1] S. iii. 423.   [2] Michelet, b. xiii. c. iii.   [3] *Ibid.*
[4] *Ibid.* L. Blanc, b. x. c. vii. Cf. M. xvii. 504, 576, 580, 584, 591.
[5] M.-T. viii. 370.

company with the mob invaded the Convention, where it now regarded the Committee of Safety as its enemy and rival.

Amid all this maelstrom of misery and faction Danton was weakened in the Sections, the clubs, the Commune, and the Convention by the absence on mission of so many of the strongest men of the Mountain. When Thuriot resigned his seat on the Committee, September 20,[1] the only Dantonist left on it was Hérault de Séchelles. But already Danton was and felt himself alone. Garat has described in memorable language his condition of mind. He had gone to Robespierre first, on behalf of the Girondins, and finding him obdurate went to Danton.

He was ill. I was not two minutes with him before I saw that his malady consisted mainly in profound grief and consternation at what was threatening. 'I shall not be able to save them' were his first words, and as he said them this strong man whom they compare to an athlete lost all self-control, and big tears ran down the face which resembled a Tartar's. He still, however, cherished some hopes for Vergniaud and Ducos.

Even Robespierre, it should be observed, would at this time have been content with the deaths of Brissot and Gensonné. The Girondins, in fact, committed suicide, so to speak, twice over, first in running away and raising a rebellion, and secondly by the craven fashion in which they conducted the rebellion. While their antagonists were present in person with every army, and scouring all France for money and men, the Girondin leaders were, said Charlotte Corday, when asked what they were doing, engaged in 'composing songs and proclamations to recall the people to union' ('*ils font des chansons, des proclamations pour rappeler le peuple à l'union*').[2] The Hébertists were now mingling cries for their blood with the people's demand for bread.

Danton had, we have seen, laid great stress on getting in the harvest before taking away the labourers for the war, and on obtaining returns for the whole stock of grain in the

<hr>

[1] M. xvii. 708.   [2] M. xvii. 246.

country. The harvest of 1793 was, happily for France, a very good one. Thuriot on August 26 said there was a sufficient supply for two years.[1] But it was only just reaped, and from other causes the temporary pinch was severe. That day a piteous deputation from Vincennes came to the Convention, and holding up some black bread said it was the best they could get, and even of that there was not enough to keep them from starving. And they asked why they might not purchase in the Paris market if Paris merchants might buy up wholesale all the corn in the neighbourhood of Paris. Thuriot in a later debate put the same case tersely when he said that country people were absolutely starving with heaps of wheat close at their doors, and that cornering must be stopped by legislation. A Committee of Five was appointed to consider the whole question.[2] Danton was one of the Five, and on September 3, after their proposals had been submitted to and discussed by the Assembly, a decree was passed fixing for the whole Republic a maximum price for corn, wheat, and the carriage of them. This had no effect on Paris discontent, however calculated to ameliorate the condition of Vincennes. On the 5th Chaumette with his following demanded that the poor of Paris should be fed, and, in order to provide food, that a revolutionary force should be created for collecting it, accompanied by a tribunal for the punishment of cornerers and speculators. Danton's appearance at the rostrum was the signal for applause from the Assembly and from the deputations, which for several minutes prevented him from beginning his speech. He said

that the Convention would be wise to turn to good account the people's sublime enthusiasm. When of its own accord it wished to march against the enemy no other measures were needed than those which itself proposed. Let there be a revolutionary army at once. The seditious plots at Paris need cause no alarm. No doubt there was an attempt to extinguish the flame of liberty where it glowed brightest, but the *sans-culottes* existed still and were the vast majority. They only had

---

[1] M. xvii. 504.   [2] *Ibid.* M.-T. viii. 368.

to be organised and they would confound all these machinations. But a revolutionary army was not enough ; the Convention must be itself revolutionary. First it must remember that men living by the sweat of their brows could with difficulty attend their Sections. They ought to be paid for attendance twice a week. Secondly, the manufacture of arms should not cease till every citizen had his musket. For every *sans-culotte* there should be a musket—nay, a cannon—and he should be told that the fatherland entrusted it to him and expected his service whenever it was required ; that each musket should be looked on as a sacred thing, sooner than lose which a man should lose his life. But, thirdly, there were traitors among them to be punished, and the Revolutionary Tribunal should be (as had been suggested) split into sections, that every day some aristocrat, some malignant should lose his head for his crimes. Lastly, the Convention should recognise gratefully, should pay homage to the sublime patience with which starving men bore privations which were the work of conspirators against the Revolution, men who would assuredly achieve the liberty for which they were content to starve.

Danton sat down amid even greater applause than that which had greeted his appearance. The whole house cheered. The spectators rose up waving their hands and hats, and on his proposals being adopted there were loud cries of 'Vive la République ! '

Several points about this speech deserve notice. Its tone of trust in the people, its flattering identification of the Assembly with the people, was the result of and the shrewdest way of checkmating Royalist manœuvres in Paris. Secondly, to pay and arm the *sans-culottes* of Paris was at once to provide bread for them and to provide a garrison. Thirdly, the sanguinary menace held out to 'aristocrats'—a term which, it should always be remembered, had by this time become a colloquial synonym for 'traitors'—can only be justly estimated in connection with the tidings told that day and the day before in the Convention,[1] how Toulon had been betrayed to the

---

[1] Cf. M. xvii. 572, 574, 575, 589, 591, and M. Stephens' *Orators of Fr. Rev.* ii. 26.

English and the King proclaimed there, how the rebels of Marseilles were boasting of the aid of thirty thousand English and Spaniards, and were threatening terrible reprisals, and how the Austrians had been tearing out the tongues and cutting off the hands and feet of French soldiers. Danton's language was mild in comparison with that which such reports elicited from men like Billaud-Varenne, who said, 'What is more important' (*than the question of food*) 'is to efface all malignants from the face of the earth;'[1] 'all your enemies ought to be arrested this very day,' &c.; and like Barère, who said, '*Plaçons la terreur à l'ordre du jour.*'

Similarly it must be remembered, with regard to the 'maximum,' that however indefensible, if judged by maxims of political economy, it was not only defensible but perhaps the only way of coping with present needs and dangers. We in our own day and in times of peace have begun to hear talk of legislation being necessary against 'corners,' but in France, where the only food to be got was from French soil, the most summary way of ensuring its approximately equal division was, short of absolute confiscation, probably the 'maximum.' It was thoroughgoing, not squeezing one class only, but millers, farmers, bakers, carriers, gardeners, &c., all alike ; and it was in a way economical, for, as a corollary of it, no one was allowed to buy more than a fixed amount of bread *per diem*. And in its primary object it was efficient. It kept down the price of the necessaries of life. It was, in short, the 'least bad' method that could be devised for unique emergencies.

Lastly, if, in view of Danton's despondency, exhibited a few days later to Garat, we are inclined to be surprised at the extraordinary enthusiasm for him in the Assembly, we have to consider that the Hébertists had not yet ventured to attack him openly, and that as an orator he, like Mirabeau, to the last dominated his audience. While he was regarded by some men as a 'Moderate,' whose day was over, there were more to whom any great movement of the Revolution seemed incomplete in

[1] M. xvii. 581.

which he did not share. '*Danton*,' said one of them next day, '*a la tête révolutionaire*,' and added that he should be placed on the Committee of Safety, whether he consented or not.

Danton, however, had made up his mind to abide by his oath never to re-enter the Committee, though he gave it ungrudging support. It had on August 29 been indirectly assailed by Billaud-Varenne,[1] who proposed that a special committee of surveillance should be appointed, to hold, as it were, a brief for the guillotine against the Executive. Robespierre immediately scented mischief, and spoke of 'a perfidious system of paralysing the Committee.' As was his wont, Danton contrived to extract something useful out of this opposition, observing

that while so many Committees must clash together and cancel each other the Committee of Safety might very well be increased by three members, whose special duty it should be to supervise the Executive. On the one hand the Executive, with eleven armies to look after, had a difficult task. On the other the Committee of Safety had passed important measures enough to occupy all its existing members, so that it might well be enlarged.

Again, on September 6 he proposed

that the Committee should be given any sum it asked in order to inspirit the Departments and countermine the enemy. Like a crank applied to a great wheel it would give a great momentum to the machine of State.[2]

And on the 13th he recommended that the Committee of Safety should appoint the Commissariat Committee, in order to ensure the proper equipment of the Army of the North.

French soldiers were not like Austrian ; they were not thrashed with a stick for a speck of dirt on their uniforms, but they could not go without clothes at all. All such sub-committees ought to be reconstructed by the Committee of Safety. No one could suspect his motives, for he would not himself serve on it. He meant to be the spur of all Committees, but to serve on none.

---

[1] M. xvii. 527.   [2] M. xvii. 596.

At the Jacobin Club he took the same line. Rossignol, the general in La Vendée, had been denounced by the Dantonist Bourdon of the Oise, and defended by Robespierre. Danton had little to say about the personal questions at issue, but he availed himself of the opportunity to make some very sound criticisms of the way in which the war was conducted.

It was ridiculous of Bourdon to describe the Vendéans as a set of swine, whom it was no honour to beat. They were men, and men who could fight well. But it was true that the war had been mismanaged. What was wanted was a central not a piecemeal war. Separation of the army inevitably presaged defeat. There were also too many commissioners in La Vendée. Their orders clashed, and some might, like the generals, be suspected of prolonging the unhappy struggle for their own ends. Two or three were quite enough. Responsibility ought to be thrown on Rossignol, the Commander-in-Chief, but with responsibility he should be given a free hand.

Rossignol was one of those bragging incapables brought by politics rather than military skill to the front; but this was not clear at the time, as it is now. Undoubtedly Danton placed his finger on the two weak spots in the plan of campaign, and undoubtedly also he was right in saying that there should be one general, and he responsible. Having done so, though Bourdon was one of his own friends, and Rossignol one of the party assailing him, he did not assail Rossignol, remembering, it may be, how too hastily he had associated himself with clamour for Montesquiou's recall on the eve of that general's successes. Moreover, the Hébertists were at this time at the height of their power, and Danton, when the fate of Vergniaud and his friends was in suspense, would not wish to come to extremities with them unless sure of his ground. Hébert was now alluding to him in the 'Père Duchesne' as the friend of Dumouriez. Danton insisted on a retractation,[1] and the two men were outwardly reconciled. But, placable and tolerant though he always showed himself, it is hard to believe that he ever said of Hébert

---

[1] Lenox, p. 240.

'*ce garçon-là que j'aime beaucoup.*'[1]　David, the Robespierrist who stood gloating over his fate as he was led to execution, and whom he called '*valet*,' is the author of the story, the intended effect of which must be judged by Hébert's venomous assertion at the Jacobins that he himself thought Danton sincere, but that Fabricius had afterwards said to him, 'You think him reconciled to you.　He is not.　Be sure he will do all he can to ruin you.'[2]　There could have been no real reconciliation.　' Danton has not in the Convention satisfied the expectations of patriots,' said Hébert.　And there is a story of Danton stamping as if crushing an insect and saying that that was how the Hébertist gang should be treated.[3]

But though he disdained such enemies he must have been glad to be quit of them for a time, when he obtained leave of absence on October 12, 'in order to re-establish his health in his native air.'[4]　As we hear nothing of him during the three weeks preceding that date he must have fallen ill in the last week of September, and was convalescent when he reached Arcis.　A letter from a neighbour of his appeared in December in the 'Journal de la Montagne,'[5] attesting that he was seen there daily in the dress and with the appearance of an invalid ; and according to tradition he spent his time feeding ducks in the Aube, planting trees in the meadow behind his house, and planning a garden.[6]　Other pleasant stories are told of him which seem to belong to this peaceful interlude in a life of storm—that it was his custom to take his meals with the windows of his house open, through which the people of Arcis were fond of gazing at their famous townsman ; that when a traveller asked for a draught of wine he would insist on his being given wine of better quality if he were an old man ; and that he tore up his shirt into bandages for a workman's wound.

It is strange that any but natural reasons should have

---

[1] *Journal de la Montagne*, quoted by Bougeart, p. 295.

[2] Bougeart, p. 294.　　　　　　[3] Gronlund's *Ça Ira*, p. 180.

[4] M. xviii. 103.　　　　　[5] Bougeart, p. 307.　　　　　[6] Lenox, p. 246.

HOUSE OF THE DANTON FAMILY AT ARCIS-SUR-AUBE

been manufactured for this brief sojourn at Arcis. He was worn out by four years of fierce and incessant conflict, the last twelve months of which had been one perpetual fever, and the fate in store for the Girondins along with the unabated rancour of parties in Paris filled him with forebodings.

Twenty times (he said) I offered the Girondins peace. They would have none of it. They refused to trust me that they might not forgo the right to ruin me. It is they who have driven us into the arms of sans-culottism, which has devoured them, will devour us all, and end by devouring itself.

But he did not leave his post till his work was done. He pinned his faith on the Committee of Safety, and he left it supreme, for on the 14th the Committee of General Security had on his motion been renewed and filled with its nominees.[1] These two Committees, with the Revolutionary Tribunal, the Law of the Suspect (to be used with circumspection), the *levée en masse*, and the maximum, were the machinery with which he trusted to beat back the allies and beat down treason. September returned him the firstfruits, October the full harvest of the seed he had sown. Hondschoote was won before he left Paris. The news of Jourdan's defeat of the Prince of Orange at Wattignies, of the recovery of Roussillon from the Spaniards, of Kléber's crowning victory over the Vendéans at Cholet reached him in October at Arcis.[2]

[1] Morse Stephens' *Fr. Rev.* ii. 543.

[2] Cholet practically decided the war. (Cf. M. Stephens, ii. 265.) Danton (cf. next chapter, first paragraph) must have regarded it as Barère, speaking for the Committee of Safety, did Oct. 23, 1793 (M. xviii. 195), when he said, '*Je viens vous annoncer aujourd'hui que la Vendée n'est plus.*'

CHAPTER XXV

1793—continued

DANTON'S IDEAL OF GOVERNMENT—WHY NOT REALISED—RETURN FROM ARCIS—REPLY TO HÉBERTISTS—ANTI-RELIGIOUS MASQUERADES CONDEMNED — 'CLEMENCY'— RESPONSIBILITY OF MINISTERS — 'CLEMENCY' AGAIN—ULTRA-REVOLUTIONARY EXCESS CONDEMNED —SCENES AT THE JACOBINS—DANTON'S SPEECH—ROBESPIERRE'S PERFIDIOUS DEFENCE

THE system Danton had built up laboriously he nevertheless regarded only as temporary, as the 'least bad' expedient possible at the moment. With the victories of Wattignies and Cholet the need of it became less pressing, and it might be hoped would soon cease to exist and be succeeded by the government of his dreams. What that was we know from Garat. It was to establish the reign of law and equal justice; to extend clemency to enemies; to pardon and restore to the Convention its expelled members; to give the Constitution practical effect; to offer peace to all foreign nations; to restore commerce by releasing it from all restrictions; to stimulate magnificently arts and science; to break down all barriers separating Department from Department; and to substitute for factitious citizenship of cards and tickets the living citizenship of the members of an honestly ruled republic. For this noble ideal '*il se montra barbare pour garder toute sa popularité, et il voulait garder toute sa popularité pour ramener avec adresse le peuple au respect du sang et des lois.*'

Already he had previsions that his dream would not be realised. Only a dictatorship could have made its fulfilment possible. Only an unscrupulous man of genius could have

made himself dictator.   Robespierre developed an unscrupu-
lousness born of fanatical belief in his monopoly of all virtue.
But he had no genius.   Danton had genius, and constructive
genius ; but while ready to sacrifice scruples, even to the point
of indifference as to his own fair fame, in order to destroy despotism, nothing would induce him to undo the work of his
own hands and assume in any shape that personal 'tyranny'
which he had denounced in all his speeches.   Nor if he had
had the will would he have been able to find a way.   The
'general middlingness' of the men of the Revolution, and their
jealousies, combined with reactionary precautions against
Monarchy, resulted in such an extraordinary system of
balanced authority that only a successful soldier, and only he
when society had become exhausted and sickened by the
Terror, could have had much chance of a successful *coup d'état.*
Danton never thought of making the attempt.   Till now the
instruments he had devised worked as he meant them to work.
Trials were fair, executions comparatively few.[1]   Between
April and September only 38 people were condemned to death
for treason ; but in October the guillotine-list increased with a
bound, and still went on steadily growing when according to
his intentions it should have diminished.   But it was not till
his execution in April 1794 that the numbers, which in August
1793 had been 5, and in September 17, and even in February
only 73, shot up to the appalling total of 257, and in the
following month to 358.[2]

The figures of October, 50, contrasting with 17 in September,
including, as they did, the Girondin Deputies, determined Danton to interfere.   It has been handed down in his family that he
was walking one day in his garden, when someone came running
with a paper in his hand and exclaiming, 'Good news ! good
news !'   'What is that ?' said Danton.   'The Girondins have
been beheaded.'   'Do you call that good news ?'   'Well, were
they not factious ?'   'Factious !   Have we not all been factious ?

<hr>

[1] *Procès,* p. 62.
[2] Morse Stephens' *Fr. Rev.* ii. 334, 544.

We deserve death as much as they, and probably we shall have to travel the same road.'[1]   Even before he left Paris, on Souberbielle exclaiming, 'Ah, if I were Danton,' he said, 'Danton sleeps, he will awake' ; and while walking with Desmoulins along the Quai des Lunettes he pointed out to him the deep red reflection in the river of the sun going down behind the hill of Passy, and said, 'Look, the Seine runs blood. Ah, too much has been shed. Come, take up your pen again; write and demand clemency. I will support you.'

But it was too late. His self-denying ordinance which excluded him from the Committee of Safety was suicidal Quixotry. When, after six weeks' absence, he returned to Paris it was to find that the Government had been proclaimed revolutionary till the conclusion of peace. He came back in gloomy mood, declaring, it is said, that the execution of Marie Antoinette was fatal to all chance of coming to terms with foreign Powers, and that Custine had been sentenced on insufficient evidence.[2]   But he was alone, or nearly alone, in these sentiments. He had never had a party, though a certain number of men more or less influenced by his sentiments may be termed Dantonists. He had been in the habit of trusting to himself, and he thought now that 'he would go, as at other times before,' and bend the Convention and the Committee as he would. But the men of the Committee, Robespierre and his *alter ego* Couthon, murderous Billaud, murderous St. Just, were his enemies there, as the Hébertists were in the streets, and instead of being able to save the lives of others it was soon plain that he would have to fight hard for his own.

He spoke in the Convention, for the fourth time after his return, on November 26, and his first words referred evidently to Hébertist slanders. A complaint against the authorities of Tours for traducing good citizens supplied him with a text. He said

the Committee of Safety must settle such things. The Convention by this time should know how to govern and to silence

---

[1] Lenox, pp. 250–1.   [2] M. xx. 162.

calumny. Some people were dubbed 'emigrants to Switzerland,' others endowed with castles in Spain. The Committee was, or presumably was, chosen from the *élite* of the Convention. It should examine all such denunciations. Meanwhile their time would be better occupied in more useful work.

Clearly there was thunder in the air.

Immediately afterwards he spoke again on the subject of priests coming to the Convention to abdicate their functions.

Such scenes should be reserved for the Committee. So much ecstasy over men merely swimming with the stream was superfluous. There was no call to show more respect to atheist priests than they had shown to bigoted ones. Instead of these anti-religious masquerades in the Convention they ought to be at work. People wanting to dedicate to the country church plate should not make sport or glorification out of it. They had something else to do than receive these interminable deputations with their floods of tautology. Everything—even congratulations, must have an end.

He went on, as anyone accustomed to his oratorical methods can, by reading between the lines, detect, to insinuate ever so dexterously the first breath of clemency, '*couvrant sa pitié sous des rugissements,*' '*pour faire plus de peur en faisant moins de mal.*'

As to *what they call* a foreign conspiracy, the Committees should prepare a report. The public willed, and with reason, that terror should be the order of the day. But it wished it to be aimed at its proper object, at aristocrats, egotists, conspirators, and traitors. It did not wish to inspire fear in men not naturally gifted with much energy, but serving their country to the best of their ability, however small. A tyrant, after having overthrown the League, said to one of the chiefs he had conquered, as he made him sweat, 'I want no other vengeance than that.' But the time was not come when the people could show clemency. The time of inflexibility and national vengeance was not over. The people required a potent, terrible strength. That strength it possessed, since with a breath it could create and overthrow its magistrates and representatives. They were politically a National Committee;

cheered by the approval of the people. And the people wished them to essay all means for enforcing and bringing into action republican government. The Committee of Safety should pay less attention to trivialities, and devote itself to these larger aims.. The people had long had to do everything itself. It was all very well for the representatives to bow before the people's sovereignty, but they should associate themselves with its glory and anticipate and direct its noble movements. The Committee of Safety, in concert with the Committee of General Security, should promptly report on the conspiracy, and on the means of instilling force and energy into the Provisional Government.

The import of these utterances, in spite of their somewhat Cromwellian circumlocution, was plain enough to his audience. Some of them would, no doubt, 'shake the head and smile with pity, as at the speech of a man apparently condemned by everyone,' for such Camille Desmoulins said was the Assembly's attitude to Danton a day or two later. Fayau, a Montagnard, jumped up and complained that

he has spoken of clemency, tried to draw distinctions between our enemies, a most dangerous thing to do now. As for me, I think that anyone, whoever he may be, who has done nothing for liberty, or has not done all he could, deserves to be accounted an enemy to it.

Danton at once appealed to and recommenced his 'rugissements.'

It is not true that I said the people were inclined to indulgence. On the contrary, I said the time for inflexibility and national vengeance was not over. I wish terror to be the order of the day. I wish stringent penalties, terrifying punishments, for the enemies of liberty, but for them only.

The sterner fanatics who listened to him may well have puzzled over the significance of some things which he had said, but they must have pondered in their hearts, most of all, his last four words. Fayau returned to the attack.

Danton talks of essaying republican government. I totally differ from him. Is not that a suggestion that the people may approve of a different sort of government? But the oath we swore, ' A Republic or death,' was no idle oath. We are for a Republic still.

Danton shortly answered that this was to twist awry the sense of what he had said. He was, and always should remain, a republican. All he wanted was to give effect to the Constitution.

Something of self-defensive autobiography may also be detected in another speech in which he argued for Ministers being held responsible.

I too have been Minister. Every evening I made myself acquainted with the net result of the work done in my office. Its head clerks had to present a summary of it. A Minister's first duty is the daily supervision of his subordinates.

In other words, he asserted that he had been a hard-working servant of the State, not the indolent do-nothing which men like Fayau represented him to be.

Two days later he drove the thin end of the wedge of clemency a little deeper. Some commissioners in the Departments had announced that in their districts failure on any one's part to bring in his gold or silver plate to be exchanged for *assignats* would be punished with death. Danton said that

it was impossible to show too much severity about such measures, especially in the case of their colleagues. Now the backbone of federation was broken revolutionary measures ought to be the necessary consequence of existing laws. The Committee had felt the necessity of supplementing revolutionary measures, and had issued decrees accordingly. From that moment the man posing as ultra-revolutionary would work definitely more harm than pronounced opponents of the Revolution. They ought to manifest the utmost displeasure at anyone exceeding the limits he had just defined. They ought to lay down that no one had the right arbitrarily to enact a law against anyone; and should safeguard the principle that a law could only emanate from the Convention, which alone had been entrusted by the people with legislative powers. Commissioners like those inculpated should be recalled forthwith. And no representatives of the nation should in future issue enactments except in strict conformity with the instructions of the Committee of Safety. The pike was, no doubt, useful for destruction, but for constructing and consolidating the social edifice the compass of reason was wanted.

This speech, illustrative of and consistent with Danton's conduct before the September massacres and before June 2, was too sensible to excite much open animadversion, but Fayau again made some objection, to which Danton replied

that he would have their policy 'revolutionary,' though the very soil of the Republic were annihilated thereby, but a little prudence would not be amiss after so much vigour, and that a combination of the two would work best for the national weal.

On the next day a citizen came to the bar of the Convention and proceeded to recite a poem in praise of Marat, to which probably the other Deputies would have listened—with much boredom, no doubt, but still would have listened. Danton cut him short. 'Marat had his good qualities, but after his apotheosis as patriot it was useless to listen every day to funeral panegyrics and bombastic orations on him.' Here again he made himself the mouthpiece of common-sense, but it was common-sense which some of his listeners knew how to use to his prejudice.

On December 3 he had to stand on the defensive at the Jacobins. A demand was made that the Convention should supply meeting-places for each popular society in the Departments. Danton opposed. He said such societies

had their natural rights and needed no stimulus from Government. No doubt the Constitution should be in abeyance while revolutionary measures were imperative, but he thought there should be a wholesome distrust of men trying to goad the people beyond the limits of the Revolution, and proposing ultra-revolutionary measures.

Coupé of the Oise retorted that the people could do what

it liked with its own property and assign convenient meeting-
places where it thought proper.

Danton said Coupé was putting into his lips poison ; he
had no wish, nor had he said a word to infringe the absolute
independence of the popular societies ; and then, replying to
some hostile sounds made on his rising—

I heard some uncomplimentary remarks. Already grave
charges have been brought against me. I claim the right to
clear myself before the people, who can easily be made to see
my innocence and my love of liberty. I summon all who may
have conceived reasons for distrusting me to specify their
accusations, for I wish to answer them publicly. I have been
met with marks of hostility on mounting the rostrum. Have
I, then, lost the look of a man who is free ? Am I no longer
he who stood at your side in the hour of danger ? Am I no
longer the man whom you have often embraced as your
friend, and who would die with you ? Have I not been made
the target of persecution ? I was one of Marat's boldest
champions. I call to witness the shade of the Friend of the
People in my justification. You will be amazed, when I
initiate you into my private life, to see that the colossal
fortune attributed to me by men who are as much your
enemies as mine dwindles to the modicum of property I have
always possessed. I defy my ill-wishers to produce against me
proof of any crime. All their attempts will fail to overwhelm
me. I want to stand face to face with the people. You shall
judge me in its presence. I will no more tear out a page of
my life than you will one of yours destined to make the
annals of liberty immortal.

It is significant that the Moniteur does not report the
remainder of his speech, which was a reply to the charges of
embezzlement brought against him, with reference to which he
demanded the appointment of a Committee of Twelve, by
whom he might be examined in public. But he was a
dangerous orator to provoke. The phrases which in print
have an air of bombast were perhaps the most effective when
thundered by his powerful voice and charged with unstudied

emotion. Now, as always, he carried his hearers away, or all of them except one; for

> On the other side uprose
> Belial, in act more graceful and humane ;
> But all was false and hollow, though his tongue
> Dropt manna and could make the worse appear
> The better reason.

Robespierre knew by the cheers amid which Danton sat down that he must be careful. But none the less he felt that his hour was at last come. Danton had once upon a time defended him. He would now defend Danton.

He began by enumerating all the current gossip about Danton, as if in irony—irony which, as subsequently he advanced it all in bitter earnest, was only assumed as a means of bringing such talk from the background into the front. With this end he unfolded a catalogue of charges—that Danton had 'emigrated' to Switzerland ; had shammed illness to conceal his flight ; had aimed at being regent with Louis XVII. as king; had been once on the point of proclaiming him ; had been chief of the conspiracy ; that not Pitt nor Cobourg, nor England, nor Prussia, nor Austria was the real enemy, but Danton ; that the Mountain was his accomplice ; that there was no need to trouble about foreign agents or imaginary conspiracies—in a word, that he was the man who ought to have his throat cut.

Then, with hypocrisy involved in hypocrisy, he hinted how impartial he was in discrediting such charges. The Convention knew his disagreements with Danton ; that at the time of the treason of Dumouriez his own suspicions had anticipated Danton's ; that he had reproached him with not pursuing Brissot and his accomplices quickly enough ; but that on his oath he had reproached him with nothing else.

In less than five months he was to represent as mortal crimes what he now alluded to as merely disagreements between friends.

After proceeding to say that all these calumnies were really the work of nobles and priests, he uttered words by which he stands self-convicted of hypocrisy and mendacity, whether they were false or true. 'I may deceive myself about Danton, perhaps, but seen in his family circle he merits nothing but eulogy.' This is the man whom he afterwards described as having before this time laughed at the name of virtue, identified it with gross excess, surrounded himself with rascals because he was so tolerant of vice, and as destitute of all ideas of morality.[1] But we know that it was what he now said of Danton's family life which was the truth.

Then he diverged, as was inevitable, to what was a more interesting topic even than treacherous defence of Danton —himself: 'Danton wishes to be judged; let me be judged too'—and ended by saying that aristocratic journals were the sources of all the stories to Danton's discredit, and that anyone there having anything to say against him should get up and say it, for this was the place where the whole truth should be told.

Did he expect some Fayau or Coupé to rise to his summons ? If so, they were overawed or unwilling to pull the chestnuts out of the fire.   There rose instead that brave man Merlin of Thion-ville, who remarked bluntly, 'What I have to say is that Danton rescued me from the clutches of Judge Larivière, that on August 10 he saved the Republic with his " Dare, dare, dare." There you have Danton.'

And so the matter ended for the time, the President giving to Danton the fraternal *accolade* amid tumultuous applause. Many may have thought Robespierre's speech sincere. Did Camille Desmoulins think so ?   He wrote of it as equal to the oratory of Mirabeau, and loaded with praise the hero who had come to the defence of the Horatius Cocles of the Revolution in his hour of need.   Camille Desmoulins was a feather-headed man, but it is possible he may have purposely tried to nail Robespierre to his 'Not guilty,' having prevision of the time when, on the same evidence, he would demand an opposite verdict.   Did Danton think so?   Thinking Robespierre less

[1] Bougeart, p. 358.

capable he may have thought him more honest than he really was. He undervalued the force of the man; he said of him, it seems, 'that he was not fit to boil an egg.'[1] Robespierre had come to measure all men by himself, all opinions by his attitude towards them, all events, pursuits, interests, creeds by the importance they assumed in his own eyes. In him was virtue. Therefore opposition to him was vice. And vice must be guillotined. Female adoration intensified his egotism. He was for ever in the pulpit and always preached from one text. Danton, tired of his monologues, 'laughed at virtue'— that is to say, at Robespierre's virtue—and said 'He who hates vice hates men'[2]—that is to say, a Robespierre has no bowels of compassion. But Robespierre failed to appreciate such quotations or to see the point of such jokes. Men of his disposition resent jokes. He intended to destroy Danton as soon as he safely could. Danton, like other people, was, though bored, still influenced by self-righteous pretensions, which if persistently urged generally do impose on others. Thinking him too self-righteous, he thought him on the whole well-meaning and loyal to the Republic. And we, if we had only Robespierre's speech on this occasion to judge by, might think so too. But *littera scripta manet.* He did not say what he really thought of Danton because the time was not yet. Calculating and cautious, he knew how to bide that time. But if the Jacobins had hooted instead of applauding the great orator he might have taken a very different tone and grappled with him at once, before demolishing Hébert.

However that may be, this scene at the Jacobins seems to have been regarded as a reconciliation between the two men, who had become estranged, though without open quarrel.

Robespierre, b. xi. c. xviii.   [2] S. iv. 61.

CHAPTER XXVI

1793-4

DECLINING INFLUENCE—VIEUX CORDELIER—DESMOULINS AND PHILIP-
PEAUX ATTACKED AT THE JACOBINS — DANTON'S APPEAL — DES-
MOULINS AND ROBESPIERRE—DANTON FOR RESPONSIBLE EXECUTIVE
—ROBESPIERRE AND FABRE D'EGLANTINE—DANTON'S INDEPEN-
DENCE AND COMMON-SENSE—LEGENDRE AND HÉBERT

IN spite of this temporary triumph at the Jacobins Danton's
influence was on the wane. It had always been greatest at
times of great national danger. As danger became less and
the petty interests of factions or individuals became the
questions of the hour, he stood aside, partly because he was not
a party man, partly from disgust. This very aloofness damaged
him. Conspirators thought he was conspiring. Friendlier
critics thought him lazy. When he did speak it was still with
the double object of supporting the Committee of Safety and
urging moderation. He advised fresh taxation of the rich
whose children emigrated ; but he wished them to be regarded
not as all equally incriminated, but as three classes, the guilty,
the doubtful, and the innocent.[1] He defended the memory
of Dampierre when he was said to have been a traitor. But
he would not support Merlin of Thionville, his friend, when
he proposed the irregular promotion of a soldier for bravery.
'It would lead to abuses. No promotion should be made not
previously submitted to the Committee of Safety.' He still
resolutely supported the Committee, because the military section
of it was doing its work so well, and because he still hoped to
modify the action of its terrorist members, who attended to

[1] M. xviii. 616. Cf. Michelet, b. xv. c. ii.

civil matters, by his own voice at the Jacobins and by Camille Desmoulins' pen in the 'Vieux Cordelier.'

The first number of the 'Vieux Cordelier' appeared on December 5, the second on the 10th, the third on the 15th, the fourth on the 20th—'that divine cry,' writes the great historian, 'which will touch the human heart for ever.'[1] It was rather the consummate presentation of a pathetic case by skilful counsel. In any case its effect was prodigious. Men stood in a long *queue* to take it from the printer's hands, and some of them thought themselves lucky to get copies at a louis apiece.[2] But, while hope shone into the prisons and into the hearts which had shuddered at the ever lengthening lists of the guillotine, tigers like St. Just and Billaud felt they were being robbed of their prey, and Robespierre saw that Virtue could never triumph if such a premature pact were made with Vice.

On the 23rd there was a stormy scene at the Jacobins. Some unnamed member gave vent to indignation at the epidemic of Moderation, and in particular fastened on Camille Desmoulins for expressing pity for the Girondins. Then Levasseur furiously assailed Philippeaux for his exposure of Ronsin and Rossignol. Danton interposed to procure Philippeaux a hearing. Philippeaux said that a measure of which he was in charge had been the means of reducing Levasseur's income, and this was the real cause of his animosity. Shouts of 'No personalities' greeted this remark, and amid a scene of great tumult Danton spoke again.

The Romans discussed in public both great matters and personal ones. But they forgot their private encounters when the enemy was at their gates. They strove then only to surpass one another in generous ardour to repulse the hordes of their assailants. The enemy is at our gates now, yet we go on rending one another. Is a single Prussian slain by all our altercations?

It was the old theme once more, and once more his

---

[1] Michelet, b. xv. c. i.   [2] *Ibid.*

audience responded to the familiar voice.   But experiences of this sort lured him on to over-confidence.   '*Il se croyait fort comme Hercule*,' says one writer.[1]   'Tua te vis perdet,' quotes another.[2]   'They would not dare,' he himself said before his arrest, and 'We will see how these fellows will appear before me' as he was being led into the presence of his judges.[3]

Soon afterwards he intervened again between Desmoulins and Hébert.   He complained

that when general interests and the public welfare were at stake there was nothing but hindrance and private squabbles. Ought patriots to torment patriots?   Time would show which of them was right and which was wrong.   But the society was met for business. Let it proceed to business and leave personal quarrels to the guillotine of public opinion.   Patriots ought to come to a compromise when they differed, for behind the scenes were their enemies profiting by such discord.   They ought to subordinate their personal animosities to the interests of all.

This time he sat down without a cheer, whereas Collot d'Herbois, with his '*Nous avons eu trop de clémence*,' was applauded.   It was as if he had said, '*Nous avons eu trop de Danton*.'   Robespierre on this occasion sided with Hébert and Collot d'Herbois, and rebuked his own brother for a spirited speech which elicited laughter at the expense of Hébert, who sat lifting up his eyes to heaven at the speaker's wickedness and muttering, '*Eh, Dieu!   Veut-on m'assassiner aujour-d'hui?*'   He was unfortunate in his imprecations.   'Justice Jacobins, justice!' he shouted ; 'I am charged with being an impudent robber.'   'So you are,' interrupted Desmoulins, and he held out extracts from the Treasury records showing that Hébert had been paid 60,000 livres of public money for copies of the 'Père Duchesne' worth 17,000.[4]   Desmoulins had reason

<hr>

[1] Vilate, Bougeart, p. 317.

[2] Courtois, Claretie's *Desmoulins*, p. 471.

[3] Ambroise Pantin's *Rapport sur le jugement de Danton-Lacroix*. Quoted *Procès*, p. 555.

[4] M. xix. 151.

for assuming the offensive then, since Nicolas, the Robespierrist, had a fortnight before said of him that for a long time he had been within 'a close shave' of the guillotine, and Nicolas and Hébert had both demanded his expulsion from the society. With his name too Hébert coupled three other Dantonists, Philippeaux, Bourdon, and Fabre d'Eglantine—Philippeaux, who had denounced one incompetent general, Rossignol; Bourdon, who had denounced another, Ronsin; and Fabre d'Eglantine, of whom he said '*serpent rusé, il se replie en cent façons.*'[1] If Fabre d'Eglantine and Desmoulins had had fewer private enemies it would have been better for Danton. It is even possible that his studiously impersonal and conciliatory language might have gradually rallied the soberer members of the Convention and the Committee to unite against the *enragés* if it had not been for Desmoulins' pen, the point of which was like a barb fetching blood. Danton no doubt prompted the 'motive' of the 'Vieux Cordelier' but he must have groaned over many of the passages on which Desmoulins most plumed himself, and perhaps never saw the most acrid of them in advance, for Desmoulins seems to have guarded some of the sheets as jealously as an opera-manager guards a catching tune before a first night. His literary vanity and inveterate delight in inflicting a sting did, in fact, infinite mischief to the noble cause for which otherwise he pleaded so nobly. Danton found himself exposed to incessant cross-fires at a time when the air was surcharged with passion from which he most desired to keep it free. Ronsin and Vincent were arrested on December 17.[2] On December 26 the Jacobins, at Hébert's instigation, decreed that action should be taken in the matter of Nos. 3 and 4 of the 'Vieux Cordelier.'[3] That same day in the Convention Barère alluded to 'periodical writers who unwittingly perhaps and unintentionally reinvigorate the contrarevolutionary party and rekindle the ashes of the aristocracy,' and by the fresh oiling of its weathercock the Convention knew foul weather was expected.

[1] M. xix. 27.   [2] *Ibid.* xix. 4.   [3] M. xix. 89.

On the 31st Desmoulins' expulsion was demanded at the Jacobins, and Hébert coupled with his name those of Bourdon and Fabre d'Eglantine.[1] On January 5 occurred the scene between the two Robespierres, Hébert, and Camille Desmoulins, already related. On the 7th Desmoulins mounted the rostrum at the Jacobins to apologise, it was thought, for the 'Vieux Cordelier,' instead of which he launched off into a discourse about Philippeaux. Such obliquity angered Robespierre, who proceeded to lecture his irritable hearer as if he were a spoiled child, telling him he was carried off his head by the great sale of his pamphlets, twitting him with his classicalities, and indulging in terribly bad puns suggested by the words philippic and Philippeaux, finally demanding that the notorious Numbers should be burned !

'That's all very fine, Robespierre,' broke in Desmoulins, 'but I will answer you like Rousseau, "to burn is not to answer."'

A Pope confuted by a text from St. Peter might share Robespierre's feelings.

'How dare you,' he snarled, 'persist in defending writings over which the aristocracy gloat? Listen, Camille; if you were not Camille one would not be so indulgent to you. Your mode of justifying yourself convinces me of your bad intentions. "To burn is not to answer," indeed ! '
'But, Robespierre,' said Camille innocently, 'I don't understand you. How can you say only aristocrats read my sheets ? The Convention, the Mountain read them. They are not aristocrats. You condemn me here, but have I not been at your house and read you these numbers, begging you as a friend to be good enough to teach me the way I should go ? '

Such ironical assumption of a child's manner to a pedagogue irritated Robespierre still more.

'You have not shown me your numbers,' said he ; 'I only

<hr>

[1] M. xix. 127.

saw two. I could not read the others, as I don't want to take sides in quarrels. One would have said I had dictated them to you.'

What Desmoulins would have further replied to this unconsciously comical supposition will be never known, for Danton interposed. When Desmoulins said to Hébert,

If foreigners wish to vilify the Republic, don't you know they insert fragments of your writings in their journals ? As if our people were as stupid and ignorant as you would have Mr. Pitt believe them to be ! As if your filthiness were the nation's ! As if a Paris sewer were the Seine !

Danton laughed, no doubt, with the rest of the world. But Robespierre, and 'bad intentions'! That was a different matter, entailing different consequences. He hastened to stop the combat, but could not refrain from falling in with Desmoulins' impersonation of the child.

'Camille,' he said, 'ought not to be frightened by the somewhat severe lesson Robespierre's friendship has just read him. Citizens, justice and calmness should always rule your decisions. While judging Desmoulins take care lest you inflict a fatal blow at the liberty of the Press.'

If Robespierre had not actually settled the fate of Danton in his own mind before, most people conversant with his character will be inclined to suspect that he settled it as he walked home from the Society between eleven and twelve o'clock that night. Danton, however, had been rendering an open outbreak harder to compass by his speech in the Convention the same afternoon. Cambon had complained that there was no getting accounts from the War Office. Danton said

it was no doubt an abuse, and the Minister of War ought not to dip into the national purse at pleasure, but nothing should be done precipitately. The matter should be left to the Committee of Safety. Europe stood astonished at the way the Government was worked by the Committee, which was in fact the Assembly. The Executive should be remodelled. He was convinced that a deliberative council was bad in principle. There ought to be a responsible War Minister, a responsible

Minister of the Interior, and the Committee of Safety ought to frame the action of the Government.

It is noticeable that again he was not cheered, but the sense of his advice was recognised, and the Assembly at once adopted resolutions in accordance with it.

Next day, amid profound silence,[1] the third number of the 'Vieux Cordelier' was read at the Jacobins. On the reader taking up the fifth, Robespierre said

it was useless to read it, that Desmoulins and Hébert were in his eyes equally to blame, and that Hébert wished the eyes of the world to be fixed on himself, instead of thinking of the national welfare, but that there were worse things in the background. Pitt and Cobourg were at work to dissolve the Convention, and how? By means of the too violent and the too clement parties, by means of the stranger within their gates (*Clootz*), by means of certain knaves seeking to resuscitate Brissotism. There was a plot on foot; thirty scoundrels were at work. There were two plots : one against the Convention, one to deceive the people,

and so on.

The dramatic point in his speech was reached when Fabre d'Eglantine, bored to death in reality, or pretending to be so, rose up in the middle of it to leave the hall. Robespierre asked the Society to stop him, and Fabre d'Eglantine seems then to have scrutinised his face through an opera-glass. ' I demand,' said Robespierre, 'that this fellow, whom one never sees without an opera-glass in his hand, enter into an explanation.' Fabre d'Eglantine naturally asked what he was to explain, but said he had nothing to do with the 'Vieux Cordelier,' for Desmoulins had been very angry with a journeyman printer for letting him have a glimpse of a sheet before publication. Groping at Robespierre's dark hints he essayed other exculpations, when someone called out, 'To the guillotine with him.' This shocked the sensitive man of virtue and his too precipitate supporter was expelled from the hall.

[1] M. xix. 183.

But men read guillotine in Robespierre's face none the less, and one by one they shrank away from the doomed man with marks of dissatisfaction at his speech.

On the 10th Desmoulins was expelled from the Jacobins,[1] though reinstated at the same meeting. Robespierre spoke of him with ostentatious contempt, which seems to have been the genuine result of familiarity with his old schoolfellow, but again delivered himself of dark allusions to other and more dangerous conspirators. On the 13th what he meant was made clear by Amar announcing to the Convention Fabre d'Eglantine's arrest.[2] Danton proposed that he should be brought before the bar of the Convention, for 'would you deprive the accused of his right to be heard?' Once more he was listened to in ominous silence, silence that was broken by ringing cheers for Vadier, who cried, ' No indulgence. Was Brissot heard?'

Danton made another attempt on behalf of his friend, hoping to procure for him, if not a hearing in person at the bar, at least a speedy report on his case, which could be discussed in the Assembly. He demanded that the Committees of Safety and General Security should inquire into and make their report on the case without delay. But he took care to add that he made no complaint against the Committee. 'To hurry would be to strangle the plot,' retorted the boding voice of Billaud-Varenne. 'Woe to him who has sat beside Fabre d'Eglantine and is still his dupe!' Robespierre doomed Fabre d'Eglantine at the Jacobins. Billaud sentenced Danton at the Convention.

Danton, however, does not seem to have taken this screech-owl warning to heart. Two days later we find him pouring a douche of cold water on the perfervid sentiment of a future member of the Committee of Safety, Laloi. Some youths appeared at the Convention requesting the presence of some Deputies at a civic fête, and one of them sang a song of his own composition. Laloi asked for the insertion of the song in

<hr>

[1] M. xix. 198, 200.   [2] M. xix. 207.

the Assembly's Bulletin. 'The Bulletin,' said Danton, 'is not meant to contain the Republic's verses, but good laws drawn up in good prose.' Laloi persisted, which drew from Danton a characteristic rejoinder.

What is the use of appealing to principles which we all recognise in order to deduce false conclusions? Of course patriotic chants have their proper use in inflaming, in electrifying, republican spirit. But which of you is competent to criticise the hymn just sung? Could you catch the sense or the words? Perhaps you will enlighten me about them, for I own I am not competent. Why then resist the Convention's taking steps to acquire competence? The proper course is to refer the matter to the Committee of Education. No one recognises more than I the necessity of encouraging the arts and the abilities of the young. We have not founded a republic of Visigoths. When its foundations are finally laid we ought certainly to look to its embellishment, but in little things, as great, the Convention should not act inconsiderately or with precipitation.

A similar scene occurred the next month. A member of a deputation began chanting some couplets of a patriotic song of which he was the author. Danton interrupted him.

The hall and bar of the Convention are meant for the serious and solemn utterance of citizens' opinions. No one should let them be turned into a mountebank's stage. I have in me, and always shall have, I hope, a fair allowance of French gaiety. For instance, I would make our enemies dance. But here it behoves us sedately, calmly, and with dignity to concern ourselves about the important interests of the country, to discuss them, to sound the war-cry against tyrants, to denounce and strike traitors, and to beat the alarm-signal against rogues. I appreciate the civic qualities of the deputation, but I move that in future we restrict to prose all that is said at the Bar.

On both these occasions Danton's good sense carried the day, but again we notice the absence of all applause. Before long we shall find it is renewed, but now he was under a cloud. In the hearing of the Billauds, Amars, and Robespierres a cheer might condemn to the guillotine.

On the 16th [1] he asserted at once his own consistency and his indifference to Billaud by claiming for an opponent, in opposition to his friend Bourdon, precisely what he had claimed for Fabre d'Eglantine, viz. a report by the Committees on his case.

On the 21st,[2] on the question being raised whether creditors of the King's brothers had any claim on the proceeds of their appanages, he remarked : ' As the proverb says, " Perish beast, perish venom." It seems to me, since these animals no longer exist, we need talk no more of appanages.'

On the 24th [3] he again opposed a friend. Camille Desmoulins in a witty speech, which, however, elicited no aughter, complained of a certain Section's foray at his father-in-law's house. ' A clock taken, because it had a fleur-de-lys-shaped hand. An old deed pounced on, the first word in which was " Louis." " Ah, ah ! " said the fellow, " the Tyrant's name. Off it goes." Another crime in the shape of an old portfolio not touched for five years, so that they had to scratch the dust off to examine it before they found the mark of the beast,' and so on. Bourdon bluntly said that the outrage was really meant for Camille Desmoulins, and moved that the Committee of Security should inquire into the matter and report. But Danton argued

that the Committee ought only to resort to such a measure in public matters. If a report was to be made in one private case it must be in others. The Committee was overloaded with work already. A revolution could not be geometrically perfect. Good citizens, if injured, should console themselves ; it was in a good cause. These inquisitorial powers had been placed in certain persons' hands when federalism was rampant, .and it was still dangerous to relax their powers. It was still necessary to combine severity with justice.

After having in his usual fashion mollified his audience by this concession he said what it was more important to enforce on them,

<hr>

[1] M. xix. 233.　　[2] *Ibid.* 273.　　[3] *Ibid.* 295.

that in revolutions of necessity arose private enmities and quarrels, and old and tried patriots were trampled on by new comers. But better give them the rein than excite in the enemy any hope of reaction. The nation was omnipotent. It could crush aristocrats. It could quell excess. The Convention was bound to do justice to all citizens, as soon as it could do so without injury to the State. Desmoulins' complaint was just in itself, but premature. If private wrongs were to be righted, priority should be given not to Deputies or their relatives, but to unhappier and needier victims of arbitrary arrests, and he commended the question to the two Committees as matter for solicitude and mature deliberation. The success of the Convention was due to its identification with the people. It would maintain it ; it would always follow and abide by the people's will.

Anyone reading between the lines of this speech will see the dexterity with which Danton inculcated a return to order and moderation while seeming to condone a wrong. This time it was he who was cheered and Desmoulins who was not. But well Danton knew that he could do Desmoulins no better service then than to place him in the light of a man who had been used harshly, and that he could do the cause of the 'Vieux Cordelier' no better service than by thus cautiously representing the poor and the friendless as its clients. There was too, in his closing sentences, a subtle reminder that the older champions of the Revolution might, if forced to do so, appeal to the nation.

He adopted the same line of argument when Dalbarade, Minister of Marine, was accused by Bourdon and another member of defying the Convention.[1] Bourdon urged that he should be summoned to the bar of the House. But Danton said

any such precipitate action was absurd. There was probably some mistake. What was the Committee of Safety for if not to see to such matters ? He noticed that members of the Convention, both with regard to Ministers and private persons, gave way to personal prejudices. Energy founded republics,

---

[1] Bougeart by mistake says 'Bouchotte.'

but it was prudence and conciliation that made them immortal. What they did not want was factious partisanship; what they did was a party of reason.[1]

Again, Raffron had moved that Chasles should be forced to come before the Convention, if he had to be carried in a litter. Danton protested against the Convention dealing with such minutiæ, which were the province of the two Committees. Chasles no doubt seemed contumacious. But he might be ill and unable to travel. Such a resolution as Raffron's would be absurd.[2]

These appearances of Danton prove that he persisted in supporting the Committees; that he never lost an opportunity of appealing to common-sense and discouraging *enragé* violence; that he acted independently of any party; that he was not the 'extinct volcano' which some historians have supposed him to be in 1794. Faction was too strong for him, but personally he was what he always was, resolute, consistent, self-reliant. It was his friends—Bourdon, Desmoulins, Legendre—not he, who were mixed up in the '*haines particu-lières*' which he deprecated in vain. Legendre's share in them has not been yet mentioned. It is a ray of comedy amid the squalid gloom of the squabbles at the Jacobins. He bitterly resented the charge—to which he might with a good conscience plead 'Not guilty'—of being an aristocrat, and Hébert, still smarting from Desmoulins' rapier-thrusts, came into collision with his pole-axe. Their respective friends attempted to assuage the combatants and suggested the exchange of a fraternal kiss; but, says the Moniteur's report, '*Legendre se refuse à cette proposition.*'[1]

<hr>

[1] M. xix. 340.　　　　　　　　[2] *Ibid.* 350

[1] *Ibid.* 339.

CHAPTER XXVII

1794 *February and March*

SINCE the overthrow of the Girondins there had been four
powers in Paris—the Mountain in the Convention, the Committees, the Commune, and the Club of the Jacobins. The
Mountain was gradually overshadowed by the Committees.
The Commune, on the other hand, habitually the Convention's
rival, long maintained its independence of the Committees.
It was represented in the Cordeliers Club by Hébert and his
gang. They again were represented in the army by Ronsin,
as the Mountain was by Westermann. In the triangular
combat which was in progress it is easy to see why Robespierre wished to suppress Hébert and Chaumette. He represented the Committee of Safety, and he wished to master the
Commune. As High Priest at the Jacobins, too, he resisted
the upstart pretensions of the atheist Hébert. It is easy also
to see why men of the Mountain, like Danton and Desmoulins,
fell foul of Hébert, who travestied their revolutionary system
and undermined their influence. Again, it is easy to see why
Hébert and Robespierre hated Bourdon, Philippeaux, Fabre
d'Eglantine, &c. It was because they resisted the power of
the Commune on the one hand, and of the Committees on the
other. But it is not so easy to see why they hated Danton.

He had no private feuds.[1] He had always been respectful to
the Commune. He strenuously supported the Committees.
But one reason in common they had for disliking him, viz. his
stronger personality, which dwarfed theirs and was apparent
every time he opened his mouth. Jealousy of his higher
revolutionary fame, and their conviction that while he lived
there would always be a formidable rallying-point for opposition, seem to have been the chief motives for his murder. As
to the means of attacking him, he was in two points especially
vulnerable. At a time when to be rich had become a crime,
gradations of wealth became gradations of wickedness.
Danton was comfortably off, sociable by nature, and equally
pleasant as host or guest. His occasional dinners at Méot's
café were exaggerated into the orgies of a Lucullus, and the
modest villa at Sèvres belonging to his father-in-law, into vast
domains for which only Verrine extortions could have paid.
He was, too, mixed up in the diplomatic negotiations which
had been going on with foreign Courts. These, in themselves
objectionable to Robespierre, could be easily twisted into
charges of plots with the stranger.

Here then, at once were the same twofold means of accusation against him as against so many other victims of the
guillotine. For his private character there was the charge of
peculation ready ; for his political character, the charge of
treasonable plots. Not even in the days of Titus Oates was a
community more credulous as to plots. There was absolutely
no ill, great or small, threatening to destroy the country, from
the treason of Dumouriez to a dearth of soap, which was not
accounted for by a plot ; and it was almost invariably hatched
by one arch-plotter. Was bread dear in Paris ? Pitt had
bought up French corn. Were *assignats* depreciated ? Pitt
had filled the country with forged notes. Was there a street-

---

[1] ' Danton eût sauvé tout le monde, même Robespierre.'—Garat. ' Ce
qui diminua sa force révolutionnaire, c'est qu'il ne put jamais croire que
ses adversaires fussent coupables.'—Fabas. Quoted by Michelet, b. ix.
c. xi.

riot in Paris? Pitt paid for it. To stir up the contra-revolutionists Pitt was at the bottom of the 'Vieux Cordelier.' To
bring the Revolution into contempt Pitt prompted 'Père
Duchesne.' To describe Hébert as a Royalist was as ridiculous as to call Legendre an aristocrat.[1] But, because ridiculous,
such charges were none the less dangerous, as Legendre knew
when he refused to give Hébert the kiss of peace.

Equally ridiculous, equally dangerous charges were being
whispered now, and had been whispered for months, against
Danton. A sentence from Élie Lacoste's report in June 1794
on the conspiracy of De Batz to rescue Louis, grotesque
though it is, is not more so than the legend that Danton
meant to set the Dauphin on the throne and act as prime
minister or regent. '*Antoinette, Chabot, Danton, Delacroix,
Ronsin, Hébert vivaient encore. Quelle ressource pour les
tyrans!*' What, indeed! This De Batz plot [2] is an excellent
illustration of the flimsy material out of which the gravest
charges were constructed, and it was of such material that the
nets now being woven round Danton were made.

Danton must have known something of what was going on.
He had erred grievously in refusing to sit again in the Committee of Safety. But Westermann was in Paris, eager to lead
once more the men he had led on August 10.[3] Had Danton
concerted another insurrection with him now, as he had then,
had he sent emissaries to the Sections, had he rallied round
him his old friends of the Mountain by one of his old fearless
speeches in the Convention, he might have turned the tables
on Hébertists and Robespierrists alike, and, instead of dying
on the scaffold in April, have been Dictator of France in
March. But that was the one thing he would not do. In his
last recorded speech he said : 'If ever private passions should
prevail over patriotism, if they should ever try to dig a fresh
pit for liberty, I would be the first to plunge into it myself.'
Invited to resist, he refused. To rise in arms against the

---

[1] Michelet, b. xvii. c. i.   [2] 'Plot of De Batz,' Appendix C.
[3] *Nouvelle Biographie*, 'Westermann.' Michelet, b. xvii. c. ii.

Committees seemed to him as if a father should draw his sword against his own son. This, and not uxoriousness or the desire to live at ease on ill-gotten wealth, is the real key to his conduct during those last two months of his life which remain to be noticed, February and March 1794.

On February 2 Voulland, speaking for the Committee of General Security, proposed to release Vincent and Ronsin, as no evidence had been brought against them. Bourdon of the Oise flatly contradicted this. Voulland replied that Philippeaux's evidence had been given to the Committee of Safety, not to his Committee. In opposition to his friends Bourdon and Philippeaux, Danton spoke in behalf of his foes Ronsin and Vincent. He said

that in a case of simple suspicion it was most dangerous and impolitic to treat as suspect any man who had been of great service to the Revolution. Philippeaux might be charged by Ronsin as contra-revolutionary, just as Ronsin might be with being incompetent by Philippeaux—that is to say, only on hearsay. There ought to be ample evidence, as he had before urged unsuccessfully in case of Fabre d'Eglantine. He still maintained in this case what he had in that; for he would defend his bitterest enemy if he had been of service to the Republic. Philippeaux was, no doubt, convinced of the truth of his charge, but under the circumstances he would surely feel that these men should be at liberty. In the early days of the Revolution he would have opposed all half-measures even with patriots. Unflinching strictness was then necessary. But now milder action might be taken. For himself, and he said so solemnly, he would divest himself of all personal feeling when called on to judge the opinions, writings, or actions of approved revolutionists. The release of Vincent and Ronsin would be a ray of hope for many men who had suffered in the common cause, and the future of liberty would be as bright and pure as it had already been victorious.

There could be no doubt of the meaning of this speech. It was the 'Vieux Cordelier' in another shape. Vincent and Ronsin were the text. But the sermon was in behalf of the two hundred thousand suspects for whose release Desmoulins had pleaded, and, by anticipation, in behalf of Desmoulins and himself.

The next day he spoke on the abolition of slavery in the colonies.

'Till to-day we have decreed liberty only selfishly and for ourselves. Now before the whole world we proclaim universal liberty, and all generations to come will glory in our decree. . . Future generations will profit by our act. To abolish slavery in the colonies is a deathblow to England.

On the 15th Robespierre fell ill, and remained so till the middle of March. But his place was filled (was it designedly?) by his bolder and even acrider lieutenant, St. Just. He had returned to Paris at the beginning of January,[1] and on February 26 read the Committee of Safety's report on the means of dealing with suspects in durance. It was a powerful, sinister, document, containing ominous allusions to Desmoulins, Danton, and Delacroix, and laden with Robespierrist syllogisms of this sort : 'Society must be purged if it is to subsist. Those who resent its purgation wish to corrupt it. Those who wish to corrupt it wish to destroy it.' He did not add what his hearers, however, could not fail to supply, 'Those who wish to destroy it must be guillotined.' But he left his meaning clear.

They had been too merciful (he said). In a year they had only put 300 scoundrels to death. What English tribunal had not slain more? And their own monarchy had swum in blood for thirty generations. Pity was treason. The first law of all laws was to safeguard the Republic. There were facing-both-ways politicians among them (*Camille Desmoulins*), sometimes for Terror, sometimes for Clemency. What was necessary was inflexibility. There were reprobates fattening on the spoils of the people (*Delacroix*)[2] who desired to overthrow the guillotine because they feared they would have to mount it. The rich were numerous, and their enemies, the poor, must be helped at their expense. Mendicity was a dishonour to a free State. It must be abolished. The property of conspirators must be given to the poor, &c.

<hr>

[1] *Nouvelle Biographie*, 'St. Just.'   [2] M. xix. 567.

He ended by proposing that everyone in durance and claiming to be set free should render an account of his conduct since May 1, 1789, and that the property of recognised enemies of the Revolution should be sequestrated. The first of these two proposals meant that the guillotine would be kept going faster than ever. The second audaciously outbid the Hébert-ists and was calculated to enlist the mass of the people on the side of the Committee.

Danton saw the snare and proposed to minimise it by an additional clause,

that every revolutionary committee should send to the Committee of General Security a list of its members, with the revolutionary record of each, for so the Committee of Security would be able to purge these committees of false patriots masquerading in the red cap, and patriots would be secure and free.

More he knew it impossible to suggest to the Assembly at the moment, for it had adopted St. Just's report by acclamation ; but by deference to the Committee of Security he succeeded in passing this rider, which he hoped would at least check the decentralisation of despotism and the otherwise infinite multi-plication of petty and spiteful acts of tyranny by the *enragés*.

Fayau said that men in durance, conscious that they could not give a satisfactory account of their conduct since 1789, might seize the opportunity to divest themselves meanwhile of their property, and therefore moved that all such transactions should be pronounced null and void since the date of their seizure. Danton replied that, as such transactions might have gone on long before the decree, retrospective action would be endless and impossible. Subsequently he recurred to the socialistic half of St. Just's proposal.

No doubt (he said) the time was near when there would not be one single destitute person in the Republic, but something immediate might be done by way of instalment. Plots of land stocked with cattle in the vicinity of Paris might be given to mutilated soldiers, and so be a constant stimulus to the patriotism of others, while filling the owners with gratitude to the Republic.

This anticipation of three acres and a cow was in itself just what would commend itself to Danton, but none the less it was probably meant as a political countercheck to St. Just. Nor could that sombre Committee-man's menaces rob him of his gaiety. The Convention, which never was averse to details, was discussing the advisability of establishing depôts of male animals to improve the breed of the most useful species, which had deteriorated during the war. Classical parallels were almost as frequent in the mouths of orators of the time as the crimes of Pitt ; but Danton's parallel was original.

After a long and murderous war the legislators of Athens, to repair the loss of so many fellow-citizens, ordained that the survivors should have several wives apiece.

He advised the Assembly in small matters with all his old shrewdness.

Landowners claiming compensation for their losses in La Vendée should be indemnified in proportion to their services to the State, and the poor on a higher scale than the rich.

A proposal to prevent petitioners denouncing members at the bar of the Convention

might lead to consequences dangerous to free speech. It was their own fault if they did not put a stop to nonsensical talk, but, that being provided against, there should be absolute freedom.

This speech was made on March 13. He spoke under very different circumstances on the 17th.

Robespierre had recovered from his illness. On the night of the 13th Hébert, Vincent, and Ronsin were arrested after a terrible denunciation by St. Just during the morning in the Convention. He did not mention Hébert by name, but every one knew whom he meant by

the scoundrel who has sold his conscience and his pen, and changes his colours according to his hopes or fears, like a chameleon in the sun ;

and when apostrophising him and his satellites he said—

Rascals, go to the workshop, to the fleet ; go and plough

the earth, infamous citizens, tools of the foreigner for the disturbance of our peace and the corruption of all our hearts ; go to the battle-field, vile concccters of calumny ; go and learn honour among those in arms for the country. But no ; you shall not go. The scaffold awaits you.

The arrest of Hébert meant the victory of the Committees over the Commune, and the overthrow of the New by the Old Cordeliers. '*Je suis vieux Cordelier*,' said Legendre at the Jacobins, when the Cordeliers sent a deputation asking him and his friends to rejoin their society, and he ended by saying they would never rejoin it till all the slaves in it had been swept out. And the Jacobins refused to have any further communications with the rival club till it was 'regenerated.'

So far Danton could not but approve. One of the charges against Hébert seems to have been calumniation of him, '*en calomniant les patriotes les plus énergiques oser même les qualifier d'hommes usés*,' and apart from personal considerations Hébert's threats of insurrection found no favour in his eyes. But on March 17 St. Just announced to the Convention the arrest of Hérault de Séchelles, Danton's last ally on the Committee of Safety, the blow being all the heavier because the grounds for arrest were so frivolous. Why did not Danton resist? Because he would not oppose the Committee ; because he did not believe that Hérault—a member of the Committee—could be in real danger of his life, not one man of his rank in the Revolution having as yet been arrested ; because he hoped to help him by what may be called constitutional means. This is what he meant when, on meeting the prisoners at the Luxembourg, of whom Hérault was one, he said, 'Gentlemen, I hoped to get you out of this.' This is why, when Bourdon attempted to get Bouchotte arrested on the 19th, Danton would not support him.

The man who threatened liberty (he said) was overthrown. The people and the Convention alike wished the guilty to be executed. But the Convention should assume a dignified attitude, and beware of confounding, by spasmodic action, real patriots with sham ones. It was an affair for the Committees, as was the conduct of all Ministers. Let the Convention use vigilance and act in unison. Let those who first spoke the word Republic, and confronted Lafayette, come there ready with head and arm to defend their country. They were each of them responsible to the people for the people's liberty. As Frenchmen let them have no fear. Liberty must boil over till all the scum was gone. The Committees were the advanced guard of the body politic; its forces must triumph when the advanced guard was on the watch. Never was the Republic, to his eyes, grander than now. A new landmark had just been raised in this sublime Revolution. When it was necessary to overthrow men who aped patriotism to slay liberty, they were overthrown at once. The Committees should jointly examine the conduct of all officials. As for themselves, each should avow his faith. He had been the first man to demand revolutionary government. At first his idea was rejected, then adopted. It had saved the Republic. It was incarnate in those he addressed. Let their watchwords be Union, Vigilance, Deliberation.

In other words, he said to the Committees—

We approve of what you have done so far. But the chief thing to aim at now is to tranquillise the public mind. Let bygones be bygones. Do not proscribe men for minor faults. The people is sovereign over us all. You may provoke an appeal to it.

For his long trust in the Committees was beginning to give way. It was about this time he is supposed to have said: 'If the tyranny of the Committees be not restrained I despair of saving the Republic.'[1]

He spoke again the same day. The Commune, overawed by the arrest of Hébert, sent Pache to protest its devotion to the Assembly. Rühl, the President, gave Pache to understand it was rather late in the day to come, but Danton declared that he believed the majority of the Commune were loyal, and that it would be a misfortune that its Deputies should go away with a bitter feeling. Then, in the last words he ever spoke in the

---

[1] 'Notes de Courtois,' Claretie's *Desmoulins*, p. 471.

Convention, he reiterated that appeal for concord with which he had so often thrilled its more generous spirits.

In the country's name let us leave no vantage-ground for dissension. If ever when we are victorious—and victory is assured already—if ever private passion should be able to prevail over love of our country, if it should again attempt to dig a fresh pitfall for liberty, I would gladly be the first to plunge in it myself. But away with all rancour. The hour is come when we shall be judged only by our actions. Masks are falling; there will be no more desire for masks. Men who would butcher patriots will no more be confounded with the magistrates of the people who are of the people themselves. Were there among all our magistrates even only one man who had done his duty, it were better to suffer anything than make him drink the cup of humiliation. But here there can be no doubt of the patriotism of the great majority of the Commune. The President's reply has been strictly just, but it is liable to misconstruction. Let us spare the Commune the mortification of thinking it has been censured harshly.

Rühl—one of the honestest men in the Assembly—told Danton to take the chair while he spoke in answer; and Danton said—

President, do not ask me to take the chair which you occupy with such dignity. My intentions are honest. If I have expressed them ill pardon the unintentional inconsistency. I would forgive you for such an error. Consider me as a brother who has spoken his mind frankly.

Rühl left the chair and threw himself into Danton's arms.

CHAPTER XXVIII

1794, *March*

A FORTNIGHT later Danton was in prison. After St. Just's
ominous speeches no one could feel at ease. The more
violent of the Dantonists determined to strike at Robespierre.
They protested loudly that the prisons were full of true
patriots, that Bouchotte, the War Minister, 'vexed the people,'[1]
and that Héron, who had arrested Fabre d'Eglantine, and,
according to some historians, had secret communications with
Robespierre, was the chief instrument in inflicting these
persecutions. Bourdon, on March 20, demanded and obtained
a decree for his arrest. Robespierre and Couthon at once
came to the rescue. Couthon inveighed against 'moderates
who wish to assassinate the Government because it is virtuous,
and to arrest Héron because he does his duty,' adding that he
had never seen Héron. Another Deputy eulogised Héron
as having brought to the guillotine 'merchants, bankers, and
other corrupt survivors of the old régime.' Robespierre spoke
next. 'I will say nothing about Héron personally,' he began.
Why should he have said this? It has been asserted that
Héron was his agent.[2] It has also been confidently denied.[3]
But clearly it was suspected at the time. He proceeded to

---

[1] M. xx. 6.   [2] By Michelet, b. xvii. c. ii.
[3] By Hamel, b. xiii. sec. 32.

say that the Committees had been informed by Fouquier-Tinville that there was not a scrap of evidence against Héron. Then, after declaring that no patriot's head should fall, he told a strange story of someone having rushed into the Committee of Safety's room the day before and, 'with fury impossible to describe, demanded three heads.' Every man in the Assembly must at once have asked himself, 'Who were the three?' and the fingers of some members must have wandered uneasily to their own necks. His vague conclusions were equally alarming ; for he became fluent about virtue, about the people's virtue and the Convention's virtue, and he never embarked on that theme without meaning mischief. In his last sentence he dealt his deadliest thrust. 'If the Convention without prejudice and without weakness will with a vigorous arm strike down one faction, as it has annihilated the other, the country is saved.'

The result of his speech was that the arrest of Héron, which had, he said, 'been illegally sprung upon the Convention,' was quashed. From that hour Robespierre's triumph was secure and Danton was lost.

It was about this time that an attempt was made by Vilain d'Aubigny to bring about a second reconciliation between the two men.[1] They were invited to dinner either in Paris or Charenton by a clerk in the Foreign Office. Vilain d'Aubigny was present, and so were Panis, Robespierre's friend, and the Dantonists Legendre and Deforgues. There are two accounts of this dinner, one by Vilain d'Aubigny, the other by Prudhomme. Neither of the two can be deemed an unimpeachable witness, but the meeting is admitted to be a fact even by the advocates of Robespierre. According to Vilain d'Aubigny, Danton declared that he never nursed any hatred, that he could not understand why Robespierre had been so curt to him for some time, that it must have been due to the animosity of St. Just, whom he had reproached with being so bloodthirsty while still so young, and of Billaud, bitter at being under an obligation to him—a couple of

---

[1] Hamel, b. xiv. sec. 4.

cowards the pair of them. Then he protested against the lies
told about his wealth, and complained that Robespierre let
himself be befooled by talk of plots, poison, and poniards,
and called on him to close ranks once more with honest
men.

This seems a very probable line for Danton to have taken.
He could not help looking down on Robespierre's tactics,
though he thought him useful to the Revolution. In allusion
to them he said

that a man always using the same materials in the end ruined
himself, and if he persisted in stirring up the mud rarely
escaped being sooner or later covered by it.

And again :

Robespierre's contempt for any great conception not his own
does not presage success for the future. He might conduct
the piece up to its fourth act, but would infallibly fail at the
climax of the fifth.'

Robespierre's reply also has verisimilitude. ' But,' said he,
' with your morals and principles there would be no convicting
anyone any more of guilt.' ' And that would not be to your
taste,' answered Danton quickly. But the reconciliation
seemed complete. They embraced and Danton showed
emotion. Everyone was moved except Robespierre, who remained cold as marble.

According to Prudhomme, Danton said : ' We ought to
crush the Royalists, but not confound the innocent with the
guilty.' ' And who,' said Robespierre, frowning, ' told you a
single innocent man has lost his life ? ' ' What ! not one ! '
said Danton ironically, turning to one of his friends. Robespierre left the room first, and Danton then said : ' We must
bestir ourselves ; there is not a moment to lose.'

If Vilain d'Aubigny's account is a fable it shows his high
dramatic ability. The disavowal of hatred, the bluff rebuke
to St. Just, the jeer at Billaud, the recurrence to that sore
spot his supposed wealth, his final appeal to Robespierre, are

all the things anyone who has read these pages will admit
Danton is likely to have said. And Robespierre's part in the
conversation is equally characteristic. Robespierre's most
thoroughgoing apologist considers both the accounts inventions.[1] He would have us believe that till March Robespierre
bore Danton no ill-will, that his defence of him at the Jacobins
was sincere, that Billaud was really his murderer, that sorely
against his will, and by dint of story after story being now
dinned into his ears, he was induced by others to agree to his
death. The Belgian dinner-napkins. '*Il le crut.*' The
'Vieux Cordelier' corrected by him for the press. '*Il le crut.*'
And now for the first time he understood the real meaning of
the Mirabeau *liaison*. '*Il se rappela.*' And of the Orleans
liaison. '*Il se rappela.*' And of the teas at Robert's house
with the Girondin general Wimpfen. '*Il se rappela.*' And of
May 31. '*Il se souvint,*' &c. All this flood of reminiscences
overpowered his affectionate nature and turned the friend into
a judge in a fortnight. And so with a painful effort ('*un
pénible effort*') and very unfortunately, no doubt ('*ce fut un
grand malheur, je n'hésite pas à le dire*'), he ' consented ' unto
his death ('*il consentit à l'abandonner*'). 'The effort was
painful, but all the grander was the sacrifice.'

One thing there is in this affecting apology which is true.
Billaud was undoubtedly Danton's bitterest enemy. It was
he who, probably immediately after his speech on January 13,
first proposed to have Danton arrested. He boasted of it
afterwards and said that Robespierre jumped up like a madman
and cried that ' there was a desire to kill the best patriots.'
But this same Billaud tells us something else, viz. that on the
very day before Danton's arrest Robespierre dined with him in
the country, and that they came back in the same carriage.[2]
To this Danton must have alluded when he said in prison that
never had Robespierre talked to Desmoulins in a friendlier
way than the evening before his arrest. If Robespierre could

---

[1] Hamel, b. xiv. sec. 3.

[2] Hamel, b. xiv. sec. 4. Michelet, b. xvii. c. v.

play the hypocrite so skilfully then why should he not have done so three months before? And what are we to think of his notes on Fabre d'Eglantine's case, drawn up that very January, in which he alluded to Danton as ' *le patriote indolent et fier, amoureux à la fois du repos et de la célébrité, enchaîné dans une lâche inaction ou égaré dans les dédales d'une politique fausse et pusillanime*' ? In the man of virtue's eyes this was vice. And at this period of his life wherever Robespierre spied vice—that is to say, opposition to himself—he meant murder. At what precise moment he pictured Danton in the exact attitude of a man being guillotined it is, of course, impossible to be certain. But that he had long hated him, and for a considerable time had determined to get rid of him, there can be no reasonable doubt. His exclamation at Billaud's proposal may have been wholly hypocritical, or partly the outbreak of a timid temperament always recoiling from sudden action. It may even have been caused by momentary remorse ; for Robespierre's nature was not always bad or cruel. It had slowly degenerated under the corrosive influence of adulation, of familiarity with bloodshed, and of self-righteous posturings. But as his notes on Fabre d'Eglantine's case show what his feelings towards Danton were in January, so his notes on Danton's case show how he had regarded him long before. In Shakespeare's plays we are familiar with the characters First Murderer, Second Murderer. Conceding analogous priority to Billaud, we shall have done full justice to Robespierre.

Danton's suspicions may have been lulled for the moment by this interview, but it is more likely that he knew his danger and was determined not to appeal to force to avert it. The famous words attributed to him expressed his resolution, ' Better be guillotined than guillotine.' Westermann, Desmoulins, and Delacroix are said to have implored him to resort to force or to fly. ' Where ? ' said he. ' If I go shall I not be thought guilty ? and if France, when she is at last free, casts me from her bosom, what country will give me an asylum ?

Does a man carry his country on the soles of his shoes?'[1]
And if he suspected Robespierre's sincerity he did not believe
in his courage. 'If I fancied he even thought of it,' he is reported
to have said: 'I would crunch up the fellow's vitals.' And
again: 'Robespierre! I will take him with my thumb and
twirl him like a top.' But rumours of what was impending
made his friends less confident. Vilate, after a treacherously
friendly visit to Desmoulins, said: "In a week we will have the
heads of the three, Danton, Camille, Philippeaux.' Vadier—
a vulgarer Billaud—boasted: 'We shall soon gut this fat
turbot.'[2]

But Danton would not move. Perhaps at the very last he
may have been in two minds. Certainly he was greatly
perturbed. On the evening of the 30th he stayed at home.
There he sat by the fireside in his study, crouching over the
grate and buried in thought. Every now and then he poked
the fire violently, heaving deep sighs and uttering broken
words, or would rise abruptly, and taking up his sister's son,
then nine years old, who afterwards related the night's events,
would kiss him passionately.[3] Late at night Panis, the Deputy,
ran in, told him the warrant for his arrest was out, and urged
him to fly. But he chid Panis for his weakness, and said:
'*Ils n'oseront pas.*' Another warning came from Robert
Lindet, with no more effect. The Committees had expected
resistance and sent an armed force in view of it. But in the
early morning of March 31 he was arrested, and, after some
delay in putting seals on his effects, was conveyed to the
Luxembourg. Desmoulins and Delacroix were brought there at
the same time. Danton saw Desmoulins sobbing, and exclaimed: 'Tears! No, no; if we must mount the scaffold, let
us do so merrily.'[4]

The prisoners of the Luxembourg crowded round them
when they were brought in. Danton bowed to them and said:
'Gentlemen, I hoped soon to have got you all out of this, but

[1] Lenox, p. 311. [2] L. Blanc, b. xi. c. x.
[3] *Procès*, p. 125. [4] Lenox's *Danton*, pp. 317, 318.

here I am myself, and how it will end no one can foresee.'
To the Englishman, Paine, he said : ' I should have liked to do
for my country what you have done for yours.' Some Royalists
jeered at Delacroix, who made no answer. But Danton
laughed back and retorted : ' A laugh is the proper answer to
people playing the fool. But if there is not a return to common-
sense soon I pity you. What you have suffered till now will
seem roses then.' [1]

Meanwhile Lucile Desmoulins was urging his wife to go
with her to Robespierre and beg him to intervene. Madame
Danton refused, saying her husband would never forgive her
if she stooped to beg for his life.[2]   And it would have been a
useless mission, as Lucile found afterwards when Robespierre
would not answer her piteous letters. She would have known it
then if she had known the events of the preceding evening.
An extraordinary meeting of the two Committees had been
convened to hear the report drawn up by St. Just from notes
furnished to him by Robespierre. Spitefuller notes or meaner
were never penned.[3]   It is not so much the graver charges in
them which excite loathing, but the evidence they furnish of
long pent-up jealousy and hatred, and of a malignant disposition. They of course accuse Danton of intrigues with Mirabeau,
Lafayette, Barnave, and Lameth, and it seems the Incorruptible had all along believed him to be bribed by Mirabeau.
They tell stories of his superior influence over Desmoulins,
clearly very irritating to the narrator ; of what Danton one
day said at dinner ; of his shedding tears merely out of jealousy
at Fabre d'Eglantine's facility in doing so ; of his having told
dirty stories about Desmoulins ; of his bribing Fabre d'Eglantine ; of his saving Duport ; of his saving the Prussian army
from destruction ; of his reviling public opinion and jesting at
virtue (in terms of which, at the time they were used, the man
of virtue had not apparently disapproved) ; of his having said
that the severe principles of their party frightened people ; of
his having been at tea with Robert, where Orleans mixed the

[1] Lenox's Danton, pp. 317, 318.   [2] Ibid.   [3] Procès, p. 467.

punch and Wimpfen drank it ; of his having supported the election of Orleans to the Convention ; of his cowardly flight to Arcis in 1792, and of his cowardice always at any crisis ; of his neutrality in the struggle with the Girondins ; of his having wanted to spare the King's life ; of his having demanded Hanriot's head and directly afterwards clinked glasses with Hanriot and cheered him on ; of his having tried to overthrow the Convention ; of his wanting to hand over French colonies to America ; of his attempt to procure a general amnesty ; of his having revised the 'Vieux Cordelier' ; of his having got pensions for the widows of enemies of the Revolution.

Never was there a baser farrago of inventions, of lies that were half the truth, of truths that were in the highest degree creditable to Danton though damnatory in the eyes of his accuser, and of stories which the sour narrator could not see really told against himself. If it condemned Danton to a quick and painless death it consigns the author to everlasting infamy. Anyone reading it must say to himself over and. over again : ' If he knew all those things why did not the incorruptible man of virtue speak at the time ? Why did he eulogise Danton at the Jacobins if his eulogy was insincere ? Why did he not denounce a man who was so dangerous a traitor long before ? The blackest blot on Carnot's name is that he signed the warrant based on such charges. And those historians, who make it a reproach to Danton that some of those who vindicated his reputation were themselves men of poor reputation, would do well to remember that the two members of the Committees who did not sign were those with the most irreproachable record, Rühl and Robert Lindet, the latter of whom, it is said, refused with the indignant exclamation : 'I am here to provide citizens with subsistence, not to kill patriots.'[1]

[1] *Procès*, p. 123.

CHAPTER XXIX

1794, *April; The Trial*

TRIAL—PACKED JURY—NO WITNESSES—DANTON'S DEFENCE—HERMAN'S
HYPOCRISY—ROBESPIERRE'S SPEECH—LEGENDRE'S DISCOMFITURE—
ST. JUST'S CRIME—LAST SAYINGS AND EXECUTION OF DANTON

THE formal interrogatory of the prisoners took place on April
1 in the Luxembourg. One by one they were called into the
hall, where a judge of the Tribunal questioned them. The
question put to Danton was : ' Have you conspired against the
French people to establish the Monarchy and destroy the
national representation and Republican Government ?' Answer :
'I was a republican even under the tyranny. I shall die
one.'

Question : ' Have you Counsel ?'

Answer : ' I can conduct my own defence.'

When Danton returned from this ceremony he found
Desmoulins foaming with indignation. He made some joking
remarks to him, and returning to Delacroix asked him what he
thought of matters. Delacroix replied that he should go and
cut his hair, to prevent Sanson touching it. 'Yes,' said
Danton, ' it will be a different affair when Sanson breaks our
necks ! I think we ought to make no answer till we are
before the two Committees.' Delacroix replied that he agreed
with him, and they must try and touch the hearts of the
people.

From the Luxembourg they were conveyed to the
Conciergerie. There Danton was overheard recalling the time
when he established the Revolutionary Tribunal, and asking

pardon for it from God and man. 'I did not intend it to be the scourge of humanity, but only to prevent the renewal of the massacre of September.'

Other things that he said there have been preserved.[1]

I leave everything in a frightful welter. Not one of them has the smallest idea of governing.

Amid so many crimes I am glad to have signed some decrees which will show I had no share in them.

They are own brothers to Cain.

Robespierre will follow me. I drag down Robespierre.

Robespierre is a second Nero. He never spoke to Camille with more friendliness than on the eve of his arrest.

Better be a poor fisherman than govern men.

I have the consolation of knowing that the man who died as chief of the faction of the Indulgents will find favour in the eyes of posterity.

When people go to execution smiling it is time to break the scythe of Death.

He talked, too, constantly, of trees and life in the country.

The trial before the Tribunal began on April 2. The jurors were not chosen by lot, but by the Tribunal on the morning of the trial. One of them was the base Vilate. One of them, according to Michelet, was an idiot, one of them deaf, one of them — Renaudin — notoriously a creature of Robespierre. Seven others were said to be his men.[2] Louis Blanc is at pains to prove that the deaf juror was only hard of hearing, that Duplay, Robespierre's landlord, was as virtuous as his lodger, and that two others were respectable—an effort in special pleading as unprosperous as his doubts about the jury having been packed. Coffinhal, one of the most brutal characters of the Revolution, furnished the minutes which Nicolas, another creature of Robespierre, printed and passed on to the journals.[3] Herman was the presiding Judge, Fouquier-Tinville the Public Prosecutor.

The prisoners were fourteen in number, including one

[1] Riouffe's Narrative. *Notes de Courtois.*   [2] *Procès*, p. 595.
[3] *Nouvelle Biographie*, 'Coffinhal.'   Michelet, b. xvii. c. vi.

Spaniard, two Germans, and a Dane; and one of the indignities to which Danton was exposed, and against which he loudly protested, was being placed in the dock in company with swindlers.

The Court opened at ten in the morning. Each of the accused was asked his name and residence, and Danton made his famous reply: 'My abode will soon be nothingness;[1] as for my name, you will find it in the Pantheon of History.' The rest of the day was occupied in reading the act of indictment against Fabre d'Eglantine &c.

On the second day the Court opened at nine o'clock. Westermann was brought in as a fifteenth prisoner. No preliminary interrogatory had been administered to him, and on his protesting, and the judge replying that it was a useless formality, Danton said that nevertheless they were for the formality, and Westermann was taken out in order that he might be interrogated in another room. It was now probably that Danton said—

If they will only allow us to speak, and speak at length, I am certain of confounding my accusers; and if the French people is what it ought to be I shall have to beg from it their pardon.

Desmoulins: Ah! all we ask is to speak.

Danton: Barère is the patriot now, eh? (*To the jury*) I am the man who instituted this tribunal, so I ought to know something about it. (*Pointing to Cambon, who was in the hall*) Do you think us conspirators? See, he laughs. He does not think so. Write down that he laughed.

On Westermann being brought back, the indictment against the Dantonists was read, and the clerk proceeded to read

[1] Does *le néant* mean *non-être* or *anéantissement de l'être* here? Danton used the words May 31, 1793 (M. xvi. 528), and during the trial again; and 'nothingness' seems to translate them on each occasion. Cf. Croker's 'Robespierre' in *Essays on Fr. Rev.* : 'We must recollect that the cemeteries bore the inscription prescribed by law: "Death is an eternal sleep."' Danton's creed was agnosticism or vague theism. Cf. note in last chapter.

the law of January 23 against false witness.[1] The witnesses
for the prosecution then withdrew to the place assigned to
them, and the President told the accused to listen attentively
to the charges. The first witness—and the only one !—called
was Cambon. His evidence was distinctly in Danton's
favour. He testified to the prisoner having denounced
Dumouriez as soon as he could have suspected his treason,
and having expressed full conviction of the ultimate triumph
of the Republic. According to the Bulletin of the Revolutionary Tribunal, he then said that Lebrun had given Danton and
Delacroix 100,000 livres secret-service money when they went
to Belgium. But the Bulletin was deliberately falsified.
Cambon could not have given such evidence, as Delacroix on
February 13 had in the Convention produced Lebrun's
written affirmation that he had given him no such sum, and
that he had never been asked for such a sum.[2] The rest of
Cambon's evidence referred to Fabre d'Eglantine, Chabot, &c.
But when Fouquier-Tinville was afterwards on his trial
D'Aubigny deposed that Fouquier told him that Danton and
Desmoulins appealed to Cambon to say if they were conspirators, whereupon Cambon replied : ' So far from saying so, I
look on them as excellent patriots who have been of the
greatest service to the Republic.'[4] Robespierrist writers
attempt to invalidate this by asserting that on October 3, 1794,
Cambon charged Danton with being a ' conspirator.' Now
what Cambon said of Danton then he said of Robespierre too,
and to say he charged either of them with being a ' conspirator '
is not true. He used no such words, and what he did say was
much too vague to constitute any valid charge. On the other
hand Danton's remark, ' Write down that he laughed,' supports
the probability of D'Aubigny's allegation. And who recorded
this remark ? One of the jury, Topino-Lebrun, whose notes
prove the dishonesty of the official report. We may conclude,
therefore, that the one witness called on the second day, so far

---

[1] M. xix. 291.   [2] *Ibid.* 551.   [3] Hamel, xiv. sec. 7.

from incriminating, acquitted Danton, and the prosecution did not dare call another.

The special charges against Fabre d'Eglantine were now adjourned, and the real trial of the Dantonists began. Danton spoke nearly all the rest of the day. The Revolutionary Bulletin makes what was in fact an extraordinary combination of reason and eloquence seem a disjointed series of incoherent and violent exclamations ; and, as the notes of Topino-Lebrun are only fragments, we have lost for ever what was his oratorical masterpiece and the grandest defence ever made by a political prisoner tried for his life.[1] He was being tried for wishing to establish monarchy and destroy the national representation and republican government. He replied by pointing to his resistance to Lafayette, Bailly, Mirabeau ; to his hindering the flight of the King to St. Cloud. As to his having 'emigrated' to England, he said he went with his brother-in-law, who had business, and when Herman maladroitly invoked Marat's name he reminded him that Marat had gone to England twice. As to his having intrigued with the Girondins, the animosity of Guadet, Brissot, and Barbaroux, he said, was his best answer. He rebutted the accusations of Orleanism and of complicity with the Court in the Champ de Mars. He admitted having gone to Arcis before August 10, and said why he went, and for how long. He went into detail as to the public money he had received and disbursed. He explained his connection with Noël and his conduct to Dumouriez. In short, he summed up the whole of his political life, answering each charge at once with overwhelming cogency and vigour of phrase. Many of his expressions are known to every reader of history.

Let the cowards who calumniate me confront me. Only let them show themselves and I will cover them with ignominy.

My life ! I am weary of it. I long to be quit of it.

Men of my stamp have no price. On their foreheads are

---

[1] So we may conclude from the effect produced by it on the audience and the judges, and from tradition.

stamped in ineffaceable characters the seal of liberty, the genius of republicanism.

Ah ! St. Just, thou shall answer to posterity for thy defamation of the people's best friend and boldest champion.

As I read through this list of horrors I shudder all over with indignation.

Let my accusers come forward, and I will plunge them into the nothingness out of which they ought never to have emerged. Appear, you impostors, and I will tear off the mask which conceals you from the people's vengeance.

Never was I influenced by cupidity or ambition. Never have my private feelings compromised the public welfare. Always for my country, body and soul, I have sacrificed without stint for it the whole of my being.

I must speak of the three shallow scoundrels who have been the bane of Robespierre.

Where are the men who were forced to urge Danton to show himself on the 10th of August? Where are those heroic beings from whom he borrowed energy?

Two days this tribunal has known Danton. To-morrow he hopes to sleep on the bosom of glory. Never has he prayed for indulgence, and he will be seen hasting to the scaffold with the serenity of an innocent conscience.

I had prepared the 10th of August, and I was at Arcis—for Danton is a good son—to spend three days in bidding good-bye to my mother and in settling my affairs.

The voice of a man speaking for his honour and his life may well drown thy bell.

Danton's voice might drown the President's bell, and did in fact swell to such volume that it was heard on the other side of the Seine. A dense crowd filled the Place Dauphine, and scarcely had he spoken in Court when his words were passed from mouth to mouth till they reached men far off at the Mint.[1] Herman grew uneasy. Some of the Committee of Security who had been looking in at one of the windows of the Court slunk one by one away. For many of Danton's appeals were addressed, as had been prearranged with Delacroix, straight to the people. What if they should rescue and revenge him ? A note was passed by Herman to Fouquier-Tinville. In it

---

[1] Claretie's *Desmoulins*, p. 334.

was written: 'In half an hour I shall suspend Danton's defence ; we must enter into greater detail.'

Accordingly, when the time was come he hypocritically invited Danton to rest awhile, as he seemed tired, and the other
prisoners must be heard.   He is also said to have promised that
he should be allowed to continue his speech next day.   That
promise was not kept, nor in any case would it have been of
any avail.   Danton had ended by insisting on being allowed to
call witnesses, and on being refused cried : ' Then I say no more
in my defence.'   Not a single document had been produced in
evidence against him, not a single witness for the prosecution
except Cambon, not a single witness for the defence, though in
several points such evidence would have been all-important to
the accused.   So ended the Third of April and the second day
of the trial.

On Friday, the 4th, a new prisoner was introduced in the
person of Lullier.   After questioning him the President proceeded to deal with Hérault de Séchelles and Delacroix.   Danton
interrupted once, when Delacroix was being charged with
having stolen linen in Belgium, to say that, so far as he was
concerned, the only property he had in the waggon containing
the linen was his own wearing-apparel, and that the official report
proved this.   The President and Prosecutor subsequently
charged him with equivocal conduct to Hanriot, a charge which
he denied point-blank.   The rest of the day was taken up by
an intermittent examination of Philippeaux and Westermann,
the accused repeatedly insisting on their right to call witnesses.
The last person to be examined was Diederichsen, the Dane.

Before relating the events of April 5 we must see what had
been meanwhile going on outside the Palais de Justice.   On
the morning of March 31 Legendre addressed the Convention
about the news which had just electrified Paris.[1]   He asked
why Danton—Danton, the saviour of the country, a man as
loyal as he was himself—had been arrested, and moved

----

[1] M. xx. 94.

that he should be heard at the bar. He was opposed by
Fayau, whose animosity against Danton has been previously
noticed.   Then Robespierre rose and delivered a speech, some
of which was really eloquent ; for when his cold blood was
fired by hate he could, as had happened in the case of Fabre
d'Eglantine, become genuinely impassioned. It so terrified
Legendre that that evening at the Jacobins 'he rolled in the
mud,'[1] declaring that he would denounce anyone who
thwarted the morning decree of the Convention.   Robespierre
demanded why more indulgence should be shown to Danton
than to Fabre d'Eglantine ; poured scorn on boastful oratory ;
charged Legendre with pretending not to know that Delacroix
was arrested because he was ashamed to defend him and
thought he might be screened by the privileged name of
Danton. 'No,' he cried, 'we will have no more privilege.
No, we will have no more idols.'   Then he warned Legendre
—and, we may be sure, many others in the Assembly sharing
Legendre's feelings—that anyone who was afraid was *ipso facto*
a criminal, for no one innocent dreaded State surveillance.
Later on he appealed with diabolical ingenuity to their selfishness, pointing out that the conspirators were only few in
number, meaning, of course, that they were not to be feared,
and therefore might be safely sacrificed. While thus working
on the baser instincts of his audience he made their cup of
shame palatable by exalting the heroism necessary to descend
so low.

No doubt courage, grandeur of soul were necessary, for
vulgar or criminal men always disliked seeing their congeners
fall, because their own turn might come next, but there were
heroic spirits in this Assembly—

such, to wit, as Robespierre, for most of the remainder of his
speech was on that old nauseous theme. Probably no other
orator since the world began would out of the murderous

---

[1] Michelet, b. xvii. c. v. : ' *Le soir Legendre aux Jacobins roula dans la
boue.*'

overthrow of a rival have evolved the following line of argument :

I have been told that Danton in time of need might be my shield. What care I for any danger? My life is my country's. My heart is exempt from fear, &c.

But Robespierre knew his audience. Though some of them, Legendre among the number, would have dearly liked to respond to this martyr for murder's sake in another fashion, they were panic-stricken and accorded him round after round of applause. (' *On applaudit à plusieurs reprises.*')

St. Just's report completed their prostration. As he stood before them, statuesque of face, hardly more than a boy in years, too much a zealot apparently to be actuated by personal malignity, his monotonous indictment seemed like 'a message of doom falling from the lips of the Angel of Death.' Yet, if its general purport had not been so sinister, the absurdity of some of its items might have provoked mirth. To charge Danton with giving dinners at 100 crowns a head must to a nimble-witted Parisian have seemed inartistic.[1] And many would have thought that a taste for dining with Englishmen, though strange and reprehensible, could hardly be considered a mortal crime. Many also acquainted with the St. Amaranthe family must have known that they were no friends of Danton. The myth of his dissolute orgies seems to have had for a basis the fact that once when they and their friends were dining at a certain restaurant he and his friends were dining in the next room, and the character of his party may be conjectured from the remark of Madame St. Amaranthe's host: 'They are graver in there than we are.'[2] But though the absurdity of such parts of St. Just's report was self-evident no one in the Convention dared criticise or oppose it, and with all its follies and infamies it was adopted amid enthusiastic cheering, the members then settling down to more commonplace topics, such

[1] *Procès*, p. 327.   [2] Claretie's *Desmoulins*, p. 437-8.

as the capture of an English 'brick' laden with oil, and the inexhaustible villainy of Pitt.

Nor on the 1st was anything said about the trial. On the 2nd Couthon announced Westermann's arrest. On the 3rd the President, Tallien, informed the Assembly that the seasons, the elements, the sun, and nature, seconded the generous efforts of a great nation, and that the ground was already firm enough to carry their armies on their way to plunge poniards into the breasts of tyrants. But he said not a word about Danton, whom a few days before he had implored to resort to force.[1] On the 4th, however, the general feeling of terror which underlay this silence was evinced quaintly by Legendre. He told the Convention how he had been warned not to sleep at home that night, as he was going to be arrested, and how out of consideration for the timidity of his wife he had promised ('*Mon épouse, qui partage la faiblesse naturelle à son sexe, me pressa d'aller coucher chez un ami. Pour la tranquilliser je le lui promis*'), but that in reality he had sought the protection of the Committee of Security, as he now did that of the Convention. Even at such a time the Convention must have smiled at Legendre's confidences and his sublime compassion for the apprehensions of his wife, but it was soon solemnised by the apparition of St. Just. In the name of the Convention he announced a letter from Fouquier-Tinville, saying 'that the rebellion of the criminals had suspended proceedings in Court till the Convention had taken measures.' Then St. Just went on—

You have escaped the greatest danger which has ever menaced liberty. All the accomplices are now discovered, and the rebellion of the criminals in the very presence of justice unfolds the secrets of their hearts. Their despair, their fury, everything, tells that the *bonhomie* which they assumed was the most hypocritical snare ever laid for the Revolution.

He went on to say that Dillon, who was in prison at the Luxembourg, had declared that Lucile Desmoulins was in

---

[1] Lenox, p. 310.

receipt of money to bribe men to assassinate 'the patriots' and the Revolutionary Tribunal. Evidently by design he so mixed up his charges against the prisoners before the Tribunal and the prisoners in the Luxembourg as to create the belief that the former were concerned in the plot of the latter. He finally demanded, on the strength of what we shall see was an abominably perfidious perversion of the truth, that the Convention should order the trial to proceed and should decree that every prisoner resisting or insulting the judicial authorities should be deprived of his normal rights as an accused man.

Immediately St. Just had finished, Billaud, before a vote on the decree could be taken, gave his account of the alleged conspiracy in the Luxembourg, about which it is unnecessary here to say more than that the chief evidence for it was that furnished by a couple of '*moutons*,' Laflotte and Amans,[1] the latter said to be an instrument of Robespierre and both of them spies on the prisoners, and in the pay of the Committees. Then the Convention unanimously passed St. Just's decree.

Now the truth is (1) that there had been no rebellion of the prisoners before the Tribunal, and that in Fouquier-Tinville's letter there was no mention of any such rebellion; (2) that they could not possibly have had any communication with the prisoners in the Luxembourg. What happened was this: Fouquier-Tinville, embarrassed by the persistent demands of the prisoners for the production of witnesses, said to Delacroix on the 4th that he would write to the Convention and ascertain its wishes, which he would strictly obey. He never wrote to the Convention. He did write to the Committee of Safety, but St. Just did not read his letter to the Convention. All that Fouquier-Tinville said in it was that a storm had arisen during the trial and that the accused furiously demanded to be allowed to call witnesses for the defence, and kept appealing to the people to note how this right was, as *they pretended*, refused them; that these persistent demands disturbed the proceedings ('*troublent la séance*'); that the

---

[1] *Procès*, pp. 423, 574.

accused openly declared they would not desist from their demands till the witnesses were called, and, he concluded: 'We beg you to define precisely how we are to treat this demand, our judicial regulations supplying no means of justifying refusal except a decree.' The demand of the prisoners, therefore, was so just that even Fouquier-Tinville dared not refuse it on his own responsibility. Neither dared St. Just let the Convention know what they demanded. So he interwove a mutiny ('*révolte*') of which Fouquier-Tinville had said nothing with the mutiny in the Luxembourg reported by Laflotte, and by this devilish trick procured from the Convention what was sentence of death for Danton.

Danton had offered no insult to the judges.[1] He had been promised another hearing. He had refused to speak unless he could call witnesses, as was his right. And when he was again brought into Court at half-past eight A.M.—before the usual time—he came confident, no doubt, that he would obtain his demand. His dismay and indignation may be imagined when the first thing Fouquier-Tinville did was to order. the clerk to read the Convention's decree of the 4th, and the next to declare that he had a number of witnesses for the prosecution, but that, in compliance with the orders of the Assembly (*which had given no such orders*), he would abstain from calling all of them (*he did not call one*); that the accused, therefore, must not expect to call theirs; that they would be judged solely on written evidence, which was all they were called on to rebut. Then Fouquier read out an account of the plot in the Luxembourg, which drew from the unhappy Desmoulins a heart-rending cry: 'Villains! not content with assassinating me, they will assassinate my wife too!'

Danton and Delacroix now claimed the right to continue their defence, but the President put it to the jury whether they had not heard enough. The jury replied in the affirmative, and the President declared the pleadings ended. 'Ended!' cried Danton; 'they are not yet begun. You have not read

<hr>

[1] *Procès*, p. 597–8.

the evidence, nor heard the witnesses ;' and he and Delacroix loudly inveighed against such tyranny. 'We are going to be sentenced unheard.' 'Quick with your verdict. We have lived long enough. Take us to the scaffold.' Danton saw Amar, Voulland, Vadier, and David gloating as they gazed, and said to his friends : 'Look at those base assassins ; they will hunt us to death.' Amar and Voulland are said to have brought the Convention's decree. Voulland sent for Fouquier, and meanwhile said to a bystander triumphantly : 'We have them, the scoundrels ; they have been conspiring at the Luxembourg.' When Fouquier came out Amar said : 'Here is what you want.' 'Something to put you at your ease,' added Voulland. 'We wanted it badly enough,' replied Fouquier, and went back into Court with a smile of satisfaction on his face.

The jurors also, it is alleged, were tampered with. Despite their composition they wavered, either overawed by the murmurs of the people or influenced by the defendants' speeches. But Herman and Fouquier showed them a letter from abroad addressed to Danton, and painted him and his friends in the vilest colours as conspirators. Souberbielle the doctor, one of the jury, has related that Topino-Lebrun said to him : 'This is not a question of law but of high policy. We are not in the position of jurors, but statesmen. Both of the two men are impossible. Is it Robespierre you would rather kill?' 'No.' 'Well that means finding Danton "guilty."' This conversation is said to have taken place on the evening of the 4th.[1] It is impossible to be sure of the truth of many of such stories, but this is related by one of the men on whose respectability the Robespierrist historian, Louis Blanc, especially insists.

Camille Desmoulins, probably when he heard his wife's arrest mentioned, is said to have flung the notes he had in his hands in the faces of his judges. And here it may be observed that whatever else may be said of Desmoulins he was no coward. He has been charged with cowardice because he had

[1] Michelet, b. xvii. c. vii.

no dignity.　Rage he exhibited, now, at his arrest, and at his execution, rage and most piteous grief for his wife—and Danton by turns rebuked and consoled him—but no cowardice. Thus much is the due of a man to whom in many respects more than justice has been done by many writers, in this respect less. But it was his childish impulse more perhaps than the manlier remonstrances of Danton and Delacroix which gave Herman an excuse for putting the Convention's decree in force and summarily ordering the prisoners to be removed.　Desmoulins clung to the bench on which he sat and uttered maledictions on his judges as he was torn away by force.　He and the others were removed to the Conciergerie.　Ducray, the clerk, soon came to announce to them their sentence.　None of them would listen.　'Take us to the guillotine,' they said; 'we are assassinated.'　While they waited there and before the jury had brought in their verdict the printers 'were setting up the types for the text of the death-sentence, so that the public criers might at once announce it to the crowd.'

From the Conciergerie they were taken to the Place de la Révolution, an armed force which had been for some time waiting at the prison escorting the tumbrels.　Some of Danton's sayings previously quoted are reported to have been uttered now.　Others more certainly belong to these last moments. Fabre d'Eglantine expressed regret at having left his comedy '*L'Orange de Malte*' unfinished.　'*Vos vers !*' said Danton with a grim jest which English cannot reproduce, '*bah ! dans une semaine vous ferez assez de vers.*'　Then he said something nobler : 'Our work is done ; let us take our rest.'　He smiled contemptuously as the executioner clipped his hair and bound him. In the tumbrel he stood between Camille Desmoulins and Fabre d'Eglantine, and Desmoulins leaned on him.　Some of the enormous crowd chanted the 'Marseillaise.'　Some were Royalists come to see the <u>Procureur</u> de la <u>Lanterne</u> die.　Others were the brutal spectators who always throng to an execution. As their yells and laughter met the ears of the condemned, Danton said : 'Fools ! they are waiting to cry " Vive la République !" In an hour the Republic will be without a head.' Desmoulins started up and struggled so violently as to tear his shirt from his shoulders, crying all the while to the people to come to the rescue. 'It was I who in '89 called you to arms. My only crime has been pity.' He was answered by jeers. 'Hush !' at last said Danton, who had been listening to him as he had often listened by their fireside, 'heed not that base rabble.' As they passed the Café de la Régence they saw David sketching them. 'You lackey !' Danton called out. The windows of Robespierre's house were closed, and Desmoulins as they passed cried : 'My assassins will not long survive me.'

The sun was declining as they reached the Place de la Révolution, where the Revolution's 'First Apostle' and its real hero were to die. It was a lovely evening of a lovely spring, such a spring as old men said they had never before known. The lilacs on the terraces of the Tuileries were in full blossom ; the air had the warmth of midsummer rather than April. The unhappy men themselves, all of them in their prime, must have felt with an additional pang that in the midst of life they were in death. Hérault de Séchelles was the first beheaded. He tried, as he passed, to kiss Danton, but the executioner's men would not let him. Danton said to them : 'Fools, you cannot hinder our heads meeting in the basket presently.' As one by one his friends were summoned he said to each some word of consolation. He himself was the last to die. Who does not know his last words? Thinking of his wife he said : 'My beloved, shall I no more behold thee ?' then, 'Come, Danton, no weakness.' And then to Sanson, the executioner : 'Show my head to the people ; it is worth while ; they do not see the like every day.'

This Danton (said an eye-witness) plays his part very well . . . .[1] At the foot of the horrible statue silhouetted in colossal outline against the sky I saw the Tribune standing

---

[1] *Souvenirs d'un Sexagénaire*, par A. V. Arnault, quoted by Claretie in his *Desmoulins*, pp. 452-4.

upright, like one of Dante's shadows, half illumined by the dying sun, and like one rising from the tomb rather than about to enter it. Nothing bolder than the countenance of this athlete of the Revolution could be imagined, nothing more formidable than the pose of the profile defying the axe, than the poise of the head, still, while on the point of falling, seeming to dictate laws. Appalling spectacle! Time can never efface it from my memory. I saw there incarnate the feeling which inspired Danton's last words—terrible words which I could not hear, but which were reported to me with a shudder of horror and admiration.

CHAPTER XXX

DANTON NOT VAIN OR CYNICAL—HIS ORATORY, TOLERANCE, COMMON-SENSE—VIEWS ON EDUCATION, RELIGION—HIS GREAT MISTAKE—HIS AIMS AND SHORTCOMINGS—STATUE AT ARCIS

To men of our day and of temperament less emotional than that of Frenchmen Danton's last words may seem revoltingly self-conscious. So may Mirabeau's 'Support that head; would I could bequeath it thee.' But to be judged fairly both men should be judged relatively to their race and time. There was plenty of theatrical eloquence then and much attitudinising in our own House of Commons, which had its dagger-scene to match Marat's pistol, and in the House of Lords, which so recently had acknowledged Chatham as its protagonist. Danton was a born orator, and perhaps there has never been a great orator who has not had in him something of the actor. But he was fundamentally neither an egotist, nor artificial, nor a cynic. What more naturally pathetic could there be than his reference to his wife? what less cynical, less self-absorbed than his demeanour to his comrades?

The egotism in his speeches, though sometimes amusing, is mostly too frank to be offensive. As in private life he was content to listen while Desmoulins talked, so in the Assembly he spoke only when he had something practical to say, not for self-glorification. Common-sense, and shrewd readiness, expressed in language of volcanic strength, are the characteristics of his oratory. So many specimens of it have been given that it is unnecessary to do more than quote Mr. Morse Stephens' appreciation.

He was the only statesman who always improvised and spoke extempore. . . . For this reason his speeches stand out as distinct from those of Mirabeau and Robespierre, Vergniaud and Barère. They are not models of style ; they are not composed with rhetorical accuracy ; they contain no balanced periods, no carefully selected words and passages. They possess all the faults and merits of extempore speeches. They are diffuse and badly arranged ; the orator jumps from subject to subject in a bewildering fashion ; he repeats his arguments and words ; and his style is brusque and rough rather than polished. But yet they have extraordinary merits. They seem to come red-hot from his thoughts ; and though they lack the care of the practised rhetorician they abound in the straight-forward eloquence of the heart.

An orator of this type could hardly be essentially a vain or cynical man. Vanity is less careless. Its speeches smell more of the lamp. It consists rather in a man's excessive estimate of his own virtues and attributes than in blunt reference to such as are accorded to him by common consent of other people. And for Danton's most tumid phrases there was special excuse. 'Nature has endowed me with the rough lineaments of liberty' may seem mere rodomontade, but when the Roland coterie spoke of his scarred visage as stamping him a villain it became an excusable retort. As to his cynicism, the notion of it is based on stories some of them palpably apocryphal, some of them brutalised in transmission, not one of them, perhaps, resting on absolutely trustworthy evidence. Everyone knows how stories beget stories and how fast they grow. Given a man devoid of all hypocrisy, humorous, apt to call a spade a spade, and he is certain to have fathered on him much that he has never said, and much which he has said wilfully metamorphosed. Riouffe avers that every sentence he spoke in the Conciergerie was interlarded with oaths and obscene expressions, and yet calmly records sentences, all of them striking, some of them noble, which are free from all such disfigurements. The truth is that Danton's habitual conversation corresponded with the dignity of his speeches,

but that in lighter moments he used the language used by
every other man whom he met in society, though perhaps with
less care as to who might be the hearers.

His strong common-sense and moderation have been often
illustrated in previous chapters.[1]   He was, in fact, intolerant on
one point only—resistance to the Republic.   Even in that he
was in practice laxer than in principle, but when once he had
made up his mind as to the necessity of a law he was for no
half-measures in enforcing it.   Thus when it had been decided
that every possessor of grain should 'declare' the amount of
his stock, he said that confiscation was insufficient punishment
for disobedience, and that the offender should be liable to ten
years' imprisonment.   And when it was urged that the law of
the maximum would work oppressively in individual instances
he replied—

This is all mischievous carping.   You must make the law
apply to all, because a legislator can only deal with the interests
of all.   The people will pay no attention to petty inconveniences
consequent on the maximum being here and there less than
the standard you are going to make universal.   But it will applaud a law which ensures food to our armies and to the State
at large.

In less vital questions he was always for tolerance.[2]   He
had little liking for priests[3] and sacerdotal mummeries.[4]   But
atheistic mummeries were, as we have seen, equally distasteful
to him, and he was strongly averse to depriving illiterate
peasants of the spiritual sustenance to which they were accustomed.   When a reduction of the salaries of the clergy was

---

[1] For another and characteristic instance, see *Moniteur*, xvi. 357.   He
proposed that no one should be admitted to the Pantheon till twenty
years after death.

[2] 'L'Assemblée ne veut pas salarier aucun culte, mais elle exècre la
persécution.'   M. xviii. 493.

[3] 'Le règne des prêtres est passé.'   M. xviii. 493.   'Le plus puissant
levier de la contre-révolution était dans les prêtres non assermentés.'
Circular of Aug. 18, 1792.

[4] M. xviii. 525.

threatened he opposed it, arguing that only those should be mulcted who refused to take the constitutional oath.[1]

To apply precipitately philosophical principles which personally I hold dear would be to turn France topsy-turvy. The people, especially the country-people, are not ripe for them.

But while he would not interfere with creeds or deprive priests of their pay he stipulated that the clergy should be tolerant too.   Bishops paid by the nation who refused to marry priests ought, he said, to be liable to dismissal, and, if actuated by treasonable motives, to one year's imprisonment.

We have safeguarded their salaries ; let them, in accordance with their founder's principle, render to Cæsar—and the nation is more than all the Cæsars—the things that are Cæsar's.[2]

His views on education were conceived in the same spirit.

The children of the poor should be educated at the expense of the State.   The great objection to this was, no doubt, the financial one, but in sowing their vast republican field cost ought not to be considered.   Next to bread education was the people's first necessity.

In another remarkable speech, which incidentally testified to his own culture, he argued that school education was preferable to education at home, in spite of what might be urged on the score of parental love.

I am a father myself, more so than the aristocrats who object, for they are not sure who are their children and who not, and in measuring my individual interest with that of the State I feel that my son belongs not to me but to the Republic ; and that it is she who should teach him his duty in order that he may serve her well.   It has been said that country-people would object to surrendering their children.   Well, do not compel them, but let them have the choice.   Let there be Sunday classes for such as prefer them.   Out of practice will grow habit. Wait for ideal perfection and you will have no education at all. . . . No one respects natural affection more than I.   But the interests of society demand that parental selfishness should not make children dangerous to society.   We ought to say to them, ' We will not tear your children from you, but neither

<hr>

[1] M. xiv. 68.   [2] M. xvii. 183.

shall you abstract them from the influence of the nation. In national schools the child will suck republican milk.'

These advanced and enlightened views on education were, however, in his eyes incomplete. To educate the youth of France in republican principles was right, but to set the seal on and consecrate the results of their educational system

there should be national games held in a vast building sacred to the purpose and embellished by the greatest artists. Greece had her Olympic games ; why should not France have her sans-culottid days, and her people festivals at which they might worship the Supreme Being? . . . For in annihilating the reign of superstition we have no intention of establishing the reign of atheism.

The above shows Danton's attitude towards religion. He was what is now called an agnostic, but was respectful to the belief of others.[1] It is said that he used to conduct his wife to the church door, though he would not go in.

---

[1] On June 21, 1791, he said at the Jacobins, ' I am about to speak as if I were in the presence of God himself.' This is evidently a rhetorical phrase furnishing no accurate clue to his own belief.

On November 30, 1792, with reference to abolition of State payment of priests, he said in the Convention, according to the *Moniteur*, xiv. 620 : ' On s'est appuyé sur des idées philosophiques qui me sont chères ; car je ne connais d'autre bien que celui de l'univers, d'autre culte que celui de la justice et de la liberté.' Here ' bien ' at first sight seems a mistake for ' dieu,' but the ' principles which he held dear ' were that no Church should be subsidised, and the train of thought seems plain enough if we read ' bien '—viz. ' I am for subsidising no particular sect, the well-being of *all* being the sole end I have in view, and liberty and justice my sole religion.' Both thought and words recall the circular of Aug. 18, 1792, in which he states his intention to preserve ' non l'égalité impossible des biens mais une égalité des droits et du bonheur.'

The *Journal des Débats et des Décrets*, however, has another version, ' Je ne connais, moi, que le dieu de l'univers, la liberté et la justice,' and places several lines before these words what in the *Moniteur* follows them. This version, with its *d*ieu not Dieu and its next words ' L'homme des champs *y* ajoute l'homme consolateur,' seems a report of words meaning, not ' I recognise only one God, the God of the universe, of liberty, and of justice,' but ' I recognise only one ruling principle for the world—

We have already seen that Danton's experience of his own profession had convinced him that the administration of justice ought by no means to rest solely in the hands of lawyers. In this and in advocating a loan on behalf of the victims of the Maison de Secours he followed the bent of a mind logical enough when logical procedure seemed practicable, but never a slave to hard and fast rule. So also he supported the 'maximum,' not, no doubt, as in itself good, but as the lesser of two evils. In finance he almost always supported the able and honest Cambon. 'Follow the example of Nature,' he said when seconding that financier's sufficiently summary proposal for dealing with 'royal' *assignats* above a certain value. 'Nature looks to the preservation of the species and pays no respect to individuals.'

In opposing the system by which public officials had to deposit caution-money as a guarantee for their probity he showed his usual shrewdness. 'You cannot ensure moral responsibility by a pecuniary deposit. Such devices are relics of the old

viz. liberty and justice'? On April 19, 1793, he said : 'Français; vous avez la liberté d'adorer *la divinité* qui vous paraît digne de vos hommages,' and 'regardez que partout le peuple, dégagé des impulsions de malveillance, reconnaît que quiconque veut s'interposer entre lui et *la divinité* est un imposteur.' M. xvi. 183. So also he said on Nov. 26, 1793 : 'Le peuple aura des fêtes dans lesquelles il offrira de l'encens à l'Être Suprême, au maître de la nature, car nous n'avons pas voulu anéantir le règne de la superstition pour établir le règne de l'athéisme.' M. xviii. 528. Now, such words as 'la divinité,' 'l'Être Suprême,' 'dieu,' no doubt indicate belief of a sort,

> 'the soul of a man, which is God,
> He adores without altar or prayer,'

but they recall Croker's comment on Robespierre : 'Any phrase to avoid the acknowledgment of *God*! Mercier's errand-boy, about fourteen years old, told him after this fête "there is no longer a God, only Robespierre's Supreme Being."' Either of the two versions, in short, points to agnosticism or vague theism rather than pronounced belief. Finally, if there were any reasonable doubt as to his belief being anything more positive, it would be dispelled by his famous words at his trial, 'My abode will soon be *dans le néant*,' words which, however explained, are incompatible with orthodox belief.

corrupt régime.   Right policy consists in appointing the right man.'

Though the sanity of all his opinions on such subjects will surprise those who have looked on him as a ' bellowing blood-drinker' it would be as absurd to contend that he was infallible in social and economic questions as to say that his foreign policy succeeded or that he realised much of his Revolutionary ideal.   His one grand success consisted in ' saving France from Brunswick.'   But his failures were almost as creditable to him as his success.   He had created, he had saved, but he could not consolidate the Republic.   He had the will but not the power.   Napoleon had the power but not the will.   Danton was rendered helpless by the jealousies and fanaticisms of meaner men.   He gave pledges of disinterestedness over and over again, resigning the Ministry of Justice and refusing to serve on the Committee of Safety even when acclaimed to it without his consent.[1]   But his personal superiority, on which he proudly relied, galled the Girondins first and the Hébertists and Robespierrists afterwards more than tenure of office would have done, while resignation of it made his enemies stronger for offence and left himself nothing to rely on except his voice in the Convention.

The last six months of his life were a single-handed struggle under hopeless conditions, aggravated by broken health and dejection at watching his hopes gradually fade away.   For it must have been dejection which dictated these among other of his melancholy words during that period :

Revolutions are like long and difficult voyages, during which you must expect the wind to blow from all quarters at once.   The open sea is often less dangerous than the harbour, for which one makes with all sails set and never a thought of the narrow shoal on which sometimes the ship goes to wreck.

The factions confronting him had no desire for peace

[1] M. xvii. 596.

abroad, because war was an excuse for keeping up revolutionary despotism at home. Danton having no personal ambition to gratify, craving only for himself a quiet country life in his old home at Arcis, would have concluded peace, would have granted an amnesty, would have restored normal government, would have fostered trade and industry, would have pursued as the proper object of a republic the comfort of the citizen. Equal law, equal chances of education, enough to eat—these were the three things which Frenchmen had not had under the Monarchy. In Danton's eyes they constituted the essence of a republic. It was the King's vision of ' a fowl in the pot ' repeated, but with something over and above possession of the fowl.[1]

Such aims stamp Danton as a true statesman apart from the genius he displayed in marshalling France against invasion. Unfortunately in one thing, without which greatness is not supreme greatness, he was lacking. Though magnificently energetic in an emergency, he was not, as the confidential letters of his own friends prove,[2] constitutionally painstaking. He was over-sanguine and unmethodical. He had not the patience to follow up a victory which he had won by a *coup de main*. To use a homely simile, he had the invention of the architect, the boldness of the builder, but was without the sleepless vigilance of the clerk of the works. He was too careless to meet ruse with ruse, to play off party against party, to seek anxiously for a personal following in the clubs, the Committees, the press. When fighting against Monarchy he courted and welcomed all allies. But, that

---

[1] In his circular of Aug. 18, 1792, to the Courts of Judicature he wrote : ' Les tribunaux me trouveront le même homme, dont toutes les pensées n'ont eu pour objet que la liberté politique et individuelle, le maintien des lois, la tranquillité publique, l'unité des quatre-vingt-trois départements, la splendeur de l'État, la prosperité du peuple français, et non l'égalité impossible des biens, mais une égalité de droits et de bonheur.'

[2] ' Oublie pour moi ta paresse ordinaire.' Delacroix to Danton, M.-T. vi. 489. ' C'est bien ta nonchalance et ta mollesse qui t'ont perdu.' Delacroix, quoted by Prudhomme, *Hist. Gen.* &c. i. 328.

battle won, he preferred to stand alone. He had plenty of friends but no party. When in his independence he procured the release of Vincent and Ronsin, when he deprecated Rühl's rebuke to the Commune, he thought he was counteracting over-despotic tendencies sufficiently. In reality he was warning and arming his enemies against himself. Confident in the un-selfishness of his own intentions and in his own strength, he could not bring himself to believe that he would fall a victim to the machinations of 'shallow scoundrels.' And indeed there is something ironical in so much force, eloquence, and popularity having been discomfited by such Lilliputian an-tagonists; something grotesque and monstrous in his having been executed on the charge of conspiracy with the foreigner against France.

On July 14, 1891, exactly one hundred and two years after the taking of the Bastille, the inhabitants of Arcis-sur-Aube saw unveiled their most famous citizen's statue. It stands there, bold and commanding as the man was in life, with one hand raised and the lips seeming still to speak. Many a pregnant and eloquent word uttered by them must have thronged to the memory of the beholders. But to those who thought how and by what hands he fell, and how history has traduced him, it may have seemed that this one of all his sayings would most appropriately be graven on the pedestal :

' Ce n'est qu'à ceux qui ont reçu quelques talents politiques que je m'adresse, et non à hommes stupides qui ne savent faire parler que leurs passions.'

APPENDICES

APPENDIX A

DANTON'S INCOME

ON March 29, 1787, he bought the office of Avocat aux Conseils du Roi for 78,000 francs + 1,050 francs for law-expenses, paying 56,000 francs down. 36,000 of these were borrowed from the Demoiselle du Hauttoir, and 15,000 from his father-in-law, Charpentier, these 15,000 being a portion of the 20,000 francs dowry he was to have with his wife.

He was enabled to borrow by his relations becoming security for him to the amount of 90,000 francs, as they might well do, the office being worth 80,000 francs and ensuring a good income.

On June 12 he paid another 10,000 francs (66,000 in all) when the formalities for the transference of the office were completed ; and on December 3, 1789, two years eight months after the purchase, he paid the remainder, 12,000 francs, though not bound to pay the whole till March 1791. A debt due to the vendor, of 12,000 francs, was included in the purchase, so that he had

> Francs
> 36,000 (borrowed)
> 20,000 (dowry)
> 12,000 (patrimony)
> 12,000 (debt to office received by him)
> ———————————————————
> 80,000 with which to pay for his office.

But how did he live ? 1, on the proceeds from his office ; 2, on the interest of his patrimony, for he was not obliged to complete the payment for his office till four years from March 1787 ; 3, on any private earnings he may have made ; 4, on his father-in-law's bounty ; 5, on that of his uncle and aunt at Troyes, he being their heir.

In 1791 he bought national land to the value of 85,000 francs. How did he pay for it ? The State repaid him 71,000 francs for his office on its suppression, and though he paid for most of his purchases (March 24, 48,200 francs ; April 12, 8,300 francs April 13, 25,300 francs) before receiving the money from the State (September 27), yet on April 14, which was the date of the suppression of the office, his certificate of having held it became equivalent to cash, as the law allowed him to purchase with it up to half its value. The rest he borrowed from his father-in-law, or as much of it as he wanted, for he must have had savings of his own, having received 90,000 francs as Avocat. His property was, therefore, in 1791, about 85,000 francs, and when executed this and some 5,000 francs personalty was all he left to his children. The above does not include such income as he derived from the various offices he filled and his pay as Deputy.[1] Madame Roland, who thought him penniless, argued that because he was penniless he was bribed. We, who know he was not penniless, might answer with more force that, as he was not penniless, he was not bribed.

The country houses he is said to have kept up belonged to his father-in-law.

By the above statement of Danton's sources of income the ground is cleared for consideration of Mirabeau's charges of venality, supplemented by those of Lafayette, in more detail than seemed convenient in the text.

1. Louis Blanc made a strong point of Mirabeau's charges occurring in a private letter to Lamarck not meant for publication. Dr. Robinet has shown that Mirabeau expressly told Lamarck that he wished his papers to be published some day.

2. Mirabeau's charge was made directly after the publication of No. 67 of the 'Révolutions de France et de Brabant,' by Camille Desmoulins. This, Mirabeau says, was inspired by Danton. In it Desmoulins talked of the passion of St. Mirabeau, and described how the sweat rolled down Mirabeau's face as he replied to the attacks made on him at the Jacobins. Afterwards he said that by this number he had forfeited Mirabeau's friendship. Here, then, is a plain reason for Mirabeau's enmity, and his enmity naturally took the shape of charges of venality.

3. To whom was Danton sold ? Mirabeau says Danton had an

---

[1] Eighteen francs a day.

understanding with Beaumetz and Chapelier. But these men were attacked by Desmoulins in No. 67, which Danton, according to Mirabeau, had inspired.

4. Mirabeau asserts that Danton was bribed, in a letter to Lamarck. Six months later, when Mirabeau was dead, Lamarck, writing to an intimate friend, bewailed the composition of the new Assembly, of which, he said three-quarters were nonentities and the rest incendiaries, and proceeded, 'A man named Danton will also perhaps be elected.' Now if Danton was a nonentity he certainly would not have got a bribe of 30,000 francs from a bankrupt Court. If he was an incendiary he was not in the Court's pay.

5. Elsewhere Mirabeau speaks of Danton as the enemy of the Court and perhaps the tool of the Lameths.

In short, Mirabeau suspected Danton of being employed by his enemies. To revenge himself for No. 67 he told lies about him.

Lafayette says Danton had given a receipt to Montmorin for a bribe of 100,000 francs, and a note in his Memoirs says that these 100,000 were nominally compensation for Danton's office, which really was only worth 10,000, so that 90,000 of the 100,000 were a bribe. He goes on to say that Danton had received other sums, *e.g.* one of 50,000 before August 10, but that Lafayette only knew of the 100,000, of which Danton himself told him at the Hôtel de Ville.

Now (1) this note is *not by Lafayette.* The charge, therefore, of the 50,000 francs bribe is an anonymous charge, based, no doubt, on gossip. Lafayette's charge is based on 'the lie which is half a truth.' Danton at the Hôtel de Ville spoke to Lafayette of what he spoke equally undisguisedly in public when elected joint deputy-procureur as '*le remboursement notoire d'une charge qui n'existe plus.*' If it had been a bribe would he have boasted of it, and to Lafayette of all men in the world?

2. In specifying the service for which Danton was paid Lafayette says it was for acting as a spy at the Jacobins and to report what went on there to the Court, a curious service to perform where everything was transacted publicly.

Bertrand de Molleville says it was to get measures passed there agreeable to the Court. If so, the art with which he went to work was most successfully concealed.

Brissot says it was to discredit the Revolution by driving it to excesses.

All three, therefore, differ as to his service, but all three agree as to his having earned his pay. Louis Blanc, however, differs from them in this, and says he took the money but did nothing for it. It is quite certain that he did nothing for it. May we not say that it is equally certain that he never took the money, and except for service rendered would never have been offered it by the Court ?

There is no sign where the money, if received, went to. Mirabeau, with his pay, bought a great library, a splendid mansion, magnificent furniture, and lavished it on mistresses. Danton lived in a small dingy house.[1] All its appurtenances were on the most modest scale. The furniture of the drawing-room was worth less than 40*l.* He was so domestic in his tastes that his revilers founded odious jests on his uxoriousness and its results. Who were his mistresses? The moment we look for facts we find there are none, nothing but stories such, for instance, as Louis Blanc tells on the authority of Godefroy Cavaignac, who gave it on the authority of his mother, viz. that at the house of Cavaignac Danton said over his wine that his party's turn was come to enjoy life, sumptuous houses, dainty morsels, stuffs of silk and gold, the ' women one dreams of,' &c., and then added, ' But do you think I cannot play *sans-culotte* with the rest of them, and,' added he with a cynical gesture, ' *montrer mon derrière aux passants ?* '

This is gossip, second-hand gossip, gossip of a woman, and a woman who would plainly not let the nature of the gossip prevent her retailing it. M. Despois, in criticising it, says that the words ' *les femmes dont on rêve* ' are not eighteenth-century words, and that Danton ' *rêvait peu.* '[2] However that may be, we know that Danton's wives were the women to whom he was devoted, and that the sumptuous houses &c. did not exist. M. Despois' article, from which much of the above is taken, appeared in July 1857, and was answered most lamely by L. Blanc.[3]

Taine (translated by Durand), vol. ii. p. 193, suggests that Danton bought property 'under third parties,' who kept it after his death, and founds himself on 'investigations of Blache at Choisy-sur-Seine, where a certain Fauvel seems to have been Danton's assumed name.' From this one might infer that

---

[1] ' Petit appartement du passage du Commerce dans la triste maison qui fait arcade et voûte entre le passage et la rue (triste elle-même) des Cordeliers.' Michelet, b. viii. c. xviii.

[2] *Vie Privée*, edit. 1865.   [3] Cf. *Vie Privée.*

' Fauvel' was merely an *alias* of Danton. In vol. iii. p. 238, however, Fauvel is represented as, what he really was, the owner of a house at Choisy frequented by Danton and other well-known men of the time. Apparently it is on the strength of the evidence of Fauvel's gardener that Danton is suspected of having bought property through Fauvel, and of having owned the house at Choisy. The evidence was of this sort : Being asked the leading question whether he had not seen Danton exercise rights of ownership in the house and its belongings, such as taking up trees &c., he answered that he had seen Danton have work done on the embellishment of the house, had seen him walking in the garden with Fauvel, and visiting with Fauvel work going on in the house as well as the garden. He said, too, that he had seen Delacroix, the two Robespierres, Didier, Benoît, &c., there. Later on he said he had seen 'them' at banquets where much wine was drunk and bottles were broken, and had seen 'them' often spend the night at Fauvel's, and that he knew Danton had lodgings there. What there is in all this to blacken Danton it is hard to see. It would be more to the purpose if evidence other than a blundering rustic's were given of property purchased by Fauvel for Danton, *and of its subsequent history*. All that can be fairly assumed is that Fauvel kept a sort of club where Danton went occasionally and slept, that he (who, as we know, was fond of gardening) suggested or directed improvements in the garden, and perhaps in other parts of the house than that in his own occupation, with Fauvel's assent.

APPENDIX B

CHARGES OF MALVERSATION IN BELGIUM [1]

ROBESPIERRE, in his notes given to St. Just, wrote : ' *Il avait la main dans la caisse de la Belgique,*' and ' *Dans le pays de Delacroix on ne parle que des serviettes de l'Archiduchesse rapportées de la Belgique et démarquées dans le pays.*'

[1] The total expenditure of the seven Commissioners in Belgium, of whom Danton was one, from November 30, 1792, to April 2, 1793, was 29,400 livres in cash, 10,600 in *assignats.*—Aulard's *Recueil des Actes du Comité de Salut Public,* i. 285. '

About these remarks we note that Robespierre makes no charge against Danton of stealing table-linen. On the contrary he seems to confine it to Delacroix. His charge against Danton refers, as far as it has any basis, to allegations of misappropriated money, confuted, on Cambon's testimony, by Danton, April 1, 1793, and, on Lebrun's testimony, by Delacroix, February 13, 1794. But as St. Just purposely mixed up the story of the mutiny in the prison with that of the mutiny at the trial, so he purposely mixed up the charge against Delacroix with the charge against Danton, insinuating that the latter was guilty of both.

What Levasseur said is more important. At the Jacobins he stated that when Belgium was being evacuated the authorities of Béthune wrote to say that they had stopped *two* carriages laden with property, as the drivers had no passports, and that these drivers said the property belonged to Danton and Delacroix ; that Danton and Delacroix got this letter handed over to them by a clerk of the Committee of Correspondence without the know-ledge of the Committee of Safety, and then came to the Conven-tion to complain of the stoppage of their baggage and procure an order for its release. In his Memoirs, published in 1831, Levasseur tells this story over again, but with more circumstance. Danton, he says, as a politician was unassailable, but as a man not of entire probity. He goes on to say that he himself at the Committee of Correspondence received the Béthune letter announ-cing the arrival of *three* carriages laden with baggage addressed to Danton and Delacroix. [*Here we see the two carriages multi-plied into three. Query—Was he on the Committee ? He was not when it was appointed in* 1792.] He goes on to say that at the time he *suspected* that this baggage contained what they had embezzled, and that he had proof of it a few days before Danton was arrested, for St. Just had come to him and asked for the letter [*of which Levasseur apparently had been talking*] ; that they went to the bureau of the Committee of Defence, but it was not to be found, and the secretary, on being questioned, said that Danton had obtained it under promise of bringing it back, saying he wanted to show it to Guiton-Morveaux, President of the Con-vention. The President denied having seen the letter, and said that Danton merely asked for a passport for his luggage, which he had given without hesitation.

This is a circumstantial story ; but, like so many stories against Danton, it collapses when pricked with a pin. Among *Danton's* papers was found (1) a letter from Dumoulin, *Commissaire aux Saisies dans la Belgique*, announcing his arrest, and asking Danton to take steps for his release ; (2) a letter from the Béthune officials saying they had made an inventory of the contents of the baggage, and had written to the President of the Convention, but getting no answer from him wrote to Danton, because the goods were directed to him and Delacroix, and they wished to know if they belonged to them.

Now let us consider the answers made by Delacroix and Danton at their trial. Danton said : '*Il résulte du procès-verbal qu'il n'y a à moi que mes chiffons et un corset de molleton. Lebas sommé m'a donné communication*'—i.e. that he had nothing in the carriages but some articles of wearing apparel, that the '*procès-verbal*' proved this, and that Lebas on being summoned communicated the facts.

Delacroix, on the other hand, admitted having some table-linen which he had bought a bargain, saying that it had to be put on the carriages laden with property carried off by the generals, and that the carriage containing it must not be confused with the other carriages which had been despatched by all the members of the Commission conjointly.

This tallies with the significance of Dumoulin's signature, '*Commissaire aux Saisies de la Belgique*,' which seems to show that the writer was *not* a man in the employ of Danton and Delacroix, but in charge of Government property.

Here, then, we have—(1) Delacroix explaining that his and Danton's property was only a portion of the goods on the carriages.

(2) Danton in Delacroix's presence denying he had any table-linen.

(3) Delacroix in Danton's presence admitting that he had the linen, and adding, ' I ' (not ' We ') ' bought it.'

Surely he thus takes the whole responsibility for the linen on to his own shoulders.

We are not concerned here with Delacroix's personal defence, but may note (1) what Legendre said when he 'rolled in the mud ' the night after Danton's arrest, viz. that he never had esteemed Delacroix as much as Danton, and (2) that it was Delacroix, not Danton, whom Herman questioned at the trial.

It is clear that an inventory was made, and that Danton appealed to it as proof of his innocence. Levasseur saw it in April 1793, and says his suspicions were aroused ; but if that

were all, how could the same document, even 'if it had been forthcoming, have become a proof of guilt in April 1794 ? Why, again,
should not St. Just have told the whole story at the trial if it were so
damning ? By itself it would have been quite sufficient to condemn
Danton to death. Why should he have left Levasseur to tell it
after Danton's death ? As for Danton's purloining the letter,
what would have been the use of doing so? It was known to
Levasseur. It was known to the Committee of Correspondence, on
which some Girondins sat, besides Fayau, whose animus against
Danton we have seen. It was known to the Committee of Defence.

Lastly, when, and under what circumstances, did Levasseur
make his accusation? He made it just after Danton's death,
when, like Legendre, many men 'rolled in the mud.' And he
made it on the direct invitation of Robespierre that anyone who
knew anything about the 'conspiracy' should get up and declare
it—an invitation to commit perjury in order to escape the axe.

It may be conjectured, therefore, either that some of the
Robespierrist gang purloined the letter, because it did *not* prove
the charge which they still meant to insinuate at the trial, or that
Levasseur (who very likely did suspect something originally,
because he may have thought that all the carriage-loads belonged
to Danton and Delacroix) said what he did at the Jacobins to
curry favour with Robespierre, and afterwards, when he wished to
justify and excuse it to a world become anti-Robespierrist, added
corroboratory details ; converted, *i.e.*, a modicum of truth into a
mendacious tale and afterwards stuck to his tale.[1]

It should be added that some doubt has been thrown on the
authenticity of his Memoirs—and that in any case they are not
regarded as wholly trustworthy.

M. Aulard's exposition of Danton's accounts has been noticed,
p. 153. It may be added here that neither the text nor an analysis
of the letter of the Executive Council, there mentioned as exculpa-
ting Danton, was entered in the *procès-verbal* of the Convention,
which simply noted the receipt of it, and to this culpable omission,
to which he was too careless to call attention, much of the subsequent defamation of him was due. M. Aulard sums up his
argument thus : 'With regard to his accounts of *extraordinary*
expenditure, I have produced them. His accounts of *secret* expenditure were received by the Executive Council, which approved
of them in detail, and notified its approval to the Convention.'

<hr>

[1] Cf. *Vie Privée.*

APPENDIX C

THE PLOT OF DE BATZ

ÉLIE LACOSTE, in the name of the two Committees, read a report about this conspiracy on May 17. He said that Chabot, Delacroix, Danton, and Basire for a long time before July 1793 met Baron de Batz four times a week at a house called the Hermitage in Charonne, and there amid drunken orgies plotted a rescue of Louis on his way to execution, and a spiriting away of the Queen and Dauphin.

The following year the Baron printed an answer to this, and in it said : ' I never saw Danton or Delacroix in my life. I had no connection whatever with them, and never sat at the same table. I defy anyone to produce any evidence to the contrary.'

For corroboratory proofs that this was the truth cf. Robinet's ' Procès des Dantonistes,' pp. 325-330.

It is very doubtful if any attempt to rescue Louis was made.

It is amusing to find Royalist writers omitting Danton's name in telling the story. Why? Either because they are ashamed to include it or because from their point of view Danton, in joining the plot, would merit praise !

Addendum

Since p. 28 was in type, the kindness of a friend has enabled me to procure from M. Claretie confirmation of what is conjectured in the note as to C. Desmoulins' residence in August 1792. M. Claretie says that he was mistaken, and that C. Desmoulins lived in a house ' située en face de celle de Danton ' : *i.e.*, it would seem, on the south side of the Rue des Cordeliers, which ran between the Cordeliers district on the south and the Cour du Commerce on the north. In any case he was living near, not in the same house as, Danton, in August 1792.

Errata

P. 107, *for* Girondins *read* des Girondins.
P. 139, *for* in December *read* December 1.

SYNOPSIS

INDEX

www.ingramcontent.com/pod-product-compliance
Lightning Source LLC
Chambersburg PA
CBHW051116120726